GUSHER!

To my beautiful wife, Linda

Some day, some time, our eyes shall see
The faces kept in memory

Daniel Robertson Lucas
1840–1907

PART I
OIL CITY, PENNSYLVANIA
MARCH 1870

FIVE DEADLY DROPS

Matthew Strong hates the boomtown and all it represents. He hates the smell of its oily streets packed with grime-caked drillers, tool pushers, roughnecks and roustabouts. He hates the pervasive waste of oil that flows from uncontrolled wells into the creeks and streams, choking them of life. He despises the encounters and confrontations with the quick-money schemers, fortune hunters, whores, misfits and malcontents lurking in shadows and back alleyways all hours of the night and day. But what he hates most is what he's doing right now: scouring the city's endless string of saloons and taverns for his father to try to convince him to come home.

Matthew stops to let a wagon pass, and a blast of wind buffets him on this blustery, cold March afternoon. He stands for a moment and watches the town blacksmith, Phineas Crump, carry a large iron anvil by its horns down the mud-laced street. Wart-riddled and red-faced, Crump looks like a muscle-bound toad, squatting and straining under the immense weight of his burden. The smithy groans, then drops the block with a grunt in its appointed place—in the middle of the intersection of Seneca and Center streets—the busiest crossroads in Oil City.

Matthew watches a crowd gather as Crump straightens up, puts his hands on his hips and begins dancing a little jig in the grease-pocked mud. He cajoles and gestures, coaxing anyone lingering around him to cough up a few coins for the show he's about to perform.

He works his way to Matthew and bends down in front of him. The lanky fifteen-year-old draws back as the odor of decay from Crump's rotting teeth assaults him.

"What will you pay?" Crump grunts, his dull gray eyes clouded with a milky film.

"Nothing," Matthew says, turning and heading to the other side of the street. "I've got to find my pa."

He stops and watches Crump hustle the crowd, his pockets now bulging with coins. After another minute or so the blacksmith appears satisfied, ready for his act, and he struts over to a wagon and stands next to it, inspecting its cargo. He begins tapping his index finger against a cylindrical tin canister dangling from the wagon's side. He taps the canister harder, and his audience edges back.

Matthew recognizes the tall, lean man bolting from the door of the nearby Down Hole Saloon and approaching Crump without hesitation. He's Jack Thackery, a teamster who delivers nitroglycerin to his father at the oil fields and sometimes to their farmhouse south of town.

"Get away from that wagon you goddamned fool, and leave that nitro be!" shouts Thackery.

"I want more than last time," the smithy barks back.

Thackery's eyes narrow. "I said step the hell away, and stop tappin' that can. You're playin' a dangerous game, Phineas."

Crump stops his tapping. "I said I want more than before."

"Three's all you get."

"I want five."

"You're crazy."

"They paid for a show."

"They'll get one, I sell you five."

"I'll pay double. On the spot."

Matthew sees the tall man study the smithy for a second. Then he hears him say, "What the hell, Crump. You want to blast yourself to kingdom come? Have at it."

Another strong gust of wind blows in, stirring the towns-folk. Crump puts his hands back on his hips and resumes his jig.

Thackery takes the canister from his wagon and walks over to the blacksmith's anvil. He sets the container in the street, bends down beside it, and unscrews its cap. Crump dances directly over him, waving his arms in circles and leaning his body backwards like he's about to slip and fall on top of the teamster.

Thackery lifts the canister by its handle, spreads his fingers underneath and slowly pours five generous drops of nitroglycerin on top of the block. He screws the cap back on, returns to his wagon, and hangs the canister back in place. He collects his money, turns and heads toward Matthew, standing by the saloon door.

"Your father's inside," he says, looking down at the boy and nodding toward the entrance as he disappears into the tavern.

Matthew's face flushes, and his stomach suddenly feels as if someone's grabbing it with both hands and tying it in knots. How many more times will he have to enter these dens of despair, to be accosted by the incoherent babble of clumsy drunkards and toothless prostitutes? How much longer will he have to feel the embarrassment of finding his father passed out in the middle of the day, and the shame of having to steady him as he staggers up the street amid the stares and whispers of the shopkeepers and other respectable folks in this god-awful town?

Matthew and his mother both know his father is on the brink of spiraling out of control. Caleb has always been a heavy drinker, but his addiction to the bottle and rapid decline have intensified since the family lost Matthew's older brother Luke to a well fire six months ago.

He takes a deep breath, walks inside and looks around.

Thick bluish bands of tobacco smoke hang above the huddled heads of drunken oil field workers sitting at packed tables and standing three deep in front of the massive mahogany bar. The persistent smell of petroleum permeates the air, as it does everywhere in the oil regions of Venango County, inside or out. Greasy boot prints blanket the wood floor, and he notices three whores standing by the stairway trying to catch men's eyes. A thin black man with white whiskers and red suspenders sits hunched over a piano, plinking its faded ivory keys.

To Matthew, the scene is all too familiar. In fact, this entire day in Oil City is unexceptional, at least so far. For no particular event has drawn the crowd to this dingy gathering spot so similar to dozens of others in town. No pay dirt hit to send streams of black gold gushing toward the sky and back to earth to drench men in dreams and desire. No farmer rushing through saloon doors to announce drinks for all and a royalty agreement freeing him from seasonal toil. No well fire raging out of control to destroy a dozen derricks, sending their owners scrambling for money already spent. No, none of these things has happened yet today.

Neither has the most feared event of all; what Matthew's father and Jack Thackery and his partner Muleface McCoy and all the others who work with nitroglycerin think about every waking moment, except when they're drunk—like they are now on this unexceptional day—postponing and blotting from their minds what they know they will soon have to do.

Matthew inches, angles and edges his way through the raucous crowd toward the table where Caleb sits drinking with his friends, and as he approaches, he can hear his father and the two other men in a heated discussion.

"Don't tell me haulin' nitro is more dangerous than shootin' wells," declares Caleb. "You have an explosion at a well, the whole field's apt to go up in flames."

Matthew often hears his father talk of his work as a well shooter, a torpedo man, one of the specialists employed by the Roberts Petroleum Torpedo Company to go into the fields and fix clogged or underperforming wells. Caleb, like so many in the oil regions who drink or gamble away their wages, often complains of the dangers of his job: the risks of filling the four-foot-long, tube-like canisters with nitro, affixing them to guide wires, and sending the devices down boreholes to the bottoms of wells. He describes how, if everything goes as planned, he drops a lead weight called a go-devil down the guide where it hits the torpedo's percussion cap, explodes the bomb, fractures the formation and releases fresh flows of precious crude oil to the surface above.

But things don't always go as planned. Sometimes the percussion cap doesn't fire and the shooter has to drop a second or even a third devil down the hole in hope of triggering a blast. If that doesn't work, the entire contraption—torpedo, cap, weights and wire—is pulled back up out of the well to be adjusted.

Caleb's partner was doing exactly that just a month ago when the rising torpedo exploded at the well's opening, blowing the man to oblivion and sending Caleb into an inebriated funk for the better part of a week.

Like other well shooters and nitro haulers, Caleb Strong steels his nerves with ever-more-frequent excursions into the town's saloons and gambling joints. They all drink together, bragging like mercenaries, drowning pent-up, inadmissible fears with endless rounds of whiskey, knowing their next job, their next torpedo at their next well the next morning might be their last day on earth.

"Least he never knew what hit 'im," they always laugh heartily, if fearfully, in memory of the latest victim in their deadly business.

Yet of late, even little setbacks make Caleb disappear into one of his favorite haunts, to return home at unpredictable hours stinking of tobacco and booze and oil. Always oil.

"You teamsters just haul the stuff," he says. "I work with it every day. I make one wrong move and an entire field's blown to smithereens."

Caleb looks up and notices Matthew standing by the table. "Well, it appears the grim reaper has arrived to take me away. I've been wonderin' when you were goin' to show."

The knot in Matthew's stomach tightens.

Caleb turns from his son and fills the men's glasses to their brims with whiskey. He puts the bottle back on the table and studies the afternoon sunlight streaming through the panes and falling on the amber liquor, immersing it in a warm, golden glow that he hopes—prays—will soon envelop him after he belts down a few more shots.

He looks out the window and watches an elderly couple cross to the other side of the muddy street, well away from the teamsters' horses and cargo. "I will say one thing," Caleb says. "People sure give your wagon a wide berth, don't they? Least those that know what you're carryin'."

"I was thinkin' people must'a run from those fellas used to haul them bodies over in Europe durin' that Black Plague, same way they run from our wagon today," says Muleface.

Caleb rolls his eyes. "Now where'd you learn 'bout that Europe plague?"

"I saw some pictures in a book about it once."

"You tryin' to show us how smart you are?" Caleb says, raising his glass.

Muleface lifts his drink and brings it up in front of him. "I may know a few things to get me by, but I've never been smart enough to quit this lousy job and move the hell out of Pennsylvania now, have I?" He flashes a toothy grin, and the three men click glasses and down their booze. Pleased not to be the center of attention, Matthew stands by their table and watches them turn and look back out the window.

"You believe what that idiot's 'bout to do?" Thackery asks.

Crump stands in the street with his back to a sixteen-pound sledgehammer, ready to show the crowd a feat of strength. With his right hand he grabs the sledge near the end of its long hickory handle, raising it into the air behind him. Crump turns his head upward and to his right, and he cocks his wrist so the sledge begins to descend toward him, his face now directly under it. He lowers it until the hammer is right over his lips, and he inches it even closer and kisses the hammer's head.

His audience applauds.

Crump cocks his wrist the opposite way and raises the sledgehammer away from his face, bringing it back down to the ground behind him. He shoots a woman in a brown bonnet a quick smile, and without a word puts his hands back on his hips and begins to dance his stupid jig. Clumps of oil-laden mud spatter his pants, and his every step stirs up the smell of hydrocarbons.

Crump stops his dancing and stands beside his anvil, sledgehammer gripped hard in his hands. As he lifts it above his head his muscles tense, and the crowd draws back. He keeps the hammer suspended straight in the air and gives the gathering a theatrical wink. Then, with all his might, Crump brings the hammer crashing down on the small pool of nitroglycerin.

The blast rocks the first two rows of spectators back on their heels, and those foolish enough to have their eyes fixed on the anvil are temporarily blinded by the searing bolt of light. The handle of the sledge splinters in Crump's hands, and its hammer flies upward with the force of a cannonball, slamming into the middle of his forehead. A thick shard of wood buries itself deep in the side of his neck.

He stands erect and motionless, eyes glazed, legs rigid, hands dangling by his sides. His arms begin to tremble and he shuffles forward, his feet plowing little troughs through the oily muck. Crump's mouth opens like he's trying to speak, and for an instant his eyes scan the crowd as if he recognizes several of the onlookers. His entire body shakes violently, and he staggers another foot and topples face-down into a shallow mud puddle.

Matthew's father and the two other men explode with laughter.

"Looks like the show's over," Caleb stammers, turning from the window and rubbing his tearing eyes.

"Permanently, I'd say," says Muleface, glancing at his partner. "So, how much you sell 'em?"

"Five drops. Big 'ins."

"Damn fool."

"Yep, but that fool just bought our bottle," Thackery replies, reaching across the table and pouring another round.

Caleb downs the drink and stares at his son. "So, did that war wagon of a wife of mine sen' you after me again? Well, consider 'er message delivered, and when you see 'er, tell 'er I'll be home when I'm damn well ready. Tell 'er I've got some business to attend to here. But aren't you supposed to be workin' on Doc Willetts' books this afternoon?"

"Yes, sir, that's where I'm headed."

"Then get your tail over there. Your mother's gonna have to wait. I'll show up in due time, and when you see 'er you tell 'er that now, hear?"

Matthew turns to leave.

"Hey, boy!" Caleb bellows. "Don't go steppin' on any dead clowns layin' out there in the dirt!" The three men launch into another bout of gut-busting laughter.

Caleb watches his son work his way back through the crowd and out the door.

"Spittin' image of you," Thackery says. "Same black hair, brown eyes, big shoulders."

"Sharp as a tack, that one, like his mother, but not near as ornery," Caleb says. "He'll be makin' more money than me in no time. Certain to be keepin' more, I'd wager, which ain't saying a whole hell of a lot. All he wants to do is work with numbers, keepin' books and the like. When my first-born, Luke, was his age, the two of us would hunt and fish all through these parts. Spend days out in the woods. This one don't want none of that. He's harder to figure out. More of a loner. Quiet as hell. Don't let you know what he's thinkin'."

Muleface interrupts him. "We ready to draw for a poke?"

"Gettin' anxious are you?" Caleb replies. "Okay, boys, throw down two bits apiece and we'll pick cards."

Muleface turns around in his chair and catches a young whore's eye. He smiles at her, drawing his thin lips wide apart to reveal a mouthful of crooked, protruding teeth.

"I tried to kiss a whore once," he says, "but she wouldn't let me. 'Fraid these buck choppers would cut 'er."

Caleb spreads a deck facedown on the table. "Draw, high card wins."

Thackery draws a ten, Caleb a three; Muleface grins and holds up a queen.

"Well, he ain't only smart, he's lucky too," Thackery says to the beaming Muleface. He pushes the coins toward his partner, who picks them up and clasps them in his hand.

Caleb glances at the whores. "Yep, you won the poke, you lucky bastard. Looks like you got a good choice of women. Go get yourself a nice one."

Muleface scrapes his chair back from the table and stands up.

Thackery slides the whiskey his way. "Here, buy the lady a drink. She just may let you sneak a kiss."

Muleface grabs the bottle by its neck and holds it to the window, gauging how much is left.

"Maybe I got enough to give 'er two. God knows, she'll need 'em."

He flashes his donkey grin, turns, and ambles toward the whores.

The smile dissolves from Caleb's face and he sits in silence, withdrawn and angry. He stares at a young man with thick black hair and diamond rings on his fingers playing poker across the crowded room.

Doc's Discovery

Matthew picks up his pace as he rounds a bend on Bissell Avenue and nears Doc Willetts' modest white-shingled home perched on a gentle slope overlooking the rushing Allegheny River. The water is always high this time of year, fed by snow melt filling brooks and streams coursing their way through surrounding, leafless hills.

Like every afternoon before he arrives for work, Matthew thinks of Lavinia and hopes she's here. They've known each other since the two of them started school together, but for the past six months he can't stop thinking about her: her neatly brushed brown hair falling down her back; her playful blue eyes and perfect fair skin sprinkled with a few light freckles; her shapely figure—getting more enticing by the day, it seems—tastefully revealed beneath her bright print dresses.

He wonders if Doc Willetts knows of his feelings for his daughter, or if he would approve of the attraction. He worries about Caleb's constant antics, and if the doc is aware of them. For if he is, he might not like this budding relationship at all. Maybe he'll tell Matthew not to come around anymore, tell him he doesn't want him doing his books any longer. Certainly, the good doctor has loftier plans for his only child than having her take up with the son of the town drunk.

He shakes away these thoughts, opens the door to the doc's first floor office and sees her standing by a shelf with a stack of medical books in her arms. She turns and smiles as he enters the room, which is heated by a stack of burning logs in a shallow brick fireplace. He closes the door behind him with an extra nudge to keep the cold out.

"Matthew, you look like you're chilled to the bone," Lavinia says, looking him over. "Go warm up by the fire. Can I get you something hot to drink?"

Matthew blows into his hands and rubs them together. "I'm fine. Here, let me help you with those," he says, walking up next to her and taking three of the heaviest books.

"Father just got them delivered, doctoring journals he plans to use, sent from Yale and Oxford."

"Yalen Oxford? Who's he, a friend of your Pa?" Matthew asks in all seriousness. "I guess he's got a lot of books to send this many." He arranges the three he's holding in a neat row on the middle shelf.

Lavinia laughs and gives him a quick kiss on his cheek. She smiles, hands him two more journals and watches him place them next to the others. "Matthew, my dear, you may have a head for numbers, but I think you need to broaden your studies a bit."

"How so?"

"Well, because Yale and Oxford are ..." The second blast of the day causes Lavinia to drop her remaining books to the floor.

The explosion sounds like it's come from far out of town, but a moment later they feel a rumbling percussion that rattles the house's windows and wraps itself around them, freezing them in place. The doc rushes out of the back room, and the three of them bolt outside, leaving the door open behind them.

Matthew knows what's happened. He knows only too well. Even at his age he's seen the devastating remnants of too many nitroglycerin blasts to waste even a second thinking otherwise.

From the street they see the dark dome of dirt and debris billowing on the horizon. The cloud glows with a devilish red and yellow hue.

Doc Willetts spins around toward his daughter. "Lavinia, go inside and wait for us. There's a patient in the back room. Please stay with her until I get back."

He turns to Matthew, who's rubbing the spot on his cheek where he received his unexpected kiss. "Let's go!" Willetts orders.

They run three blocks to the livery where a stable hand is already hitching up Willetts' two black stallions—high-headed, muscular steeds, the fastest team in Oil City.

"I knew you'd be coming, just like always," the young stable worker snickers with a vulpine grin.

"These trips are far too frequent," replies Willetts.

"Lost the smithy earlier," the kid mumbles, the smile still creasing his lips.

The doctor flashes a stern look. "I'm not saying he had it coming," Willetts says. "Far from it. Crump was an honest, hardworking man. But he courted trouble. I told him so time and again while patching him up after his various stunts, yet the braggart never listened, he always wanted to show off, play for a crowd, bully a few bucks out of those stupid enough to take in his act. Even so, he didn't deserve what happened to him."

Willetts secures his medical bag in the back of the buggy, and he and Matthew climb aboard. The doc guides his team through the wide open door and into the street.

He reins back the horses, stops the carriage and glances over his shoulder at the stable hand.

"I want you here when we get back. I don't want to come looking for you like last time, understand? I'll need my horses brushed and put up proper for the night. We won't be long."

The kid nods and smiles again. He knows the doc and his young companion won't be long at all.

As the carriage speeds out of town, Matthew feels the last rays of the late afternoon sun on the side of his face, and he looks at the round, whitish moon suspended and just visible in the graying sky. His mind races with the horses, and Willetts glances at him out of the corner of his eye.

"You look like you're carrying quite a weight on those shoulders of yours."

"I was thinking about my brother, Luke, and the well fire six months ago. I pray he went fast. Pa has never said, but then we're not talking much lately."

"You and your father do things together?"

Nothing I can tell you about, thinks Matthew. "Not much," he answers. "I was always second fiddle to Luke. He and Pa were close."

Willetts adjusts his grip on the reins. "I remember when you got sick."

Matthew turns away and stares at the passing trees. "Yeah, the time me and Pa and Luke were supposed to go fishing on Pollywog Run. Pa had lined up a friend's boat, and we were going to camp, just the three of us, sleeping outdoors, catching fish, hunting game, but I broke my arm the day before and had to stay behind with my mother. But that was just the start. You remember I came down with rheumatic fever that same week and was in bed for two months, even after the fever broke, getting my strength back?"

"I recall you were in bad shape, but you overcame it."
Willetts replies. "I remember it took a while."

"I had to stay in bed, and that's how I learned my numbers, my mathematics, out of boredom. There was nothing
else to do. If I hadn't got hurt, and then sick, things would
have been different. We all could have spent more time
together."

Matthew turns back to the doc and says, "I think I missed
my opportunity, and the three of us never had another one.
I hate this town, you know, and I hate the waste and destruction and death by the business that runs it."

"There's more to the oil business than what you see in
this town," Willetts replies. "There are people making for-
tunes in it. Just look at Rockefeller."

"Who?"

"John D. Rockefeller from Cleveland. He's making
money hand over fist, and I bet he hasn't spent more than a
day in an oil field his entire life, or drilled a single well for
that matter. From what I hear, he's far on his way to control-
ling the entire trade, from the field to the kerosene lamp."

Matthew looks the doc in the eyes. "I want to be rich
someday, like him."

"No reason you can't be," Willetts replies.

Matthew shifts in his seat and thinks of Lavinia. "I also
want to thank you for letting me keep your books, Doctor
Willetts, and I appreciate it more than you know. You've
been very good to me and I won't forget it."

Willetts chuckles. "When you're rich, you mean."

"Right…I mean no," Matthew says. "I don't forget it
now."

"You haven't had it easy, son. That's why I've tried to
help you get a start, give you work this past year, not only so
you could earn a few extra dollars, but also to get your mind

off things, especially after your brother passed. I know what it's like to lose a loved one. I can't tell you how hard it was on us when the cancer took Lavinia's mother. None of us saw it coming, and there was nothing anyone could do, it was on her so fast."

Matthew notices a small red fox scamper into the forest's cover. He looks up again and searches for the moon, barely apparent as they near the site of the blast, and he takes a deep breath of the crisp afternoon air, getting cooler by the minute. The doc heads the wagon off the road and up to the rim of a shallow valley where stands of towering pines once grew close together. They survey the destruction below, and watch the glowing cloud continue to coat the sky above them.

Willetts guides his horses around the stumps and ground fires, and he draws back on the reins and slows the horses to a trot as he and Matthew continue deeper into the valley that is now a cratered, smoky wasteland. The smell of smoldering pine and burned dirt assaults them, and the trees, most denuded of bark and branch, stand broken and twisted, shattered masts beckoning a path to hell. Dozens of small fires burn in the depression, some with flames shooting skyward in gaseous bursts as if fueled by pockets from inside the earth. Scattered everywhere are mounds of glowing embers of all shapes and sizes. They remind Matthew of fiery beacons.

The doctor brings his carriage to a halt in a swale that somehow was untouched by the blast and flames. Matthew jumps to the ground and feels the brittle wintry grass crinkle under his polished black shoes.

Willetts stands up in the carriage and scans the crater for evidence of human remains, sniffing the air to detect any hint of burning flesh or hair, but there is none, and he climbs from the wagon and joins Matthew. They begin walking in no particular pattern amid the desolation, and the fires around them hold the encroaching darkness at bay.

"There aren't any survivors, that's for sure," Willetts says as they make their way to the outer edge of the scarred terrain.

Matthew walks with the doctor in a broad circle around its perimeter, marking its size and limits in his mind, calculating the extent of the blast and conflagration. "I reckon it had to be a fully-loaded wagon," he says, "probably carrying a dozen nitro canisters or more and a team of two men. What do you think set it off?"

"They probably left the road and came down into this hollow," Willetts replies. "Why, I've no idea. Maybe their horses needed a rest. I'm guessing the horses spooked before they could unhitch them and that jostled their cargo, igniting the blast. Or maybe their wagon overturned."

The two make their way up a steep grade to the northeast corner of the depression, where a stand of majestic pines marks the beginning of the forest wall, and forms a line of demarcation between normalcy and the sweep of destruction behind them.

The doctor walks to the base of one of the trees, and Matthew notices him breathing hard as he stops for a moment and pulls a cloth handkerchief from his jacket pocket. Willetts wipes his perspiring brow and closes his eyes. He turns and faces the forest, breathing in the crisp aroma of the pines.

Matthew, too, takes a deep breath of the aromatic air, a welcome respite from the hydrocarbon and smoke smells so common to the countryside around Oil City. He can see the doctor's breathing is now less labored, but he notices a bright red streak trickling down the doc's left cheek. He moves closer to him. "Are you cut?"

Willetts opens his eyes and rubs his hand across the side of his face. He holds his hand in front of him and through the fires' glow Matthew sees blood smudged on the tips of the man's fingers.

"What the ...?"

The doc dabs his face again, but there's no wound. Another drop of blood falls on his forehead. Matthew looks up into the pine tree and then at one of its lower branches. Draped across it, barely apparent in the darkness, is a portion of a jaw. A sliver of jagged white bone is visible, as are five teeth, some skin and a two-inch reddish brush that Matthew supposes was once part of a man's beard. The doctor steps aside just as another trickle of blood hits the ground.

Matthew bends over and picks up a stick. He throws it upward toward the pine limb, but it misses its mark and comes back down beside his feet. He grabs it again, judging his target once more, and sends the stick end-over-end toward the dripping remnants. It hits the remains squarely this time, dislodging them from the limb. The bloody mass falls through the blackness and flops to the dirt.

"Leave it be, I'll take care of this," orders Willetts, kneeling and opening a scuffed wooden cigar box he carries for these occasions.

He lifts the piece of jaw from the ground and places it inside the box. "We'll find out who he was," Willetts says. "And his family, if he had one, will at least have something to bury. May God have mercy on his soul."

BLANKET OF SNOW

L ater that night on the outskirts of Oil City in the kitchen of a small ramshackle farmhouse his family rents from an absentee oil concessionaire, Matthew sits at a home-made wooden table practicing his multiplication exercises. He holds a stubby pencil in his right hand, and three other pencils of varying lengths and thicknesses rest on the table-top beside a two-foot ruler and a stack of unlined white paper.

He loves escaping into his numbers, and after his schoolwork and part-time job and daily chores are finished he'll lose himself in them, some nights practicing division or decimals or fractions or complex calculations by the light of a candle until his mother Rebecca calls into the kitchen and implores him to go to bed.

But the predictability and power the numbers help him exert over his otherwise uncertain world are nowhere to be found on this night. He can't concentrate, can't shake the day's events from his mind: Crump facedown in the mud; the dripping jawbone in the tree.

He hears a groan outside the window, and he puts his pencil down beside the others and rises from his chair. He opens the back door and scans the blackness of the night, adjusting his eyes to the dark. It's snowing hard, and he can see the grayish-blue flakes swirling and twisting in the sky, falling to the ground. Suddenly, he sees a figure laying in the yard. It's his father, who lays coated and curled up on his side.

"Pa!" Matthew shouts, rushing from the doorway and kneeling beside Caleb, who lifts himself up on one elbow, but then falls back, dissipating his blanket of snow.

"Help me up, boy. I slipped and riled this trick knee of mine and I'm havin' trouble walkin', negotiatin' this path. Help me up, now."

Matthew reaches under Caleb's arms and tries to raise him, but his father's sheer size and bulk prevent it.

"Pa, stand up. Here, take my hand."

Caleb shakes his head and rises to one knee as his son grabs his hands to steady him and help him get up.

"Have you eaten anything?" Matthew asks.

"I ain't hungry," Caleb replies, dropping his head to his chest and draping his heavy arm around his son's shoulders as they make their way toward the back door and up the stoop.

At least no one can see us here, Matthew thinks.

"Let's get out of this cold and find you something to eat," he says, guiding the big man inside and over to the kitchen table, where Caleb collapses into one of the big wooden chairs.

"Get me a drink," his father mutters.

"I'll make a pot of hot coffee. That'll warm you up."

"I've got...a job...tomorrow...shootin' three wells...Farris fields." Caleb's words are slurred and stifled.

He looks down at Matthew's paper and pencils on the table. "It's good...you practicin' them numbers like you do," Caleb says. "When you're older, you ought to get a job keepin' books...work inside in an office...wear clean clothes and keep dry...keep safe and warm on days like these...doin' anything other than the godforsaken labor I've been sentenced to." Caleb picks a pencil off the table. "These the only things you got to write with?"

"Preacher Hill from church gives me any extras he has," Matthew replies. "He knows I go through a lot of them, although most times the ones he gives me are so small I don't get much use out of them. Glad to get them, though. Saves some money."

"So you use 'em...'til they're no more than a nub of lead?" Caleb says, waving the pencil in front of him mock ingly. It's sharpened down to less than an inch in length. "You know what I'm goin' to do? I been thinkin' about it. I'm goin' to get you one of them fancy fountain pens to work with."

"I don't need one of those, Pa," Matthew replies. "These pencils work just fine for what I'm doing. I'm not making real entries in a journal. I'm doing nothing permanent, just practicing."

"I know where to get it, too. It's got a real diamond in it. A big one."

"No need, Pa. Besides, if I used a pen, I'd have to buy ink. But thanks for the offer, anyway." Matthew smiles at his father.

The aroma of the brewing coffee infuses the small kitchen, and Caleb's eyes hold a faraway look as if he's try-ing to gather his thoughts, and he takes a deep breath.

"Every bookkeeper worth his salt ought to have himself a good-lookin' pen, a writin' instrument he can be proud of," Caleb says. "It's expected in business. Don't you think I know? I see the office workers at the Roberts Company car-ryin' pens in their pockets. It shows success, and I got just the one in mind. It's made of onyx and gold, and has a big

diamond in it. But I think I already told you that, didn't I?
I know the man who's got it. I saw him playin' poker today
at the saloon."

"Talk of gifts is one thing when you're able to afford
them, but we've got rent to pay."

Matthew looks up to see his mother standing in the
kitchen doorway. She's a beautiful woman with long dark
hair, but her face is worn and worried, and Matthew realizes
that he hasn't seen her smile since Luke died.

Caleb rubs his eyes and answers his wife. "The
boy deserves somethin' of value. He carries a lot of
responsibility."

"You've gambled your wages away again, haven't you?"
Rebecca says, walking over to the table and gathering up
Matthew's paper and pencils. She places them in a tattered
folder and glares at her husband. "I asked you a question. I
said the money's gone again, isn't it?"

"Not gone…merely being held until I can retrieve it,"
Caleb answers, snickering at the irony.

"It may be a joke to you," Rebecca snaps, "but I don't
think Mr. Kincaid is going to find it funny that we're behind
on his rent. We owe him eighteen dollars. Where are we
going to get that amount of money?"

Caleb rises from the table, walks unsteadily over to the
cupboard and pulls out a bottle of whiskey.

Rebecca's eyes narrow, and she walks up to her husband.
"You don't need any of that," she says. Caleb turns his back
to her and pours a healthy shot into the bottom of a glass,
polishing it off with a quick gulp.

Matthew gets his father a cup of coffee. "Here, Pa, have
this instead," he says, putting the cup on the table.

"Listen to your son!" Rebecca shouts.

Caleb spins around.

"I ain't listenin' to anyone anymore, least not to the likes of you! If I want to get the boy a gift, I will. And I'm sick and tired of sendin' my hard-earned money every month to Kincaid. Like he needs it, or even expects it. He's got his. A year ago he was a dirt-poor farmer askin' me for a handout like so many other bastards around this hellhole until they found oil on his property and bought him out."

"That was his good fortune," Rebecca retorts.

"And my curse!"

"He expects his payment."

"He left a year ago."

"He gave us an address to send the money. And we haven't paid him in three months. What are you thinking?"

"Pa, drink your coffee."

Caleb ignores his son. "So Kincaid's rich and livin' worry free, and I'm left behind shootin' wells, courtin' death so he can line his pockets with more blood money?"

Caleb pours himself another shot. He downs the booze and flashes Rebecca a fiery look. "Let me tell you somethin'," he says. "Every day there's leaseholders and speculators fillin' the saloons lookin' to sell their holdin's. Most of their properties are played out, flushed of their oil too quick, or least the owners think so. But I know better. Those wells never been fracked, never been opened up, because the speculators spend the money too fast and have nothin' in their pockets to put back into the fields to keep 'em producin'."

Caleb steadies himself on the cupboard and pours another. "One of these days I'm goin' to come home with a concession. I'm goin' to walk through that door with our future in my hands." He downs his drink.

Rebecca shakes her head. "Whatever you're looking to bring home, you're not going to find it by carousing and gambling the way you do, that I *will* tell you."

"Pa, why don't you let me help you?" Matthew says. "I have some money."

Caleb doesn't answer him. He just smacks his lips and says, "In fact, I have a feelin' there's a deal waitin' for me right now."

Rebecca glares at him. "The only deal you'll find tonight is your usual, a deal at the card table, and the result will be the same as always."

Caleb grabs the bottle and heads toward the door. Matthew runs in front of him, blocking his way.

"What do you think you're doin'?" Caleb growls.

"Stay, Pa. You need your rest for tomorrow. You need to eat something."

"Step aside, boy!"

"No, Pa. You stay here."

Caleb lifts his hand as if he's going to slap his son, and Rebecca comes up in back of him and grabs his arm.

"You so much as lay a finger on that boy and you won't have to worry about a torpedo killing you. I'll do it myself!"

"Get the hell away from me, woman!" Caleb shouts. "I don't want any part of you. Don't you think I know what you're up to durin' the day when I'm gone?"

"What's it to you?" Rebecca hisses. "You abandoned me for the bottle years ago."

Caleb hoists his whiskey in a mock toast to his wife. Then he turns and looks down at Matthew. "You save your money, son, and keep studyin' your numbers. Don't worry about those stubby pencils, or the preacher's charity. You're goin' to have somethin' nice to work with real soon."

He shoots a strained smile at his wife and staggers out of the house.

Matthew stands on the stoop and watches his father disappear into the cold darkness. He feels so small and helpless.

At ten minutes to midnight Caleb struts back into the Down Hole Saloon. A few solitary drinkers stand at the long bar. A group of Pinkerton guards—fresh off their shifts patrolling the oil fields in search of rogue well shooters who operate in violation of Roberts Company patents—are eating a late dinner of stew and bread at a large round table in the middle of the room. At another table by the back wall a poker game is in progress, and Caleb makes his way over to the five men immersed in the wagering.

"Johnny, I've come to play for your pen," Caleb says.

A young man, still in his twenties, looks up from his cards. He has on a dark, tailored, but heavily wrinkled three-piece suit made of expensive European fabric. There is a large diamond stickpin in his right lapel, and the top two buttons of his white shirt are unfastened, revealing his hairless and tanned chest. He brushes his unruly, jet-black hair off his forehead with a quick sweep of his hand and fixes his penetrating blue eyes on the man standing before him.

"Well, well, if it isn't Caleb Strong, come to play me not for my money, but for my pen," Coal Oil Johnny replies, smiling, reaching into his shirt pocket and removing the would-be prize. He holds it up for Caleb and the other men at the table.

"I saw you staring at it earlier this afternoon," he says. "I had this special requisitioned for me in Switzerland a few years ago after I'd made my first million. It's polished black onyx and gold, and this diamond inlaid in the cap here is one full carat, mine-cut of impeccable clarity and color. Can you see?" Johnny lifts the pen higher, rotating it in a slight circle, and the rainbow brilliance of the jewel radiates under the glow of the candlelight from the chandelier suspended above him.

"Like I told you a dozen times before, Caleb, I'm not putting this into play for just any penny ante game. You're going to have to lay some healthy wagers on the table if you're to have any chance of acquiring this beauty, and as usual I doubt you have the money to run with the big dogs. But dream on, my good man, I certainly can't fault you for that." He puts the pen back into his pocket, looks down at his cards and prepares to resume play.

Caleb reaches into his jacket and pulls out a thick wad of bills. "Tonight's different," he says. "I've been cleanin' house at every stop I've made workin' my way here, and I'd expect I can hold my own in any game you fellas want to play."

Coal Oil Johnny feasts his eyes on the cash. "Well, well, what have we here? Looks to me like this mongrel has what it takes to join the pack. Why don't you have a seat, Caleb, and play a few hands with us? We're not ready to bust our game up just yet, are we boys? Sit down and let us deal you in. We'll play some five-card for awhile and, if you have any money left afterwards, you and I will go one-on-one for the big prize."

Caleb turns his back to the table and flags the bartender. "Bring us six glasses and a bottle of whiskey on me. We're goin' to be here for a spell!"

He lets the five men at the table finish their hand, and then he sits down across from Coal Oil Johnny. Caleb looks him in the eyes, withdraws more money from his pocket and says, "Yep, I'm feelin' mighty lucky tonight, mighty lucky, indeed. Let's get goin', boys. Who wants to cut for the deal?"

A MAN REMEMBERED

The night's snowfall has turned into a driving, bone-chilling rain by sunup, and Caleb, coatless and drenched, groans as he strains to remove the last bolt from the valves and piping connected to the top of Farris Well Number 1 in an oil field just north of town.

He latches a large steel hook to the wellhead and uses both of his calloused hands to pull on a chain affixed to a pulley at the top of a sturdy tripod rigged directly over the well. With another groan, he hoists the head off the well and into the air, immediately noticing there's no pressure or force coming from the hole. A moment later an anemic trickle of brackish crude begins gurgling up, and Caleb watches it spread like spilled molasses across the water-soaked, grassless ground toward his feet.

He walks over to his wagon, removes an empty torpedo, and brings it to the open well. He returns to the wagon, raises the top of a wooden utility box, and thrusts his hand inside to check his percussion caps. Satisfied, he closes the lid to keep out the rain, now pounding down harder.

Caleb removes a canister of nitroglycerin hanging from a hook next to the utility box and sets it beside the torpedo. He walks back to the wagon and searches among the tools, spools of guide wire, wet gloves, boots and other clutter for a go-devil weight. Finding the one he wants, he picks it up and puts it beside the torpedo and canister of nitro. He's soaked through, and the wind begins to blow, yet he feels neither cold nor discomfort.

Caleb bends down on one knee and unscrews the top of the torpedo. He steadies the device in his left hand and with his right takes the lid off the nitro canister. He grabs its handle, tilts it up and fills the bomb to its brim. He screws the top back on, and with both hands lays it on the ground like he's returning a baby to bed. The rain intensifies, and streams of water now mix with the oil and mud at the surface of the well.

Caleb rises and walks over to his horses. As is his custom whenever he shoots a well, he unhitches his team from the wagon and takes them a good ways away from the work site. His head begins to throb and his hands shake from his dawn-to-dawn drinking, but he reaches his spot and drapes the reins around a small tree, tying them in a loose knot to keep the horses in place.

"You two stay here awhile," he says, rubbing the mare's wet nose and then his own.

Back at his wagon, Caleb reopens the utility box, removes a percussion cap and takes it over to the well. He bends down and affixes the cap to the end of the bomb. He grips the cap hard, double-checking it to make sure it's positioned just right. Then he picks up the torpedo.

The blinding rain pounds down even harder now and dirty, wind-whipped water swirls and churns in the mud-gullies at his feet. He cocks his head to curse the formless sky, but as he does his legs shoot out from beneath him. His huge frame falls toward the ground, and he tries to cradle the torpedo to protect it from the impact he knows is coming. He watches the earth approach. It is the last thing Caleb Strong ever sees.

✤ ✤ ✤

The stable hand has the black steeds hitched and ready when Doc Willetts rushes through the barn door.

"I'll be here when you get back," the boy says, flashing his sly smile. He's already spending the latest tip he'll soon receive from his best customer.

"I expect you will," the doc replies sarcastically, raising his collar in anticipation of the cold rain about to pelt him. He cracks the reins, and his team speeds off into the lightless day.

A short ways out of town he sees Matthew running down the road toward the Farris fields, and Willetts slows his wagon and comes up beside the boy. "Get in, son. We'll ride together."

Matthew keeps running, but turns toward the doctor. "I know it's him!" he shouts. "Pa went back out soon after he came home last night. He never came back. He told me he had a job this morning shooting the Farris wells. The blast came from that direction!"

The doc pulls his team to a halt. "Come on, get in, son. We don't know anything yet."

Matthew stops running. "I do. I know. I have no doubt it was him," he says, climbing into the wagon.

As they near the field they ride by two horses standing side by side in the rain next to the road. Matthew says nothing, but he turns to look at them as he and the doc pass. Drenched and dripping, the mare stares back at him with forlorn eyes.

The sight and smell of destruction are everywhere. The air hangs heavy with the smell of burnt dirt, splintered timber, heated mud and oil fires that spit defiantly at the wet day. An opaque, smoky haze covers the area, trapped by the falling rain. Two small buildings on the far corner of the tract have been blown into oblivion. All that remain are smoldering and broken fieldstone foundations.

"You walk the perimeter that way," Willetts says, "and I'll head in the opposite direction. We'll meet up and then cover the blast area together. Holler if you come across something."

Matthew climbs off the wagon and begins walking the edges of the blast. He's soaked, and he feels as if he's inside a dream, locked in a state of unreality where nightmare and premonition converge.

Why couldn't I have gotten him to stay? If he had, this wouldn't have happened. This is my fault.

Tears stream down his face, but he continues on, even though he knows his search is senseless. He scans the tree line for a fragment, a remnant, anything recognizable, something to take home, something to keep and to hold, but the pounding rain blurs his vision and thoughts, and he feels light headed and his legs become unsteady. He falls to his knees, opens his fingers and presses his hands into the mud and throws up. He feels like a trapped animal, and the feeling burns his insides. He wants to escape, to run, to fly away, to soar and not look back, never look back, to knock on the door and be welcomed inside, to race through the grass on a summer's day, to recapture opportunity lost, time passed by, to be greeted on the street with respect and pride, to make a mark, to be a man ... remembered.

A man remembered. That's all I have left of him. The thought keeps repeating itself in his head.

He gets up from the ground, and through the smoke and destruction he can barely see the black silhouette of the doc standing by a burning well. He makes his way down a washed-out furrow toward him.

"There's nothing here, son," Willetts says, holding the cigar box under his arm. "Not a trace of anyone or anything. I've looked all over."

"I know," Matthew whispers, and the two of them begin making their way back to the carriage.

"We have no proof your father was the one caught in the blast," Willetts says. We have no proof of that, no proof that he was even here."

"Yes, we do," Matthew replies. "Those horses we saw are Pa's."

The boy surveys the destruction one last time, and through the wall of rain he catches a dull glimmer out of the corner of his eye about fifty yards away. He stops and looks again, turning to the doctor.

"Sir, you go ahead. I'll follow as soon as I can and meet you by the carriage. If you have to leave..."

"No, you do what you have to do," Willetts says. "Take as long as you need."

Matthew walks back alone toward the far edge of the barren circle. The glimmer becomes brighter and more distinct with every step, and his pace quickens. He fixes his eyes on the object in the mud and begins to run. His footing is steady now, and he runs faster, closing in and covering his ground with great speed and agility.

Then he stands over it.

The diamond's brilliance cuts through the dark day like a beacon on a hill, radiant in its power, its brightness intensified against the black onyx and gold. Even in the smoky haze, the stone attracts light and breaks it into vibrant rays of red, green, blue and yellow. To Matthew, the rainbow shines through the darkness in search of a soul, ready to reveal the way, protect the lost, assure the fearful, heal the hurting, show the path home, open the future.

He bends down and picks the pen up out of the mud. He cups it in his hands, brings it to his chest and closes his eyes.

The rain pounds down harder. Matthew doesn't care. His father had kept his promise.

Three days later in the early morning Matthew secures the last box of his family's possessions in the back of the wagon and walks over to Lavinia. She and Doc Willetts, who's inside with Rebecca checking and locking up the house, have come to see Matthew and his mother off. Lavinia starts to cry, and Matthew guides her by the arm a short distance away so they can be alone.

"Both our families have lost so much, lost people we loved," Lavinia says. "I'm so sorry."

I feel I'm going to lose you, too, Matthew thinks.

"Why do you have to go?" she asks him, dabbing her eyes with a hankie.

"Because there's work in Cleveland," Matthew says. "I have to take care of my mother now, and I can make more money there. There's more opportunities for jobs in a big city."

"I'm going to miss our afternoons," Lavinia says. "You're my best friend, Matthew, whether you know it or not. I'm going to miss *you.*"

"I'm going to come back, I promise," Matthew says, leaning over to kiss her, but then drawing away as he notices the doc and Rebecca emerging from the house.

"I know what you were about to do," Lavinia whispers. "I wish you'd just go ahead and do it. I wish you'd kiss me goodbye."

But he doesn't. "I'll write you," Matthew says. "I'll write you as often as I can. Maybe you and your father can visit us once we get settled."

"Why won't you? Why won't you kiss me?"

Doc Willetts and Rebecca join them. "You ready, Matthew?" his mother asks.

Matthew shakes the doctor's hand and thanks him, looking at Lavinia one more time as he and his mother head to their wagon.

He climbs up onto the seat next to Rebecca and reaches for the reins. His eyes are clear and his grip strong and steady, but they mask the sadness that consumes him.

Rebecca turns to her son. "So much of Caleb died when the fire took Luke, and with his passing your father slipped farther away, despite us trying to pull him back. He was headstrong and proud and a wonderful man deep down. But the sins of the bottle killed him, as he knew they would. As I think he wanted them to."

Matthew scans the brightening horizon and thinks of his father.

I remember the smell of the lather when he'd shave, the wisps of hot steam rising from the washbowl, and the sound of his brush bumping the side of the shaving mug. He'd look down at me and smile with his face full of white foam, and I can hear the razor sharpen against the strap and the water swirl as he cleaned the whiskers from his blade. He'd towel himself dry and pat on cologne to close the nicks, and he'd reach out and my hand would disappear into his. We'd walk outside where Luke was already waiting and we'd stand in the morning sun, just the three of us. It was warm and green under the cloudless cobalt sky and I wasn't afraid of anything: I thought the day would last forever.

Matthew breaks away from his thoughts and prepares for the journey ahead.

"It will take us three days to get to Cleveland, Mother," he says. "We'll put up in a boarding house until I find a job and we can get settled somewhere better. I'm going to ask Mr. Rockefeller for a position in his company."

"Who?"

"Mr. John D. Rockefeller. He owns a big refinery in Cleveland, and now he's buying oil fields in Pennsylvania and Ohio. I hear he's changing the business, bringing order, stopping the destruction. I plan to finish my schooling in the mornings, and work afternoons or nights at one of his plants."

"Now, how do you expect to meet a man like that?"

Matthew looks down at the pen in his pocket and takes in the rainbow.

"I don't know how, Mother, but I know I will."

He glances at Lavinia and her father a final time. He flicks the reins, the horses come alive, and his wagon begins to roll.

ATTACK ON THE ALLEGHENY

Augustus Clapp and his men emerge from the murky night with weapons in their hands and murder on their minds.

Clapp, a pot-bellied brute with black soulless eyes, grips a thick wooden club coated with dried blood and hair. A second man cradles a twelve-gauge shotgun in gnarled, big-knuckled hands, and a third, a few steps away, clasps a three-foot, steel-link chain that dangles to the dirt.

Bringing up the rear, panting with raspy breaths, limps a Pinkerton guard. A holster and revolver hang from his frayed brown belt, and he holds a flaming torch.

Clapp opens his mouth to reveal two rows of tiny, rat-like teeth, but he doesn't utter a sound. He merely motions to the Pinkerton and to the man holding the shotgun, and they split off toward the bow of a flatbed barge that's wrapped in a shroud of fog.

Crammed with more than eighty barrels of oil stacked three high across its broad-planked deck, the vessel sits low in the water, waiting to make its run down the Allegheny River from Franklin to Pittsburgh at sunup.

The brute beckons the man with the chain to come with him, and the two slip into the shadows on either side of the door to the crew's sleeping quarters.

The man with the shotgun wipes his dripping nose across his sleeve and checks his load. "You ready to teach these pole pushers a lesson?" he says, planting his feet wide apart on the dock and aiming his gun at the bottom row of barrels.

"We warned 'em, sure enough," the Pinkerton answers, smiling as he watches the flame dance atop his torch.

The buck pellets burst through an oaken cask, creating a gaping hole that spews blackish-blue crude over the worn wooden deck. The shooter places a second round into a top barrel, splitting it in two. Its disgorged contents cascade over the cargo like a glistening waterfall, coating the barrels' sides in a viscous sheen.

The Pinkerton pitches the torch on top of the oil. The other man pumps a couple more rounds into the inferno, and the fire leaps across the front of the barge, its flames a twisting tower in the veil of midnight mist.

On the opposite end of the vessel, Clapp nods his head toward the crew-shack door. He hears voices inside, muffled at first, but becoming more distinct. A voice is approaching, and the teamster grips his club with both hands and draws it back.

"Leave it to me to see what the commotion is," a man inside says. "Likely drunkards whopping it up on their way home, which is where I wish I was now, as I believe I must go back to me dear County Clare to get a good night's sleep. God knows I'm getting none here."

The thugs wait in the shadows as the door opens. Out comes a roundish, freckled-faced man with a checkered shirt and carrot-colored hair. He freezes in his tracks.

"Blessed be Jesus! Fire! Fire!" The man turns toward the door. "Will, get up! The barge's on fire!"

The club cracks across the middle of the Irishman's back, and he melts to his knees with a curdling groan. The steel-link chain cuts through the darkness, whipping across his face. Clapp jams the end of his bat into the man's belly, doubling him over, and the whip-chain descends across his back in unrelenting, skin-ripping fury.

The Irishman tries to crawl toward the rear of the deck, away from the blows of the club and chain, and from the fire that now engulfs the front half of the barge. He raises his eyes to Clapp. "Who you be? What deeds have we done to deserve this wrath?"

"There's but one way a bringin' oil outta these parts, and that's over road by wagon!" Clapp shouts, swinging his bat around in a wide arc and slamming it into the right side of the man's head. "When you barge scum gonna know that?"

The teamster steps up the power and speed of his swings, as if relishing every sickening contact of club to flesh, every crack and crush of shattered bone and brain.

The Pinkerton jumps onto the boat, revolver in hand. He limps past what's left of the Irishman and into the crew shack.

"Well, lookie here," he shouts to the others outside. "This one's got a whore 'tween the sheets."

The man with the chain appears in the doorway, his muscled frame illuminated and shimmering in the fire's glow. He calls to the Pinkerton, "This flatbed's gonna blow. We gotta shove 'er to the river and get the hell outta here!"

The Pinkerton points his pistol at the young girl and twitches it a couple of times. "Yeah? Then she's comin' with us. We'll drag her up in the woods and have some fun." He eyes the girl. "Get up."

She looks at the man beside her.

"I said, get up goddamn it!" the Pinkerton shouts.

The man in bed remains silent, appearing unafraid.

The Pinkerton feasts his eyes on the naked girl as she draws the sheet back and gets out of the bed. "Mexicano," he mutters, "one of them hot bloods. Oh, yeah, we're gonna teach this one a new trick or two."

It's the diversion the man is waiting for. His right hand springs from the covers, and he takes dead aim at the Pinkerton with his Colt revolver. The bullet tears the top of the guard's head off, and he flys backward and collapses against the wall. The thug with the chain in the doorway turns to run, but a second shot cuts him down cold.

The gunman springs out of bed and runs toward the door. He bolts on to the deck, holding his Colt before him. A shotgun blast tears through his shoulder, and he falls on his side, writhing in pain but still gripping his weapon.

Clapp and the man with the shotgun stride from the shadows and stand over the wounded man. They peer down at him, and the teamster readies his club. "Your Mick buddy won't be makin' any more river trips," Clapp says. "And guess what? You ain't gonna be neither."

A night wind descends from the hills and jumps across the water, fanning the flames higher into the sky. Billowing black clouds, dripping with soot, curdle above the mirrored Allegheny, and a sheet of heat radiates and blankets the back of the barge.

"Let 'em burn, Clapp!" the other thug shouts. "He's half dead anyway, and the whore, she ain't going nowhere. If you an' me don't get the hell outta here now, we'll end up blown to smithereens 'long with this boat. I say let's watch the fireworks up the way."

The teamster lowers his bat and glances inside the crew shack. He eyes the girl, who sits on the side of the bed wrapped in the sheet, a dazed look on her face. "Right, the hell with 'em," Clapp grunts.

Clapp jams his club into the wounded man's wrist. The Colt falls to the deck and he kicks the gun into the water. "You won't be needin' that," he sneers. "Matter of fact, in a second or two, you won't be needin' nothin'." Clapp turns to the other man. "Let's get the fuck outta here."

They jump from the deck as the fire burns the retaining ropes securing the front end of the boat to the dock posts, and the current draws the bow of the barge away from shore out into the river. Clapp undoes the two remaining lines and pushes the flaming vessel from the dock with his club.

The man with the shotgun again draws his snot-filled nose up the length of his sleeve. "Let's head up the bluff and get a bird's-eye view," he shouts.

They trot off the wharf and onto a dark trail leading up a hill. The ground is slippery and wet, and they hunch forward with their arms low for balance as they ascend the mud path, breathing hard. The trail opens onto a clearing that overlooks the river, and the men slog around clumps of tall, greenish-blue grasses, bent heavy with droplets of night dew.

"Well, I'll be damned, Clapp, look at that," says the man with the shotgun. The teamster pulls a half-smoked cigar from his shirt pocket, puts it between his lips and lights it.

The barge, now nearly consumed in flames, is a good two hundred yards downriver, carried fast by the churning current. At its stern, the men see the outlines of the naked girl and the wounded man, and they watch the girl support him as they make their way to the very back of the boat.

The pair jump into the river. The barge draws away from them, and a series of explosions tears apart the vessel, sending barrels skyward and dotting the obsidian waterway with pools of burning petroleum.

Augustus Clapp, enforcer for the teamsters, clamps his tiny teeth around his squat stogie and takes in the scene with the detached curiosity of a bored housecat. He watches the fires flash and spurt. He scans the brightened sky, teeming with violent illumination. He sees farm families and other river dwellers come out from their homes and run to the water's edge to catch a glimpse of the floating inferno careening by. He watches the escapees paddling their way to shore, closing in on a crescent-shaped cove nestled among moss-covered rocks.

Clapp takes a deep puff, tilts his head back and exhales rings of smoke from his mouth. "Not to worry, not to worry at all," he says, drawing the club to his nose, closing his eyes and smelling the fresh blood. He brings the bat down and taps it twice on the ground. "We'll run into those two again real soon, you bet your ass we will. And when we do, mark my words, I'm gonna make sure we finish the job good and proper."

MONEYMEN

John Davison Rockefeller stands at the window of his fourth floor office and stares across the Cuyahoga River. He's watching the twenty or so barges waiting to be loaded at his refinery on Kingsbury Run on the outskirts of Cleveland's busy commercial district.

The thirty-year-old has on pressed gray trousers, a starched white shirt buttoned at the collar with a black wraparound bowtie, a tailored black jacket with thin blue stripes, and polished brown shoes laced tight and high. His shirt cuffs extend a half-inch below the sleeves of his jacket, revealing two polished gold cufflinks, each inscribed with the letters "JDR." He has groomed chestnut hair and a precisely trimmed auburn moustache cut just above the top half of his thin lips. Neat sideburns extend down each side of his angular face.

Though thinly built and of medium height, the young man has a somber, somewhat threatening appearance, and his face is contemplative and unsmiling. But the most astounding feature are his eyes: bright, clear, intelligent, piercing, gray-blue. Eyes it's said that size up men and situations in an instant; eyes that look at you and inside you at the same time; cold, calculating, otherworldly eyes reflecting a genius intent on imposing his vision of order on the wasteful, dangerous, freewheeling oil business he's about to dominate.

There are three other men in the room with him, all original stockholders of the Standard Oil Company: Henry Morrison Flagler, seven years JDR's senior and dashingly handsome, whip-smart and a master at negotiating contracts; Steven V. Harkness, Flagler's gruff-looking stepbrother and moneyman who made his fortune selling liquor before a new Ohio sales tax was passed; and William Rockefeller, JDR's younger brother, who runs Standard Oil's export operations from New York City.

A small fire crackles in the plain brick fireplace, dispelling the morning chill.

Harkness, relaxing on a black leather couch with a copy of the magazine, *Frenzied Finance*, breaks the silence. "Have you heard what this rag is saying about us?"

Flagler smiles. "They're calling us a monopoly. Imagine that."

"I have no use for such drivel," snaps JDR, waving a telegram in the air. "What concerns me is that one of our crude shipments was hit again last night, and we think the teamsters are behind the attack. Probably that lug, Augustus Clapp. Perhaps we need to teach him a lesson or two!"

"I've heard of him." Flagler says. "He's an enforcer, big as a mountain and mean as a snake, not a man to be trifled with. I hear he and his gangs are responsible for just about every act of sabotage in the oil regions. They've even begun ripping our pipelines out of the ground."

"Looks like the haulers are doing everything they can to corner crude movements out of the fields," JDR says. "Trying to muscle in on any competition, mainly the river carriers, but also the pipeline builders."

"I've sent word to Daniel O'Day to tell his workers to be extra careful," Flagler says, "and we've boosted Daniel's security force to more than two dozen men."

"Daniel's a good man," Rockefeller replies, "one of the best we have. Do you know he was an amateur boxing champion?"

Harkness smiles and chimes in. "Yes, he's *our* enforcer. And, I agree, maybe it's time to set him loose on this Clapp chap."

JDR stares back across the river. "The teamsters are doomed to failure, though none of them are smart enough to know it. The railroads are extending farther into the oil fields every day, and soon our tank cars and pipelines will be carrying all the crude from our wells to our plants, despite the haulers' interference."

"Try as they may, they can't rip all the steel from the ground, now can they?" says William, sitting up in his chair and smiling at Harkness. "But let's talk some good news, gentlemen. I'm happy to report that exports to Europe are growing by the month. Last year we shipped twelve million gallons of kerosene abroad, and this year we're on pace to export fifteen million by the end of December. The English, French—even those hard-ass Germans—simply can't get their hands on enough illuminant. They burn it as fast as we can deliver it."

"Make sure they don't get their hands on any crude exports," JDR says. "I don't want the Europeans refining any oil themselves. I want to make sure no new competitor gets into our business. And if they try to, we'll crush them."

"We're setting up sales centers in all the European cities," William says, "and I've got most all the transatlantic crude ships chartered for the remainder of the year, so they're locked up."

"How's our man Andrews doing on the refining front?" Harkness asks to no one in particular.

"Lubricants, grease and specialties continue to grow," JDR replies, "and Samuel's setting up equipment that will expand the volume of every barrel we process. Soon we'll be getting more products in greater volumes from the same amount of oil."

"Sam's a good technician," William says, "if somewhat short-sighted on the bigger picture. Is he still fighting our expansion plans?"

JDR nods. "Despite Andrews' objections, we've bought a large piece of property to build a refinery at Bayonne, just outside of New York. We've acquired the trading house, Bostwick and Tilford, which gives us an oil-commodities business, a network of barges and shuttles, and a 780-barrel-a-day refinery at Hunter's Point on the East River."

"In the next month," adds Flagler, "we're going to buy every competing refinery in and around Cleveland, Pittsburgh, elsewhere in Western Pennsylvania as well as several on the East Coast. We'll operate only the most efficient, and shutter the rest."

"You're talking a consolidation?" Harkness asks. "The independents will never go along. They'll fight us tooth and claw."

"We need fewer plants so we can control supply and keep demand high," JDR replies. "We're also consolidating our shipments with the railroads. Our plan," Rockefeller says, with the look of a fox, "is to play one road against another for our business."

"Jay Gould has already given us a fifty-five-cent-a-barrel rebate on all our crude carried from the regions on his Erie line," Flagler says, "and we're getting the same amount for refined products sent from here to the coast."

"In a few minutes," JDR adds, "Henry and I are meeting General J.H. Devereux, the new head of the Lake Shore Railroad, which, as you know, is a spur of Commodore Vanderbilt's New York Central. The Lake Shore offers a direct link to Buffalo and the Erie Canal, with the Central giving us a rail route to Albany and then south to New York City."

JDR looks at Harkness. "We're going to strike an even richer deal than we did with the Erie. Yes, gentlemen, we intend to bring old General Devereux in for a good sweating. I just hope he has a strong heart, so he doesn't keel over on us!"

The men laugh, then Harkness asks, "How's our capitalization?"

"Within the last two weeks," JDR replies, "we've brought in several new investors who've bought significant blocks of stock. Bankers Truman Handy, Amasa Stone and Stillman Witt, as well as Benjamin Brewster, who made a fortune during the California gold rush. Our available capital now exceeds three and one-half million dollars, gentlemen."

Harkness rises from the couch. "It sounds like you and Henry have matters well in hand, John. I'm going to let you two get back at it." He turns to William. "What do you say we walk over to the Empire Hotel for a platter of steak and eggs? I'd like to hear more about those European expansions." They leave Rockefeller's office by a secret side door.

A few minutes later there's a knock on the office door, and a clerk opens it and announces that their guest is here. General J.H. Devereux, president of the Lake Shore Railroad, strides past him sporting the cocksure manner of a man on a mission.

The three black walnut chairs in JDR's office are arranged in a neat semicircle, and Rockefeller and Flagler sit on either side of the general like a couple of vultures ready to swoop down from a tree limb and peck away at a dead rabbit. The men are in to the second hour of their meeting and Devereux, a portly man with a red face and a mane of thick white hair, is indeed beginning to sweat.

"What you ask is heresy, gentlemen," Devereux stammers. "It's unheard of in the history of railroad operations."

"Don't be so sure," Flagler replies.

"My board would string me up by my balls if I were to accept your proposal."

"Quite the contrary, General," JDR says, leaning closer to him. "Your board will herald you as a conquering hero. What would you say if the Standard guaranteed you sixty carloads of crude oil a day from the regions, every day, with the exception of Sunday, of course. And the same number of carloads of refined products for shipment to the coast?"

Devereux looks at Rockefeller in disbelief. "How can you possibly commit to that much cargo?" he says.

"There's more, General," JDR replies. "We're also prepared to consolidate the loading and unloading of these shipments through our network of terminals in Franklin, Cleveland, Buffalo, Albany and New York City."

"I can go two dollars forty cents a barrel for the full transit," Devereux declares. "Not a penny less!"

"The key here is to not get fixed on the per barrel rate," JDR says, "for that will be more than offset by the volume of cargo the Standard is going to ship with you. As we said earlier, we're looking for a rebate from the Lake Shore of seventy-five cents on every barrel shipped."

"That would leave us with a gross rate of a mere dollar sixty-five a barrel!" Devereux replies.

"In addition," Rockefeller says, "we will require a drawback of twenty-five cents a barrel payable to us for all competitive barrels transported on Lake Shore trains. That includes any crude oil not controlled by Standard Oil that's brought out of the regions, and any refined product shipped by refineries in competition with us."

"I don't understand," Devereux says.

"It's simple," Flagler says. "You charge our competitors the Lake Shore's posted rate to carry their barrels, say that two-dollar-and-forty-cent figure you cited a moment ago, and you drawback from that amount twenty-five cents a barrel and pay us for every barrel of competitive oil transported."

The general shakes his head. "Who's going to keep track of all that?"

"*You* are," snaps Flagler. "And, in addition to that, we will expect weekly reports on how much oil and kerosene our competitors are shipping, and where they're shipping it to."

"That's spying, gentlemen!"

"We prefer to describe it as competitive intelligence," JDR says. "Simple information shared among friends."

Rockefeller continues. "Another aspect of all this that's going to work to both our benefit is if the Lake Shore converts from carrying wooden barrels of oil strapped on flatbed railcars to the more efficient tanker cars."

"But my railroad doesn't own any cars like that." Devereux declares.

"We do," Flagler says, smiling for the first time at the general.

"And we're ready to loan you one hundred cars to modernize your fleet, with more to come as needed," JDR adds. "Offered at a modest per mile rental fee, of course."

Flagler's smile widens. "By the same token, we're going to require the requisite leakage allowance that you apply to barrel shipments."

"But tanker cars are made of steel!" Devereux exclaims. "They don't leak!"

Flagler's smile fades. "General, think what we're giving you. That leakage fee is something we deserve. Why in the world would your railroad give it to our competitors, and not extend the same courtesy to us, who deserve it, and who are doing everything we can to work with you?"

Devereux looks down at the polished wood floor and shakes his head in disbelief.

JDR taps him on the knee. "I believe, sir, by the time we've ended this meeting you're going to see the light."

Devereux looks up at him. "You're saying we're not done?"

"Just two more relatively minor items," JDR replies. "We expect any empty Standard Oil barrels or railcars brought back to the regions from Cleveland for refilling to be transported at no charge. The same goes for our empty drums of kerosene. Of course, you'll continue to charge your other customers the going fee for empty cargo."

Devereux sighs. "And the final request, Mr. Rockefeller?"

"Not a request, but a small token of our friendship," JDR answers, rising from his chair and walking over to his desk.

"This morning, the Lake Shore's stock is trading at ten dollars a share," Rockefeller says. "Isn't that right, General?"

"Yes, sir."

"Well today, Standard Oil would like to purchase twenty-five hundred shares of your railroad," Rockefeller says, reaching into a drawer and withdrawing a cashier's check for $25,000. He walks back over to the general and gives it to him. "You can consider that just the start of our investment."

Devereux's jaw drops as he looks down at the check, and JDR extends his hand. He shoots to his feet and stands ramrod straight, a trait ingrained from his military days. He wipes the inside of his right hand on his trousers and clasps JDR's hand.

"So, where do I sign?" he asks.

Flagler rises and stands beside the other two men. "Like Mr. Rockefeller said, you can expect today's stock purchase to be the first of many more coming your way. And as for a contract, we'd prefer to keep this a verbal agreement, committing nothing we've discussed here this morning in writing. Our broker will be in touch with yours to take care of the formal transfer of shares. But, again, everything should be kept secret. No public announcements."

"Good bye, General," JDR says, leading him to the door and opening it. The clerk who'd escorted Devereux in earlier is waiting for him in the hallway.

They walk down the stairs, with the young man leading the way. As they approach the third-floor landing, Devereux reaches forward and taps the clerk on his shoulder. "I've never met such tough negotiators."

"They have few equals in that regard, or so I'm told," the clerk replies.

Devereux swipes his forehead with his sweat-soaked hankie. "I've no doubt that's true," he says. "But I'm leaving here with the feeling I may have just made a deal with the devil himself!"

PRAYER IN THE PARK

"There's no work here," says the skinny, pock-faced man with a tingle of pleasure. "This firm isn't taking in new hires! Don't you know the country's in a depression? Or are you too young to understand that? We're not hiring, I tell you, and neither is anyone else!"

In the six weeks since he and his mother arrived in Cleveland, Matthew has encountered his kind before: these low-level clerks and office boys, a cut above apprentice, the self-appointed, self-consumed keepers of the gate, the palace guard dogs inflated with ego and fear whose bark, Matthew knows, is so much more cutting than their bite, yet the words hurt all the same. During his days of knocking on doors, searching for work and getting rejections from countless commodities firms, banks, trading houses, transit companies and other businesses lining the narrow streets of Cleveland's commercial district, he'd met his fill of these selfish, protective, paranoid little men.

He takes a deep breath and looks this one straight in the eyes. "If I can speak to the owner, I won't take much of his time."

"Oh, really! You want to meet the owner? Well, he's not in. Will the manager do?"

Matthew nods. "Yes, I'd appreciate that."

"Well, guess what, he's not here either," the clerk smirks. "So, there's no way around it, you're just going to have to deal with me and, as I said, this is a closed shop. There's nothing here for you, so be on your way."

"Then at least let me see the head bookkeeper," Matthew says, not backing off. "Maybe he'll put me on his list for a future job."

The clerk's expression dissolves into a scowl, and his moustache twitches as he speaks: "Don't you understand English, you impertinent ass? Are you deaf as well as dumb? Leave now, or I'll throw your sorry soul out the door and into the street myself!"

Matthew wishes he'd try, for he'd love to take this boorish fool down a peg or two. But instead he takes a calming breath and just studies the anemic-looking clerk, with his flushed face and too-short trousers.

"You should learn to treat people a little better," Matthew says. "Because you never know when you're going to be looking for a job yourself."

He turns and walks down the front stairs of the brick building to the sidewalk and looks around.

Although the United States is in the midst of a downturn, an economic storm that's brought bank failures, personal bankruptcies, growing unemployment and the freezing of wages, one wouldn't know it by the activity in Cleveland's commercial center or on its waterfront.

Superior Avenue, Ontario Street and Lakeshore Drive bustle with packed, horse-drawn trolleys traveling back and forth in never-ending streams, carrying workers to their jobs. Well-dressed businessmen file in and out of the rows of brokerage and trading houses, speculating on salt, lumber, iron ore, grain, beans, pork bellies—anything that can be planted, harvested, raised or extracted from the earth.

On the banks of Lake Erie, tall-masted sailing ships and cargo steamers line the docks and wharves, and longshoremen scurry over their decks, popping into holds like frenetic ants to retrieve crates of dry goods, cured meats, bricks, nails, building supplies, clocks, carriages, furniture, fabrics—all the necessities needed by this growing Midwestern city.

Parallel to the shoreline, dozens of boxcars packed with vegetables and other perishables are parked next to one another on side rails waiting to be unloaded. Steam locomotives, black as the course coal that powers them, sit in nearby switchyards preparing to whisk barrels of petroleum products to the Eastern cities, or to the busy hubs of Chicago, Louisville and St. Louis.

Everywhere the acrid odor of the refining process fills Cleveland's air with a pungent- amalgam of heated hydrocarbons, steamy chlorides, vaporous sulfur, naphthalenes and the tarry tang of the asphalt-coke residuals scraped from the bottoms of industrial boilers.

A factory whistle blows, and lines of employees file from refinery offices, laboratories, storage areas and docks, finishing their day, only to be replaced by a another wave of workers ready to begin the night shift.

Yet Matthew isn't a part of any of it. For he's on the outside looking in, a country boy knocking on doors, barred from entry. He feels so out of place, like a giant hand has plucked him up and put him in this unreal world. He wants to close his eyes and rest, but the hand keeps grabbing him again, shaking him awake, lifting him—only to drop him alone once more in this alien land.

Matthew shakes off these thoughts, and heads a couple of blocks west toward the Cuyahoga River. He threads his way through the stream of carriages and wagons on Superior Street, and enters a small tree-lined park, a sequestered remnant of a quieter time.

He sits on a wooden bench, takes a deep breath and looks up at the midday sky. The sun's rays stream through the unfurling virgin-green leaves of oak, poplar, maple and beech trees bursting awake from winter's dormancy. The dappled light filters through the foliage and dances on a slope full of butter-yellow daffodils popping alive by the water's edge.

Matthew reaches in his pocket and takes out a letter that he got yesterday from Lavinia, and he reads it for what has to be the tenth time.

My dearest Matthew: While I am excited with the news I'm about to tell you, I am also saddened because it is going to put more miles between us, and it will be harder to visit each other if that chance ever comes, which I pray it will someday soon. But I hope you will be glad and support me in what I'm doing, for I've come to realize that since you left Oil City there is nothing keeping me here anymore or stopping me from accepting this unexpected opportunity, which my father has arranged.

Just as you have struck out to find your fortune in Cleveland (father told me you want to be as rich as Rockefeller, and I have no doubt you will be some day), I know there is more for me to do and contribute in my life. I've never told you this, but after my mother died I have thought a lot about becoming a doctor and helping the sick, especially those with incurable diseases like cancer.

My father's long-time friend, Dr. John Spencer, has agreed to have me come to Chicago and live with him and his wife so he can begin teaching me his specialty, which is studying and treating the terminally ill. Father tells me that Dr. Spencer is renowned throughout the Midwest for his work with cancer patients, and I will be learning from the best as I progress through my studies, which as you can imagine will be a long road and involve much time and work. But father believes I am ready to embark on this path, and he has told me that medicine is something you should learn while you are young. As I said earlier, I am very excited but also quite worried (and a little guilty) about leaving father, but he assures me he'll be just fine.

I also worry about you, and I treasure the letters you have sent me during the past weeks. I have thought about you every day (and night) and know that our time in Oil City was not just an ephemeral moment, but that someday we will be together and our circumstances will not force us to be apart like we are now. I have come to understand that I love you more than words can express, and I pray that we will be able to make a life with each other, a wonderful life where we can be together all the time. I hope you believe that, too.

I will write again soon, after I get settled in Chicago. I leave next week by train—my first trip of such distance! Good luck with your job search, and please keep your chin up, as I know you will find something good any day now. Know that I think of you constantly, and my affections are only for you, now and forever.

Love,
Lavinia

P.S. Yalen Oxford says hello!

Matthew folds the letter and puts it back in his jacket. *I'm going to lose her,* he thinks. *I have to get to Chicago. But I can't just up and leave mother.*

He raises his head to the sky and whispers a favorite passage:

"Forgetting what lies behind and straining forward to what lies ahead, I press on toward the goal for the prize of the upward call of God in Christ Jesus."

A light breeze ripples the waters of the Cuyahoga, caressing the shore, feathering the daffodils, bending them in gentle sway.

He lowers his head and looks across the river at the two refineries on the opposite bank. They're the largest of many that dot the outskirts of the city and, although he's never visited either one, Matthew is familiar with both of them.

Rockefeller's Kingsbury Run fans across a cut of land that juts out into the river, bordered on three sides by water. Matthew can see that incoming barges, those loaded with supplies, moor at the wharves constructed on the cut farthest upriver on the south side of the refinery. The primary docks, used for outgoing shipments, and located on the main waterway on the eastern side of the complex, are by far the biggest and most active.

Even now at noon, when most people take a break to have some lunch and rest for a few minutes, Rockefeller's docks remain active, with workers rolling barrels onto barges, and ships disembarking every few minutes, bound down river to Lake Erie. The northern docks look to be used for overflow traffic, or, Matthew supposes, as a mooring area where vessels berth while waiting for specialized or custom cargoes, out of the way of the steady movements of the other ships. He can see a network of rail lines flanking the western end of the complex, and a massive unloading terminal with ramps spanning fifty yards of track, designed for railcars to drive right through the middle of it to speed the transfer of incoming crude and outgoing kerosene.

He takes a bite of an apple he's brought with him and looks upriver at the sprawling Star Works refinery, owned by Clark, Payne and Company, Rockefeller's biggest competitor in Cleveland. He doesn't know much about that operation, only what he's read in *The Plain Dealer*, articles focused on its principal owner, Colonel Oliver H. Payne, described as a decorated Civil War veteran and a descendant of Cleveland's founders, whom, like Rockefeller, the paper lists as one of the city's richest men.

Matthew stares at the Star Works, and thinks it looks pretty much like any other large refining operation with its crude oil storage tanks, processing buildings and smokestacks belching soot and steam. But its noonday docks are deserted, barge traffic is standing still, and there's no activity at the rail areas either.

He looks back over to Kingsbury Run. While time seems suspended at Payne's refinery, Rockefeller's is running with clockwork choreography, with workers visible everywhere.

Matthew sits for a minute longer, and he reaches inside his jacket and runs his hand across Lavinia's letter. He gets up from his bench and walks a short ways across the park to a black-iron hand pump. He takes a tin cup hanging from the pump's spout, holds it in his left hand, and with his right begins moving the long, wooden handle up and down. After a few seconds, cold, clear water gushes from the pump, and he places the cup under it.

He drinks about half, and pours the rest over his fingers, rubbing his face and forehead, enjoying the coolness, and as he does he feels the tension dissipate and his resolve return.

He hangs the cup back on the pump and walks quickly out of the park in search of work.

A Fractured Woman

Rebecca Strong stands alone in front of her boarding-house mirror and runs her thin hands down her body, straightening the wrinkles from her plain white petticoat. Her bright-green eyes—eyes her father once described as "having the eternal sparkle of the highest, sun-blessed meadow on the Emerald Isle,"—now reveal only strain and weariness, the dulling toll of the loss and uncertainty of the past six months.

Yet, at thirty-six Rebecca is still a stunningly attractive woman, a tall Irish beauty with smooth porcelain skin, high cheekbones, full lips and long, flowing black hair. Even the few stray white strands, intermingled with the dark, give her a distinctive, almost regal air that doesn't detract from the sensuality she exudes with every breath.

She runs her hands across her body again, feeling her breasts, firm, supple, sensitive under the soothing, soft cloth. She steps back from the mirror, clasps her fingers around her waist, and smiles, shaping the petticoat to the contours of her still-slim figure, studying herself.

A deep crack running vertically down the mirror's glass divides her reflection in two. Rebecca's expression dissolves, and she stands dead still, staring at the fractured woman before her.

She appears to recognize the image on the left, and for a moment seems comforted by the person staring back at her: for it's Rebecca Strong, mother, homemaker, stable rock that raised the children, tucked them into bed at night, heard their prayers, nursed them when they were sick, helped them on their way as they began to grow and test their wings and venture from the nest. Yes, it is Rebecca Strong, wife of Caleb, a handsome, headstrong husband, a man who meant well, yet always had to have his way, a boy-man with grand schemes and ready failures, but *her* man nonetheless, despite their indiscretions. Now that man is a fading memory.

She continues to study the image in the glass. She sees a woman who's cast aside her silent suffering after Luke's death, a woman who's become more opinionated, more confrontational, a woman who's been in a battle against time and fate to gain control, fighting to keep her family together, hoping to protect them, wanting to make things whole, but ultimately failing in her efforts. Now, she sees only a woman who finds herself falling backwards into a place of no return.

Yes, it's Rebecca Strong reflected in the boardinghouse mirror. Or *is* it? She steps closer, closer to the image on the right side of the glass.

She leans forward, peers at the figure, and shudders, as if in disbelief at what she sees. For the woman in the mirror is a girl, Rebecca McCann, the feisty fourteen-year-old, landing in Philadelphia so many years ago on the British steamer, *Destiny's End*, after a two-month trip from Liverpool: Rebecca McCann, precocious, restless, inquisitive, forced from her home by the misery and upheaval sweeping across Donegal and the entire Irish countryside in 1848—a girl aware of the wider world and ready for a new start, hoping to grab a piece from the land of opportunity, something special just for herself.

No doubt, it's Rebecca McCann in the mirror. The freckled-faced girl who would forever remember the pestilence, the dying souls lying on the roadside wracked with cholera and typhus; the filthy, stinking, half-naked hordes of starving peasants, clinging to life, invading her parents' cottage for shelter and anything edible, even clumps of grass and garbage, normally fodder for goats and swine.

Her world had turned upside down, and Rebecca, first child of an Irish father, Brendan, and a Scottish mother, Morna, was driven away with her family by the blight and crushing tax laws of the English, booking passage to America with what little money they had left, a miserable journey, yet a far cry better than the voyages of the coffin ships run by the Irish lines; Rebecca, who two years later had turned into a promiscuous, rebellious sixteen-year-old, shunning her parents' wishes, enticing boys into back alleys and running away with the first man that came calling, an exciting man six years her senior, but ending up penniless and pregnant with Luke in a wharf-side tenement inside of a few weeks. The right side of the mirror reveals that girl again in all her defiant glory.

Rebecca draws back from the looking glass. She slips on a white high-necked blouse, buttoning it all the way up. She walks across the room, and reaches for a long, brown wool skirt, which she'd laid out earlier on top of her bed. She puts it on, along with a pair of high-topped shoes that lace up the front. She lifts the lid to the corner trunk, removes a green shawl, and drapes it over her shoulders.

She opens the door to her dressing room, stopping to study the two images in the mirror one last time. Which woman—Rebecca Strong or Rebecca McCann—is about to venture outside to the maze of Cleveland streets, the city that's now her home, where she hopes to stake claim to a better life? She smiles, winks at the reflections, and whispers, "Maybe both of us."

The afternoon rush on Superior Avenue is busier than ever, and each time Rebecca stops to watch a trolley pass or look at an impressive building or notice another woman in a particularly fancy dress, she's bumped and jostled by the crowds making their way up and down the crammed sidewalks. Merchant carts, some pushed by hand, others drawn by scrawny horses, line the streets, their purveyors hawking everything from fish and chickens to salt pork and cabbage.

Rebecca makes her way over to an apple cart. The afternoon sun is still high in the sky, and its warming rays drape across her as she approaches a short, portly, red-faced man standing next to the cart.

"I need three good-sized baking apples," she says to him. She can smell horse manure wafting from the front of his wagon, its earthy odor mixing with the sweet aroma of the fruit.

"You'll need more than three apples if you're baking a pie," answers the man, "You'll need at least six. You can see these Baldwins are running small, so I'll give you a good price on a half dozen."

"I'm not making a pie."

"Oh, if you're just looking for something sweet to eat, how about a bagful of these Ralls Genet? You can't beat them for taste. Thomas Jefferson grew this variety." The man reaches for one.

"No," Rebecca says, "I need a good baking variety. I'm making an apple-cherry rum cake. It's for a special occasion."

"Then we're back to the Baldwins," replies the merchant, "or these Wagener's over here."

Rebecca looks at the red and pale-yellow Wageners mounded in the center of the cart and points to them. "Let me have three of these, please."

The man picks out three plump ones and puts them in a small brown-paper bag. "That'll be six cents."

"Would you take a nickel?" Rebecca asks, opening a small leather change purse. "It's obvious they've spent some time away from the orchard."

"Nickel it is, lady. I'm feeling generous this fine day, and who knows, maybe I'll make a steady customer of you."

"Do you know where I can buy some sugar and baking soda?"

The man points about a block up the street. "McKelvey's Dry Goods and Provisions," he says. "You can get dried cherries there and just about anything else you'll need for your cake. I hope to see you back, now, and don't forget the discount I gave you!" He watches her walk away.

Rebecca crosses Superior Avenue and dodges a fast-moving carriage speeding down the center of the street. She steps up on the sidewalk and climbs the wooden stairs leading to a long porch running the entire length of McKelvey's storefront. On the porch are crates and cartons of goods waiting to be unpacked and shelved. She opens the screen door at the front of the store and walks inside, letting the door spring back with a bang behind her.

The trim, blonde-haired man behind the counter with a short-sleeved tan shirt and white apron is about Rebecca's age, maybe a couple of years older. He looks up when he hears the door slam, and his eyes seem to widen as she approaches.

"Welcome to McKelvey's," he says. "I'm Jim McKelvey, proprietor. What can I help you with today?"

"I need some ingredients for a special cake I'm going to bake. It's a surprise for my son. It's his birthday."

"Looks like you've bought something already."

"Just some apples," Rebecca answers, smiling, placing her sack on the counter. "I'm going to need cherries, flour, baking soda, eggs, sugar and some rum."

"Well, let's get you set up so you can get back home and get everything ready for the party," McKelvey says, bending down and picking up a small wire basket from behind the counter. He begins walking up and down the store isles, loading up the needed items. Rebecca wanders close behind, watching him.

"You and your family new to the neighborhood?" he asks, turning toward her.

"It's just me and my son," she says. "We've only arrived from Oil City in the past few weeks."

"Your husband must be in the oil business. What did he do, stay behind with his work?

"My husband died in an accident going on two months ago," Rebecca replies. "And, yes, he was in the oil business. He was a well shooter, worked with nitroglycerin, worked for the Roberts Company."

"I'm terribly sorry," McKelvey says, placing a bag of flour in the basket. "I've heard how dangerous that kind of work is, read about all the accidents in the oil regions. It's a shame they can't find a better way to keep those wells flowing without blasting them with nitro. So, how old's your boy?"

"My son, Matthew, turned sixteen today," Rebecca says, watching another customer enter the store. "Can you believe I let him leave this morning without wishing him happy birthday? I'd completely forgotten what day it is."

McKelvey smiles at her. "Of course I can believe it. When you suffer a loss like you have, you tend to forget things like that for awhile. I know. I lost my wife two years ago to a heart condition, and it takes time to overcome the pain, assuming you ever really do. I hope your husband's company compensated you for the accident, not that anything could replace the loss."

"Nothing to speak of," Rebecca replies. "They claimed he shouldn't have been working in the rain that day, said he shouldn't have been out there by himself. But from what I understand they always come up with some excuse to avoid paying the families much of anything."

They walk side-by-side back to the counter, and McKelvey empties the basket, laying the items out before Rebecca. "I think we've got everything you'll need; butter, eggs, flour, sugar, tin of baking soda, and a quarter-pound of dried cherries."

"That should do it, Mr. McKelvey," Rebecca says. "Thank you very much for all your help. You have a nice store here, with good, fresh provisions. I hope to come in again."

"I hope you do, too," McKelvey replies. "I'm going to have one of my clerks carry this home for you. And, please, call me Jim. Let me ask you something, Mrs..?"

"Strong, Rebecca Strong."

"Mrs. Strong. I'd be happy to open up a store credit, if that would help you. You can pay me when you can, take your time until things get a little more settled for you and your son."

Rebecca shakes her head. "I can't ask you to do that."

"You haven't asked," McKelvey says. "I'm offering it to you, and happy to do it. I know how difficult things can be when you lose a spouse. As I said, it takes time to sort things out, get on your feet, get life back to normal again."

Without another word, McKelvey turns and pulls a blank card from a file he keeps by the register. He writes Rebecca's full name in bold letters on the top of the card and then jots down a description and price of the items she's just purchased. As he writes, McKelvey looks up at her. "Has Matthew found work yet?"

"He's been out looking every day from sunup to sundown since we got here," Rebecca says. "But he hasn't found anything."

"That doesn't surprise me," McKelvey says. "Many businesses aren't hiring, especially young boys, because of the slump. But I don't understand that because Cleveland seems to be doing just fine."

"I can tell you Cleveland's a far cry from Oil City, Pennsylvania," Rebecca says, smiling. "And, it's going to take awhile before we'll feel at home."

"I have an idea," McKelvey says. "Why don't you have Matthew come by tomorrow morning and talk to me; there's plenty of work around here he can do. I'm sure you noticed those unopened crates on your way in."

Rebecca smiles at him again. "He's a big, strong boy, and a dependable worker. He'll be thrilled when I tell him, and what a surprise this will be on his birthday. I can't tell you how grateful I am for all you're doing. I just happened to come into your store, and here we find ourselves talking like this. It's the best thing that's happened to me since arriving in the city."

McKelvey nods and smiles at her.

"Oh!" Rebecca exclaims, "I almost forgot. I'm making an apple-cherry rum cake, and with all the talking we've done, I nearly overlooked the most important ingredient.

Would you happen to have a small bottle of rum? My recipe doesn't call for much."

"Of course I do," McKelvey replies, walking a few steps to a shelf behind the counter containing a small assortment of spirits. He grabs a bottle of dark Jamaican rum and puts it in a brown bag. He adds the liquor to Rebecca's bill and motions to one of his clerks.

"I hope to see you again soon, Rebecca," he says. I want you to know your credit is good here at McKelvey's, and if there's anything more I can do to help you, I hope you won't hesitate to ask."

"You've done too much already, Mr. McKelvey."

"Jim."

"Jim," Rebecca says, looking into the eyes of the attractive man who's being so kind to her. "I have a feeling you're going to see much more of me."

"And your son," he adds.

James McKelvey places his hands on the smooth grocery countertop and leans forward, watching the alluring Rebecca Strong walk out of his store. The clerk carrying her groceries hustles ahead, opening the screen door for her. She walks onto the front porch, takes a deep breath and looks up and down Superior Avenue. A broad smile covers her face, a genuine smile, the first in many months.

The clerk steps out onto the porch, and the screen door slams shut with a bang behind him.

A Step Up

Matthew walks home after another fruitless day, turning the corner at the lower end of Superior Avenue, the area down by the docks. He crosses a wooden footbridge suspended above the western finger of the Cuyahoga River leading to Whiskey Island, the poorest section in Cleveland.

His narrow street is lined with rows of brick tenement buildings, tiny walkups and unpainted, gray wood rooming houses stacked one next to the other. This is where the immigrants live—Irish and Italians mostly—but also newcomers to the city like Matthew who are unemployed with next to no money.

He's tired, tired of rejection, and the sight and sounds around him seem like a reoccurring dream. From every building cheap towels and worn garments of all shapes and colors hang from open windows, drying in the late-afternoon breeze. Dirty-faced kids squat and play by the gutters, rolling marbles or scuffed wooden balls back and forth to each other. A few persistent fish merchants, desperate to unload their fast-spoiling stock before nightfall, stand by their wagons, shouting to anyone passing by.

Matthew approaches his rooming house and notices a thin young man with dark hair sitting on the stone steps leading up from the street to the building's drab front stoop.

He's never seen him before, but he places the fellow at about eighteen or nineteen. The stranger wears a white pullover shirt partially unbuttoned, with his sleeves rolled up. A silver chain containing a small figurine hangs from his neck. He has on brown workman's trousers and old black boots with worn heels covered in red dirt. He has olive skin and looks to be in good shape.

He watches Matthew walk up the steps. "Hey, fella," he says, "you look like you just came from a funeral."

Matthew looks down at the older boy, who leans back and stretches his long legs out in front of him.

"Why don't you sit down and talk awhile?" the boy says. "I've got an hour or so before I've got to get to work."

"I ought to get inside," Matthew replies.

"Come on, sit down," repeats the boy on the steps. "You live here? I got a room here. I bet we're neighbors."

"My mother and I only moved in two days ago," Matthew answers. "We lived a couple of streets over before that, but the landlord raised the rent on us."

"That's why I haven't seen you, then," the other boy says, motioning toward the steps. "Come on, sit down. You look like you could use a rest, take the weight off."

Matthew turns and says, "Maybe that's not a bad idea." He backtracks and takes a seat next to the older boy, who extends his hand and says, "I'm Remo Carbone."

"Matthew Strong. You Italian?"

"Pope Catholic?"

"I don't know a whole lot about the Pope."

Remo laughs. "You think I do? All I know is he lives in a big place in Rome. But I never been there. I'm from south Italy, from Sicily."

"So, you work?" Matthew asks.

"I keep busy," Remo says.

"I've been out knocking on doors every day since my mother and I moved here from Oil City, but I've had no luck," Matthew says. "I'm running out of money."

"What you lookin' to do?"

"I want to work in an office, maybe at one of the refineries, doing something in the oil business. I want to try and get a job with John D. Rockefeller. I was at his building a week ago, but couldn't even talk my way past the guards on the first floor."

"Rockefeller?" Remo says. "You talkin' about the millionaire? He's a Bible thumper, real religious, you know, like a priest or preacher. He teaches a Bible class every Wednesday night at a church up on Euclid Avenue. He hires people outta that class. I know, I went there once."

"Today's Wednesday!" Matthew exclaims. "Do you know if he's there tonight? Does he still teach his class?"

"Don't know," Remo replies, watching one of the fish merchants pack up his wagon. "So, like I was sayin'…"

"What church is it? Do you remember the name of his church?"

"Real plain, simple-lookin' place," Remo says. "Wooden walls, no windows, real uncomfortable seats. Hard on my ass."

"On Euclid Avenue?"

A dark expression falls across Remo's face. "Yeah, Euclid Avenue, that's what I said. How many more times do I have to tell you?"

"Sorry," Matthew replies, "but I'm thinking if Mr. Rockefeller still runs his Bible class on Wednesday nights, I'm going to go there tonight and try and meet him."

Matthew hears footsteps coming down the wooden-floored hallway inside of the boardinghouse. The front door opens, and Rebecca walks out onto the stoop. She doesn't say anything, just looks down at Matthew and Remo.

Matthew gestures toward Remo. "Mother, this is Remo Carbone. He lives here."

"Let me guess," Rebecca says, "you're talking about John D. Rockefeller. He's all Matthew talks about."

"Right," Remo replies, smiling at Rebecca, then back at Matthew.

Matthew stands up and notices Rebecca has a faraway look in her eyes. "Mother, are you okay?"

She takes a second before answering. "Oh, honey, I'm just thinking about things. Did you tell your friend it's your birthday today?"

Matthew rolls his eyes. "I didn't tell him, since it's not a special day, not for me, anyway. It will be a special day when I get a job."

Remo smiles and pokes Matthew in the ribs. "Birthday, huh?"

"I've cooked some lamb stew," Rebecca says, placing her hand on Matthew's shoulder, "and I have a special surprise for you." She glances down at Remo. "Have you eaten yet?"

"I haven't had a good meal in a couple of days," Remo replies. "I got some time before I got to be anywhere."

"I've baked a loaf of bread, and I have a quart of fresh milk, which will be good for you boys," Rebecca says, turning toward the front door.

"Count me in," Remo says, jumping up from the steps. Rebecca starts for the door, but Remo cuts in front of her, reaches out and opens it. "Least I can do," he says to her, grinning and bowing from the waist.

Rebecca smiles back at him. "It will be nice to have some company for a change, nice for you to celebrate Matthew's birthday with us, Remo."

A few minutes later, after they're seated at the table, Matthew watches his mother push around several chunks of lamb in her bowl. Every so often she eats a small piece of meat or potato, but for the most part she merely plays with her meal, which Matthew finds strange.

"I need to get going soon," he says to her. "I have to find where Mr. Rockefeller's church is, and I can't be late."

"Late?" Remo shoots back. "What are you talkin' about, 'late'? That meetin', if they even have it anymore, don't start until seven o'clock, so what's your hurry? You got over an hour, and all you got to do is hop a trolley at Euclid and you'll be there in no time. Me, I'm the one ought to be sweatin'. I got to be at the horse track in a half hour, over on the other end of town."

Rebecca looks up from her food. "Neither of you boys can leave before you have dessert. It's Matthew's birthday cake, apple-cherry rum, made fresh this afternoon."

She gets up, gathers their empty bowls, and places them by the sink. Then she opens the cupboard and brings out the cake, covered in a moist cloth towel to keep it from drying out. She puts it down on the table, cuts two generous pieces and puts them on plates, which she sets before the two boys.

Remo looks up at her. "You ain't havin' any? You went to the trouble of bakin' this, and you ain't havin' any?"

"I'm just not hungry tonight," Rebecca says. She walks around the table behind Matthew, puts her arms around him, leans over and kisses him on the cheek. "Happy birthday, son. You're sixteen now, and just look at you. You're getting to be as big as your father!"

Across the table Remo gobbles down his cake, then looks up at Rebecca with a smirk on his face. "I thought you said this is a rum cake? I ain't tastin' no rum. Where's the kick?"

Rebecca frowns at him. "That's because, Remo, it's a rum cake in name only. The recipe doesn't call for more than a dash or two of liquor, just enough to spice it up a bit."

"Then you might as well have kept your money for all the punch this thing's got."

Matthew glares at him. "What are you complaining about? I didn't hear you say you had any better offers for a meal tonight. Here my mother invites you to eat with us, and you were mighty quick to say 'yes,' weren't you? Now you sit here and complain how her cake tastes?"

"Hell," Remo says, shrugging his shoulders, "all I said was this damn cake got no taste. What's it to you?"

Matthew pushes his chair back and stands up. "Watch your mouth around my mother."

Remo jumps to his feet. "What? You gonna make somethin' of it?"

"Maybe I am," Matthew shoots back. "That's up to you." He can feel his stomach tighten and his muscles tense up, but he's not afraid. While Remo is older and at least a head taller, Matthew has broader shoulders and a heavier, more powerful build. He looks like a bull ready to charge.

He locks eyes with Remo. "Come on, you have no idea how I'm itching for a fight."

Rebecca appears shocked at the unexpected turn of events. "Boys, I want you to stop this right now! This is supposed to be a birthday celebration, my son's birthday. What's wrong with you two?"

Remo stands dead still, sizing up Matthew, deciding what to do. Then he shakes his head and starts walking toward the door.

"I give you a tip on how to meet Mr. Moneybags, and this is what I get? I'll tell you what, fella. You steer clear of me and I'll steer clear of you. Got it?"

"I wasn't looking for trouble," Matthew says to him. "But I don't like how you spoke around my mother. Just keep away from us!"

"You're in the city now, bumpkin," Remo shoots back. "You need a thicker skin."

He opens the kitchen door and walks out, slamming the door behind him.

Matthew looks over at Rebecca, and sees that she has her head in her hands and she's crying. He rushes over to her.

Tears cover her cheeks. "I wanted it to be special, your birthday, and look what's happened," she says.

He bends down and hugs her, and he can feel her body convulsing as she cries harder and buries her face in his chest. She's lost her oldest son and her husband, and Matthew wraps his arms around her, stroking her hair with a gentleness that surprises him, hoping to comfort her, but knowing what she needs most is for the pain to go away, if only for a moment. He shuts his eyes and draws his mother close.

Later that night Matthew stands in the shadows in the alleyway on the east end of the church. Rockefeller's carriage is parked in front of a side door leading from the building, and two kerosene lanterns fixed on the coach cast wide circles of light around it. After a few moments, the church door opens and JDR walks out alone. His driver pulls open the carriage door, and Rockefeller heads for it. Matthew runs up to him as he is still a few feet away from climbing inside.

JDR stops, turns toward the young man and says, "Sir, I'm afraid our session is over for this evening. Perhaps we can discuss whatever's on your mind next week."

"Mr. Rockefeller," Matthew replies, "I'd like to show you something." He opens a notebook and holds it under the lanterns' light. "I am very good with figures, if you can take a moment to have a look at my work. I've brought my practice journal. I'm seeking a bookkeeper's job."

JDR takes the ledger and fixes his eyes on Matthew, and the boy is taken back, for he's never seen a look of such intensity.

The oil king looks at him up and down, riveting his eyes on the large diamond pen glistening in Matthew's shirt pocket.

Rockefeller thrusts the notebook back into Matthew's hands and heads back toward his carriage. "I think not," he says to Matthew, who hurries after him.

"Sir, if you're wondering about this pen, it was a gift from my father. He left it to me the day he died."

JDR stops and turns to him. "I'm sorry to hear about your father," he says.

"He died in an oil-field accident," Matthew replies. "As did my older brother."

"Son, I *am* truly sorry for your losses," Rockefeller says. "But that pen of yours is ostentatious and garish, and I must tell you it has no place here on the grounds of the Lord. I'm surprised you haven't shown better judgment, and left it at home in its box where it belongs."

"My father thought it would help me in business."

"I can tell you right now there's no one at Standard Oil who owns a pen like that, not even our trustees and shareholders, let alone our bookkeepers," JDR says.

He climbs into his coach, and his driver shuts the door, and Matthew sees his opportunity slipping away as the carriage begins to move down the alley.

I've got to stop him, he thinks. A second later he shouts: "I noticed a difference between your Kingsbury Run refinery and the Star Works!"

He sees Rockefeller motion his driver to halt. JDR leans out the window and looks back at Matthew. "Tell me, what might that be, young man?"

"I watched them both from the park by the river at noon today," Matthew says, running forward and again standing beside the carriage.

"And what did you see?" JDR asks him.

"I saw all the activity at Star Works stop for a good twenty minutes, while work at Kingsbury Run continued as usual."

"Why do you think that is?"

"Because you stagger your crews' lunch breaks, while at the Works, all the employees stop and eat at the same time."

"Quite inefficient, wouldn't you say?" JDR says with a slight smile.

"Yes, sir, I would. I saw barges backing up at your competitor, but at your refinery, loadings continued, both coming and going."

JDR extends his hand out of his carriage toward Matthew. "Let me take another look at your notebook." He opens it to a random page, takes a pencil from his jacket pocket, and puts check marks beside five entries. "Tell me the sum of the numbers I've just marked," he says, handing the notebook back.

Matthew scans the figures: $12,567.55, $16,793.96, $22,533.38, $10,885.71 and $43,020.22. A second later he gives JDR the answer, "One hundred and five thousand, eight hundred dollars and eighty-two cents."

"Correct," Rockefeller replies. "Give me your book again," JDR says, and Matthew hands it back to him.

"Your penmanship, and the care you've taken making your entries, are impressive," JDR says, marking ten larger numbers. "I've made it a bit more difficult for you this time. Are you able to tell me what the answer is?"

Matthew plugs the figures into his head and adds them up, answering nearly as fast as the first time, "One million, three hundred eighty-seven thousand dollars and sixty-six cents."

"Divide that by three," instructs JDR.

"Four hundred sixty-two thousand, three hundred thirty-three dollars and fifty-five cents," Matthew replies without hesitation.

JDR flashes Matthew another wry smile and corrects him. "Fifty-five and three three three cents," he says. "At the Standard, we carry the decimal out five places, rounding up." Rockefeller's expression turns serious. "There's no doubt you're quite proficient with figures. You say you're looking for a bookkeeper's position?"

"Yes, sir," Matthew says. "I can't tell you what it would mean to work for Standard Oil, and I want to learn everything I can about the business. Maybe someday I'd have a chance to do more than keep numbers."

"The keeping of numbers is an important and critical role in a company like ours," JDR replies. "Don't underestimate its value."

"I know a bookkeeper's job is a good starting point to enter a business and learn its workings, especially a business as big as the Standard," Matthew says. "All I'm saying, sir, is someday I'd like to contribute to the firm in an even bigger way."

"Doing what?" JDR asks.

"Maybe work on oil wells in your production fields, or on a pipeline crew, or sell kerosene, or maybe work at a refinery. I'm sure there's much to do, more than I can even imagine. I want to learn it all."

Rockefeller studies the young man standing outside his carriage door. "Tell me, what do you know about the oil trade?"

"My father was a well shooter, a torpedo man, and my brother worked on a drilling-crew. We lived in Oil City for a little more than five years. I know how dangerous the business is, and I saw the waste and destruction, and I hated it. I saw men become millionaires, and then lose everything and go begging for jobs as field hands or tool pushers soon after striking it rich."

"But what did you *learn?*" Rockefeller asks him.

"If I learned anything," Matthew replies, "I learned what not to do."

"Well, you're certainly an ambitious and knowledgeable young fellow," JDR says.

"I have no choice, sir. I've got to take care of my mother, now that my father's gone."

"I know what it is to grow up without a father," JDR says, staring into the night. "What's your name?"

"Matthew Strong, sir."

"Answer me another question, Matthew Strong. What is it that you *really* want?"

Matthew looks straight at JDR. "I want to be rich, very rich, like you, Mr. Rockefeller."

JDR reaches into the inside pocket of his jacket, withdraws a business card and hands it to Matthew.

"Mr. Strong, do you know where our offices are?"

"Yes, sir."

"Come by promptly at nine tomorrow morning. Present this card to the attendant who will be waiting for you in the downstairs lobby. I believe there's a good chance we will be able to find a position for you in our company. I suspect, though, you still need to finish your schooling. Is that right?"

"Yes, sir."

"Then we may start you out part-time until you complete your courses. We'll determine appropriate hours for you."

It's happening, thinks Matthew. *I can't believe it's finally happening.*

"One last thing," JDR says. "Your ledger is quite impressive, and it's obvious how much care and practice you've put into it. But do you also keep a little personal journal, a book to capture your personal income and disbursements?"

"No, sir, I don't."

"Start. You'll be surprised at what it tells you," John D. Rockefeller replies as his coach begins to roll down the alleyway.

"Thank you, sir! I'll be at your office at nine o'clock sharp!"

JDR sticks his head out the window. "And wrap that pen of yours up and put it in a safe place. Be sure you leave it at home!"

Tomorrow's Promise

Matthew hops off the Superior Avenue trolley at the end of the line across from Whiskey Island.

The fog, common this time of year, is beginning to roll in off Lake Erie, and he gazes at its encroaching wall of mist and at the dancing reflections of the city's gaslights on the water. He takes a deep breath and sniffs the primal smell of the docks. He listens to the sounds of the groaning ships in their berths, the clanging of their bells and flapping of their flags, caressed by the gentle waves and wet springtime breezes.

He feels so alive, so confident, so unburdened by the churning weight of worries he's carried inside him for so long. His chance has come, and he will make the most of it, doing everything in his power to set himself apart. He can't wait to give his mother the good news because she won't believe he's really done it, but he has, and he knows how relieved and happy she'll be. It'll take a few months, he's sure, but they will soon leave the rooming house and own a place of their own, a respectable home with a picket fence and grassy yard and front porch and cozy, warm rooms to protect them from the world.

Matthew runs over the footbridge to the other side of the river, racing past the tenements and clusters of urchins playing in the dark. It feels good to run, and he feels the sweat trickling down the side of his face as he bolts up the curvy, damp street. He comes to his place, leaping up the front steps two at a time. He opens the front door, catching his breath and gathering his thoughts as he climbs the stairs and walks the down the narrow hallway to the room he and his mother share.

As Matthew reaches for the door, he stops, steps back, and listens in disbelief. Inside, he can hear laughter, Rebecca's laughter, a purring, childish, cattish laughter he's never heard from his mother before, accompanied by the deep, guttural tones of a man talking. He turns the knob, but the door's locked.

"Mother, what's happening? Is someone in there with you? It's Matthew. I'm home."

He hears muffled voices from inside.

"Who's there?" says Rebecca.

"It's me, Mother, Matthew. What's going on?"

"Son, you can't come in right now. Be a good boy and go for a walk. Come back later."

"Yeah, get lost, kid," the man shouts.

Matthew can't fathom what he's hearing, can't believe what's happening. He grits his teeth, raises his right leg, and kicks open the door.

Rebecca and the man are in bed, and his mother pulls the covers up to protect her naked body. Matthew looks at the small nightstand and sees two glasses and the empty bottle of rum Rebecca had used to flavor his cake. He looks back at the bed, but it isn't a man lying beside his mother. It's Remo Carbone.

"Get the hell outta here," the Italian snarls.

"Or what?" Matthew shouts, running toward him. "What are you doing here? What are you doing with my mother?"

Carbone sits up and throws a punch at Matthew, but his fist slams into the bedpost instead. Matthew grabs Carbone's wrists with the strength of two vise grips, and he drags the young man from under the covers. He knees him in the groin, and Carbone doubles over, screaming in pain. Matthew's fists pummel the Italian's face in quick, vicious thrusts, and blood begins to stream from his nose onto the bare wooden floor. Matthew appears possessed, trying to purge from his very being all the pain, uncertainty and setbacks he's experienced during the past year.

"Matthew, stop it!" his mother hollers. "You stop this right now, you're hurting him! I invited Remo in. This is not his fault."

"Yes it is," Matthew snaps. "He was supposed to stay away from us, and now I'm going to teach him a lesson he won't forget." He kicks Carbone in the face, and the Italian groans, falls on his back, and lays motionless.

Matthew gathers up the intruder's clothes with his left hand, and with his right clasps a thick clump of Carbone's hair, pulling him across the floor as the Italian boy screams again and arches his back, propping himself up on his heels and palms. Matthew pulls him into the hallway, and Carbone looks like a stranded crab as he crawls backwards behind his tormentor, trying to keep up, trying to ease the pain of his pulled hair.

"You son-of-a-bitch," Carbone shouts, crouching over and spitting blood onto the floor by the top of the stairwell. "You're goin' to pay for this. You can count on it. I'll get you when you least expect it, so you better watch your back." A few boarders stare at them through cracked-open doors.

"Maybe so," Matthew replies, looking down at the beaten and bruised Carbone. "But payback ain't coming my way tonight, now is it?" He kicks him in the ribs and the Italian tumbles head first down the stairs. Matthew runs madly after him, kicking him several more times as Carbone crawls and curses his way out the front door onto the stoop. Matthew throws his clothes in a heap beside him.

"Now, if you're smart, you'll pack up and leave this place tonight!" Matthew shouts. "You'll get as far out of Cleveland as you can go and not come back. That's if you're smart. Because if I catch you touching my mother again, I'll kill you."

Matthew watches Remo gather up his garments and limp off into the darkness of Whiskey Island. He turns and walks back inside.

Rebecca is dressed and waiting for him as he enters their room. At first neither says a word, but Matthew walks over to the table, raises the empty bottle of rum, and waves it in front of his mother.

"What's this?"

"None of your business."

"The bottle killed Pa, and I'm not going to let the same thing happen to you."

"I think that's entirely up to me, wouldn't you say?"

"No, we're in this together."

"Maybe in *your* mind," Rebecca snaps. "But has it ever occurred to you that you and I have different ways of handling what we've been through, what we're going through ... different ways of dealing with the hurt?"

Matthew feels his anger return. "Yeah? Well by God this is not one of them!" He throws the bottle against the far wall, and it shatters to pieces on the floor. "What were you doing with that lowlife? What were you thinking?"

"Again, that's none of your business," Rebecca says.

Matthew lashes out. "The hell it's not! Have you been with him before?"

"How dare you ask me that question!" Rebecca sneers. "I'm not only your mother, I'm a woman with my own needs. And you're my son, not my keeper!"

"Were there others?" Matthew asks. "Others in Oil City when you were married to Pa? I heard him accuse you the night before he died. Were you with other men? Is that what drove him to drink?" Tears stream down his cheeks.

Rebecca stands in front of him. "You shut that mouth of yours! Truth is, he neglected me in favor of the bottle. I loved him, but he was no saint!"

"How many were there, Mother? Remo's not the first, is he?'

Rebecca's hand flashes through the air, slapping Matthew hard on the side of his face. He just stands there with his eyes closed, trembling.

His mother appears shocked. "Oh, my dear boy, I'm so sorry."

Matthew takes a deep breath. "I had some wonderful news to tell you tonight, Mother. I wanted it to be a surprise, and I wanted you to be happy for us. I finally got my opportunity with Mr. Rockefeller. I have an appointment with him at nine in the morning, and I believe he's going to offer me a job."

Rebecca reaches out and runs her hand over the spot where she's hit him. "I am happy for you, Matthew, I truly am. I know that's what you've wanted, what you've set your sights on. But you also must know I'm going to do what I'm going to do. I have to take care of myself, now. I have choices, and I have decisions to make. You're not always going to be around. This job of yours is going to take you away, whether you know it or not."

"I'm going to look after you, Mother," Matthew says. "I promise it won't be long before we are able to leave here and buy a house, a better place to live."

"Remember what I said, son," Rebecca says to him. "Each of us will do what we have to do. I'm not getting any younger, and if I have the chance to find some security, some happiness, a good provider, I'll seek that out, just as you are going to follow your course as well."

"But your future's not Remo Carbone, Mother."

"Why don't we put him behind us?"

"Because you deserve better, and you know it."

Rebecca also takes a deep breath. "We deserve what we make happen. Each of us. Now come on, let's stop fighting and get this broken glass cleaned up."

She grabs a broom from the corner, and Matthew holds a metal dustpan and bends down as his mother sweeps the jagged green shards of the rum bottle into the pan. They work in silence, having said all there is to say, having released their pent-up venom. The cracked mirror on the wall catches their reflections, image of mother and son, trying to make it right, trying to mend their broken lives, each about to pursue separate paths, each seeking the promise of tomorrow.

PART II
TOLEDO, OHIO
SEPTEMBER 1881

ANNUITIES

Matthew sits in the elegant dining room of the Whittington Hotel across from Frederic Fleshner, the three-hundred-pound president of Toledo's city council, watching him inhale a breakfast of a half dozen eggs, three thick slices of smoked ham, six sausage links, a side dish of fried potatoes with crispy red onions and, for good measure, five freshly-baked, piping hot biscuits slathered in lumpy brown gravy.

In front of Matthew on the starched white tablecloth sits a patterned China bowl containing half a grapefruit. A matching plate holds a piece of unbuttered rye toast, and alongside the plate is a cup of steaming black coffee. A pair of polished silver salt and pepper shakers, creamer and sugar bowl also rest on the table beside a candlestick holding a tall lit tapered green candle. Next to the candle is a small round crystal vase containing three orange, yellow and red nasturtium blooms floating in a pool of turquoise water.

Fat Freddie, as just about everyone calls Fleshner behind his sizable back, slides a hunk of sausage dipped in egg yolk off his fork and into his mouth. He motions his head toward Matthew's meal as he chews. "A breakfast like that isn't any way to start the day, if you ask me, which I know you didn't. But there's nothing on that plate of yours to put meat on your bones, give you energy to get you going, you know, get you through what you have to do."

"You're probably right," Matthew chuckles, taking a sip of coffee and eyeing Fleshner. At six feet two and 190 pounds, the trim twenty-seven-year-old doesn't have an ounce of fat on him. He's bigger and stronger than his father, inheriting Caleb's rugged good looks, dark skin and muscular build. But he also mirrors his mother in appearance with his thick black hair, patrician features and a raw sensuality that turns women's heads across crowded rooms.

Fleshner appears fixated on Matthew's meal, or lack of it. "You a drinking man?" he asks.

"Not really." Matthew says.

"My running buddies say you can't trust someone who's got no appetite … or doesn't drink, and I for one tend to believe them." Fleshner bites into a hunk of biscuit, leaving a gravy trail dribbling down his chin.

"Believe me, I have appetites, Councilman," Matthew says, shooting the fat man a sly smile, his chestnut-brown eyes sparkling. Like JDR's, they're clear, intelligent eyes, unpolluted by alcohol, opium or tobacco, and they are such a deep shade of brown that when he's angry, they take on the appearance of polished obsidian. But now they playfully return Fleshner's scrutinizing stare and skeptical frown.

"Oh, I'm certain you have at least one," Fleshner replies, stuffing a forkful of potatoes and onions into his mouth. "Like all the Standard men, you have an appetite for making money, am I right?"

Matthew spears a wedge of grapefruit. "I think that's a passion we share, sir." Working with JDR, he's developed the titan's ability to size a man up in seconds of an introduction, and he suspects that bringing this glutton around will be child's play.

Fleshner draws a green cloth napkin from his lap and wipes his mouth. He lifts a pitcher of buttermilk from the table, fills a tumbler to the brim, and chugs the milk down in a couple of gulps.

"AAAAAAHHHHHH." Fleshner keeps his eyes on Matthew. He again brings the napkin to his mouth, wiping a white milk-ring from around his corpulent lips. "So what do you do for the Standard?"

"I'm senior vice president of operations."

"You seem young for that position."

Abandoning all modesty, Matthew decides to impress the fat fuck with the full weight of his lofty relationship with John D. himself.

"I was hired eleven years ago by Mr. Rockefeller, who's always taken an interest in my career. But I've worked hard for what I've earned, and I have a head for numbers."

Fleshner smiles, and Matthew notices clumps of egg and sausage wedged between his teeth. "Head for numbers, huh?" he says. "Then I guess you've figured out what this breakfast is going to cost you."

"I have." Matthew replies.

Fat Freddie studies him for a second. "So, what exactly does 'senior vice president of operations' mean? Are you like a second or third bank vice president, spending your days in hotels like this, chasing accounts, hobnobbing at businessmen's lunches, glad handing with politicians like me? What exactly do you do?"

"I've done just about everything in the business," Matthew says. "I started out as a bookkeeper, then worked as a supervisor at one of the company's refineries. I've built pipelines and run oil fields, and I'm now in charge of Standard's activities in West Virginia, Pennsylvania, Ohio, Indiana, Illinois and part of Kentucky. That involves production districts in the six states, eighteen hundred miles of pipelines, twenty-five crude-oil railroad terminals, a fleet of barges, sixteen refineries, trading agencies, as well as a sales force of six hundred tank wagons and drivers on the road six days a week, delivering kerosene to customers and middlemen."

"How do you determine if you deal with a middleman?"

"Population, mainly," Matthew replies, not surprised at the question. "In the cities, we distribute through middle-men. Drugstores, grocers, hardware shops—you know, any place city people might go to get their kerosene lamps refilled. In the country, the tank wagons deliver direct to the farm houses, selling door-to-door. It's more convenient for rural folks that way."

"Middleman," Fleshner repeats, smiling again at Matthew. "I like that concept. That's kind of like what I am, don't you know, a middleman." He plops another eight ounces of buttermilk into his tumbler, splattering a portion on the tablecloth.

"Sir?"

"Toledo's a big city, isn't it?"

"Yes it is, Councilman."

"So if someone wanted to do something, say something in a city the size of Toledo, it would stand to reason he'd go through a middleman, don't you think?"

Matthew folds his hands on the table and leans toward Fleshner, who has his head cocked back downing the second glass of milk. "I think, sir, depending on the situation, seeking the services of a middleman is not only advantageous, but a very prudent and intelligent way of getting something done."

"AAAAAAAAAHHHHHH." Matthew can smell Fleshner's breakfast and buttermilk breath as it wafts across the table. He doesn't flinch.

"I also believe, Councilman, that if one wants to accomplish something, say something significant…something that would be of great benefit to the citizens of Toledo, he doesn't just trudge ahead assuming all will be fine, or that he won't run into obstacles if he doesn't lay the proper foundation."

"Quite the contrary," Fleshner interjects, motioning to one of the black waiters standing just outside earshot of their table. The waiter approaches, and Fat Freddie looks up at him. "Boy, get me a refill on this pitcher. And while you're at it, I'll take six more biscuits with gravy. And make sure they're hot!"

He turns back to Matthew. "You were saying?"

"I have the view, as I'm sure you do as well, Councilman, that to accomplish something of value takes allies, persons who not only can help you get what you want today, but also those you can count on tomorrow. Friends who are there with you for the long haul."

"Relationships," Fleshner adds, popping a potato in his mouth.

"Precisely."

"They're the name of the game," Fat Freddie mumbles, gobbling the potato down.

"Which is why I appreciate this opportunity to speak with you today," Matthew says. "The Standard has a proposal we believe you'll want to consider."

"I'm always open to new and interesting ideas, especially those that benefit my constituents," Fleshner replies. He begins to smile, but then frowns as the waiter places the fresh pitcher of buttermilk and a half-dozen biscuits in front of him.

"You forgot my gravy."

"It's on its way, sir," the waiter says, taking a few steps back from the table. A moment later a second waiter approaches with an oblong plate holding the serving dish of gravy, along with a silver ladle.

Fleshner watches him place it on the table. He brushes his fat hand through the air, waving both waiters away. "Leave us," he says. "This will tide me over for the moment. I'll call if I need more."

He stares at Matthew. "Okay, let's dispense with the pussyfooting and get down to it. Talk to me, Mr. Strong. Tell me something I'm going to like as much as these fresh biscuits here."

"As you may know," Matthew begins, "Standard Oil holds significant oil and gas leases in and around Lima. We are expanding our natural gas production, and are laying pipelines to supply that gas to customers."

"What kind of customers?" Fleshner asks.

"Large ones. Cities and municipalities, factories, bakeries, any large concern that needs a steady source of fuel for illumination, or to run furnaces, burners, those kinds of things," Matthew explains.

Fleshner bites into a biscuit. "I've read where cities all across the East are putting in gas streetlights so people can see at night."

"A project like that would be ideal for Toledo, especially with ample supplies of gas so nearby," Matthew says.

"I was also reading about this Edison chap and his light bulb," Fleshner adds, "how he's built an electric generating plant in lower Manhattan, how he's supplying electricity to light offices on Wall Street. I'm sure it will be just a matter of time before we'll see electric streetlights everywhere. Imagine that!"

This whale isn't as stupid as he looks, Matthew thinks.

"Matter of fact," Fleshner says, "just in the last week I was thinking of contacting Edison's folks to talk about doing something similar, here in our city."

"Then it's fortuitous, sir, for us to be talking now."

"It is, huh?" Fleshner replies. "Then let me ask you, Mr. Strong, what possibly could interest me in convincing the council and the mayor, both of whom, by the way, I have considerable influence over, as I'm sure you know, or why else would you be here?"

"Councilman..."

"I mean, just a year or so ago you guys were burning off natural gas in your fields as a waste product, a nuisance, something you were pissed off to find and couldn't get rid of fast enough. Am I right? Now, all of a sudden, you want to sell it to the city of Toledo? And recruit my help in doing so?"

"Councilman, if I may..."

"What could something like that possibly be worth, considering such competition on the horizon?"

The men stare at each other for a moment. The nasturtiums float motionless. The dining room clock strikes 9 a.m. The waiters watch from a distance, poised, perhaps expecting a beckoning hand.

Matthew speaks first. "Sir, it can be worth your getting in on the very ground floor of a new start-up company the Standard is forming here in Toledo, the Northwestern Ohio Natural Gas Company."

Fleshner ladles a spoonful of gravy over another biscuit. "I said it once, and I'll say it again. Talk to me, Mr. Strong."

"You've been recommended to us by Mr. Charles Foster," Matthew tells him.

"Our former governor?"

"The same."

"He's been out of office for three years now," Fat Freddie says. "Been involved in your type of business, as I understand. Pretty successful, too, from what I hear. In fact, he's building a gas-processing plant outside of town, with the same idea you have, to supply natural gas to Toledo."

"He owns the Fostoria Illuminating Gas Company," Matthew says.

"So why aren't you talking to him?"

"The Fostoria company *is* building a plant," Matthew says, "and it owns a few wells, but not nearly the number required to supply Toledo, especially if your gas needs were to expand beyond streetlights, say, to municipal buildings like the city hall, your courthouse, hospitals, schools, the waterworks plant, your police station."

"So, like I say," Fleshner replies, "why don't you talk to Governor Foster?"

"We already have," Matthew says. "In fact, we've purchased his company. We're merging it into Northwestern Ohio Natural Gas, and building seventy-five miles of pipeline from our wells in Lima to Toledo."

Fleshner drops his fork on his plate and shoots Matthew a cold stare. "Aren't you putting your cart before your horse?"

"We don't believe so, sir. Northwestern is going to need a board of directors to oversee the company and make sure it thrives."

"Who's going to head it up?"

"Governor Foster, of course, and he's assembling his board as we speak. He's recommended, and the Standard wholly endorses, your appointment as a founding director in Northwestern Ohio. That's why I requested our meeting this morning."

"Go on," Fleshner says, eyeing another potato.

"As a member of the board, you'll receive founding shares of preferred stock, a generous yearly compensation for your services, a lifetime annuity, plus additional monies

GUSHER!

for every committee you serve on. In fact, Governor Foster is going to recommend that you head up the Municipal Trade Committee, to help us grow in Toledo as well as in Bryan, Bowling Green, Findlay and other cities in this part of the state."

"I have a question of you, Mr. Strong."

"I'm not quite finished, Councilman," Matthew says with a slight gesture of his hand. "If you'll let me, there's one last thing. The board will conduct meetings every three months in different places across the country. "Saratoga in the summer, Nantucket in the fall, Augusta in the winter, other destinations to be determined, all first-class. Your travel, accommodations and costs of attending these meetings would be at the expense of Northwestern. Oh, and you can bring your wife, or whomever you want to join you, and Northwestern will pick up the tab."

Fleshner takes a drink of ice water, and then says, "This is an extremely generous proposition, Mr. Strong, and I appreciate the consideration. The beauty of all this is that it's not a full-time job, so I can keep my position on the city council. That makes a lot of sense to me. I like everything about it. Please convey my enthusiastic acceptance to Governor Foster for his gracious offer, and tell him I look forward to contributing to his new enterprise as soon as he needs me."

"That will be my pleasure, Councilman," Matthew replies.

They shake hands across the table, and the waiters perk up.

"I still have that question for you, Mr. Strong."

"Sir?"

"You must have done your homework, didn't you?"

"I don't follow, Councilman."

"Well, if that wasn't the case, then how did you know I was looking for an annuity, something predictable and reassuring for the future? I mean, had you come in here and acted like so many of the others who seek an audience, those short-sighted pipsqueaks who offer me some sort of one-time pittance, some insulting, under-the-table payola, and then expect me to jump at their every whim and perform never-ending favors, well, let's just say this meeting would not have lasted as long as it has."

"Or come to such a successful conclusion," Matthew adds, smiling at Fleshner.

"So how did you know? How did you know, having not ever met me, to come here today with an offer that clearly would be of interest?"

"Councilman, a man reaches an age where it's not about money per se, because he's set his sights on other things, like knowing his family will be taken care of, that there's sufficient, regular funds coming in to meet the uncertainties of the future, funds that can accumulate quickly, perhaps to the extent that he might be able to leave a legacy, his name on a library or on a school or museum, perhaps provide funds for a generous endowment to a hospital or university."

Matthew lets the thought sink in, then he continues. "You were right earlier, sir, I do have an appetite for making money, and I'm willing to take great risks to achieve that. But all of us eventually seek more than the almighty dollar. It's just a question of when that happens, and what form it takes when it does."

"There's givers, then there's takers," Fleshner says, staring at Matthew, "and I suspect you and I fall into the latter category for the most part. Am I right?"

Matthew beckons the waiter to bring him the check. "If there's any truth to that," he replies, "I think we can say there's a very nice change coming to at least one of us, Councilman, wouldn't you agree?"

The men stand up and shake hands again, and Matthew watches Fredrick Fleshner waddle out of the Whittington's dining room. He signs his name and suite number on the tab, then reaches into his pocket and pulls out some silver coins, giving each waiter two bits, thanking them for their service.

Matthew checks out of the hotel, walks three blocks to the Western Union telegraph office and approaches the clerk inside.

"I want to send a telegram. I'll write it out for you."

"Yes, sir, here's the form."

Matthew rests an elbow on the counter and writes:

To: Executive Committee
26 Broadway
New York City
Gentlemen: Weather in Toledo perfect. Made fruitful visits to all points of interest. Expect brighter days (and nights) ahead. M.

He gives the note to the clerk, who sends it over the wire.

Ten minutes later, Matthew climbs the stairs to the railroad station to catch the 10:15 a.m. train to Chicago. A trim muscular man with a face that looks like it's chiseled from granite stands on the platform waiting for him; it's Daniel O'Day.

O'Day projects the erect, confident air of a military general, a natural leader, a commander of men accustomed to overcoming great obstacles to accomplish missions. In the realm of the Standard empire, that's exactly how he's regarded.

The tenacious O'Day, in charge of building and operating Standard's sprawling network of crude oil and natural gas pipelines, can be charming one moment and ruthless the next. Matthew has seen him dismantle opponents in seconds with his lightning-fast fists and hammer punches, honed from his boxing days through-out Europe. O'Day's forehead sports a deep scar as testa-ment to one of his back-alley brawls. He's about fifteen years older than Matthew and more experienced in the business, having arrived in the oil regions from Ireland right after the Civil War.

Matthew approaches the Irishman and shakes his hand.

A broad smile flashes across O'Day's face. "So, Matthew, what's this I hear about you marrying a Wharton? I suppose if you do, you'll never have to work another day in your life. They're worth millions."

"Word travels fast," Matthew replies, annoyed at O'Day's inquisitiveness, but trying not to show it. "It's true I've been under some pressure from the bosses to settle down and begin a family. They think that's the way it should be for a vice president, someone my age, and Flagler introduced me to Melissa a few months back. We've seen each other a couple of times, done some things, but marriage isn't in the picture, that I can tell you."

"Well, I didn't mean to pry," O'Day says. "But I wanted to be the first to congratulate you, if the rumors were true."

Matthew changes the subject. "Daniel, any progress on our problem?"

O'Day's blue eyes flash with anger. "You talking about that German prick, Helmut Weiss?"

"Yeah."

"I've offered that bastard everything New York authorized. Outright purchase of his dairy farm for twenty-five thousand dollars, a back-end royalty stake in all production, a straight lease agreement for just the mineral rights so he can continue to raise his precious cows, formation of a holding company, a separate operating unit, if you will, to oversee all exploration and production activities on his property, with Weiss as a principal shareholder complete with voting rights, even ownership in the pipelines. You name it, I've offered."

"And he didn't bite at any of it?"

"He's rejected every single proposal we've presented. I've got a fair mind to drop in on him one night and let these do the talking," O'Day says, holding his fists up in the air.

"Does he have any idea how much oil could be under his property?"

"He doesn't care. He hates our business and he hates us, thinks all we do is spoil the land, rape it, pump the riches out of the earth as fast as we can, and damned if we care what we leave behind."

"The money doesn't interest him?" Matthew asks. "Because I think I'm going to get the okay to up the ante to fifty thousand."

"He's got plenty of money," O'Day replies. "All he wants and needs, or so he says. I think he came from money in the old country, and rumor has it he's got the first dime he ever made over here."

"How old you peg him at?" Matthew asks.

"Late forties, I'd say. He's a widower, raising two teenage boys, ne'er-do-wells, from what I've observed."

"Maybe there's a way to him through them," Matthew says.

"Don't count on it. Weiss has some sort of pastoral vision as to how things should be. He believes his land is sacred, his way of life a part of nature's grand scheme. He gets up at dawn, milks his cows, gathers his hen's eggs, makes his fucking dairy deliveries. He lives for that, and seems intolerant to change."

Matthew can hear the train's whistle in the distance.

O'Day continues. "At our last meeting, I said to him, 'Okay, Helmut, forget about the sale of your property. We'll take that off the table. But at least grant us a right of way, so I can run a pipeline from our fields south of your farm north to Toledo.' I assured him we'd bury the line deep, so he'd never have to see it, or even think about it, that we'd compensate him handsomely, put every blade of grass we'd disturbed back into place, and that in a month after we finished, his cows would be grazing on top of that pipeline, none the wiser, certainly none the worse."

"What did he say to that?"

"He stuck his finger in my face, looked me straight in the eyes, and told me to shove my pipeline up my ass," O'Day says, shaking his head. "He told me in no uncertain terms that no part of the oil business would ever encroach on his little piece of almighty heaven. He said if I tried to lay a line on his land, or anywhere near it for that matter, he'd hire his own private police force to rip it out of the ground. He said that he isn't afraid to take us on, that he'll sue Standard Oil for everything it's worth."

The men watch the train pull into the station and grind to a halt in front of them. Two porters jump out to assist passengers with their luggage. Matthew picks up his suitcase and turns to O'Day as he boards. "Sounds like the prick needs a bit of convincing."

SEDUCTION

With thirty-minute stops in South Bend and Gary, Indiana, Matthew's train chugs into Chicago's newly opened Union Depot a little after 4:30 p.m.

He's still chafing at O'Day's comment about Melissa. It's true that if he marries her he'll probably never have to worry about money again, and he thinks about that a lot. But he's now making a good salary, and he loves Lavinia—or at least thinks he does—even though he's consumed with work and hasn't seen or written her nearly enough. But somehow he always expects her to be there.

She's been busy, too, first becoming a leading researcher of terminal diseases under John Spencer's guidance, and now a recognized doctor with a busy practice of her own. Her letters have tapered off as well, and the last time they were together, nearly eleven months ago, he sensed a growing distance.

I don't want to lose her, he thinks. *But if I don't make a commitment, and soon, I will.*

He walks through the grand lobby of the gabled terminal and out the door onto Madison Street. A large American flag flutters in the afternoon breeze from the highest peak of the depot, and he can smell the nearby Chicago River as he waves down a passing livery carriage.

"Sherman House, corner of Randolph and Clark," Matthew directs the driver as he climbs inside, getting more excited by the minute at the prospect of seeing Lavinia.

The carriage moves at a good clip through the late-afternoon rush and in a few minutes pulls up in front of the hotel, the most elegant in the city, a seven-story renaissance-style structure with three hundred rooms. A doorman and bellhop greet him, and one of the men grabs Matthew's suitcase and heads inside toward the front desk.

A little before 5 p.m. he's checked in and is standing in front of a silver-trimmed oval wall mirror in his spacious seventh-floor suite. He takes off his shirt and lathers his face with shaving cream, and he dips the straight-edge razor into the white porcelain washbowl filled with steaming hot water. Even though he really doesn't need a shave he feels like giving himself one, and after he's finished he's glad he did, since his face is smooth and refreshed.

He splashes a couple shakes of cologne into his hand and rubs the fresh-smelling fragrance on both cheeks and across his chest. He walks over to the dresser, removes a starched-white shirt and puts it on.

As he is tying his bowtie there's a rap at his door, and a young black man sticks his head inside after Matthew calls out for him to enter. "You ordered a shine, sir?"

"Over here, please," Matthew says, and the man comes in and begins polishing his black shoes. Matthew remains silent, wondering what he's going to say to Lavinia. He suspects she's arriving this very moment, and is being escorted to the quiet corner table he reserved in the ornate restaurant just after he arrived at the hotel.

When the shoeshine man finishes Matthew pays him, takes his black suit jacket from the closet, puts it on and heads to the elevator.

The cozy oak-paneled dining room, nestled in the back of the Sherman's first floor, is lit by dozens of candles, and the polished silver and crystal glasses on the tables sparkle under the warm illumination. His eyes are immediately drawn to Lavinia as he walks through the arched entrance past the maître d.

She's wearing a fitted blue dress with a string of opera-length pearls that accentuate her shapely body, and her lustrous black hair is pulled up with tortoise-shell barrettes, which make her bright blue eyes seem larger, even from across the room. A few strands of her hair escape the barrettes and cascade down her stately neck. She takes his breath away.

Lavinia smiles as Matthew approaches their table, leans down and kisses her on the cheek.

"Don't you look nice tonight," she says, their eyes locking as he sits across from her. "It's wonderful to see you, Matthew."

"It's great to see you, too, Lavinia," he says. "It's been way too long."

"Too long," Lavinia repeats softly as a waiter approaches.

"Tea or coffee?" Matthew asks her.

"What are you having?" she replies, and Matthew looks up at the waiter.

"Would you bring us a pot of Ceylon tea?" The man nods and disappears into the kitchen.

"Matthew," Lavinia says, 'I'm very much looking forward to having dinner with you tonight, but…"

"I know I haven't written as often as I should," he says. "I'll work on that."

"We haven't seen each other in almost a year, and we haven't written in nearly six months. That's not what I'd call a close relationship."

"I've been so busy at work. The Standard Oil crowd demands a lot, especially from someone my age. But I think about you every day."

She shakes her head. "That's not what we need to discuss. That's not really even the point. Thinking about each other is very different from being together, making a life together, living like two normal people, not two souls separated by hundreds of miles and huge gaps of time between them."

Matthew looks over at the waiter approaching with their tea. "We had to do what we did, Lavinia. There was nothing for us in Oil City."

They both fall silent as the server arranges the cups and tea on the table.

Matthew leans toward her after the man leaves. "You know I love you. I've always loved you."

"I've been on my own since I was sixteen," she replies.

"I have, too," Matthew says.

"I think it's time my situation changed," she says. "I'm twenty seven now, and I have an opportunity in front of me that if I don't take it seriously, it may not come my way again."

"Look what you've achieved," Matthew says. 'You're a doctor, and you should be very proud of that. What possibly is there left for you to accomplish?"

"And look at you," Lavinia answers, taking a sip of tea. "How much more do you have to attain, Matthew? You're a vice president of Standard Oil, for goodness sakes. How long is it going to be before you settle down and start a family?"

What kind of father would the son of the town drunk and a mother that fools around make? he thinks.

"It's time things changed," Lavinia says. "This just isn't working."

Matthew stares at her. "What are you talking about? What do you mean?"

Lavinia places her teacup on the starched white table-cloth, folds her hands and lowers her voice to just above a whisper, even though the dining room is empty and the waiters are nowhere to be seen.

"I never told you this before," Lavinia says, "but five years after I arrived at Dr. and Mrs. Spencer's home here in Chicago, just before my twenty-first birthday, Mrs. Spencer became pregnant with her first child. It was a difficult pregnancy from the start, with her having severe pains and hemorrhaging throughout most of the time she was carrying the baby. I was with her a great deal during those days, trying to ease her discomfort, but I could see the worry in John's eyes because I believe he knew things weren't right, and there wasn't anything he could do to correct them."

"What happened?" Matthew asks.

"The child came prematurely, a breeched birth that caused a massive loss of blood over several hours. Both mother and baby died and, as I said, neither John nor I could do a thing to save them."

Why is she telling me this? Matthew thinks. *What's this have to do with us?*

"From the start," Lavinia continues, "the Spencers were very kind to me, taking me in as they did. My father sent them money, of course, for my room and board, and for my medical books, but we became close, close friends really, with John especially patient in teaching me about the different diseases and ways of treating them. In the six years since he lost his wife and child, we've developed an even greater affection toward each other."

Matthew's eyes darken. "I don't believe what you're saying. How old is this Doctor Spencer, anyway?"

"Forty eight."

"Good Lord, Lavinia, he's old enough to be your father! How can you be attracted to a man that age?"

"He's not that old, Matthew, and not only is he one of the kindest men I've ever met, I can't tell you how much I respect what he's doing for the sick, and the plans he's proposed for us. He wants us to combine our practices and open a clinic for people who need special care."

Matthew feels the anger welling up inside him, but he's also gripped with a feeling of intense fear, a gnawing realization of how alone he really is, and how he's about to lose the one person in this world he truly loves.

"I bet he has more plans for you two than that," he says.

"You're right," Lavinia says softly. "He wants me to marry him. He wants children, and so do I."

The waiter comes up to their table with the menus.

"Not now!" Matthew says, waving the man away. He looks Lavinia in the eyes. "There's something I need to tell you, but I don't want to do it here. I have a suite upstairs. Come up with me for a few minutes."

She shakes her head. "I don't know, Matthew."

"I love you, Lavinia, and you love me, too, and you know it. We are meant for each other, and I'm going to make it right between us."

"Why has it taken you so long, Matthew? I've waited all this time, being faithful to you. Can you say the same?"

Matthew stands up, reaches in his pocket and pitches a silver dollar on the table. He extends his hand to Lavinia. "Please, I need to say some things, but I need to do it in private. Come with me."

Lavinia takes his hand and gets up from the table. Her mere touch makes his fear disappear, and an excitement rushes in, filling him with a burning anticipation. Her hand feels warm, and he notices her face is slightly flushed, but she makes no effort to remove her hand from his as they leave the dining room and make their way to the lobby elevators. In fact, she seems to be squeezing it tighter with every step.

A couple minutes later they walk into his suite, and Matthew shuts and locks the door behind them.

Lavinia looks around the room, first at the over-stuffed chairs and couches in the sitting area, and then at a huge vase of roses on the polished table beside the big four-poster bed.

"That's beautiful, Matthew," she whispers.

"I had them delivered while we were downstairs," he says.

"How did you know I'd come up?"

"I was hoping..."

She takes a seat, and Matthew sits down across from her.

"This Dr. Spencer," he begins, "he's not for you. He may want to marry you, but I do, too, and I've known you a lot longer than he has. We're meant to be together. We always were. Think of what we've been through."

"I thought that as well," Lavinia says, "but you've never mentioned anything about it, either in your letters or the times we've seen each other. As much as I'd wished it, and I did for as long as I can remember, I've come to believe it's not going to happen, that it's just not going to be."

Matthew shifts in his chair, and he runs his fingers through his thick black hair. "Listen, Lavinia, I have something I have to take care of in Cleveland."

"A woman?"

"Yes, but no one I really care about. I wouldn't even call it a relationship. We've been with each other a few times, social situations and that kind of thing, get-togethers that had to do with business. Believe me, she's nothing special, just an escort so I'm able to walk around a room with somebody on my arm."

He sees the tears welling up in her eyes. "Why didn't you want me to be with you?" she asks.

"Because it was just work, always just work, and I knew you were busy, too. I knew you were building your practice, and that you couldn't come to Cleveland every time I had some boring social thing. I've been with her at most a total of a few hours, that's all."

"You didn't even ask me," Lavinia replies.

Matthew stares at the floor, not saying anything.

Lavinia finally breaks the silence. "I told you downstairs that I've been faithful to you all these years. I asked you if you could say the same. You didn't give me an answer."

Matthew looks up at her. "Of course I have."

"What's her name?" Lavinia asks.

"Melissa. Melissa Wharton."

"And you've been faithful to me with her?"

"I've been faithful to you from the first day we met," Matthew says. "Now, I'm going to go back to Cleveland and tell Melissa that you and I plan on getting married in the next few weeks. I want us to make a life together, Lavinia. I want to protect you and be with you forever. I want you to be my wife. Will you tell Dr. Spencer that?" He comes over to her and kisses her tenderly.

"Matthew, I don't..."

He clasps his hands around her waist and eases her up from the chair, wrapping his arms around her, holding her tightly, kissing her again. "Will you marry me, Lavinia?"

"Matthew, I've waited so long."

"There's no reason for us to wait any longer," he breathes, drawing her even closer, feeling her body's heat and growing passion as she presses against him.

"I want to be with you," Lavinia whispers to him softly, and he sweeps her up in his arms and carries her from the sitting room and gently places her upon the large bed. Matthew begins undressing her, kissing every part of her luscious body as he takes off her dress.

The room is warm, and he guides her back on the bed until her head rests on the soft pillows, and he quickly strips off his clothes and lets them fall to the floor.

They embrace, and he lays beside her feeling their bodies become one, taking in the delicious taste of her full lips. His kisses and caresses cover her with gentleness and appreciation, for he's so happy to be alive, so happy to finally be with her, so grateful for the exquisite tenderness of her arousing touch.

He draws himself into her, and they make love beside the lush bouquet of roses that have infused the room with the fresh spirit of life and sensual renewal.

THE SUMMONS

B y Tuesday of the following week, Matthew is back in
Cleveland and working at his desk when his chief assistant
raps on his office door. The young man opens it, and walks
into the corner room overlooking Cleveland's Public Square.

"This just arrived for you, Mr. Strong," he says, handing
Matthew an envelope, then turning to leave.

"Stay a minute, will you James?" Matthew replies, knowing by the canary-yellow color of the envelope that it contains a telegram. He picks up a letter opener off his desk,
slices the envelope open and reads what's inside:

> To: M.S.
>   Standard Oil of Ohio
>   Cleveland
>   Request presence at ECM.
>   26 Broadway. 8 a.m. Thurs. 22 Sept.

Matthew looks at his assistant. "They want me in New
York at an executive committee meeting on Thursday.
Interesting they don't say what it's about."

"They're probably going to congratulate you on your
gas deal with Fleshner," the young man says.

"I doubt it," Matthew replies. "Better get me a report on
our production volumes over the past three weeks, state by

state, and pull together the same period for August in case they ask for a month-to-month comparison. Same goes for refinery runs, and kerosene and specialty sales."

"Anything else, sir?"

"Yeah, book me a compartment on the afternoon train to Philadelphia, with a direct connection to New York. Contact the Buckingham Hotel, and tell them I'll be there around noon tomorrow. Have them prepare my rooms for a couple of nights. Oh, and have my carriage brought around."

The assistant walks toward the door and says, "Where would you like the reports dropped off to you?"

"Have someone deliver them to me at the train station. I'll be on the platform about fifteen minutes before I have to leave."

Matthew watches the young man leave his office and shut the door behind him. He finishes signing several contracts and other documents, and he puts the papers in a neat stack on the side of his desk. He gets up, puts on his overcoat and top hat, and walks down the four flights of stairs to his waiting carriage.

His driver opens the door. "Where to, Mr. Strong?"

"Hollenden Hotel."

It's a little past 10:30 a.m. as the polished black-wood and canvas-topped carriage pulls away from the Standard Building. As he travels down Superior Avenue, Matthew peers out his window to see a man in the center of the public square, lowering the American flag to half-mast.

The horses gather speed, and the carriage approaches the corner of West 6th Street, where a crowd mingles in front of the Cleveland Herald Building. Matthew leans forward and slides open a small window in back of the driver's seat. "Stop here a minute; I want to find out what's going on."

The man reins the horses to an abrupt stop, and Matthew jumps from the carriage.

"Have you heard?" someone shouts, "President Garfield has died!"

"After all those weeks of suffering," hollers another, "he'll finally be coming back to Cleveland."

"He fought the good fight, God rest his soul," adds a third.

Two young boys rush out the front door and down the steps of the building, each with a heavy stack of newspapers under his arm. They stake out separate spots on the packed sidewalk, shouting: "President dies! Read it here in the *Herald*! Get yours now!"

Matthew watches two more flags being lowered as he stands in line for a paper. After a few moments he gives one of the boys a nickel and takes a copy from the lad's outstretched hand. The headline reads:

PRESIDENT DEAD
Succumbs to Assassin's Bullet

As Matthew climbs back into his carriage, the driver leans to the sliding window and asks, "Still want to go to the Hollenden, Mr. Strong?"

Matthew looks up from his reading. "Yes, Gus, my plans haven't changed." The carriage starts off again, and Matthew continues reading the article.

The president's condition had been on everyone's mind, especially those in Cleveland, since he was born not far from the city and was a long-time Ohio senator. He *did* put up the good fight, Matthew thinks. He'd hung on for eighty days after being shot twice by a deranged lawyer, Charles J. Guiteau, who'd become incensed when Garfield rejected his repeated requests to become an ambassador.

Guiteau shot the president as he waited at the Baltimore and Potomac Railroad Station in Washington, preparing to leave for a trip to New England to see his ailing wife. The first shot was superficial, grazing Garfield's arm. But the second bullet pierced his vertebrae, coming to rest so deep in the president's body his doctors couldn't find it. During the course of his ordeal, Garfield's physicians probed for the bullet with unwashed fingers and unsterilized instruments, managing to expand what was a three-inch wound into a twenty-inch gash.

Infection set in, blood poisoning destroyed his last defenses, and he died of a massive heart attack late last night on September 19th, the *Herald* reported.

Matthew finishes the article as the carriage pulls under the ornate porte cochere of the imposing Hollenden Hotel on the corner of Superior and Bond.

Encompassing a full city block, the thousand-room Hollenden is Cleveland's newest and most lavish hotel, with its public areas and special rooms adorned with crystal chandeliers, brass-studded tufted leather chairs, plush sofas, fanciful Persian rugs, and the finest redwood and mahogany paneling with hand-carved fittings. The cavernous dining room and adjoining bar and smoking nooks are always a hub of activity, attracting the city's elite and politically powerful at every meal and well into the evenings.

Matthew keeps a permanent suite of three rooms on a private floor at the top of the building. He retains similar residences in Philadelphia, Baltimore and New York.

One of three doormen rushes over and opens his carriage for him. "Good morning, Mr. Strong, you're back early today."

"Not for long, I've just stopped to pack a bag, and I'm off to New York for two days."

"I lowered our flag a few minutes ago," the man says, "after I heard about the president. Terrible thing."

Matthew nods. "Tell my driver to keep the carriage out front," he says, handing the man a quarter.

"By the way, Mr. Strong," the doorman replies, "Miss Wharton and three other young ladies are having brunch in the conservatory."

"I know," Matthew answers, "she mentioned she was coming downtown. They're celebrating her friend's birthday."

He walks through the hotel's entrance and into the Hollenden's vast lobby, removing his top hat. He heads straight into the dining room, waving away the tuxedoed maitre d' and acknowledging several business contacts with a quick nod as he strides by the still-busy tables.

Matthew stops a few feet from the entrance to the octagon-shaped conservatory, which is built of glass and hand-rubbed teakwood. The greenhouse, set apart from the main dining area, has a pyramid ceiling. A thirty-foot Princess palm, potted in a huge Chinese porcelain planter, dominates the center of the room. A sea of pink and purple petunias mounding from the planter trail to the tiled floor. Lush green ferns, multi-colored impatiens, yellow begonias, flowering cannas, miniature citrus trees—some bearing cumquats and Meyer lemons—and an array of other tropicals set the exotic garden scene.

I'll tell her that we have to end it today, he thinks. *It was my mistake, leading her on like I did. I want to be with Lavinia, and I know that now more than ever.*

As usual, Matthew hears Melissa Abigail Wharton well before he sees her.

"Daddy treated me to a trip to Paris on my eighteenth birthday," he hears her say, "and I've been after both mother and him for months now to take me back, ever since I turned twenty-one. But this time I want a longer trip—London, Budapest, Rome, Florence and, of course, Paris all over again. I want to see castles, visit the shops, the fine hotels and experience the thrill of the transatlantic crossing again."

"You can't imagine the beauty of the Sistine Chapel," Matthew overhears one of the women say, "the incredible frescoes of Michelangelo, until you see them with your own eyes."

"Or lose yourself under the stars at sea sipping champagne on the top deck of the *Britannic*," Melissa replies. He hears the crisp clinks of crystal glasses.

Matthew walks around a marble urn containing the unfurling fronds of a large Australian tree fern, and he spots Melissa and three of her friends sitting at a round white wicker table with matching red-cushioned chairs. They're consumed in conversation, oblivious to everyone else in the room, and he stands there for a few seconds looking at Melissa.

Her blonde hair is pulled back straight off her face into a tight round bun centered on the back of her head. She has intense, cat-like green eyes and pouty, sensual lips that seem made for kissing.

She may not have my heart, he thinks, *but she owns every other part of me. I'm going to miss her.*

She has a tall, thin, shapely figure and an upward curl to her small nose that make her appear all the more aristocratic, particularly when she's fashionably dressed, which is most of the time. Today, Melissa wears a stylish, long ivory-colored dress with a red cashmere shoulder wrap that's draped around her shoulders and frames either side of her small but perfectly shaped breasts. She has on polished short-heeled shoes laced high up the front, the identical color of her dress. A long, wrapped strand of white pearls and an emerald and gold ring with matching broach round out her wardrobe.

Matthew walks up to their table. "Missy," he says.

The women stop their conversation and look up at him. "Why, Matthew," Melissa says, appearing surprised, "I didn't expect to see you here this morning. I thought you were at the office."

He glances at the bottle of champagne nestled in an ice bucket, and Melissa says, "It's Priscilla's birthday today, and it's a special one. She's turned twenty-one, just like the rest of us. We're comparing stories about trips to the Continent."

Matthew shows no reaction. "Do you know President Garfield is dead?" he says.

Melissa arches her manicured eyebrows. "No, we haven't heard a word about that. No one here mentioned a thing. You're the first to tell us. When did it happen?"

"No, we certainly hadn't heard he had died," Priscilla adds. "But, I did read where Alexander Graham Bell…"

Melissa interrupts her. "Who?"

"He's some sort of inventor," a third woman at the table says.

"As I was saying," Priscilla continues, "this Alexander Graham Bell character invented some sort of metal-detecting device to locate the bullet in the president's back."

"The bullet's been in him all this time?" Melissa asks.

Priscilla glances at her, then looks at Matthew. "They've never been able to find it, despite his doctors' working on him," she says. "So, like I was saying, they rolled the poor president over on his stomach and scanned his back with the detector and, sure enough, the machine gave a reading."

Melissa takes a slow sip of champagne. "So, they did find it?"

"Not really, but they thought they did. The machine's dial showed there was metal all right, and the doctors cut open the president on the spot, but when they did, they still couldn't find a bullet. The thing was actually detecting a metal spring in the mattress *under* the poor man."

"I'd say this Graham fellow doesn't have much of a future as an inventor, if you ask me," Melissa says.

Matthew walks over to her chair. "Missy, will you come with me for a few minutes? I have to tell you about a change of plans."

Matthew takes her by the hand, and they walk out of the conservatory, into the main dining room and over to the private elevator that services the top-floor suites.

"You're still coming to dinner tonight, aren't you?" she asks him. "The family's expecting you, and mother's having a special meal prepared."

The elevator doors opens, and an attendant draws back the metal grating. "Good morning, Mr. Strong, Miss Wharton. Good to see you both again."

Matthew nods at the man, but Melissa turns her back to him. "You know you have something to discuss with my father, Matthew," she says. "You promised you'd speak with him as soon as you got back to town."

"It can't be tonight, Missy. I'm going to New York for a couple of days."

"This wasn't just Priscilla's special day," Melissa says, frowning. "It was supposed to be mine, too. It was supposed to be the day you asked my father's permission to marry me. Did that ever cross your mind?"

The elevator comes to a stop on the tenth floor and the attendant slides open the grating.   "Did you hear what I just said?" she asks Matthew, who doesn't answer her.

He opens the door to his suite, and she shadows his every step.

"What's going on, Matthew? I want to know."

"I told you, I've been summoned to New York."

"Summoned? Oh, really! So John D. Rockefeller calls, and you drop everything you're supposed to do and run to his side like some sort of trained lap dog begging for scraps? You cancel all your plans, just like that, forget about your obligations to me? I told Daddy you have something important to ask him. He's staying home tonight just to see you, *expecting* to see you, and you won't disappoint him."

She walks up next to him, takes his hands and places them around her waist.

"Missy, I've been thinking," Matthew says, keeping his hands where she's put them.

"You have, have you?" she whispers back, pushing her body closer to his. "Thinking about what?"

"I'm thinking we should postpone our engagement."

"Really?" she replies, drawing back and flashing a taunting smile. "You really want to give up what I do for you? I don't think so. You're like me, you like it too much. You can't tell me you don't."

She can turn from an aristocrat to a whore faster than I can shut the bedroom door, he thinks.

"So, how long are you thinking of 'postponing' our plans?" she asks him.

"I don't know," he replies, "but I want to give it some time. Things have changed with me."

"You've got it all figured out, don't you, Matthew?" she snaps, pushing him away. "You think your only consideration is what's good for you, not what's best for us, the life we planned to make, what it would mean to my family. Oh no, I don't suppose you've thought about any of that, because all you care about is what Matthew Strong wants. And where has that gotten you? I mean, look around, you live out of suitcases in hotel rooms in how many cities? I've lost count. You're twenty-seven years old, and you don't even own a home."

"I want us to give it some time, that's all, and I don't want us making a mistake," he says, searching for his suitcase.

"Well, Matthew, you've already made one."

He turns to her. "What did you say?"

"Mistake. You've already made a mistake."

"How so?"

"I can tell you that you now have far more to think about than just yourself. I can tell you that your days of coming and going as you please are over for good. You talk about being summoned to New York? Well, my dear, here's another summons for you. You now have two other people beside yourself to concern yourself with. Two others to spend your time with, share your money with, show your affections to, you name it, because now you have something more in your life than your precious Standard Oil."

"No..."

"Yes, Matthew, I'm going to have your baby."

Melissa's green cat eyes bore into him, and her soulful mouth twists into a devious, half-smiling smirk.

PERILS OF HONESTY

Matthew walks through the doorway of the top-floor conference room at the Standard Oil Building in New York City and stands alone in the vast space. The room's most imposing feature is the twenty-five-foot polished table made of carved black oak. Twelve matching oak and red leather chairs are placed around it, five on each side, with two chairs positioned at either end. Three large gas chandeliers hang from the ceiling over the table, bathing the room with light.

Matthew doesn't take a seat, preferring to stand and wait for the others to arrive. It's three minutes to eight.

He hears someone whistling *Onward Christian Soldiers* in the hallway. The melody becomes louder as the whistler approaches, and the door opens, and in walks John D. Archbold, the rising star of the Standard organization.

"Good morning, John," Matthew says, attempting to assess the mercurial man's mood, always a challenge this early in the morning.

Archbold, like so many other Standard Oil executives, is the son of a preacher, and had come from nothing after his father abandoned his family when he was ten. He's brilliant, but the balding, one-hundred-thirty-pound, boyish-faced Archbold isn't cut from the typical executive mold. He's boastful and brash, has a reservoir of jokes, and a quick wit around the office. After hours he craves whiskey, tobacco and late-night poker games, exchanging stories with his cronies until the early hours of the morning. For reasons Matthew can't understand, this behavior only seems to endear him even more to the stoic, teetotaling Rockefeller, who treats him like a son.

To Matthew, the arrogant Archbold has come out of nowhere to leapfrog in front of him on his path to eventually succeed the forty-two-year-old founder of the oil empire.

Archbold gives him the once over and says, "Why, Matthew Strong, how are things in Cleveland? It's such a progressive city. I hear they just passed a law there making it a crime for women to wear patent-leather shoes. Seems they're afraid guys like you would be able to see the reflection of a poor girl's panties in them. Imagine that?"

"I hadn't heard," Matthew says.

Archbold raises his right hand. "God's honest truth. There's more laws there than you can keep track of. They even tell me you need a hunting license inside the city limits to kill a mouse."

"I don't think the same applies to rats, John," Matthew replies, flashing a sarcastic smile.

The hands of the conference room clock point to 8 a.m. The door opens and in walks John D. Rockefeller, followed by his brother, William, and Henry Flagler. Matthew comes around the table to greet them.

The men exchange courtesies, and William Rockefeller takes a seat at the head of the table. To his left sits Flagler, and next to him is JDR, then Archbold. Matthew sits on the opposite side across from JDR, who looks at everyone and says, "Gentlemen, shall we begin?"

"Before we do," William says, "I think we should congratulate Matthew on his Toledo gas deal."

Matthew smiles at him. "Thank you, sir. I think our Ohio investments are going to pay us back handsomely."

JDR doesn't say a word and immediately changes the subject. "Speaking of investments," he says, "has anyone seen the price of oil this morning? It's more than doubled from yesterday, with a barrel trading at four dollars and eight cents." His cold eyes bore into Matthew. "I trust your financial folks anticipated the price spike and capitalized on the gain?"

Archbold puts his arms on the conference table and leans forward. "Seems everyone was counting on a big strike out of Pennsylvania, with the bears driving prices down over the last couple of weeks. But everybody bet wrong. Those wells were dry holes."

JDR's stare is still fixed on Matthew. "How about your Treasury people, Matthew," he asks. "Were they plugged into the situation?"

"I'd have to check, sir."

"You mean you don't know?" Archbold interjects.

"John, as I said, I'll have to look into it, and get back to you," Matthew replies. "Treasury isn't my primary area of responsibility."

Archbold shrugs and rolls his eyes. "I thought you were a numbers man, Matthew. Isn't that how you got hired here?"

JDR turns to Flagler. "How many oil certificates do we have, Henry?"

"Somewhere in the neighborhood of seventeen and a half million, John."

"Give the order to cash out eighty percent. Let's do it today, before the bubble bursts. Plug the money into our cash reserves."

"I'll take care of it right after our meeting, John," Flagler replies.

"Let's talk about the German," William says.

"Ah yes, our friend, the infamous Helmut Weiss," Archbold adds.

JDR folds his hands on the table. "Daniel O'Day has given us regular reports, but what's your take, Matthew?"

Matthew leans back and takes a breath, relieved the discussion is moving off the subject of certificates. It's true he's done some personal speculating, quite a bit actually, on the oil markets. He's even used some inside knowledge. What's wrong with that?

But how does the old man know?

"The German is everything we're unaccustomed to in a negotiation," Matthew begins. "Money doesn't seem to interest him; a proposed equity position in future production falls on deaf ears, as does an outright offer to pick up his farm and move it lock, stock and barrel to bigger, better, greener pastures."

Archbold stops him with a wave of his hand. "We know all this, Matthew."

"There's oil under his property," William says. "We've sent scouts there at night for surveys, and we think there's a ton of oil, probably just as much gas, underneath his land."

Archbold leans forward again, places his elbow on the table, and points a finger at Matthew: "Land, I might add, that's in *your* district, Matthew, and, therefore, *your* responsibility to acquire."

"We *want* that future production," Flagler reiterates.

"Gentlemen, please," JDR says, rubbing his eyes, then looking at Matthew. "I'm authorizing you to offer Mr. Weiss fifty thousand dollars for his property," he says. You can even cut him in for an equity stake, if he wants one. We'll leave the particulars up to you."

"I'll be on it right after this meeting, Mr. Rockefeller," Matthew says. "I'll head to Lima this afternoon."

"Just get it done," Archbold sneers.

Matthew holds his tongue, but his blood boils.

JDR rises from his chair and looks down at the group. "Another reason I called this meeting is that several developments have cropped up that are bothering me, gentlemen. Things we need to discuss." He reaches into his jacket pocket, pulls out a thick pamphlet and throws it on the table. "Would anyone care to read the title?"

Archbold cranes his neck sideways. "*Black Death*," he says. "John, is someone here going to meet an untimely demise?" He shoots a glance at Matthew.

Flagler frowns. "I wish the author would."

William leans over and picks up the booklet. "Well well, it's written by our old nemesis, George Rice. Is he still trying to extort seventy-five thousand from us for his refinery, which is worth a tenth of that?"

"Yes," JDR replies, "he's nothing but a common blackmailer."

William thumbs through the pamphlet. "He's more than that, John. His foul treatise dredges up every accusation that's ever been leveled against us, from market manipulation and price fixing to charges of insider deals and kickbacks with the railroads."

Flagler's still frowning. "This loudmouth is calling for a federal probe of our railroad rebates, and if that happens nobody's going to understand the reasoning behind our arrangements."

Archbold looks across the table at Matthew. "Rice's refinery is in Marietta, Ohio," he says. "Looks like you've got *another* problem in your district that needs your attention, Matthew. What are your plans to solve it?"

"I've already taken steps, John," Matthew replies. "I'm in the middle of negotiating an agreement with the Cleveland and Marietta Railroad that services Rice's plant. We're closing in on a deal with the road to charge Standard a dollar fifty a barrel for transport, as opposed to one-seventy-five for Rice and the other independents. Cleveland and Marietta will also credit us another twenty-five cents for every barrel Rice ships."

"I want this devil squeezed!" JDR says, pounding his fist on the table.

"How about the marketing front, Matthew?" William asks. "What's happening there?"

"We've instructed all our subsidiaries and agents to undercut Rice by whatever it takes. We're recruiting his wholesalers and distributors by giving them a lower bulk rate, so they can fatten their margins."

"Sounds like a start," Archbold says, not appearing to mean it.

"What about this Henry Demarest Lloyd character?" JDR asks, "I trust you've all read his drivel in *Atlantic Monthly*?"

"Dutch bastard," Flagler says.

"He calls us 'The Octopus'," William adds.

"So," JDR asks, "what are we doing about these attacks?"

Flagler answers. "A positive move we've taken is to have one of our intermediaries purchase the *Oil City Derrick*, which, as you know, has been nothing but critical of us from the start, especially in fanning the tempers of the producers. We've hired Patrick Boyle, a Standard ally, as the magazine's editor."

"We've also retained a press bureau," William says, "to write and place favorable articles in various newspapers. We, of course, disguise these pieces as independently written."

"Still, this public animosity disturbs me," JDR replies. "I want your reaction to something I received last week from a trustee, William Warden, for whom up until now I've had the highest respect. He ran one of the most efficient refineries in Philadelphia before we bought him out during our acquisitions ten years ago. We took him into our company as an ally, giving him a generous stock position, I might add."

JDR again reaches into his coat pocket and takes out two sheets of writing paper, which he unfolds. "I'm going to read a portion of Warden's note, and then I want to know what you think about it."

"'We have met with a success unparalleled in commercial history, our name is known all over the world, and our public character is not one to be envied. We are quoted as the representative of all that is evil, hard hearted, oppressive, cruel (we think unjustly), but men look askance at us, we are pointed at with contempt, and while some good men flatter us, it's only for our money and we scorn them for it and it leads to a further hardness of heart. This is not pleasant to write, for I had longed for an honored position in commercial life. None of us would choose such a reputation: we all desire a place in the good will, honor and affection of honorable men.'"

JDR looks up. "Now, I won't bore you with what comes next: Warden's rambling proposal for a profit-sharing plan with the producers that Standard would underwrite. He thinks it would promote goodwill between us. Can you imagine such lunacy? I'm not going to even waste my breath reading it to you, but I'll convey his conclusion.

"'Don't put this down or throw it to one side, think over it, talk with Mrs. Rockefeller about it — she is the salt of the earth. How happy she would be to see a change in public opinion and see her husband honored and blessed. May he whose wisdom alone can put it in our hearts to love our fellow men, guide and direct you at this time. The whole world will rejoice to see such an effort made for the people, the working people.' "

Rockefeller tosses the letter on the table. "There you have it, gentlemen. Comments?"

"The damn ingrate," Flagler begins. "It's easy to be sanctimonious when you've made the kind of fortune Warden has. What he forgets is where his money comes from!"

"Or who's behind him getting it in the first place," William snorts. "The man's a Judas."

Archbold stands up and begins to pace. "It's apparent Warden has lost his mind. The producers have always been a greedy lot, unable to control output from even their most prolific wells, and their pattern, ever since Drake stuck his first bit into the ground, has been to flush this precious resource from the earth, with no regard to the future, other than to get their grubby little hands on as much oil as they can, as fast as they can."

"John's right," Flagler adds. "Not only can't these people manage their good fortune, but don't forget, we're talking about competitors here. Years ago, when we restricted our activities to running refineries, our relationship with the producers was different, albeit tenuous. But now the Standard is in the business of owning and operating oil and gas fields. We're looking to beat these people at their own game, and I can't comprehend giving them money that will only end up being pooled to work against us."

"Or spent in saloons and pissed down the drain," William says. "Remember how fast these morons destroyed

Pithole, flushing the reservoirs dry in less than ten years, while drinking their profits away."

"We have always guided our enterprise based upon a higher calling, a moral imperative, if you will," an agitated JDR says. "And Warden's proposal doesn't rise to that level,"

Matthew swallows hard, for he knows what the reaction will be to what he's about to say. "There's a movement emerging here, gentlemen, and if we don't take it seriously, we do so at our peril. If we don't respect its power, it will turn into a groundswell that will bite us like a snake rearing its ugly head from the grass."

Archbold freezes, and turns to him. "What did you just say?"

John D. Rockefeller stands with his arms folded across his chest and looks down at Matthew with an impassive, expressionless stare.

"I travel extensively through the producing regions, the cities as well as Washington, D.C." Matthew says.

"You're saying we don't?" Archbold retorts.

"No, John, I'm not saying that at all. But I can tell you trouble's brewing. I've had too many people corner me, whether it's a cash-strapped field owner or an irate shopkeeper or a U.S. Congressman."

"Politicians be damned!" Archbold shouts at him. "What the hell do we care. We own them all anyway."

"Because they can hurt us!" Matthew shoots back.

"I view those bloodsuckers in the same manner as Mark Twain," William says. "Remember his great phrase? 'There's a Congressman, I mean a son-of-a-bitch, but why do I repeat myself?'"

"What are you hearing, Matthew?" Flagler asks.

"Sir, earlier this morning I was reading an article about this very building, twenty-six Broadway. On the surface, the account is ludicrous, it likens the place to the inner chambers of the Spanish Inquisition. But there's a reason for that perception, and that's what concerns me."

Archbold looks over to William. "I have to confess, there have been mornings here when my head has felt as if it's been placed in a vise."

William laughs. "I think we all know the reasons for that, John."

"Has anyone heard of Ida Minerva Tarbell?" Matthew asks.

"Tarball?" Archbold quips, and William buries his face in his hands, muffling another laugh.

Matthew ignores the taunt. "She's an editor with *McClure's Magazine*, and you should read what she's writing about us. Her father was in the business but lost it all, and she blames the Standard for her family's bad fortune."

"But, back to what's being said about us," Flagler repeats. "What specifically are the accusations?"

Matthew realizes the dangers behind the door he's just opened, but there's no backing off now.

"If I were to sum them up, Henry, four recurring charges: one, that our agents are engaged in espionage on competitors and are using that information to coerce them; second, that people are wising up to, and resenting, our use of secret companies."

Archbold interrupts him. "Oh, bullshit! It gives the perception of choice, and that provides people a degree of comfort."

Matthew ignores him. "Third, we are being charged with flagrant competitor buyouts, where we are accused of paying inflated prices to bolster our market dominance; and last, there's a belief among our marketing agents and distributors that we indulge in price favoritism to chosen retailers, and that we 'zone price' by cutting what we charge in one region, only to make up for it by setting excessive rates in another location."

Archbold rolls his round eyes and raises his hands. "And all that would be bad, because ...?"

"It was the independents who threw the glove at our feet in the first place," JDR says. "These people did not want cooperation; they wanted competition, and when they got it, they didn't like it."

"How soon they forget," Archbold adds.

"Right," JDR replies. "They forget the Standard was an angel of mercy, reaching down from the sky and saying, 'Get into the ark. Put in your old junk. We'll take all the risks!'"

"So, Matthew, what are you recommending?" Flagler asks.

"I'm saying, sir, we should take these accusations seriously, we should be more forthcoming in our public positions, and we should examine a number of our business practices."

Archbold stares down at him. "You're as loony as Warden."

"I say we can't discount public opinion," Matthew replies, "for it drives public policy, it influences politicians, and it sets the stage for how laws are made."

"We're running an oil company, Matthew, not a bloody charity," Archbold retorts. "I don't give a damn how people *feel* about us. I do give a damn about whether or not they buy our kerosene!"

JDR catches his brother's eye and gives him a slight nod.

"Matthew," William says, "we do wish you well on your negotiations with the German. But would you excuse us, please? We have some private business, trustee issues, that we need to discuss. You understand, don't you?"

Matthew rises, feeling as if the wind's just been sucked out of him.

"Yes, good luck bringing Weiss around," Archbold says, escorting Matthew to the door. He pats him on the back and flashes an insincere grin. "We're counting on you, son."

After Matthew leaves, Archbold sits back down and says, "He's enthusiastic, and I'll even go so far as to say he's capable."

"There's no question as to his capabilities," Flagler says.

"But where did he acquire such seditious thoughts?" Archbold asks. "It concerns me having someone like that in a position of such responsibility."

JDR turns to him. "Don't let it worry you, John. Let's see how Matthew takes care of our German friend. Then, I have a project involving both of you that will leave no doubt as to where he stands with the company."

John D. Rockefeller leans back in his chair and casts a sly smile at the three men surrounding him.

DOUBLE TROUBLE

Matthew boards a trolley heading from lower Manhattan to Park Avenue, and he feels a sinking feeling in his stomach as he peers out an open window at a string of barges being towed down the East River.

The way the meeting ended, so abruptly, upset him, and yet... they'd concluded their business, hadn't they? Besides, public perception is an issue that needs to be talked about. After all, the oil king brought the subject up in the first place.

Or was he just opening the door for a condemnation of Warden? Matthew thinks. *Either way, they let me hang myself.*

After a few minutes the trolley stops at Park Avenue and 53rd Street, and Matthew steps off onto the crowded sidewalk. It's a little past 9:00 a.m.

He walks two blocks and crosses the avenue to its west side, stopping in front of an imposing, four-story mansion built of brown rough-cut granite. He walks up the front stairway, reaches for the brass door knocker, and raps it three times. He stands for what seems like an eternity, and then, the thick wooden door opens and a small, gray-haired women in a black dress and white apron peers out.

"Good morning, he says, "Mrs. Philip Fenner please. I'm expected. It's Matthew Strong."

"Oh, yes sir, please come in."

The maid leads him down a long central hallway running the length of the first floor and as he walks, Matthew looks down at the rich Persian carpet with its intricate designs of swans, lions and crossed shamshir swords in deep burgundy, blue and ivory colors. The white walls of the hallway are lined with large oil paintings of English country scenes in burnished walnut frames. Finally, they stop at a closed black-walnut pocket door, and the maid places her hands into its slots and slides it open. "You may go in, Mr. Strong," the woman says. "Mrs. Fenner is waiting for you."

Matthew enters the mansion's library, which contains hundreds of leather-bound books arranged in neat rows on floor-to-ceiling shelves. The grand room has several clustered reading areas with sofas, ottomans, overstuffed chairs and electric-powered Tiffany lamps sitting on top of imported European side tables. The largest of these sitting areas is in front of an ornate, white marble fireplace set into the polished oak-paneled walls and bookshelves.

A woman stands by a huge bay window framed with ruby-red drapes and backed with delicate long-laced curtains. She appears to be staring at the passing carriages outside. She has on a beautiful emerald-green dress with stylish black-healed shoes, and her hair falls to her shoulders, which are covered with a rich purple and gold-silk shawl. She turns from the window as Matthew walks toward her.

"Hello, Mother," he says.

"Matthew," Rebecca replies with a passive, perfunctory smile, angling her cheek so her son can kiss it.

They haven't been close during the past eleven years, and they've drifted even farther apart after Rebecca left Cleveland five years ago to live in New York. Once in the city, she met and married Philip Fenner, a widowed investment banker twenty years her senior. She and Matthew didn't make a habit of seeing each other during his regular visits to 26 Broadway, and they hadn't laid eyes on each other since the summer of 1879, more than two years earlier.

"Let's sit by the fire," Rebecca suggests, leading the way to two large chairs set ten feet apart and facing one another. Between the chairs is a low table. "Would you like some coffee or tea?" she asks him. "I'm going to have some."

"Tea would be fine, if it's no trouble," Matthew says.

Rebecca smiles, reaches for a small brass bell on the side of the table and rings it. Within a few seconds, a maid appears. Rebecca orders them tea and scones.

"Well, Matthew, this is a rare surprise," his mother says. "I gathered from your telegram you have something you need to talk about."

"I do, Mother, but I feel badly just appearing out of the blue, coming to you like this for advice after all this time."

"You shouldn't," she says. "We both have known where to find each other, how to get in touch, if we'd needed to."

Matthew smiles at her. "You're looking fabulous, by the way."

"Why, thank you, son. A woman always appreciates a compliment."

"How's Philip?"

Rebecca doesn't answer.

Matthew looks around the room. "I'd say he's treating you well."

"Do you really care?"

"I care if he's treating you right."

"Care so much you've been knocking on my door every week to make sure now, haven't you."

"That's not fair, Mother. You know I had to go my own way."

"And so did I," Rebecca replies.

"You said as much that night in the boardinghouse," Matthew says. "Remember?"

The maid comes back with a tray containing their tea, four scones, two starched white napkins, utensils and a small silver bowl filled to its top with orange marmalade. She places the tray on the table between Matthew and Rebecca, arranging the items in front of them.

"Will there be anything else, Mrs. Fenner?" the maid asks.

Rebecca shakes her head, and the woman leaves the room.

She waves her hand at the books, artwork and other ornaments in the opulent library. "Well, as you can see, I've come a long way from that boardinghouse we shared on Whiskey Island."

"I have too, Mother."

"I know, Matthew, and I'm proud of you," Rebecca says. "As you said, we both knew we had to go our separate ways, and if we hadn't, we would have pulled each other down with the anger we were carrying at the time."

"So, what's he like?"

"Philip? What's it to you?"

"I want you to be happy."

"He's not abusive, if that's what you're getting at. He's gone most of time, travels for long periods on business. I run this house, and his country estate in Greenwich, much like I did before we married."

"I didn't like him from the first time I met him at your wedding. There's something about him I don't trust."

"Well, that's not really the point, now, is it?" Rebecca says.

"He's the reason I haven't been coming around."

"Oh, come on," Rebecca says, reaching for her tea. "I just told you he's never here, so don't try and use him as an excuse, because I don't buy it. All it would have taken is one visit on your part, and you would have known you could come by most anytime, that Philip most likely wouldn't be here."

"I still don't get it." Matthew says.

"What's there to get?" Rebecca replies. "He hired me to be in charge of his household when his wife fell sick. The cancer consumed her fast, but while she was ill, Philip and I began spending time together, going out for dinners, getting away from here, that kind of thing, mainly to get his mind off the situation, which was becoming worse by the day."

"Don't get me wrong, Mother. I'm happy you're secure and don't have to worry about things, but I've had the feeling from the moment I laid eyes on him that he wasn't right for you."

"Matthew, it's an arrangement, okay?" Rebecca says, shrugging. "I administer the staff and other things at the two homes, not insignificant chores, I'll tell you. And Philip needed someone after Kathleen died, so he made a proposal, and I accepted. It's as simple as that. He just happened to make me an honest woman in the process."

"What about his children?"

"Both grown and gone, with kids of their own. They don't come around. Kind of like you. But you're right, Philip and I lead separate lives. He has, shall we say, certain proclivities he doesn't share with me, and I have no illusions about that. But I have my interests as well, my lady friends, lunches, volunteer work, those sorts of things. Believe me, I keep busy. I do pretty much whatever I want."

"Mother," Matthew interrupts, "I'm in love with Lavinia."

Rebecca takes a sip of tea. "Oh, Matthew, don't you think I know that? I've know that since you two were teenagers."

"But I've made a horrible mistake."

"By letting her remain a single woman all these years, and not going after her?" Rebecca says. "Let me guess, she's found someone else."

"I wish it was that simple. I need to get married."

His mother smiles at him. "So what's so bad about that, if you love her? Besides, a man your age should be settled down with a wife and family."

"But I don't love her. And it's not Lavinia."

Rebecca doesn't react.

"It's someone else, and she claims she's pregnant," Matthew says, shaking his head, looking at the floor.

Rebecca smiles and takes another sip of tea. "And you believe her?"

"It's too early to tell, but I can't see her making something like that up."

"Maybe she's after your money."

"No, that's not the case, trust me. She comes from millions. One of the Standard Oil men introduced us six months ago. He told me he'd heard great things about the job I've been doing, and how he thought it's time I should be thinking about taking a wife, having a home and children. He said it would help my career and all that. He told me that he knew just the woman, fine family and all."

"Well, Matthew, it sounds like you've got yourself in quite a situation now, haven't you?"

"I can't believe how stupid I've been."

Rebecca corrects him. "Not stupid. But you did make your own bed, and now you're going to have to sleep in it. What's her name, by the way?"

"Melissa. Melissa Wharton."

"I take it you don't love this Melissa now, but do you think that's something that will come later on?"

"I can't see it."

"The baby will change that," Rebecca says. "Believe me."

"What do you mean?"

Rebecca reaches for a scone. "It's been my experience," she says looking over at Matthew, "when a man has a child, even in a relationship that has its problems, he finds emotions and feelings that he never knew he had. That's especially true with his first child."

"Was that the case with pa?"

"Of course," Rebecca replies. "It's the case with just about every man. I can tell you right now, it's going to happen to you. So you better prepare for it."

"I hope you're right," Matthew says. "I know I have no choice but to marry her."

"You don't, so you better make the most of it, and understand most marriages don't come easy. I hope you also understand that you need to break this news to Lavinia in person, not in some letter. You owe her that, Matthew, if you're the friend to her that I know you are."

He nods and Rebecca studies him.

"Speaking of Caleb," she says, "whatever happened to that pen he got you? I didn't see you wearing it at my wedding, and I don't see you wearing it now."

"I don't wear it," Matthew replies. "Mr. Rockefeller thinks it's gauche."

"That's ironic, wouldn't you say, coming from someone with his money? I'm sure you remember, I fought Caleb when he said he wanted to get it for you because we had so many other needs for what little money we had. How he got it, I'll never know, but I didn't realize at the time that would be his last act for his family. I'm glad he did that for you, Matthew, and I'm pleased you still have his gift after all these years."

"I can't imagine anything that would make me part with it."

Rebecca glances at the mantel clock. "Matthew, I hate to rush you along, but I have a garden club meeting across town, and I'm a speaker. I'm going to have to leave since I'm already running a little late. You understand, don't you?"

"Of course, Mother. I just needed to talk with you about this. You've confirmed..."

"What you already knew," Rebecca says, smiling at her son again, and rising from her chair. Matthew gets up as well.

She looks at him from head to toe. "I can't believe how you've grown. You're the spitting image of Caleb when he was your age."

"Mother, I will try harder to come by more often. I've missed you. I really have."

Rebecca rings the bell again, and the maid appears. "Please have them bring my carriage around," Rebecca says to her. "I have a meeting on the west side. I'm giving a lecture to a hundred women on how to cultivate roses, if you can believe it." She glances at the clock again.

"Today was a start," she says to Matthew. "You know you're welcome here anytime, son. Can I drop you somewhere?"

"No thanks," Matthew replies. "I have business nearby, and it's a short walk." He comes over to Rebecca and hugs her. "Thank you for today, Mother. I appreciate your advice."

"As I said, I didn't tell you anything you didn't already know," she replies, putting her arms around him and holding him close. "You know more than you reveal, just like me," she whispers, "that's the McCann in you. Your father wore everything on his sleeve. But you and me, we keep it all inside. We know how to keep a secret now, don't we?"

Matthew kisses her. "I can be my own worst enemy."

"I know what you mean," Rebecca answers, kissing him on the cheek. "But, I guess you could say that we're both making our own beds now, aren't we?

Twenty minutes after leaving his mother's mansion, Matthew walks into a branch office of the Oil Exchange on the corner of 45th Street and Third Avenue and approaches one of the clerks.

"My account number is seven, five, eight, zero, three, nine, two. The name's Strong, Matthew Strong."

The clerk checks Matthew's account and quickly replies, "Yes, sir. What can I do for you today?"

"I want to cash out six thousand shares at the current price. Please transfer the money into my cash balance."

"I'm doing it right now," the clerk answers. "That's twenty four thousand, four hundred and eighty dollars to your cash holdings, sir." He writes out a receipt and slides it to Matthew.

Twenty blocks away, Rebecca's carriage passes a slaughterhouse in the Hell's Kitchen section of the city. She hears the squeal of pigs coming from inside, and she smells the stench of butchered animals, the stink of the intestine vats, the foul odor of lifeless blood flowing like rivers into the sewer drains.

Her carriage travels a short distance farther down Eighth Avenue, and she catches glimpses of the Hudson River between the brown multi-story tenement buildings, grog shops and bordellos lining the street. Her driver stops at one of the rundown walkups.

Rebecca gets out and runs up the front steps. She enters the darkened building and begins climbing the narrow, creaking stairs, and she smells rotting garbage placed in the hallway outside some of the rooms. She stops on the third floor in front of Room 310, opens the door and walks inside.

"You're late. Where the hell were you?" Remo Carbone is stretched out on the bed smoking a cigarette. He's stripped, except for a pair of white underpants.

Rebecca takes off her shawl, lays it on a chair and begins unbuttoning her dress. "You'll never guess who came by today," she says, flashing a glance at Remo.

He takes a drag on his cigarette. "I don't give a flyin' fuck if the Queen of England visited you today. Like I said, you're late, and I got things to do."

"Like what?" Rebecca snaps back, slipping off her dress, then taking a seat and unlacing her shoes.

Remo eyes her. "Okay, I give up. Who was so important you made me cool my heels for an hour?"

"My son, Matthew, that's who."

"That son-of-a-bitch?" Remo replies. "I ask myself every day why I don't have someone break his legs. I can't fuckin' believe I've let him slide all these years, after what that bastard did to me."

Rebecca yanks off her second shoe, drops it to the floor and stands up. "Now you listen to me, Remo, and listen good. If you so much as lay a finger on my boy, I'll kill you, do you understand? I'll track you down and kill you. Matthew was young and hot-headed, and he caught us in a situation that set him off."

"If I hadn't been layin' buck naked in bed with my dick up and my defenses down, it would have been a different story, that's for sure," Remo sneers. "The prick sucker punched me."

Rebecca can hear the screams of the pigs from the slaughterhouse down the street from Carbone's open window. She walks over to the bed and lays down beside the Italian. "So, you've been cooling your heels, waiting for me?" she asks him, grabbing his crotch and whispering in his ear. "I'll bet everything isn't cooled off. And even if it is, I think I can find a way to get things heated up real fast."

Carbone snuffs out his cigarette. "Don't worry about your precious son. I'm just lettin' off steam. I ain't goin' to touch a hair on his pretty little head. I'm all talk when it comes to him. You should now that by now."

He pulls Rebecca's petticoat off and begins kissing her breasts and the rest of her still-beautiful body.

Fifteen hours later and 600 miles due west of New York City, Augustus Clapp sits on the edge of the bed in a dingy upstairs room of a two-bit brothel set on the outskirts of the tiny hamlet of Cygnet, Ohio.

His shirt's off, and thick blotches of black hair coat his chest and huge potbelly. His dirty britches and boots are still on, and he grips his club, now stained a permanent reddish-maroon, colored with the blood of countless victims.

Two nude whores, a skinny blonde and a chubby brunette, dance and gyrate on the bare wood floor in front of him. Clapp's mouth is wide open because he's acquired the habit of breathing through it. His rat teeth, most missing, are decayed, and his gums are coated with pockets of pus and infectious ooze. The women keep their distance, because he stinks so badly.

The syphilis, contracted in the mid-70s, has begun showing its symptoms in the past year, eating his brain away, making it impossible for him to hold a job or lead any semblance of a normal life. He's left the teamsters, and now he drinks to keep the constant pain at bay, drifting from one town to another, living in woods or alleyways, stealing food, never bathing, harassing the innocent, or anything else that crosses his path.

An old Pinkerton connection set him up with work on Helmut Weiss' private security detail, figuring Clapp is just the kind of loose cannon the German needs to intimidate the Standard Oil men scouring the countryside surrounding his dairy farm.

His dead eyes lock on the dancing girls, and with his free hand he reaches over and grabs one of several photographs he's spread out on top of the bed. Clapp raises the photo so the women can see it. It's an image of himself taken years earlier. He's naked, and over his head, suspended straight up in the air like a pair of barbells, is a woman who must have weighed at least two hundred fifty pounds, also wearing not a stitch of clothing.

"I like the fat ones," Clapp mumbles as a reddish-yellow drop of drool falls on his pants.

The brunette twirls in a circle, points at the picture and begins laughing.

"What you findin' so fuckin' funny?" Clapp barks, jerking his head up.

"Well, look at yourself," the girl says. "It's like you don't have a pecker."

Clapp turns the picture around. The girl's correct. His drooping bands of belly fat obscure his genitalia, and his flabby breasts, hanging halfway down his chest, make it appear as if two huge women are performing a feat of strength.

"She's right," says the blonde, "that picture's like two people you'd see in the circus."

"Yeah, the freak show," adds the chubby one, giggling again. "Is that why you carry around that pole of yours?

Reminds you of what you should have dangling between your legs?"

"You don't think I got one?" Clapp shouts at the brunette. He points to his pants. "Git over here; I'll show you what I got!"

"In your dreams, mister," answers the woman. "You know what you bought. Just the dances. You said you didn't have money for anything else when you paid us."

"I got more money."

"Let's see it," the blonde replies.

"Not on me."

"Then dancin's all you'll get," says the brunette, "not that you'd be able to do much of anything else, even if you did have a wad in your pants, wad of money, that is." She raises her arms above her head and does another twirl, this time balancing on her other foot in the opposite direction.

The club flashes through the air, striking her in the center of her face as she completes her rotation. She falls to her knees, and Clapp rises from the bed. The blonde freezes in fear as Clapp glares at her: "You're next," he growls.

He grabs the bat with both hands and brings it down hard on the brunette's back and she crumbles to the floor. "You bastard," she cries, attempting to raise herself to her hands and knees. She spits two bloody teeth from her mouth.

The blonde bolts for the door, swinging it open and running into the hallway. "Leave her be, you crazy son-of-a-bitch! You're gonna kill her!" She takes off down the stairs, screaming for help.

Clapp stands over the crippled girl and looks down on her as she tries to crawl away, but her legs aren't working anymore. "Don't worry, I ain't gonna kill ya," he sneers. "I'm just gonna make ya wish you were dead."

He brings the club to his nose and takes a long whiff. Then he slowly draws it over his head, preparing for another blow.

CHOICE AND CONFRONTATION

By Saturday afternoon, Matthew is back in Chicago to meet with Lavinia, and he's now waiting for her across the busy boulevard from the clinic that she runs with John Spencer on North State Street. It's a clear, blue-skied, late- September day, warm yet breezy, and he can see the endless expanse of Lake Michigan between the sturdy brick buildings lining the city's downtown, an area rebuilt after the Great Fire of nearly ten years ago next month.

He dreads what he has to tell her—the Melissa thing—and yet, as he stands watching people go in and out of her office, some looking healthy, others obviously very sick, he feels so proud of her, proud of all she's achieved, proud of how she's pulled herself away from that Western Pennsylvania hellhole into which they both could have easily fallen, only to begin an inevitable descent into routines unchallenged and limited, the only bond between them one of sameness and struggle.

He stares at the painted sign bolted to the bricks over the door to her building:

Dr. John Spencer - Dr. Lavinia Willetts
Physicians for Care

He's done the same thing with Lavinia that he has with his mother—pushed away a person he loves, justified as necessary, something he had to do to find his calling.

He knows in his heart Lavinia has pursued her goals for similar reasons, but now he's about to take some of that away, about to hurt her, about to destroy her dream of making a life with him. And for what? A few nights of gratification with a woman he really can't stand? Not to mention the other one-nighters he's had at various times and places over the years.

He feels as trapped now as those early days in Oil City.

"Matthew," Lavinia says, kissing him lightly on the cheek. "You look lost in thought."

He hadn't seen her come out of her building, and it takes him a couple of seconds to regroup his mind to where it needs to be. He doesn't say anything for a moment, and he notices that she appears tired but as beautiful as ever.

He glances back at the sign and says to her, "I was standing here admiring that, thinking how far you've come from your father's house on Bissell Avenue. How is he, by the way?"

"He's fine, busy as ever patching up oilfield workers, a never-ending job he tells me. Do you know he and your mother write each other regularly? He's kept her up on the comings and goings around town."

I'm surprised she'd want to know, Matthew thinks.

"I never told you this, Matthew," Lavinia says, "but there was a time I thought your mother and my father might marry. He visited her a few times after she moved to New York, you know. I always felt there were sparks between them."

"She's remarried," Matthew mumbles.

"He hasn't," Lavinia says, "and I used to think how nice it would be if the four of us were married and were one big family. Wouldn't that have been something?"

"That's why I've come," Matthew replies.

"I know," she says. "I've some things to say to you as well. Why don't we walk a bit?"

They head east down State Street with the sun at their backs.

"Matthew," Lavinia begins, "I've been doing a great deal of thinking."

"So have I."

"And I want to begin by saying our night at the Sherman House was beautiful, being together like that, feeling the closeness, the tenderness of your touch. I'll never forget it."

"I won't either; we'd waited so long."

"Too long," Lavinia says. "And while I discovered emotions and feelings I never dreamed I had..."

"I feel the same way," Matthew says, turning his head toward her for a moment as they walk. "I've always held those feelings for you. You know that."

"I mean, maybe I imagined I had them," she says, "but I never realized they were so pent up inside me, or understood how strong they were, or how much I needed them to be released. I certainly never had experienced anything like that until that night with you."

"We were always meant to be together. We've always said that."

"But those emotions you brought out have also made my choices clearer," Lavinia replies. "They have made me understand the decisions I know now I have to make. That night was wonderful, Matthew, and at times I wish it would have lasted forever. But it also put everything in perspective for me, defined what I have here in Chicago, made me realize I can't just walk away."

"I'm in the same situation," he says. "I have circumstances I can't turn my back on either."

"The difference between us that night in your room is something I can't get out of my mind," Lavinia says. "Everything was new to me, exciting and unknown, but you seemed as if you'd had a lot of practice at it. You were too experienced, too smooth with your kisses and the other things you did to me."

Matthew looks down at the sidewalk. "I travel all the time, Lavinia. It's been lonely, those hotel rooms, the strange cities. Things happened that I didn't set out to do, that I wasn't expecting. But I never meant to hurt you."

She grabs his arm, stops him and looks him in the eyes. "And you really haven't, Matthew, because my life is here now, and we represent the past, and not even a tangible past, if you think about it. More of a past manufactured in our heads. We both know that, I think."

"You didn't tell John Spencer what we agreed to at the Sherman House, about our plans, did you?"

"I didn't," Lavinia replies without hesitation. "I wasn't about to hurt him in that way. You're talking about a man who I owe my life to, a kind and gentle man whom I've come to love, not just for taking me away from Oil City, but for what he's taught me. His patience, his support in helping me become a doctor so I, like him, can do some good in this world."

Matthew mumbles something under his breath.

They begin walking again, and Lavinia turns and says to him, "You don't have any idea what I'm talking about do you, Matthew? Has it even occurred to you that John was there when you weren't? He was there for my birthdays, for Christmas and the other special times. He was with me when I got my certificate to become a physician and he was with me, encouraged me actually, when we decided to build a practice together. You can't say you were a part of any of that."

Matthew feels a gnawing emptiness inside. "So, you're set on marrying him?"

"Yes, Matthew, I am. John's a wonderful man, and he will make a wonderful father to our children."

He doesn't know what to say to her, and his thoughts are a blur. Finally, he utters, "Lavinia. I'm getting married as well and, in fact, we're going to have a child. I came here to tell you that."

She stops in the middle of the sidewalk and faces him. "How long have you known?"

"I just found out."

"I don't know if I believe you, Matthew. How can I believe you?

"Because it's true," he says.

"I believe you about the baby," she replies. "I'm sure your future wife *is* going to have a child. What I'm not so sure about is when you found out about it."

"Just in the last few days, I swear," he says, noticing a strength and resolve in Lavinia's expression that he's never seen before.

"The more important issue is that you lied to me at Sherman House, didn't you?" she says. "You know you did. You told me that your relationship with Melissa was platonic, simply social, that she was an arm piece to bring to dinners and dances, nothing more. Then you seduced me. So why should I believe anything you've told me?"

"Because it's true."

"Matthew, I think the only thing I can say is that until you understand yourself, until you begin doing what you say you're going to, treating people—especially those closest to you—with the respect they deserve, you're going to be one lonely and unhappy man for a very, very long time!"

She begins walking away.

"Lavinia, please, you don't understand! Let me explain!"

"Leave me alone, Matthew," she says. "I want to walk back by myself. Don't write me again, and don't come to see me again, because I don't want to hear from you or see you. Ever!"

She stops a second later and turns back toward him. "I do have one question. Whatever happened to that young man who left in the wagon that spring morning from Oil City with such purpose and promise in his eyes?"

Lavinia doesn't wait for an answer. Rather, she turns and walks briskly across the street.

"He died with Luke and Pa," Matthew whispers.

He stands on the sidewalk for a minute, watching her disappear into the crowd. Then he begins walking slowly toward Union Depot to catch the evening train to Lima, Ohio, to make an offer to Helmut Weiss.

The construction camp is nestled in a hollow about three miles north of Cygnet. It is set up military-style, with five long tents providing sleeping quarters for twenty men each; a large mess hall capable of serving fifty meals in two shifts; open latrines dug sixty yards or so down slope from the camp; a small infirmary staffed with a doctor and assistant; and private living areas set apart from the workers for Daniel O'Day and his crew bosses.

As is his custom, O'Day has risen at 4 a.m.—an hour before most of his workmen—and prepares for his day over coffee and a hardy breakfast in the mess tent. He's finished eating and is studying a topographical map of the pipeline route when his chief supervisor, Tom Miller, joins him.

"Morning, Daniel," Miller says. "What's the day look like?"

"Our loggers will be starting work about five miles south of Bowling Green," O'Day replies. "It should be smooth sailing for them, since just about all the land in our right of way toward town is already cleared. The crews should make excellent progress today."

Miller pours himself some coffee and looks over O'Day's shoulder at the map. "Yeah, I've scouted it out," Miller says. "Not a lot of trees, mainly farms, flatlands, fields, that sort of thing. I see you're routing the line well east of town."

"Right, the German's dairy operation is over here," O'Day replies, drawing a large circle with his pencil northwest of Bowling Green. "I'm giving that moron a wide berth so we don't rile him up."

"You mentioned we're going to make another run at his property?"

"Yeah, Matthew Strong's coming down from Chicago and should be talking to him tomorrow.

"How do you see his chances?" Miller asks.

"About as good as me getting a personal invitation to a private lunch at the White House with the new president," O'Day replies, not smiling.

Two hours later, about 6:40 a.m., all the workers are at their various jobs, advancing the line northward. O'Day and a mechanic are replacing a broken chain on one of the steam shovels, when the Irishman looks up to see Tom Miller coming toward him fast on horseback.

Miller stops ten feet from the two men and jumps to the ground. "Daniel, can I speak with you a moment?" he says.

O'Day turns to the mechanic. "Get Flannigan to help you finish this. Something's up."

"We've got trouble!" Miller says to O'Day. "We need you at the front of the line, sir."

"What kind of trouble?"

"Our men are being blocked from going any farther."

"Blocked? How the hell can that be? We own all the rights of way from here to Toledo!"

"Apparently not anymore," Miller says. Appears one of the landowners reneged, and there's an army of fifty men standing in our path."

"You got to be shittin' me!" O'Day says, stroking a Colt .45 cradled in a brown leather holster strapped to his side.

"No," Miller replies. "I've seen their paperwork, and it seems in order,"

"Screw the paperwork!" O'Day shoots back. "Let me have your horse. You hitch a ride back to camp and muster as many men as you can. Have them bring rifles."

O'Day jumps on Miller's horse and digs his heels into its sides, and he covers the two miles in less than seven minutes. The loggers have done their jobs well, clearing the corridor of trees and brush, so O'Day has a straight path to where the trouble is.

He exits the woods and rides into a meadow that slopes to a small stream where he can see the two groups of men. The Standard Oil loggers are huddled together on the side of the stream closest to him. Across the creek are more than fifty other men, most armed with rifles and shotguns. He guides the horse down the slope and jumps off.

"What the hell's going on?" O'Day hollers to one of the loggers.

"We finished cuttin' the path through the woods this mornin'," the man reports, "and we jus' begun stakin' out the route over the field, when our guys looked up to see these men gatherin' across the way. There was jus' a few at first, but then they kept growin'."

"Who's in charge?" O'Day demands.

"Appears to be that skinny guy in the brown uniform," the logger says, pointing across the stream. He's the one with the notice."

O'Day squints towards where the logger's pointing, and he sees a man no bigger than a rail with slicked brown hair and a severe part running down the left side of his scalp. The man has darting eyes and a thin moustache, and he, too, wears a pistol on his side.

O'Day walks to the edge of the stream, and he jumps on several exposed rocks and makes his way across. He approaches the little man in the brown outfit.

"I'm Daniel O'Day."

"I know who you are," the man replies.

"Well, then, who the fuck are you?"

"The name's Snipes. Tendrick Snipes."

O'Day looks beyond the group of armed men. Behind the crowd, off by himself, is Augustus Clapp. The brute has taken his shirt off, and he stands with his feet apart, raising and lowering his club over his head. Every few seconds he grips the end of the bat with both his hands, grunts, and swings it in a wide circle. His eyes look like they're disconnected from his brain.

"I see you brought the village idiot with you," O'Day says.

Snipes glances over his shoulder, then turns and smiles at the Irishman. "You never know when someone's going to need some special persuasion."

"Yeah, well, that can work both ways," O'Day answers. "What's going on here, Snipes? We have a valid right of way to cross this stream and bury our line on this land."

"*Had* a right of way, you should say," Snipes says, handing O'Day a document. "As you can see the new owner got a court order nullifying your agreement. Helmut Weiss holds the contract now, and you're looking at a dead zone, sir."

Snipes points to his right, then to his left. "Mr. Weiss controls this entire strip for a mile that way and a mile the other way. You're not laying your pipeline anywhere near here, so I'd say you're looking at a major re-route. Of course, you don't know what other land he controls nearby." Snipes smiles at him a second time.

O'Day finishes reading the court's directive. "Son-of-a-bitch!" he shouts, throwing the paper to the ground. "We're not anywhere near his farm. Why the fuck would Weiss stop our line this far from where he lives?"

"Simple," Snipes says. "He doesn't like you oilmen. He thinks all you do is ruin things."

"You want to talk court orders?" O'Day says. "We'll take this land under writ of eminent domain."

"That may be," Snipes answers, "but that's going to take time, time I don't think you have, sir."

O'Day stares at him. "That's where you're wrong, Snipes. When it comes to dealing with people like you, and that vindictive German bastard you work for, Standard Oil has all the time in the world. You both are going to find that out, sooner than you realize. And it's going to cost you both."

O'Day leaves Snipes, makes his way back across the stream and approaches his men. "Okay, there's not a whole hell of a lot we can do out here right now," he says to them. "Let's head back to camp, until we can see where this is all headed."

He takes a final look across the creek. He can see Augustus Clapp glaring at him like a deranged black bear poised for a kill. O'Day shakes his head and spits on the ground. He jumps back onto his horse and rides off at a fast clip.

THE ATTENTIVE TWIN

Matthew guides his carriage through the gates of Helmut Weiss' five-hundred acre dairy farm thinking this crisp fall morning is about as perfect as it can be: clear blue skies, no humidity, temperatures hovering in the high sixties.

The pastures extend on either side of the roadway as far as he can see, and separating the fields, which are still covered with patches of thick green grasses, is a meandering network of stone walls, hand built by Weiss, Matthew figures. Dozens of spotted black and white cows graze in the pastures, milked earlier that morning and now content to simply spend the rest of the day munching on the ground's bounty, or cooling off in one of the small ponds the German has built in this section of his farm.

Matthew spots a solitary man facing one of the stone walls quite a ways off to his right. He has a rifle in his hand, and on top of the wall appears to be a dozen or so tin cans lined up in a row. The man is about fifty yards from his targets, and Matthew can see him take aim, and then he hears the crack of the carbine as a can flies to the ground. Sometimes the man crouches to make the shot, but he never misses his mark, knocking five cans off the wall in rapid succession.

Matthew drives his carriage up a sweeping hill between two rows of oak trees toward a modest white-planked house and several dairy barns, painted dark green with brown trim. He hears the burst of the carbine again, and in the branches above him he can sense a bullet whizzing through the limbs. Matthew glances back to the field where the man has been taking target practice, but he's nowhere to be seen. Another shot rings out, and a pencil-sized twig breaks from the tree and falls to the path about ten yards in front of him.

He's not trying to kill me, Matthew thinks. *Because if he was, I'd already be dead.*

So he fights his instincts, not panicking or jumping from his carriage to take cover but instead driving the horse and buggy to the front of the main house. He steps out as if nothing has happened, walks to the front door and knocks on it several times with his fist.

A sleepy-looking young man with shaggy blond hair and blue eyes opens the door a crack and peers out. Matthew places him about seventeen, probably one of Weiss' sons, he figures. The kid doesn't say anything. He just stares at Matthew with a sullen look on his face.

"My name's Matthew Strong, and I have business with your father. Was that him out in the field target shooting?"

The boy doesn't acknowledge his visitor at first. Finally he says, "No, that was Klaus, my brother. Pop's workin' in the barn."

"Will you take me to him?"

"I suppose."

"Your brother looks like he can handle a rifle," Matthew says, trying to make small talk with the kid as they head for the largest barn not far from the main house.

"We both can."

"Out of necessity, huh?"

"Huh?"

"I'm saying you and your brother probably like to hunt, bring back game for your meals, you know, bring back something to cook to go with all that milk you make here."

"Something like that," the kid says. "So, what kind of business you got with my Pop? You gonna try and get him to sell the place?"

"I'd like to talk to him about that, yes."

"Then you're gonna get the same answer he gave that Mick who used to come by."

"Maybe he'll like what I have to say to him more than what he's heard before," Matthew says. "By the way, what's your name?"

"Deiter."

Matthew extends his hand but the kid doesn't take it. "Well, Deiter," he says, letting his arm drop back to his side, "I appreciate you letting me talk to your father."

They enter the huge green barn, and the moist, still air inside the structure smells of dried hay and manure, which Helmut Weiss is shoveling out of the cow stalls into a wooden-sided wheelbarrow.

Weiss is stooped and stocky, but muscular, with short-cropped blond hair with specks of gray sprinkled around his sideburns and temples. He's sweaty and red-faced from shoveling his cow shit, and he wears a collarless white shirt and denim coveralls with straps that loop around his thick shoulders. His brown boots are covered with fresh dung and strands of dried straw.

He looks up as his son and Matthew approach, and he rolls his eyes and jams his shovel to the barn floor, staring at Matthew. "Vhat must I do to find peace from you bloodsuckers?"

"Can we take a walk outside, sir?" Matthew asks.

"Vie?"

"Because it's cooler out there, and I think you'd be more comfortable hearing what I'd like to propose to you."

"You people have zed it all before, and my answers have always been zee same. I am not zelling my farm to you. I'm not zelling my farm to anyvon. Ven vill you understand that?"

Weiss turns to his son and points to a large steel vat at the far end of the barn. "Deiter, I vant you to stir zee milk. Zee vagons vill be back soon to fill up so zey can continue zeir deliveries."

"In a minute, Pop. I want to hear what this guy has to say to us."

Matthew turns to see the second son enter the barn. He grips his rifle in his right hand with the barrel pointing to the floor.

"You must be Klaus," Matthew says. "I see you're quite a shot."

The young man looks exactly like his brother: same age, build, color hair, eyes. Identical twins, Matthew thinks.

"What's goin' on, Pop?" Klaus asks.

"Another zalesman zent from zee oil company, looking to buy us out."

Klaus casts a cold stare at Matthew and says, "You want me to get rid of him for you?"

Matthew moves closer to Helmut Weiss, and the sons take a step toward Matthew, so they are now standing right behind him, the four forming a tight circle in the breezeless barn.

"Sir, Standard Oil is prepared to pay you fifty thousand dollars cash for your property."

"I don't care if you offer me fifty million dollars!" Weiss shouts. "My land is not for zale!"

"Fifty thousand is a considerable sum, Mr. Weiss," Matthew replies. "And our company would also help you relocate to even better land."

Weiss approaches Matthew and looks him in the eyes. "Let me tell you somezing, Mr. Who Ever You Are. My wife and I came here twenty years ago from zee old country. We found ziss land, walked every acre of it together, decided to build a home and business here. She gave birth to my sons in za house you saw outside. She died in zat house, and is buried on top of vone of zose hills you passed on the vey here. Zoe, I ask you: Vie vould I possibly zell this place zat means so much, zat holds so many memories here for me and my boys?"

"Because with the money we would give you," replies Matthew, "you could start a new life somewhere else. An easier life, one you might enjoy more. You wouldn't have to work as hard as you do."

"I like to verk. I verk, just as my sons vill verk after me. Zat is the vey it is, zat is the vey it is meant to be."

"You speak of your sons, Mr. Weiss, but think of the inheritance you would be giving them, if you were to accept our offer."

The German throws his shovel to the barn floor. "You talk of inheritance! Vhat kind of legacy are you oil people leaving our children? I have been to Pennsylvania and zeen vhat you have done to zee land zere, vhat you have left behind. It is dead land, nothing lives vhere you have put your oil vells. I zee you doing za zame zing in Lima, turning farmland into vasteland. Is this zee *inheritance* you are leaving behind for my children and, someday, my grand-children? I hate vhat the oil companies do, and I hate zee people who verk for zem!"

"I grew up in the oil fields, sir," Matthew says. "I have seen the waste, and I hated it, too."

"Yet, look how you make your living?" Weiss snickers. "You are no better zan a cheap whore."

"But things are changing, Mr. Weiss," Matthew argues. "The pipelines and tank cars are solving the spill problems we had when we carried the oil by wooden barrels and wagons. We have better drilling rigs now."

Helmut Weiss picks up his shovel. "I vant you to go." He turns to Deiter and points to the vat. "And I vant *you* to stir zee milk. Zee vagons vill be here soon."

Klaus grips his rifle with both hands now. "You heard my Pop, he wants you to get out of here." The son points the barrel of his carbine first at Matthew, then at the barn door.

Matthew shakes his head but says nothing more. He draws his lips together, looks at the ground and storms out of the barn.

Several minutes later as he travels down the main drive off Weiss' farm, his carriage rounds a bend. Standing in the middle of the road is Klaus Weiss with his gun cradled in his arms, and Matthew reaches for his rifle, which he keeps underneath the seat beside him.

"You won't be needin' that, mister," the kid says to him. "I aim you no harm."

Matthew feels the first sense of relief since the twin had taken the potshots in the trees above him an hour earlier.

"You said something in the barn that got me interested," Klaus says.

"What's that?" Matthew asks.

"Talk of my inheritance. Me and Deiter are named in Pop's will. If anything happens to him, the farm goes to us."

"I think that's a long time coming, son," answers Matthew. "Your father looks to me like he's going to be around awhile."

"Yeah, but if he weren't," Klaus replies, "my brother and me would be the ones to decide whether or not to sell the farm, right?"

"If you and Deiter had legal rights to the property through the probate of your father's will, that would be correct, yes."

"Would you still pay fifty thousand dollars if we owned the place outright?"

"I don't see that changing, no matter who holds title to the land," Matthew replies.

"Maybe we can convince him to give us our inheritance before it's due," Klaus says with a faraway look in his eyes. "After all, it'll be comin' to us sooner or later, and he has to know we got no inklin' to keep the place runnin' after he goes."

"Inheritances usually don't work that way." Matthew points out.

He sees Klaus Weiss smile for the first time since he met him, a vacant, joyless expression, hard to figure.

"Deiter and me are goin' to talk to Pop right now. We'll let him know how we feel. You should stick around. I think we can convince him to sell."

Matthew reaches in his pocket and hands the boy his card. "I'm spending the night in our camp just north of Cygnet. You can reach me there if something changes."

He cracks the reins to his carriage and begins heading down the road again. A few moments later he turns, looking back at the spot where he had talked to Klaus. The boy hasn't moved, and he's standing there dead still watching Matthew depart, the odd smile still stuck on his face.

A Shot in the Dark

Daniel O'Day and Matthew sit by themselves in the mess tent eating an early supper of beef stew. It's a bit past 4:30 p.m.

O'Day reaches over and rips a hunk of bread from the loaf between them on the table and dips it into the hot brown gravy in his bowl. "You can't look at it as failure, my friend," he says to Matthew, "because there's no way in hell the German's going to part with his land. Everyone knows the run I put on him, and I tried everything, to no avail. You could have offered him the sun and the moon, but it wouldn't of made any difference. You might as well been pissing in the wind. Besides, it's not a case of him just selling his land. He's made it personal with us."

"About as personal as it can get," Matthew replies. "It's one thing to refuse to sell and then go about your business. But this guy has hired an army."

"Including that moron Augustus Clapp. Ever heard of him?"

"That troublemaking teamster? Yes, you bet I have," Matthew says. "Our crew's sitting idle with their thumbs up their butts, all because the German has taken it on himself to lock up a two-mile-long dead zone south of Bowling Green."

"That's what we're talking about," says O'Day, swallowing some stew and grabbing another wedge of bread. "He's

165

moved this fight beyond his property. But let's stop our bitching for a moment, and go over what we *can* control here."

"First," Matthew says, "we own most of the state judges in Ohio, and we can seek an injunction claiming restraint of trade. That'd probably be the fastest way to come at this, quicker than condemning the land under an eminent domain order."

"He'll appeal," O'Day replies.

Matthew stabs a chunk of beef with his fork. "Then we call on our friends at the federal level."

"This is all going to take time."

Matthew nods. "I agree, Daniel, and that's the problem. We can't even have the men divert the line in a new direction because we've no idea what other property the bastard has bought around here. Plus, we're dealing with natural gas. If we were moving crude, we could run the pipe to the nearest train depot and set up temporary transfer into tank cars. Sure, it's expensive and time consuming, but at least we'd have a way to get product up north. With gas, we've no choice but to run it by pipeline, and until we work this out, we're screwed."

O'Day frowns. "Meanwhile, you've made delivery commitments to Toledo, those municipal contracts Fat Freddie's setting up for us ... and the clock's ticking."

They hear voices outside the mess tent and Tom Miller parts the flaps, rushes inside and approaches Matthew. "There's a Tendrick Snipes here, sir. He wants to speak to you."

"Who?" Matthew says.

O'Day puts his fork down and leans back in his chair. "Well, isn't this interesting? Come on, I'll introduce you. We'll find out what the worm wants." The men get up from the table and walk outside.

The little wisp stands nervously by his horse, still decked out in his brown uniform, and O'Day walks up to him. "So, Snipes, where'd you leave your army, and to what do we owe the dubious honor of this visit?"

"I'm here to see Matthew Strong. I've a message from Mr. Weiss."

"That's me," Matthew says.

Snipes turns to him. "He wants to talk to you."

"When?"

"Tonight. Apparently, you two spoke earlier today?"

"That's right."

"He wants me to tell you he's reconsidered your offer."

O'Day narrows his eyes and gives Snipes the once over. "Why didn't he come himself? Why'd he send you?"

"Because he's finishing up his chores," Snipes replies. "He couldn't get away right now."

"Do you know if his sons spoke with him?" Matthew asks.

"I've no idea," Snipes answers. "All I know is when I went to see him about an hour ago to give my daily report, I was all set to tell him about my encounter with Mr. O'Day down by the creek this morning…" Snipes shoots at look at the Irishman, "…when he interrupts me to say he's not interested in any of that, just get the guy who came by earlier who made me the fifty thousand dollar offer."

Matthew starts walking to his carriage.

"I'm going with you," O'Day shouts. "Hold on while I get my rifle."

"He asked that Mr. Strong come by himself," Snipes says.

"Are you going with him?" O'Day asks.

"No, I'm headed to Bowling Green to join my men. Mr. Weiss told me he wants to speak with Mr. Strong alone."

"It's okay, Daniel," Matthew says. "I talked with one of the sons after my meeting with Weiss. He and his brother were going to talk to their father, and I bet they've convinced him what the money we're offering can do for the family."

"I don't like it," O'Day says. "I don't like any of it."

"Daniel, this could be the break we've been waiting for," Matthew says. "Think what it's going to mean to bring this deal home. I have to see what Weiss has in mind."

He climbs into his carriage and rides off.

O'Day watches his friend depart, then turns and glares at Snipes. "This better be on the up and up," he says. "Because if it's not... do you see that little gun of yours you wear on the side of your little waist? If anything happens to him, I'm going to hunt you down like a dog, and take that gun, and empty it up your little ass!"

By the time Matthew approaches the Weiss farm, it's night-fall. He'd stopped his carriage about thirty minutes earlier and fired up the two lanterns bolted on either side of the surrey to help him navigate the pitch-black backwoods path.

He hears the rustling of the dried fall leaves quivering in the night breeze, and in the distant hills he can make out the faint howling of wolves. He looks up to see if there's a moon, and catches the huge, fleeting shadow of a horned owl gliding like a silent specter between the treetops, the nocturnal predator out for its hunt. The great bird hisses at him with a sound like an angry snake.

The farmhouse is dark and deserted as Matthew pulls up and stops his carriage near the spot where he'd parked that morning. He keeps his lanterns lit so he can make his way to the front door.

Maybe they're in the back kitchen having dinner, he thinks.

He knocks on the door. "Mr. Weiss? It's Matthew Strong. Are you home? Klaus, Deiter, are you in there?"

He tries the knob, but the door is locked. Matthew sees a dim light coming from the barn, and he begins walking toward it.

Finishing up his chores. That's what Snipes said he was doing.

He enters the building, and it smells much the same as it did that morning, the aroma of manure-caked straw floating in the still air, but now there's a pervading closeness, an animal odor, and as his eyes adjust, Matthew realizes the stalls are filled with cows. He can hear them mash the hay in their mouths, and he also hears the occasional stream of urine or burst of feces hitting the barn floor.

The door to the huge structure creaks shut. Matthew turns to see who's coming.

"My friend and me was hopin' you'd show." The massive frame of Augustus Clapp emerges from the shadows. He holds his club up with his right hand, and walks toward Matthew.

Matthew takes a couple of steps backward as Clapp approaches. "My business is with Helmut Weiss," he says, not believing he's been so stupid as to have left his rifle in the carriage.

"Me and my friend here are gonna be doin' the talkin' for Weiss. He says it's time to teach you oilmen a lesson ... one you ain't gonna forget." Clapp brings the club to his nose and smells it, all the while keeping his eyes glued to Matthew, who scans the stalls for something he can defend himself with. He sees the shovel the German had used earlier leaning against a wall.

"Listen, Clapp. You and I don't have a fight."

"Oh, yeah we do," Clapp answers. "We was gonna fight when I got me this job." He begins coughing, a thick, mucous-filled cough, and out of his mouth shoots a clump of bloody phlegm that lands a couple of inches from Matthew's boot.

Matthew makes his move, running toward the shovel, but Clapp springs after him with surprising quickness. The bat crashes into the side of Matthew's head.

When he awakes, he realizes his arms are tied above his head from a rope suspended from one of the beams of the barn. He's stripped naked, and he's raised about a foot off the floor. His forehead throbs with pain and the ropes cut into his wrists. He tries to move his hands to see if there's any play in the knots but there isn't. He feels like an animal ready for slaughter.

Clapp stands in front of him, mouth ajar, lips coated with dried drool. Matthew smells the brute's malodorous stench, and he can also feel the streams of sweat gushing from his own underarms, running in rivulets down the sides of his bare chest.

Clapp looks up at Matthew's hands, still trying to work their way free, and says, "Don't think I don't know how to tie a knot. You ain't going nowhere."

He draws his club back with both hands and thrusts the end of it into Matthew's stomach with all his might. "That's fer the first offer you made Weiss that he turned down," he says.

Matthew's mouth shoots open, and he begins to gag and convulse because he can't breathe. He gasps for air, but nothing's coming. He is suffocating.

"This is fer your second," Clapp grunts, gripping the club like a baseball bat. He spreads his feet apart and brings the bat crashing into Matthew's left side.

Matthew can hear the cracking of his bones, and his insides feel as if they're being punctured by a dozen knives.

He tries to scream, but he still can't make a sound. All he hears is one of the cows pissing.

Clapp comes closer and looks up at him. "Weiss told me you oilmen made eight or ten offers, so we've a ways to go. 'Course there ain't gonna be much left a 'ya."

Clapp disappears behind him and Matthew prepares for another strike, but it doesn't come right away, his tormentor apparently content to watch him hang. Then the club creases his back, and this time Matthew does scream, for the pain is unbearable.

"Son-of-a-bitching bastard," Matthew says under his breath.

Clapp walks back around in front of him. "What'd you say? You callin' me names, now? You hadn't be callin' me names. My friend and me have somethin' we do to people call us names. You know what it is?"

Matthew looks down at him and shakes his head, thinking for the first time that he is about to die.

"We knock their teeth out."

Clapp ambles over to one of the cow stalls and picks up Weiss' milking stool. He carries it back to where Matthew is hanging and sets it on the floor about five feet from him.

"I like this distance," Clapp says, stepping up on the stool. "Gives a good angle. Gonna let me get the club workin' real good to pop them teeth of yours and break your face."

A voice comes from behind him. "Augustus... I've brought your money."

Matthew looks up through half-shut eyes to see Daniel O'Day standing in the barn doorway with a suitcase in his hand.

Clapp spins around. "Money? What you talkin' 'bout, O'Day?"

"Well, we figure it this way, Augustus," O'Day says, walking toward the brute. "Since Weiss doesn't want the fifty thousand we offered, we think you should have it."

"You shittin'?"

O'Day smiles at him. "No, we're not, and all you have to do to get it is stop beating on my friend. You have to understand, Augustus, he was just doing his job, just like you do your job. You can't fault a man for that now, can you?"

Clapp steps off the stool, eyes the suitcase. "You got money in there?"

"Yes, I do. And since Weiss doesn't want it, we might as well give it to you. We've got nothing else to do with it." O'Day is now standing beside Clapp, and he puts the suitcase down on the barn floor.

"What do you mean you got nothin' to do with it?" Clapp says, moving his eyes from the suitcase to O'Day.

"You saying you don't need it, Augustus?" O'Day says, glancing at the club. "Think of all the things you could buy with such a fortune. Why, you'd never have to work another day in your life."

"I ain't never seen that kind of money."

"You want to take a look? Go ahead, open the case."

Clapp bends down on one knee, setting his bat beside him. He flips the suitcase latches up with his thumbs and opens the top. There's nothing inside.

"You lyin' bastard!" Clapp shouts, reaching for his weapon, but O'Day slams his foot down on top of it. He brings his fist around at the same time and smashes it into Clapp's face, and the force topples the brute onto his back.

O'Day picks up the bat and throws it out the barn door. "Get up, Clapp," he orders.

The enforcer rises like a giant beast from the floor, and O'Day assumes the balanced stance of a boxer with his feet spread, and his fists cocked just under his chin. Clapp lets loose a wild, roundhouse swing, but O'Day steps to one side, and the would-be blow misses. He moves in to pummel Clapp with six successive jabs, and with every punch the man's head flies backwards, and his nose begins to pour blood.

Clapp charges O'Day, who sidesteps him again, landing three rapid punches to his head and ribs. The Irishman is on him in an instant, covering the man's face, chest and gut with a vicious series of furious blows, aiming for the eyes, nose and mouth, beating him senseless.

Clapp's face is a bloody pulp in less than a minute. The brute just stands there, weaving, eyes half shut.

O'Day reaches up, grabs a hunk of Clapp's hair and leads him over to the vat of milk in the corner of the barn. He keeps his grip on him with his right hand, and he throws open the lid to the vat with his left. Then he punches Clapp three more times square in the face.

O'Day grips Clapp's hair and chin with both hands and submerges his head in the milk. As the brute's blood mingles with the white liquid, his arms begin to flail and his body starts to shake, and O'Day raises his head from the vat.

Clapp tries to catch his breath, but O'Day dunks him again. The milk is now a reddish-cream color, and the air bubbles expelled by the helpless man rise to the surface and pop like volcanic corpuscles. The life seems to be draining from Clapp before the Irishman pulls him out and throws him to the floor.

The old teamster coughs, spitting blood and milk from his lungs as he gasps for breath. O'Day kneels beside him. "Augustus, can you hear me, Augustus? Do you know who has your money? Weiss does. He decided to take it after all. And he wanted me to let you know, he won't be needing your services anymore. He wanted me to tell you, you're done working for him."

Clapp coughs up more milk. "That German son-of-a-bitch, he double-crossed me," he says, still coughing. "I'll kill the bastard. I swear I will!"

O'Day stands over him. "Good, you do that, Augustus. You'll be saving a lot of people a lot of headaches." He jumps up on the milking stool and cuts his friend down.

Matthew is doubled over in pain, but he can still walk, and O'Day throws a blanket around him and guides him outside where Tom Miller and another worker are waiting in a wagon.

"Get some more blankets and a couple of pillows from the house, and put them in the back of this rig. Make Matthew as comfortable as possible," O'Day orders. "Go easy on the ride back, and get him to the infirmary tent right away. I think his ribs are broken."

"Are you coming with us?" Miller asks.

"No, I've got unfinished business in Bowling Green," O'Day shouts, jumping into Matthew's carriage and riding off into the night.

Forty-five minutes later he kicks in the door of a corner room in a flop house on the edge of town. Tendrick Snipes is standing on a worn carpet taking a piss in a tin bedpan. He looks up in horror at O'Day.

"Remember what I said I was going to do, if you did anything to Matthew Strong?"

Snipes screams and drops his bedpan, spilling its contents on the rug. O'Day enters the room, shutting the door behind him.

The following morning, Helmut Weiss is up as usual before sunrise to milk his cows. He finishes his breakfast of oatmeal and eggs, walks over to a washbowl, and places his empty dish in the soapy water. He scrubs the plate clean and dips it in a second bowl to rinse it off. He wipes it dry and sets it back in his kitchen cupboard.

The German pours himself a mug of steaming black coffee and heads for the front door. He opens it, and steps outside into the darkness, stopping to breathe the fresh morning air. He takes a long, slow sip of coffee.

The barrel of the rifle appears from behind the stone wall, and the shooter takes aim. The shot pierces the silence of the dawn, and Helmut Weiss collapses to his walkway with a bullet to the brain.

NESTS

The hornets' nest has been sliced in half from top to bottom, revealing hundreds of paper-gray chambers—some folded shut, others open and dark, a few flapping and bidding entree as if kissed by smoky clouds. The nest hangs from a splintered and debarked tree maimed by a nitro blast. But the insects are long gone. Dead or taken flight, nowhere to be seen.

In their place Matthew can detect movement deep in the layered vaults, and he hears what sounds like screams coming from the catacomb maze. He squints and tries to focus his mind in hopes of seeing what's inside, asking his eyes to adjust before the fast-falling night wraps the hive in darkness.

Suddenly one of the paper layers parts like the parched lips of a dying man, and Matthew freezes in terror as a snake-like creature emerges, suspended in the air and coming toward him. In the blackness he detects the deformed face of Phineas Crump with his cataract-coated eyes and fractured forehead, his reptile claws clasping a sledgehammer.

"What will you pay?" the thing croaks before sliding back into its nest.

Out of a second chamber comes the face of Caleb smiling at his son, nodding like everything will be all right, and inside a third Matthew can see Lavinia, but she isn't facing him; all he can make out is the back of her head as she quickly disappears into her vault. His father slides forward, and now Matthew can see the scales running down the side of his serpent body, and in his hand Caleb grips a torpedo. A second later the bomb slips through his fingers, and father and son watch as it falls silently into an endless abyss.

A flame flashes from one of the cave-like rooms, and a portion of the nest begins to burn and peel away like crinkled parchment. Inside the fire Matthew recognizes his brother Luke, hovering for a moment in the heat and then opening his mouth, and as he does a dozen fat pollywogs squirm from his throat and fall flopping to the floor, tails wiggling back and forth like a pack of hairless dogs at the end of a winter hunt.

Matthew feels the top of his head being stroked, and he looks to Luke's left and sees the menacing form of Augustus Clapp emerging from the nest. The serpent body of the one-time teamster is larger than the others, and his hands hold a club dripping with blood. Matthew feels the arms of his naked body stretched above him, tied to the barn rafters, a prisoner with no escape. He watches as Clapp runs the end of his club lightly across his dark hair and down each side of his face, a prelude of the pain to come. He feels the club touch his head again and he sees the clawed reptile hands of the brute draw the bat behind his back as he prepares for the strike.

"Matthew...Matthew, I'm here," he hears the voice say, and he feels as if he'd drowned and is now revived, propelled to the surface of a roiling spring. "Matthew, Matthew," comes his name again, louder now, and he feels the club stroke his hair a second time, but how can that be? Clapp is swinging it toward him with all his might. "Get the club workin' real good," he hears the brute sneer, "pop them teeth of yours and break your face."

He braces for the blow that never comes, and he wakes with a jolt and a shout, but instead of Clapp he sees Melissa sitting on the side of his bed. She's rubbing the small portion of his head that isn't wrapped in bandages.

Standing behind Melissa he can make out the hunched form of the camp doctor, and he hears him say, "He's been in and out of consciousness for the past three days, and we've been administering laudanum every few hours or so for his pain, trying to make him as comfortable as possible, considering what he's been through."

Matthew feels a constant throbbing in his head from the concussion he's sustained, and it's difficult to take a deep breath because of the broken ribs on his left side. The bandages around his midsection provide some support, but the bolts of pain shooting through him when he makes the slightest movement border on the unbearable.

"I've taped his back extra tight," he hears the doctor say, "since I believe he's got at least one cracked vertebrae."

"Mirror," Matthew says, raising his head from the pillow and running his tongue over his teeth.

"Oh, Matthew dear," Melissa answers, stoking his head some more, "there's no need for that now."

"Please, Missy," he says. "I need to see something."

"Can't do him any harm," the doctor replies, reaching for an oval-shaped, wooden-handled mirror sitting on the table next to Matthew's bed. He holds it up in front of Matthew so he can see himself.

Matthew parts his lips and is relieved that all his teeth are still there. But a bolt of pain pierces his head like a nail driven through his skull, and he can also see that the right side of his face is covered in a mask-like blackish-yellow and blue bruise, and his eye is swollen shut in its shattered socket. The doctor puts down the mirror, and Matthew's head falls back on the pillow.

Melissa leans close to him and whispers, "The doctor says all that's going to heal and you're not going to have any lasting scars. All it's going to take is time and rest, and I'm going to take you back to Cleveland so we can get you well even faster."

"She's right," the doctor adds. "We're limited to what we can do for you here, so the sooner we get you to a real hospital for the treatment and attention you need, the quicker you'll be back on your feet and the better you'll recover from all this in the long run."

"Where's Daniel?" Matthew asks.

"He's in New York," the doctor replies, "reporting on what happened to Mr. Flagler, so I'm told."

Matthew looks up at him. "Did he kill Clapp?"

"Might as well have," the doctor says. "He beat him to within an inch of his life."

"So, Daniel's okay?"

"Yes, but the German's not. They found him dead in front of his house the morning after Clapp beat you."

"Dead?"

"Shot dead," the doctor answers.

Matthew shakes his head slowly and whispers, "No, oh no! What did I do?" Melissa leans over and kisses him on his forehead. "There's no need to trouble Matthew with all this now," she says, turning to the doctor. "And, if you'd be so kind to leave us, there are some things Matthew and I need to talk about in private."

The doctor nods and walks toward the flap of the tent, which is pulled closed. "I'll check back in on him later. He'll need another dose of laudanum before the night's out."

Melissa reaches under the blanket and puts Matthew's special pen in his hand. "Here, I brought this for you. I know what it means to you, and I thought it would give you strength."

Matthew nods at her, but keeps his eyes closed.

"You just rest now, my darling," she says. "Don't try and talk, because there's no need for you to say anything. All you have to do is listen."

"I'm awake," Matthew says. "I've been sleeping too much anyway. I can talk, at least for a while. Wake me if I drift off on you."

Melissa smiles at him. "Well, the first thing I want to tell you is that Daddy has bought us a wedding present."

"What kind of present?" Matthew asks, opening his one good eye.

"The most wonderful gift you can imagine. He's bought us the Huntington estate. We're going to have a grand home to live in after we're married!"

Matthew tries to frown but it hurts too much to move the muscles in his face. "Are you talking about the Huntington estate on Lake Shore Boulevard?" he asks. "Why in the name of God did he do something like that? It's a fifty-room stone castle on seventy acres. How much did your father spend on it?"

"Close to twenty-five thousand dollars," Melissa answers, adding, "Of course, it needs a great deal of work. And besides that, I want new furniture, carpets and artwork, and the stables need repairing, and I want a formal rose garden with statues and fountains. Oh, and I want the ballroom completely redone. But when I'm through, it's going to make a proper place for us and the baby."

"We don't need a place that big, and how could you think I'd want to be beholden to your father for that kind of money? Do you know me at all?" His head throbs with every word.

"I'm beginning to think sometimes I don't have a clue." she shoots back, her body stiffening as she sits beside him on the bed.

"And we're supposed to be getting married?" he asks. "Supposed to be forming a partnership? A union? Doesn't that tell you something?"

"You can be as sarcastic as you want, Matthew, but you'll get no sympathy from me. Has it occurred to you that your precious business deals, and your never-ending travels are now going to have to take a back seat to your primary obligations, which now are to me and the baby? How could you have put yourself in the kind of danger you did, knowing I'm carrying your child? You could have been killed for goodness sakes, and then what would I do?"

"No one ever said the oil business doesn't have risks," he replies wearily, closing his undamaged eye a bit.

"Yes, well, here's what's going to happen," Melissa says. "You're going to leave Standard Oil and come to work for my father. He's going to make a place for you at his commodities firm. I've already spoken to him about it, and we've got it all set up. It's a far safer job than what you're doing now, and I can at least expect you home at night where you belong."

"Throw away my career for some glorified banker's job?" Matthew says. "It's not going to happen, Melissa."

"And we *are* getting married, Matthew, make no mistake about it. The ceremony is six weeks from this coming Saturday. I've reserved the church, and the reception will be at my parents' estate. So, in the morning we're traveling to Cleveland so we can get you back in shape. No if, ands or buts!"

He feels a sinking feeling in his stomach. "Not going to happen," he mumbles, squeezing his pen and drifting into semi-consciousness.

Melissa ignores his protest and says, "When you become presentable again, we have things we'll be expected to do socially, events and parties to attend where I'll want my husband by my side, not off on some ill-fated crusade for the almighty John D. Rockefeller."

"No way, by God, can we live at the Huntington estate," he says, straining to make the words come out. "It's bigger than Rockefeller's home. I'd be breaking every rule in the book."

"I told just you, it doesn't matter," she replies, stroking his hair again, leaning over and kissing him a second time. "You're leaving his company."

That's what you think. He barely hears her as she rambles on.

"It will be the biggest and most beautiful wedding Cleveland has ever seen. All the Whartons will be coming, and my father's business partners and, of course, my best friend, Priscilla, and the other girls. Do you think your mother and her husband will want to come in from New York? I'm going to practice my piano so I can give a wonderful recital at the reception, maybe a sonnet by Mozart. What do you think of that? What kind of flowers should we order? I'll need a seamstress to start on my dress and..."

Matthew has slipped back into a deep sleep and hasn't heard a word. But beneath the supposed calm bringing comfort and cure, beside the flickering lamp casting a warm glow in his tent, under the non-stop babble and plans of his soon-to-be wife, the twisted fang-bearing snakes open their eyes and begin to rustle around their nests, appearing once again from the haunted recesses of his mind.

CASPIAN BOUND

Though the rains have stripped the trees of their fall foliage, the third week of November in Cleveland finds Indian summer still bringing welcome mild days and tolerably cool nights to the southern shores of Lake Erie. The frigid bands of Canadian air haven't descended over the Midwest yet, so everyone is savoring the respite from the four-month icebox just around the corner.

Matthew is especially upbeat, since it's only seven weeks after his attack, and his wounds are healing faster and better than he could have imagined. His energy has returned and he's feeling stronger with each passing day. He has dodged death, or at the very least a horrible disfigurement, and as a new husband and future father he realizes each hour is a gift to be cherished, an opportunity for contribution and giving of thanks.

Melissa was right when she predicted their wedding would be the grandest affair Cleveland society had ever seen; more than 600 of the city's upper crust attended the event, which spanned three days of dinners and receptions, music recitals, a luncheon for the bridal party, private gatherings for the family and, of course, the ceremony itself.

They'd moved into the old Huntington place, and Melissa, true to her word, began revamping everything, from the front gate to the rear stables, hiring maids, cooks and other household helpers, spending money like it was printed on a perpetual press in the cellars of her castle. She, of course, was incensed when Matthew told her that he was not leaving the oil business and going to work for her father, Charles Wharton. But her wrath had quickly subsided, and he's now getting used to having a place to call his own, having meals prepared and waiting for him when he arrives home after his day's work.

He looks out the window of his office at the sidewalk below, and he can see most people aren't even wearing coats because of the warm weather. He takes a generous drink of laudanum from a silver flask, but a knock on his door pulls him from his thoughts, and he quickly slips the flask back into his jacket pocket.

His advisor, James Harris, enters the room and says to him, "I'm not interrupting anything, am I, Matthew?"

"Not at all, James, I'm just sitting here thinking how good it is to be back."

"Well, sir, I have to tell you something that's either going to make your day even better, or … I suppose there's always the opposite possibility."

Matthew laughs. "And what's that?"

"Mr. Rockefeller wants to see you."

"Where is he?"

"Forest Hill."

"Did he say what he wants?"

"His telegram doesn't mention anything … just that he'd like to see you, at your convenience. He doesn't even specify a time, which is unlike him."

Matthew rises from his chair. "As usual, I'm sure he'd prefer to see me sooner than later. If there's something we need to talk about, it's best to get to him right away and take care of it, so he doesn't have to worry about it longer than he has to."

"You driving out by yourself, or would you like some company?"

"No, I'll go alone," Matthew answers, heading for the door. "I don't know how long I'll be, and you'd just have to wait around until I'm done."

A few minutes later, Matthew climbs into his surrey in front of the Standard Oil Building. Its top is down, and harnessed to the carriage are two thoroughbred stallions, one brown, the other a magnificent midnight black. He snaps the reins and takes off.

He guides the carriage down the middle of Euclid Avenue at a fast clip. The street is immaculate as usual, and Matthew admires the fine homes and rows of broad oaks with their gnarled brown trunks and twisted branches intertwined like a canopy of outstretched arms.

JDR's Cleveland estate, Forest Hill, is a seven-hundred-acre paradise set on a rise overlooking Lake Erie, and during the oil king's visits to the city, this is where he stays. The secluded compound is a good four miles east of Euclid Avenue, and Matthew gives the horses a tap of the reins to keep up their pace.

Soon he approaches the entrance to the property. The black wrought-iron gates, which are closed, are attached to two twelve-foot high cut-granite columns. On top of each column is a massive marble urn containing dark-green ivy cascading down its side. Running to the left and right of the columns and curling into the woods on the periphery of the estate as far as Matthew can see is a ten-foot iron fence set into sections of stone. Planted behind the fence are shrubs obscuring any view of the property.

To the left of the entrance is the guard house. It's a large two-story structure with a terracotta tiled roof, built of the same quarried granite as the front columns. The roof is peaked, and two huge chimneys protrude from each end of the building. An attached porte cochere extends over a section of the estate's main drive.

An armed guard approaches the gates and opens them. "Are you Matthew Strong?" he asks.

"I am."

"Can I see your business card, sir?"

Matthew hands the man his card and he looks it over.

"Mr. Rockefeller has sent word he'll meet you at the west end of the property, at the nursery," the guard says. "The way to get there is to travel up the entrance road through the woods about a quarter mile to the main house. Once you're there, bear right, and follow that road as far as you can go."

Matthew thanks him and guides his carriage between the gates and up the drive.

His surrey crosses a stone bridge constructed of the gray granite he'd seen at the entrance, and the bridge spans a gulley with a fast-moving creek flowing through it. Beyond the bridge the forest ends, and acres of cut green lawn come into view. The carriage continues up the slope, and Matthew turns, catching his first panoramic view of the great lake behind him, the water shimmering a deep blue under the clear morning sky.

He comes up to the Rockefeller home, a rambling, four-storied wooden Victorian sitting atop the hill with wrap-around porches, white-lattice railings and towering gables. A team of painters works on the third level, and he passes several groundsmen preparing rose beds for winter.

As the guard had instructed, Matthew heads his horses to the right of the mansion, down a drive leading to the western portion of the estate. The lawn falls away, and he re-enters the woods, which are denser and less cleared than the more manicured and mulched forest he encountered on the drive in.

He travels another twenty minutes, crossing two more arched bridges. As the surrey draws closer to the spot JDR had said to meet him, Matthew hears machinery in the distance. The road hugs the edge of a drop off, and he looks down the ridge to see another stream tumbling toward the lake.

The woods end, and he enters what he estimates are one-hundred acres of cleared land, most of it hillside. Planted in neat rows in the open space are more than a thousand Scotch pine and Norway spruce trees ranging in size from ten feet to more than fifty feet tall.

Matthew pulls his horses to a stop to take in the scene.

Ten mechanical shovels belch steam into the air as they excavate the soil around the roots of the largest trees. About eighty laborers are engrossed in a variety of jobs. Some work next to the steam diggers with shovels, widening the holes around the trees, exposing their root balls. Others are assigned to derrick-like hoists, affixing ropes at various points around tree trucks and using pulleys and mules to coax the green behemoths from the earth.

The workers use the same hoist and pulley arrangements to place the trees on special flatbed wagons. Teams of powerful oxen, some with horns spanning four feet, pull the wagons off the hillside. Several crews with long fire hoses moisten down the roots and pine boughs as they're readied for transport, pulling water from the nearby brook with steam-powered pumps. The noise from the machines and shouts of the men reverberate through the wooded valley.

Matthew looks down to the base of the ridge and sees a small white house on about an acre of fenced-in land. A man, and his wife and young daughter are standing in their yard looking up at the activity. The woman's holding the girl's hand.

Encircling the entire perimeter of the landowner's fence are more than a hundred huge holes, and at several of the holes Matthew can see crews raising the uprooted trees off the flatbeds, and planting them in place. Men with wagons full of dirt fill in the depressions, covering the root balls and tamping the soil with heavy steel tools. More laborers with hoses give the transplants a drink.

Matthew looks back up the hillside. Standing alone at the top of the ridge, taking it all in, is John D. Rockefeller.

He eases his surrey just off the road away from the commotion and stops it next to JDR's horse and carriage. He climbs out, secures his team, and begins walking up the slope to join his boss.

Rockefeller extends his hand, and Matthew clasps it as he reaches the top of the hill. "Matthew, I am so very pleased you're feeling better and your injuries are healing like the doctors hoped."

"Thank you, sir, I'm coming along quite well. It's good to see you."

JDR releases his grip and points to the workers. "I suppose you're wondering what's going on here."

"I have to say it's quite an operation, sir."

"Yes, saving and moving large trees is becoming a new hobby for me, and I'm finding the work very satisfying."

Matthew nods his head toward the family standing in their yard. "Excuse me, sir, but it looks like you're moving your spruces just down the hill, and planting them so they surround that poor soul's house."

JDR folds his arms over his chest and looks down at the family in disgust. "Oh, that fiasco... I'll explain about them in a moment. But come on, let's walk up here and take in the view. There's something else I need to speak to you about first."

JDR and Matthew walk side by side along the crest of the ridge toward a peak about fifty yards away. The older man doesn't say anything during the short walk. Then they come to an opening in the woods with magnificent views of Lake Erie to the north, and to the east, the tended grounds and imposing home that is the centerpiece of Forest Hill.

JDR stops and turns to Matthew. "In the mid eighteen-seventies, when I first purchased this property, it consisted of the original house and about two-hundred acres. Since then, I've expanded the estate by some five-hundred acres, acquired, for the most part, through fair and civil agreement with some fourteen landowners. Sure, there were a few holdouts who tried to pump up the value of their holdings. It didn't take a genius to figure out I was the buyer, even though, as always, I was making the offers through intermediaries."

From this vantage point Matthew takes in the full breadth of JDR's land: the leafless treetops stretching for miles around him; the bridges, roadways and paths curving through the grounds; the bands of sunlight dancing on the rippled waters of a lake so grand its borders touch the sky.

It's exquisite, he thinks. *This is something I could have had, should have had, if only I'd waited awhile, built a place with the money I earned, not been given... but look what I have instead.*

Rockefeller grabs hold of Matthew's elbow and guides him back toward the hillside where the workers are removing the trees, and Matthew can see the family in their yard, still watching the activity around them.

"Yet," JDR says as they reach the spot where they'd begun their conversation, "even if I felt I was being asked to pay a premium for the land I wanted, we always seemed to be able to come to an agreement in the end as to what that price would be, and the transaction was successfully completed. While we may have had differing views as to what the property was worth, we could always reach an accommodation satisfying both buyer and seller."

"Not unlike our Standard acquisitions, sir."

"Exactly," Rockefeller says, pointing at the family in the valley. "But even considering some of the characters we've had to deal with in the building of our business..."

"One of whom, I understand, has met an untimely demise," Matthew interjects.

JDR ignores the comment. "But, I have to say that family down there, the Fowlers I believe is their name, are the most stubborn, obstinate and greedy people I've come across in a long time."

"I can see why you want their land."

"Can you?"

"Yes. You own everything around them, and I bet a deed covenant on the adjoining parcel gives them full use of that road to enter and exit their home anytime they want. I figure the right of way is restricted for that purpose and that purpose only, and if the property were yours, you could tear down that shack they live in, extend the road to the base of your nursery, and transport the trees off your land without having to travel through the heart of your estate."

"You're very astute, Matthew," JDR says with a wry smile. "Of course, I suppose I could build another road bypassing the Fowler plot, don't you think?"

"But that would be time-consuming and expensive, sir, not to mention inefficient. Why build a road when you've got one already?"

"My sentiments completely."

"So, I can see you're letting them think about their decision."

"Yes," Rockefeller replies. "I'm going to let them stew on it for a spell...contemplate their position, so to speak," "They can think about it as long as they want. Of course, they'll be doing their thinking in the dark. For, as you can see, I'm surrounding their house with the largest trees in my stock. I'm going to encircle their property in such a way that no light falls on their land, day or night. I'm going to build a barrier so they'll live in perpetual darkness, never seeing the sun or the moon, unless they venture off their plot."

"That should get their attention, Mr. Rockefeller," Matthew says as he watches a crew position another huge pine in one of the holes. "I can tell you, sir, it would certainly get mine."

"I want that egress because I'm thinking about buying several more places to live, and I think we could be developing an active trade moving these trees between my various homes."

"I understand completely," Matthew says.

"But where are my manners, Matthew? I've been doing all the talking. How is *your* new wife and home? I hear you and Melissa purchased the Huntington estate, so that must be keeping you two quite busy."

"It's a never-ending job, sir."

"How large a staff do you have?"

"Twenty-eight and growing."

"Would you believe I have one hundred and thirty-six people working at this place? Of course, that includes the eighty men you see here dedicated to the nursery."

JDR raises his hand to his chin. "Listen, I have an assignment for you."

"What's that, sir?"

"As I'm sure you know, Matthew, Standard Oil exports about seventy percent of the kerosene we produce here in the states."

"Yes."

"We've been fortunate for many years to have those European and Far East markets all to ourselves, and we've built an extensive network of brokers and distributors to sell our products."

"Standard kerosene lights the world," Matthew replies.

"I worry about how long we are going to be able to retain that dominance," JDR says.

Matthew can see the homeowner in the valley shaking his fist at the two of them. If Rockefeller notices the man, he doesn't let on.

"I know the crude output from Caspian Russia is growing beyond our wildest dreams," Matthew says. "I heard of one recent well expelling more than twenty-four hundred tons of oil before it was able to be capped."

"I read the same report," JDR replies, "and there are refineries springing up like mushrooms all throughout Baku and elsewhere in Europe. It reminds me of the uncontrolled competition we were forced to tame in Pennsylvania in the seventies."

"What do you need, sir? What can I do?" Matthew asks.

"There are several players capitalizing on this Russian windfall who are moving fast to squeeze us out of our foreign territories," Rockefeller replies.

"I know who you're talking about."

"Alfred, Ludvig and Robert Nobel, and Baron Alphonse de Rothschild," JDR says.

Matthew nods. "They operate through the Nobel Brothers Petroleum Producing Company, and the Rothschilds run the Caspian Black Sea Petroleum Company," he says. "What about Marcus Samuel ... we can't overlook him?"

"He's a relatively fringe player at the moment," answers JDR, shaking his head. "A former merchant, peddler of shell boxes, if you can believe it. But he's working on an arrangement with the Rothschilds to sell their kerosene in the Orient, and he's building special bulk tanker ships for transport. So yes, the Jew bears watching."

Matthew can see the landowner in a scuffle with two of JDR's nurserymen, and in a few seconds a third worker joins the row, punching the man in the face. He falls to the ground, and Rockefeller's men pick him up and carry him back to his property. They lift him in the air, and throw him over his fence. The man's daughter rushes to his side.

"I had wanted to ask if you were willing to join John Archbold on a special assignment," JDR says. "But with your recent injuries and marriage, I don't think the timing's good for you to leave right now, do you?"

"That's not the case at all, Mr. Rockefeller. I'm very able to travel and take on any assignment you have in mind."

JDR searches Matthew's eyes. "Are you sure a European trip won't pose problems at home ... especially with your new purchase of the Huntington place? I hear there's quite a bit of work to do on it."

"No problems at all, sir. I can be ready to leave in a day or two ... as soon as we book passage."

"Okay, then, here's what I'm thinking," replies JDR, looking down stoically at the homeowner, who's sitting on the ground with his wife and daughter beside him.

"First, I want you and John to travel to London where you'll meet our chief foreign operative, a fellow named

William Herbert Libby. I've had Libby on a two-year study assessing market conditions throughout Europe, Arabia and China. I've directed him to give you both a briefing on his findings thus far."

"Excellent," Matthew says.

"Then, I've asked John to travel to Paris to meet Baron Rothschild, and I want you to go to Baku to set up a face-to-face with the Nobels. Libby will join you there to give you additional information about the family, although I want you to deal with the brothers alone. The purpose of each of these meetings will be to strike an agreement with both parties, whereby we work together to eliminate the foreign independents and, ideally, parcel out global marketing territories for the benefit of our three companies."

"And if they balk at our proposals?" Matthew asks.

JDR smiles. "If that's the case, we'll hit them with a price war on every front that will make their heads spin."

"Mr. Rockefeller," Matthew says, smiling, "I want to thank you for this opportunity... it's an honor to have been chosen for such an assignment!"

JDR extends his hand. "You deserve it, Matthew. We've been very impressed with your work and accomplishments."

"I won't fail you, sir."

The oil king remains silent and merely nods as his employee bids him goodbye. Matthew begins walking down the slope to his surrey, and in the valley below he sees the landowner heading back toward his tiny house, flanked by his wife and daughter. The man's face is covered with his hands, and he appears to be crying.

Matthew reaches his horses, unties their reins from the tree and looks back into the valley. The nurserymen are positioning another giant pine in place next to the others, and the little white house begins to disappear behind the vast green wall.

He glances back up the ridge as he rides off to see John D. Rockefeller standing alone, arms crossed, surveying his current and future domain.

THE CROSSING

John D. Archbold sits at a round felt-topped table in the cozy teakwood-paneled smoking room of the first-class section of the luxury steamship *SS Britannic.* He has a deck of cards in his hands, a pile of money in front of him and a tall glass of single-malt Scotch whiskey by his side.

Four other men join him at the table, all dressed, like Archbold, in formal dark suits and neckties. Matthew, similarly attired, relaxes in an overstuffed chair in the corner reading, now and then looking over at the group to take in the action. Though he's never played poker, he wants to learn the game, and these evening sessions provide a good introduction.

Archbold glances at the mariner's clock affixed to the far wall. "It's going on twelve thirty, gentlemen. What do you say we each do one more hand around the table?"

The men agree, Archbold deals the cards and says, "So, I'm boarding the ship in New York, when I come across this kid on the docks—I'd place him about ten—dressed in all black with a patch over one eye. He's wearing a pirate's hat with a big feather sticking out of it. And I walk up to him and say, 'Are you a pirate?'"

The oilman takes a slow sip of scotch, smiles at his companions for a moment and continues his story. "So, the kid replies, "Yeah, I'm a pirate, what's it to you?" And I say,

You're a pirate, huh? Well, if you're a pirate, then where are your buccaneers? And the kid looks me straight in the eyes and says, 'Where the hell do think they are...under my bucking hat!'"

The men roar with laughter, and Matthew joins them. After a few seconds, the player to Archbold's left studies his cards and says, "Open for ten."

Matthew closes his book and sets it in his lap. He's enjoying the easy-going fellowship of this small group who had been strangers at the beginning of the crossing, but, thanks to Archbold's breaking the collective ice, now dined and unwound together for each of the past four nights during their journey across the Atlantic.

He's also soaking up the charm and wit of John D. Archbold, which surprises him since he'd expected their time together to be strained and guarded. But the Standard Oil executive is making an effort to educate him, sharing tips for Matthew's upcoming negotiations with Robert Nobel, telling stories of his early days in the oil patch, revealing insights into the inner workings of the trust, and the expectations and quirks of its reclusive founder.

Furthermore, the trip is allowing Matthew to put some of his worries behind him. When he told Melissa he was going overseas, the anticipated firestorm never occurred, although she was far from pleased that he didn't have a clue as to how long he'd be gone, and they were both upset that he might not be back for the birth of their first child.

One worry he can't shake, however, is Melissa's penchant for spending money like it bubbles up from an eternal spring. He fears she's going to bankrupt him, force him to go to her father, hat in one hand, kid in the other, begging for a loan. All the back-slapping, clubby camaraderie with Archbold and his new-found friends can't tear his mind from the terrifying notion his money is draining away faster than it's coming in; that he'll return home, whenever that might be, and his savings will be gone.

He reaches into his pocket, pulls out his flask of laudanum and downs a couple of shots. He puts the flask back in his jacket and takes out his lucky pen, and as he studies it he thinks it looks more beautiful than ever, as prized possessions so often do. The rainbow from the radiant diamond sparkles in the subdued amber of the gas-lit lounge, cutting through the tobacco smoke in the small room much like the jewel's colored rays had pierced the wet gloom and explosive residue hanging over the Farris fields that horrible day eleven years ago.

You opened the future for me with this gift, Pa, he thinks, *and it's guided me with light ever since.*

Matthew cups the pen in his hand and looks down at it, recalling one of his favorite poems from Shelley:

> When the lamp is shattered
> The light in the dust lies dead –
> When the cloud is scattered
> The rainbow's glory is shed.

He hears footsteps approaching, and looks up to see Archbold standing beside his chair.

"You've never tried a drop of alcohol, have you Matthew?"

"No, sir, I haven't."

"You don't know what you're missing," Archbold says, raising an unopened bottle of Chateau Margaux wine. "I have here an eighteen sixty vintage, going on twenty-two years old. It should be exquisite. What do you say? Join me topside for a glass under the stars."

"We better get our coats." Matthew suggests, "It's freezing out there."

GUSHER!

"Forget the coats," Archbold replies. "I know a warm spot out of the wind, right next to the smokestacks. Besides, after a taste or two of this, you'll be plenty warm."

He walks over to a cabinet and takes out a pair of Bordeaux glasses.

Once on deck, the men sit side by side in two chairs on the upper level of the ship. Archbold was right: the heat from the stacks has warmed the surrounding area, the structures protecting them from the biting night wind.

"I have a feeling you've come here once or twice before, John."

Archbold smiles, pulls a wine opener from his vest pocket and cuts the foil from the top of the bottle. He inserts the tip of the opener into the cork and begins turning the coiled screw so it disappears inside. With a quick flick of his wrist, he removes the cork with a loud pop.

Matthew looks at the sky, and stretching above him is a canopy of stars, a curving crown of sparkling lights reaching to the horizon's edge.

Archbold leans toward him and pours a bit of wine into his glass. He then serves himself an equal amount.

"What you want to do is raise the temperature just a touch, to release the flavors, and you also want the wine to breathe," Archbold says. "The way to do that is to cup the glass in your hand like this, and swirl it around, but before you taste it, sample what they call 'the nose.'"

He rotates his glass with a slight circular motion, watching its contents bank and cascade back down the inside of the glass. A moment later Matthew does the same. Archbold waves the rim of the Bordeaux glass under his nose, savoring its aroma. "See what I mean?"

Matthew smells the wine, without the show and flourish of his colleague.

"Yes, it smells like grape juice."

"Grape juice from the gods," Archbold replies, laughing. "Take a taste, and keep it in your mouth for a moment before you swallow."

Matthew takes a sip as Archbold instructed, and his eyes widen. "Oh my, this is delicious!"

"Do you sense a chewiness, a lingering flavor in your mouth?"

"Yes."

"That's the maturity of the grape. Can you detect an earthiness underneath the fruit flavor?"

"I do."

"That's because with a fine and complex wine like this one, the grapes take on the characteristics of the soil and conditions where the vines grow, in this case in the southwest of France."

"How did you learn so much about wine, John?"

"Practice, practice, and more practice, my friend. Tomorrow night I'll give you a lesson on fine Scotch." Archbold smiles and pours another dash into their glasses.

"We'll be arriving in Liverpool in three days," he says, "and I've tried to tell you a little about Ludvig Nobel. Prepare you for your meeting. I guess to sum him up, I'd say he's smart… he's a chemist by training… and he's tough, with a somewhat dour disposition. He's going to be a hard-assed negotiator, not willing to give up much. One problem you're going to run into is he won't make a move without the consent of his brother, Alfred, or the Czarist government. The great Russian Bear is the real force pulling the strings behind Baku's oil riches."

"You know the American politicians and newspapers call Standard Oil, 'The Octopus,'" Matthew says.

Archbold takes a sip of wine. "Yes...the Octopus is about to meet the Bear," he replies. "Should be an interesting encounter, wouldn't you say? But I can tell you, I'm going to have an easier time dealing with the Rothschilds because they're more open to negotiation than the Nobels, who take orders from the government, like I said."

"I don't think the Russians are going to be too keen on opening their doors to an American company," Matthew says, taking another drink.

"I think you're exactly right," Archbold answers, "and John D. understands all this, which is why we're moving quickly to revamp our marketing system throughout Europe and Asia. We're going to stop working through brokers and middlemen.

"Good," Matthew says, "I figured he was going to make a change. He's going to the way we do it in the states...working through affiliated companies, right?"

"Yeah, that's the plan. If you want to know the truth, we probably should have done that sooner, but we're ready to run with the new organization now."

"Well," Matthew says, "it will put us in a better position to cut prices when and where we need to. How much of this can I use as leverage with Nobel?"

Archbold pours them both another spot of wine. "You can threaten him with a price war, but don't get into specifics on what we're thinking or how we're going to do it...nothing about the new affiliate organization at this point. Let's get it in place first."

"Of course," Matthew says.

"But enough of that," Archbold replies. "We've got a couple more nights together to prepare for our meetings, and besides, after we hook up with Libby in London, he'll go to Baku with you and help you further prepare for your talks. We can discuss the Nobels another time."

Matthew takes a long, slow sip of his Bordeaux, and he begins to feel very relaxed. "God, this is good," he exclaims. "Incredible, in fact!"

Archbold smiles, raises his glass and clicks it against Matthew's. "See what you've been missing all these years?"

"John, let me ask you a question," Matthew says. "I was with Mr. Rockefeller a week ago."

"Yeah, I know, at Forest Hill."

"And I probably shouldn't have, but I made a reference to Helmut Weiss."

"Right, you shouldn't have done that."

"I guess I was looking for some sort of recognition, some sort of compliment from him for solving, you know, our problem."

"You didn't solve the problem, Matthew," Archbold answers. "The problem solved *itself.*"

"But I knew I'd made a mistake, because Mr. Rockefeller didn't acknowledge my comment," Matthew replies, taking another drink. "He glossed right over it, in fact. Kept on talking like I'd never even raised the subject."

"Look," Archbold says. "Everyone knows what you went through in that barn trying to negotiate an honest deal with that German bastard. He double-crossed you, led you into a trap, and as far as I'm concerned the prick got what he deserved."

"But the sons sold us the farm ... lock, stock and barrel," Matthew says. "We're going to drill wells there, and that's what we wanted, what JDR wanted, right?"

"Of course it was," Archbold replies. "But John D. can't be brought into any conversation about Weiss. He must be able to disavow all knowledge of the affair, if there were a legal inquiry and he was called to testify."

"I don't see that happening," Matthew says.

"For Christ sakes, Matthew, the son-of-a-bitch was murdered walking out his front door!"

Archbold appears blurry to Matthew, and he blinks his eyes a few times and says, "Well, we didn't do it."

Archbold stares at him. "Yeah, but somebody did ... probably one of his idiot sons ... or maybe Clapp, but I doubt it, after the shellacking Daniel gave him."

"What if *you* were subpoenaed, John?" Matthew asks. "We were both there when it was discussed at the executive committee meeting in September. What would you say?"

"I would plead ignorance, for the most part, although I might admit I was vaguely aware we wanted to acquire additional production fields in Northwestern Ohio, but that's about as far as I'd go. I'll level with you, Matthew ... if I were called to testify, I'd characterize the Weiss offer and acquisition as a decision made at the *district* level, not something New York was involved in."

Archbold takes a sip from his glass and his eyes narrow, as if he is trying to read Matthew's reaction, but his colleague has a faraway look.

"You'd serve me and Daniel up, just like that ... like lambs for slaughter?"

"What in the hell are you talking about?" snaps Archbold. "You're making no sense, Matthew. *If* there were a legal inquiry, which I doubt there ever will be, and you or Daniel were called to testify, you'd tell the truth ... it's as simple as that."

Matthew brings his glass to his lips, spilling a bit of the Bordeaux on his white shirt. "All neat and pretty, huh, John?"

"Yeah, it's all very straightforward," Archbold says, looking Matthew straight in the eyes. "Let me lay it out for you. Standard Oil of Ohio wanted more production acreage, and you identified the Weiss property as a prospect. You made several good-faith offers to purchase the land. The fact that the owner was shot and killed while these discussions were occurring is unfortunate, but unrelated to whatever business we were conducting with him at the time."

Matthew looks down at the red stain on his shirt. "All neat and pretty."

"What the fuck is bothering you about this?" Archbold shouts. "I just laid it out! Is there something I'm not getting?"

Archbold surveys the remaining wine in the bottle, and he pours some more in his glass, ignoring Matthew.

Matthew attempts to focus his eyes on the stars. "You say it's simple, John, but tell me how simple this is: when I was recovering from my run in with Clapp, and I was told Weiss had been murdered, what do you think was the first thing that went through my mind?"

"I'll tell you what went through mine," Archbold shoots back. "I said it earlier, and I'll say it again: when I heard about it, I thought, our problem has solved itself."

Matthew smirks. "That's easy for you to say. I'll tell you what I thought: I thought I caused the death of an innocent man, and I still think that."

"Get over it," Archbold says coolly, sipping his wine.

Matthew stares at the heavens, not noticing the scowl on Archbold's face.

"I set it in motion, John. I put the prize in front of those two idiot sons of his, those two loose cannons. Can you imagine what fifty thousand dollars meant to a couple of teenagers who were on the outs with their father, who had no intention of following in his footsteps?"

Archbold straightens up in his chair and says, "I'm getting damn tired of hearing this crap, Matthew. I'm telling you right now!"

Matthew turns and faces him. "Do you want to know what haunts me the most, John? I think I *knew* what I was doing. I think I knew *exactly* what I was setting up."

"Bullshit!" Archbold hollers. "What happened was an unintended consequence. Has it ever occurred to you how many properties the Standard buys and sells every day? How many refineries, terminals or plants we purchase, build or demolish? How many leases we negotiate, or not, making some people rich beyond their wildest dreams, while others are left stuck in their tracks?"

"That happened to my father," Matthew mumbles, looking back up at the sky.

"You, better than anyone, know how we can make or break a railroad when we threaten to book our business elsewhere," Archbold says.

"Neat and pretty, right, John?"

Archbold shakes his head. "So why am I wasting my time telling you this, Matthew? I'll tell you why. Because it's important for you to know that in every one of these situations I've just named, there are winners and there are losers. Good God, man, we've been accused of putting widows out on the street in the middle of winter, driving men to suicide, turning bustling cities into ghost towns because a production field runs dry, or we built a pipeline that closes a refinery or terminal, throwing hundreds out of work. Christ, we've been accused of all the world's ills at one time or another, and I bet we always will be."

Matthew gulps the remainder of his wine. He attempts to put the empty glass beside him on the deck, but he jams it down too hard, breaking the base off its stem.

Archbold shakes his head again and rises from his chair. "You're screwing up, my friend, and now I'm going to hit you with a few facts, and I want you to listen to what I'm going to say, and think about it hard and long. First, you demonstrated exceptional naiveté in showing up by yourself at Weiss' farm that night. You should have smelled a trap and taken some men with you, or at least a fucking gun. Do you think Daniel O'Day would have put himself in that position?"

Matthew frowns and stares at the deck.

"Shit, it was Daniel who got you out of that jam," Archbold says. "And if he hadn't, we wouldn't be having this conversation right now, would we?"

Matthew shakes his head, but remains silent.

"Second, your little performance at the executive committee meeting in September didn't exactly ingratiate you with the trustees."

"What I said was true ... public opinion matters, and we have to understand it can hurt us."

"Truth be dammed, Matthew! We have a business to run and we have to make tough decisions that often affect a great many people. But, never forget, we operate for the greater good, bringing light and cheap energy to those who've never had it before. Hell, that's our divine mission!"

"Our critics are growing, John, and they're plotting against us, scheming to bring us down."

"Screw the critics," Archbold snaps. "We do the hard part ... all they do is sit back after the decisions are made, after the actions are taken and ... *criticize*. Do you know my opinion of critics? A critic is a man who knows fifty ways to have sex ... but doesn't know any women."

"I thought I had an obligation ..."

Archbold cuts him off with a sweep of his hand. "Matthew, you have to understand John D. is especially sensitive to criticism, and he doesn't like it when someone brings up the kind of pansy-assed bullshit like you did in that meeting. Don't get me wrong; he's willing to tackle any organizational problem that comes up ... but nebulous crap like you were throwing out? Well, you better be very careful with that kind of thing in the future, I'm telling you. And, while we're at it, your third screw-up was what we touched on earlier: never, ever talk about anything to Mr. Rockefeller that could compromise him from a legal standpoint. Always operate on a need to know basis, in communicating both up and down the organization. For Christ sakes, use some damn judgment!"

Matthew looks down at the deck, sees his glass lying on its side, and picks it up. "Can I have a little more wine, John?"

"Fuck no!" Archbold bellows. "What are you, nuts? Have you heard anything I've just said? You know, when I invited you up here tonight, I thought I was going to open your eyes to a new experience. I thought I was going to give you a bit of education on the finer points of wine. What I didn't think I was going to have to do ... was teach you how to act after you'd drank some of it!"

Matthew throws his empty glass overboard. Archbold turns away, bottle in hand, and begins walking toward a door leading inside the ship.

Matthew watches his colleague depart. "Good night, John," he shouts. "See you tomorrow."

Archbold doesn't answer, and Matthew leans back in his deck chair and scans the sky. The stars swirl like a candied confection in a black morass.

He pulls out his flask and downs a healthy swig of laudanum, and he thinks about Lavinia, wondering what she's doing right now. He wonders if he'll make it home in time to be with Melissa for the baby's arrival. He doubts it.

He feels his stomach sink, and he peers up at the black smoke belching from the ship's stacks. As he had earlier in the evening, Matthew recalls the day his father died. He feels like he's wandering through the Farris fields all over again.

His eyes draw shut, his head droops, and he enters the haunted path of his nightly journey to hell.

THE OCTOPUS AND THE BEAR

The arctic winds are called *Khazri*, and they rise from the Russian tundra like angry winter zephyrs to begin their seasonal assault on the barren tip of the Apsheron Peninsula and the ancient city of Baku.

They race along the Ural Mountains and across the giant Caspian Sea, churning the salty water into an agitated caldron of brownish-gray, white capped waves. The winds blast the land with such force that for centuries, before the Nobels started planting them, not a single tree could be found on this arid coastal plain.

Matthew stands on an outcrop above the city watching dozens of refineries by the water's edge shoot black soot into the air. Surrounding the factories are miles of decrepit wooden derricks and rusted pipelines spewing oil onto the dead, otherworldly ground.

A wall of wind whips up from below, pounding him with the force of a hammer, infusing the odor of petroleum and stinging sulfuric smoke into his nose and eyes, and he turns away from the irritants, carried upward by the *Khazri's* power, and he coughs, covering his face in the crook of his arm.

William Libby, the Standard Oil operative, hunches beside Matthew and shouts, "Some have likened it to living inside a chimney pot!"

"I thought Oil City was a dump," Matthew hollers back, "but this land is something you'd expect to find on the moon!" He points to a deep crater cut into an outcrop a short distance away. "What's that?"

Thick brown mud gurgles inside the depression, which looks like a lake of bubbling liquid dirt. The fluid rises in huge balloon-shaped balls that appear to be the size and shape of whales' backs, and the balls expand, then burst, shooting their outflow skyward. Encircling the larger cavity, smaller craters burp and spit more roiling muck from the earth. Leaping from several of these are dancing columns of fire stretching thirty feet into the air.

"They call them, *salses*, mud volcanoes," Libby says, reaching into his coat for a cigar and nodding toward a tent on the side of the largest crater. "You see that? Let's walk over there. I'll show you something else."

William Herbert Libby is a small, stocky man with a furrowed face and tiny ears pinned back to his rather large head. He has short hair, cropped eyebrows and round brown eyes, giving him the look of a bulldog. He is the ideal intelligence gatherer, since his appearance is not memorable, which allows him to blend into crowds unnoticed and overhear conversations.

They enter the tent, and inside, huddled around a coal stove, are six men seated on stools with their shirts off and their chests wrapped in large towels. Four of the men are old, probably in their seventies or eighties, and two are younger, maybe between thirty and forty, Matthew figures. Their necks are coated with mud, and a seventh man, the proprietor, makes his rounds with a wooden bucket in his hand, attending to the men, smearing new layers of volcanic silt in circles under their chins and around their necks.

"What the hell's going on?" Matthew asks Libby.

The mud purveyor, stooped and grizzled, raises his head. His emerald-green eyes flash in his leathery face, and he shoots a quick glance at his visitors as if he's sizing them up.

"*Boyunbağı ücün gəlmisiniz?*" he asks, motioning his head toward two vacant stools in the corner of his tent.

"*Xeyr,*" Libby answers, "*başqa vaxt. Bu gün, elə-belə baxırıq.*"

"What'd he say to you?" Matthew asks.

"He wanted to know if we're here for collars, and I told him we weren't, that we are here only to look." Libby pitches the proprietor a coin, which the man catches with a quick swipe of his muddy hand. "They believe these collars promote blood flow to their brains, making them smarter. You find an interesting mix of cultures here in Baku. These men are Azeri natives, but you also have Armenians, Iranians and, of course, Russians."

"Quite a melting pot," Matthew replies, as Libby leads him out of the tent.

"I'm going to take you to a special place up the road called *Yanardagh*, or Fire Mountain," Libby says. "The entire hillside is ablaze with perpetual flames, and there's a café at its base where we can relax and talk."

After a few minutes, Libby reins his horse to a stop in front of a small teahouse, and he and Matthew climb out of the carriage. They enter the little square building made of stone and thread their way around several customers seated at tables and engaged in heated conversations. Tobacco smoke and the aroma of herbal teas fill the tiny room.

Libby opens a back door, gesturing for Matthew to walk through first, and the men stand next to each other for a moment behind the teahouse taking in the strange scene.

There are a dozen round tables with chairs spaced a good distance from each other on the coarse bare dirt. Three of the tables are occupied. About twenty yards from the café, forming a natural back wall, is an escarpment rising forty feet into the side of a mountain. The entire lower half of the cliff is on fire, and the flames, shooting from the rocks, extend along the base of the rise some sixty feet, making the hidden patio behind the teahouse warm and pleasant.

"Well, I'll be damned," Matthew says. "Looks like a natural gas seep."

"They tell me it caught fire in the seventeen hundreds, and has been burning ever since," Libby replies, motioning toward an open table. "Let's take that one over there."

He and Matthew grab the sides of a table set apart from the others, and they lift it up and move it closer to the fire. A young black-haired woman with a hook nose and piercing dark eyes approaches them, and they order two mugs of tea. They sit across from each other with their chairs angled toward the heat.

"I hear Robert's brother, Ludvig, is in town," Libby says. "So I suspect he'll join your meeting this afternoon. He's the real brains behind the family's success."

Matthew eyes the flames. "What do you know about him?"

"The three brothers don't get along all that well," Libby replies. "They each have differing views on how their business should be run. While Robert's the oldest, he holds the least power, probably because he's had a history of failed businesses before he was in on forming the brothers' current company."

"But it was Robert who bought their first refinery here, right?" Matthew says.

"Right, but that was not part of his original instructions."

"Instructions?"

"Yeah," Libby replies. "As the story goes, Ludvig had sent him on a mission to the Caucasus to buy walnut wood to be used as stocks at his rifle-making plant. But instead, Robert ends up in Baku, using that walnut money to buy a refinery. Even though oil has made them a fortune several times over, I suspect Ludvig has always resented that Robert went ahead and made that move without asking. On the other hand, Robert feels it was his foresight that got them into the oil business in the first place, and he sees Ludvig's complaints as meddling in something he began, and by all rights should be running on his own."

The dark-haired woman returns, setting two steaming mugs of tea in front of them.

"What about Alfred?" Matthew asks.

"Somewhat the same situation, except the relations are more strained between Alfred and Ludvig. Alfred has never forgotten how their father, Immanuel, went bankrupt when the Russians pulled a contract from him to build underwater mines. The father was stretched moneywise, and when the Czar terminated the agreement, everything came crashing down."

Matthew sips some tea. "So, Alfred's the cautious one, while Ludvig pushes ahead as fast as he can go, buying refineries, terminals, railroads, ships, you name it."

"Right," Libby replies. "That's why Ludvig's called the 'Oil King of Baku.' Believe me, he's a tough adversary, and in many ways, as much a visionary as John Rockefeller."

Matthew leans closer to Libby. "Give me the big picture, William, and tell me how I can use these divisions between the brothers to our advantage in my negotiations."

"First of all, Matthew, you should know Mr. Rockefeller is very concerned over the inroads Russian oil is making on the Standard's global dominance. It wasn't that long ago we controlled ninety percent of the world's exported kerosene, but that figure has plummeted. Ten years ago, Russian crude production was only six hundred thousand barrels a year. Now, they're approaching eleven million barrels, nearly a third of the entire U.S. output."

Matthew takes another sip of tea. "I heard talk of one gusher they call *Droozba*," he says, "which I think means 'Friendship' in Russian. They say it's flowed at over forty thousand barrels a day for the past five months, without showing any signs of slowing down. It's obvious their spigot isn't going to run dry anytime soon."

"Certainly not," Libby answers, "quite the contrary. We can only expect more of the same, and we'd be foolish to think otherwise."

"What about their refining operations," Matthew asks, "or the quality of their products. How do they compare to ours?"

"Not many chinks in that armor either," Libby answers. "Robert and Alfred are chemists, and they've perfected a continuous-distillation process that, in some ways, makes their kerosene cleaner and better burning than ours."

"Then we'll start a smear campaign to undermine their brand," Matthew says, gesturing to the dark-haired woman for more tea.

"That may be all well and good," Libby replies, "but here's what worries me the most. What's to stop the Nobels and Rothschilds from forming an alliance against us? Think about it. Their wells and refineries are practically side by side right here in Baku. There's potential for a sharing of their various transportation systems—pipelines, terminals, railcars, tanker ships and the like. They maintain great relations with heads of state, giving each family access and protection not only in Russia, as is the case with the Nobels, but throughout Europe, which is the unquestioned domain of the Rothschilds."

Matthew stands up and walks a few steps toward the burning wall. He stretches his hands out to warm them, and he glances back over his shoulder at Libby. "I'll camp out in this city if I have to until we convince the Nobels to come on board. I gather John Archbold is committed to the same goal with the Rothschilds in Paris?"

"Yes, Libby replies. "He's operating under the same instructions as you are."

The little bulldog also rises from his seat, and he glances at an old Armenian man in a tattered coat at a nearby table hunched over a bowl of gruel. The man guides a large spoon to his mouth with shaking hands.

"Of course, there is one difference between your assignment and John's."

"What's that?" Matthew asks, searching Libby's eyes.

"The food's a hell of a lot better in Paris!"

The surrey makes its way off the mountain and over the volcanic, petroleum-laced trails snaking through the heart of Baku's oil fields. Matthew can hear the horses' hooves and the carriage's steel-banded wheels crushing a sea of hardened cinders scattered about their path. Columns of refinery soot climb skyward, occasionally whipped into black tornadic funnels by the fury of the *Khazri* winds.

He's amazed at the bone-shuddering bleakness of this hellish place. Everywhere he looks, hundreds of wooden oil derricks dot the barren, treeless wasteland in a schizophrenic patchwork of tar-encrusted spires. Rotting, maggot-covered mule carcasses line the roads, their bluish-yellow bodies and bones made all the more grotesque by the corrosive effects of spilled petroleum chemicals strewn across the pocked, pitted earth. Other work animals, oxen and horses, lay dead or dying in ditches filled with ghoulish-green liquid crude.

As he and Libby leave the oil fields and draw near the shores of the Caspian, Libby points to a palatial home looming in the distance. The residence looks like a castle with its marble columns, its dozens of windows bordered by intricate carved facades, and the sixty-foot stone turret towering high above the main house.

"The brothers named it Villa Petrolea," Libby says, "in honor of the fortune they've made from oil."

"It sounds like they live, sleep and eat this business," Matthew replies. "I don't know if that's good or bad as far as my negotiations with them are going to go."

"Well, whatever happens, I know you'll do your best, Matthew, and I wish you success."

"Wish me some luck, too… I'm going to need it. Why don't you drop me here, William? I'll walk the rest of the way."

The two men bid one another goodbye, and Matthew jumps from the carriage and heads toward the Nobels' home. After a few minutes, he sees a solitary figure standing in front of the villa, and as he gets closer he recognizes the man. It's Robert Nobel.

He walks up and introduces himself. "I'm Matthew Strong."

"Yes," Nobel replies, shaking Matthew's hand. "My brother Ludvig and I have been expecting you."

Matthew doesn't answer, but instead looks a hundred yards or so beyond the villa where several dozen workers are planting trees next to huge piles of rich, brown soil. "So, what are you building here, Robert?"

"I'm not building anything," he replies. "That's all Ludvig's work. He's got it in his head we should have trees here in Baku, just like in our native Sweden, so he's started a planting project. He's making a park."

"Where do the trees come from?" Matthew asks.

"Germany."

"What about the dirt?"

"From Iran," Robert answers. "Ludvig set up a taxing system on the Persians. For every tanker of kerosene we deliver to them, they must fill the return ship full of dirt, at no charge to us. That way we get good, fertile soil. After all, the holds would just go empty on the return voyage, would they not?"

"So, you get free soil for Ludvig's park, plus ballast for the vessels," Matthew says, looking at the endless rows of trees. "You must have more than a thousand here ready for planting, Robert."

"Ludvig figures we'll have transported and planted more than eighty thousand by the time he's finished. He's even hired a full-time botanist, who's created many of the parks and gardens in Warsaw."

"Why do your planting this time of year?"

"Winter is a great time to plant," Robert says. "The trees may look dead without their leaves, but they're very much alive."

"I'm surprised the ground isn't frozen," Matthew says. "I'm surprised you're able to plant this time of year."

"It's milder here than people expect," Robert answers. "That's because of the warming effects of the Caspian, but the ground is also heated by the hot gases and oil that's just beneath the surface."

"Where are you going to get the water for all your trees?" Matthew asks. "The Caspian's full of salt, and what little water you have here in Baku, I doubt you'd want to use it for watering trees."

Robert looks at him and smiles. "Do you always ask so many questions?"

"Just when something interests me," Matthew answers, smiling back.

"See that pipeline being built over there?" Robert replies, pointing to a second crew of men laying pipe. "That's Ludvig's solution to greening his park. He's developed a system of condensing steam from our nearby refinery, and he's piping the water here to irrigate the trees. Ingenious, wouldn't you say?"

Matthew shakes his head in amazement. "Brilliant ... just brilliant."

Robert Nobel takes his pocket watch from his vest and presses the latch to pop the cover open. "Let's go inside," he says. "We'll meet Ludvig there. We've had some refreshments prepared for you."

They enter the gates of Villa Petrolea and walk down its main drive past dozens of giant Italian cypresses lining the entrance to the estate. Matthew notices scores of smaller homes built at varying distances from the villa, and he looks at the refinery spewing filthy smoke into the sky. He can see dozens of oil wells and pipelines, and a second refinery farther away in the distance.

Robert sees him taking it all in. "We chose this portion of the Black City, as it's called, because Ludvig thinks it's important to be close to our operations. He wants his staff and managers right here, too, so if there's a problem at the refinery they can get to it quickly. We know this isn't the way Mr. Rockefeller lives. He seems to put as much distance between himself and the source of his fortune as possible, wouldn't you say?"

Robert flashes Matthew a sarcastic grin.

"Mr. Rockefeller operates at a high administrative level," Matthew answers. "He oversees the broad aspects of our business, making the big decisions, not getting bound up in the day-to-day activities."

"Not getting his hands dirty like we crude Europeans. Is that what you're saying?"

"I'm not saying that at all, Robert. I'm surprised you'd think such a thing."

Two servants stand in front of the huge wooden doors leading inside the villa, and they swing them open in unison as Robert Nobel and Matthew approach. The men enter the grand salon of the mansion, decorated in a formal Renaissance style with a floor of tiled white Italian marble flecked with black mica. Six ornate crystal chandeliers hang above them in perfect rows lining either side of the room, and massive oil paintings by German and Dutch masters grace the walls in gilded gold-leaf frames.

"We're going to meet Ludvig in the dining room," Robert says, gesturing to Matthew with his hand. "It's this way."

"And Alfred?" Matthew asks.

"Traveling," Robert replies.

As they reach the far end of the great room, another servant parts two intricately carved oak pocket doors leading to the dining room. Standing beside a long polished cherrywood table is Ludvig Nobel.

"Mr. Strong," he says, "welcome to Villa Petrolea. You're younger than I expected."

Matthew and the second Nobel brother shake hands, and the three men take their seats at the table. Ludvig sits at the head, with Robert to his right. Matthew takes his place opposite Robert.

A side door opens and three maids enter. One carries a silver ice bucket containing what looks to Matthew like a chilled bottle of water. Another carries a tray holding three cut-crystal shot glasses and three small plates with utensils. The third servant walks in carrying a tray with a round silver bowl filled with what appears to Matthew to be tiny black buckshot. Her tray also holds little plates of chopped onions, boiled and diced egg whites and yolks, and small round green-like vegetables Matthew takes for peas, except they're darker and smaller, and a plate of toast tips with the crusts cut off.

"I take it, Matthew, you've never had caviar?" Ludvig says.

"Can't say that I have."

The maids place the meal on the table in front of the men.

"Like many things, it's an acquired taste," Robert notes. "You're looking at the best there is, Beluga caviar, taken earlier this morning from fresh-caught Caspian sturgeon."

Ludvig appears bored by the small talk, and he turns to Matthew and says, "So, Mr. Strong, what can we do for you?"

He reaches for the bottle of vodka, fills the shot glasses with the chilled, clear liquor and he places a glass in front of Matthew, then slides the second one over to his brother.

"Actually, Ludvig," Matthew replies, "I was thinking our conversation would be about what Standard Oil can do for you."

Ludwig's ice-blue eyes bore into him. "Were you now? Why would you think that?" He raises his glass, and Matthew and Robert do the same.

"May I propose the toast?" Matthew asks.

Ludvig nods. "By all means. You're the guest."

"Here's to a fruitful conversation that will help us strike an accommodation between our two companies, making the foundation for future growth and prosperity."

Matthew draws his glass to his lips, then notices that Ludvig has set his back on the table.

"Let's postpone consummating the toast," Ludvig says. "I have one to offer up myself, after I ask you something." Matthew and Robert place their glasses down and look at Ludvig.

"*Accommodation*," Ludvig begins, "that's an interesting word, isn't it? What exactly do you mean by that, Mr. Strong?"

Matthew studies the two brothers for a second, folds his hands in front of him and leans forward. "Let me answer your question this way, sir. When you have two great and powerful organizations like Standard Oil and the Nobel Brothers' Petroleum Producing Company, there are basically two ways we can go about our business. We can be enemies, fighting and undermining each other every chance we get, or we can say to ourselves, 'it's a big world out there with limitless opportunities for each of us,' and we can divide up those opportunities between us for mutual benefit. I think this second option best describes what I mean by accommodation."

"And I think I'm ready to propose our second toast," Ludvig replies, raising his glass again and training his eyes on his guest.

"We welcome our visitor from America who joins us with such high expectations. We are businessmen, the three of us, trained to listen and evaluate opportunities that come our way. We pledge to do that, realizing an industrial enterprise is a living thing. It grows, works to become stronger, seeks associations and allies as it pursues its goals, tries to avoid mistakes. But when it does stumble, it learns from such missteps, vowing not to repeat those errors. Much like a person, an enterprise will seek cooperation, or as you like to say, Mr. Strong, *accommodation*, when such action serves its purpose. But, also like a person, the organization will ultimately be guided by its self interest and preservation."

"Well said, Ludvig!" Matthew replies, clicking his glass with his hosts and downing his vodka along with the two other men. "What I like most about your toast is when you said you'd 'listen' to what I have to say. That's a start, and maybe that's all I can ask."

"That's quite a pen you have there," Ludvig says, eyeing Matthew's pocket.

"It was a gift from my father," answers Matthew. "It's always brought me good things in business…deals, agreements, those sorts of things."

A maid glides around the table, pouring more vodka.

"Let me show you how to eat caviar," Robert says, spooning a small portion on a piece of toast, then adding the chopped onions, eggs and capers. Matthew follows his lead.

Ludvig again appears impatient. "So, Mr. Strong, tell me what you have on your mind."

Matthew dabs his mouth with his napkin. "Let me begin by saying that I have great respect for what you and your brothers have built here in Russia in such a short time."

"I'm sure you do," Ludvig replies, taking a sip of his vodka, then fixing two pieces of caviar toast.

"Absolutely," Matthew says. "And I know you're proud of how far you've come, and how excited you are about the opportunities ahead. But, as we all know, the future's very uncertain, especially in our business."

"We're well aware of the unpredictability of the oil trade, Mr. Strong," Ludvig replies. "And we know how to prepare and manage for it."

"But you can weather those storms in an even stronger position, Ludvig," Matthew says. "And you can achieve that by accepting a cash infusion from my company."

"What are you proposing?" Robert asks.

"Standard Oil is prepared to buy a substantial block of Nobel Brothers' stock at its current par value, in addition to an agreed-upon, good-faith premium, as a way of aligning our two companies," Matthew says.

Robert begins to speak, but Ludvig cuts him off. "What possibly would interest us in doing something like that, Mr. Strong?"

"For one thing, Ludvig, you are in the midst of major acquisitions...ships, railcars, terminals and so forth as part of your expansion plan, and you need cash to accomplish that."

"Our access to funds is more than sufficient," Ludvig replies.

Matthew downs another shot of vodka. "Is that a fact?" he says. "I don't doubt what you're saying, Ludvig, but I go back to the risk factor. If something were to go wrong..."

Ludvig's eyes narrow. "What are you getting at?"

"I'm simply saying you never know when a train might derail, or a refinery catch fire, or an oil well blow up, or a tanker runs onto the rocks. God forbid, if any one of those unfortunate things were to happen, you'd have to shoulder the cost entirely on your own."

Ludvig's eyes get even smaller. "For your information, Mr. Strong, Nobel Brothers' stock is privately held. It's not for sale."

Matthew pushes on. "You realize, gentlemen, you're not just competing with Standard Oil. You have the Rothschilds to consider as well, along with the smaller independents that are operating all around you, making money that should be yours, wasting precious product with their inefficient and shoddy operations. They're making inroads as we sit here, doing business in countries each of our companies counted as our own. You both know there's strength in combination, and we should work together to tamp down the competition."

"We've battled the Rothschilds for quite some time now, sir," Ludvig says. "I don't see that changing, and I haven't heard anything you've said this afternoon that would cause me to think we're any less equipped to continue to deal with them, or anyone else for that matter, as we have from the very beginning."

"It's not a question of being *less* equipped," Matthew answers. "It's putting yourself in a position where you are *better* equipped to counter their competitive threats."

Robert pipes in. "I agree with Ludvig. Nothing you've said has changed my mind, either."

Matthew takes a drink of vodka and slowly shakes his head. "Tell me we are not going to start a price war, gentlemen."

Ludvig fixes his cold stare on him. "Are you trying to intimidate us, Mr. Strong?"

"Not in the least, sir. But I am saying, one action the Standard will always take when dealing with stubborn negotiators is to undercut prices, most always gaining customers and market share. We find once customers form an allegiance and loyalty to us, they rarely go back to their former supplier."

The maid pours more vodka, and Matthew downs another shot. "You know, gentlemen," he says, "we're talking to the Rothschilds as well."

Ludvig pitches his head back, emptying the rest of his drink. He sets his glass in front of him and smiles. "We would have been disappointed if you'd said otherwise."

"When an alliance is struck with them," Matthew says, "we don't want the Nobel brothers left out in the cold."

Robert looks at him and smiles. "As I told you outside, Matthew, it never gets too cold here in Baku...at least not for us."

The men rise from the table.

"Can we talk again tomorrow?" Matthew asks as he gets up. "I'd like to expand on a number of things we touched on today, and perhaps offer up some other ideas."

Again, Ludvig's eyes bore into his visitor. "Maybe," he says.

"Maybe?" Matthew replies.

"That's right, Mr. Strong," Ludvig snaps. "I said, 'maybe.' And if you want to know why I'm equivocating, it's because I don't especially like you, Mr. Strong. I find you arrogant, ill-prepared, and strangely casual in your negotiating style. And I resent your threats against my company. I don't think we have anything more to talk about today, and perhaps not tomorrow, or next week...or ever!"

Matthew is floored. "I'd hoped we could reach an understanding," he says. "Perhaps if you give my proposals some more thought, or I sweeten the pot a little."

Ludvig glares at him. "What part of what I've just said don't you understand, Mr. Strong? I just told you, our discussions are over for now, and very likely from here on out!"

Once outdoors, the vodka kicks in full bore, and Matthew feels dizzy and he begins to sweat. He reaches for his flask of laudanum, but once he has it in his hand he realizes the container's empty. "I can't believe I walked out of there with nothing," he whispers. "What am I going to tell the executive committee? How am I going to explain this to Mr. Rockefeller?" He puts the flask back in his pocket and reaches for his pen.

The cypress trees and walls of Villa Petrolea start to spin, and he closes his eyes and shakes his head to regain his bearings.

Why did I drink so much? he thinks. *After that night with Archbold, I was sure I had the liquor under control.*

The *Khazri* whips off the water and Matthew steadies himself, shocked at the reality of his first business failure. He walks unsteadily through the gates of the estate and onto the street. The Nobel brothers stand beside each other at the top of the villa's tower, laughing as they watch him stagger away.

REUNION

The afternoon of Monday, September 25, 1882 is cold and wet in Cleveland as Matthew pulls his bags out of the carriage that brought him home from the train station. He stands for a moment in the drizzling rain staring at the front entrance of his mansion, not believing he's been away for the better part of ten months.

He notices all the new stone and iron work Melissa has commissioned, and, with a twinge of annoyance, calculates the money he knows she's spent. But his real anger is reserved for old man Rockefeller, who'd insisted he stay in Baku when it was obvious that the Nobels were not interested in striking any sort of deal. To add to that insult, JDR had sent him to Singapore and then on to London and Brussels to negotiate new kerosene contracts that tacked on another five months to his already extended overseas stay.

And for what? he thinks. *All I accomplished was missing the birth of my daughter in April. Did the old man do that to me for speaking up that day in front of the executive committee? Some sort of vindictive payback?*

Matthew can't shake the thought.

The only positive things he can look back on during his absence is that he's kicked his laudanum habit cold turkey, and he seems to have his drinking under control. Plus, he and Melissa had begun writing each other weekly, growing closer with time and distance between them, developing a better understanding of one another, or so he hopes.

He's going to make Standard Oil pay for the pointless diversion. Just like his side deals with the oil certificates that channeled extra cash into his secret account, he's hatched an idea to invest in high-risk Texas oil wells that could put even more money in his pocket. He will move forward on that idea tomorrow when he returns to the office.

He stares through the mist at a crew of workers in the rose garden erecting a large marble statue that looks like some sort of Greek goddess. He shakes his head, ascends the cut-granite front steps and enters his house.

He can hear lovely piano music coming from the conservatory, the kind of classical composition that Melissa likes and has mastered. He places his bags in the foyer and walks quietly to where she's practicing, not announcing himself, wanting to surprise her.

Her back is to him and he stands listening to her play in the circular teak-paneled room with the tall bay windows overlooking the garden. He watches her fingers caress the keyboard, her quick, delicate touch alternating between the upper and lower ivories, filling the space with a rich but haunting melody.

"Shubert?" he says.

Melissa stops in mid measure. She looks up at him with surprise for a second, then rises from the piano bench. "Good guess, my long-lost lover," she says, smiling at him. "Actually, it's Franz Liszt. It's his Sonata in B Minor."

"Beautiful," Matthew says, moving to her.

"It alternates between major and minor movements," she replies. "It's very complicated."

"Isn't everything?" he whispers, throwing his arms around her, noticing her body has become more shapely, softer, sexier since he's been gone. He feels her push closer, thrusting her breasts and hips against him, and he kisses her firmly on her moist lips. She breaks away for a breath. Then she kisses him again long and hard.

Flames rise from the stack of crackling logs in the curved fireplace dominating a far wall, filling the room with waves of heat as Matthew runs his hands through Melissa's hair and down her back. He begins to remove one of her barrettes to let her hair down, and she smiles and puts her hand over his. "There's plenty of time to make up for these months," she whispers in his ear. "It's the perfect rainy night for it."

"I was thinking sooner than later," Matthew says softly, as she presses herself against him again.

"I can see that," Melissa answers. "But don't you want to meet your daughter first?"

He keeps holding her, not wanting the feeling to end. "I'm dying to see her," he says. "You're right, let's go up and visit Maddy together before she goes to sleep."

"It should be just about her feeding time," Melissa replies.

"Then let's come back here so you can play me the rest of that song," Matthew says. "That is, if you can keep your mind on the music."

"Why, Matthew Strong," Melissa taunts, taking him by his hand and walking him past the windows over to a hidden stairway leading to the second floor nursery. "Do you have something that might distract me?"

Matthew glances at the workers erecting the statue. "Who's our new guest?" he asks her, pointing outside.

"She's going to look so beautiful when the roses bloom in the spring, don't you think?" Melissa says. "Her name's Demeter, Goddess of the Harvest. She'll bring good luck to our garden."

"Never heard of her," Matthew says.

"She's had somewhat of a sordid past," Melissa explains, stopping for a moment beside him before they climb the stairs. "She never married, although she had an affair with Zeus, and they had a daughter together called Kore. But then Hades, Lord of the Underworld, abducted Kore, and Demeter searched for her in vain for many months. Finally, in her wrath she cast a spell on the world that threw it into eternal winter, so nothing could grow."

"Hell hath no fury like a woman scorned," Matthew says, smiling. "What happened?"

"Hades finally released Kore, and Demeter ended her spell on Earth, and things began to grow again. But every year Kore revisits the underworld for several months, and winter comes back with a vengeance."

She pulls Matthew close to her and whispers, "I feel I've been in an eternal winter without you."

"Play that sonata for me later and spring will be here before we know it," he replies with a wink.

They climb the stairs together, and just before they get to Maddy's room Matthew stops and turns to her. "Missy, I want to apologize for being gone so long...for not being here with you when the baby arrived."

Melissa looks him in the eyes. "Matthew, this may not make a lot of sense to you, but I'm not mad at all. Actually, I understand."

"You do?"

"I know what your work means to you. Good Lord, it almost got you killed. And the more I thought about that while you were away all these months, and the more I missed you, I realized that your calling is to the oil business, and I'd be making a huge mistake to try and force you out of it. I've come to realize that your job is going to separate us now and then, and I should get used to that and be happy for the times you are here."

"Missy, I can't believe what you're saying."

"Do you want to know something else, Matthew? Maddy has made me more understanding. Maybe it's the experience of having a child, being a mother, having something so helpless be so dependent on you, I don't know. But she's changed me ... for the better."

"Maybe she'll change both of us," Matthew says.

A sly smile crosses Melissa's lips. "I'll tell you a secret. That statue we were talking about a few minutes ago, Demeter?"

"What about her?"

"She's not only the Goddess of the Harvest; she's the Goddess of Fertility. That's the real reason I had her placed in the garden, to bring us luck in making babies. I want more of them, Matthew. I want a large family."

He reaches for her, kisses her tenderly. "That makes two of us," he says softly.

A moment later they break their embrace, and Matthew opens the door to the nursery. Their nanny, Thelma Jean, has just finished feeding Maddy and is sitting in a chair holding the baby, gently dabbing the infant's mouth with a moist towel.

"Oh my God, look at her!" Matthew exclaims. "Look how big she is! I'd no idea!"

"She's growing by the day," Melissa says, as Maddy spots her mother and begins to squirm in Thelma Jean's lap.

"Can I hold her?" Matthew asks, leaning over and extending his arms toward his daughter.

"Of course, sir," Thelma Jean replies, handing Matthew the towel. "But why don't you put this over your shoulder first in case the little one spits up."

Matthew does so, and then reaches down and cradles Maddy in his arms. He kisses her on the cheek, and puts his face next to hers. He hugs her and rocks her back and forth a bit, kissing her a second time. He extends his finger, and the baby smiles and grips it with her tiny hand.

"Madeline Abigail Wharton Strong," Matthew whispers. "What a beautiful name. What a beautiful girl!"

"She has your eyes, dark and intelligent," Melissa says, smiling and studying her husband as he stares at their child, obviously lost in his thoughts.

He hasn't heard a word; for he's holding his miracle and realizing love, perhaps for the first time. His mother had been right; fatherhood is going to make him a changed man.

He cradles Maddy ever so close. He can feel her heart beating against his chest, and he smells her milky-sweet breath. Matthew feels as if he's holding his very life in his hands.

Night falls, and the rain stops, but the fall air carries a cutting chill, a chiseled reminder of Demeter's coming wrath. The workmen have long-since left, and Matthew and Melissa stand before the imposing statue, her white-marble form draped in the dappled glow of moonlight drifting through scattered, ever-changing clouds.

"Do you see those shadows?" Melissa asks, nodding at the statue. "See how they move across her … never staying the same?"

Matthew looks up at the sky. "The clouds are moving fast tonight. A front's coming in."

"Sometimes I feel like that."

"Like what?"

"Like shadows are moving across me," Melissa replies. "Like they've penetrated me…as if they're inside me, covering me all over. I sometimes feel like I'm wrapped in a darkness that I can't run away from."

Matthew steps beside his wife and puts his arm around her, and he can feel her shaking.

"I have dreams," Melissa whispers. "More and more lately."

Matthew nods and draws her closer. "I do, too. Ever since the beating."

"I question things," Melissa says to him. "Like I'm not in control…like I'm being drawn down a strange path, and I have no idea where I'm going."

"I felt that way in Baku," Matthew says. "For the first time, I felt that I couldn't close the deal. I've always been able to do it before. Now I'm not so sure. I've lost my confidence."

"I want more children, Matthew," Melissa replies, again looking up at Demeter. Through the darkness the statue appears cold, like a pillar of ice.

"I'd like us to have a son," Matthew says, as thoughts of Luke and Caleb rush into his head.

"Do you know what I said earlier about your job taking you away from me, and how I'd be okay with that?"

Matthew nods.

"I lied. I can't bear to be alone anymore, Matthew. It can't be like it's been, because when you're gone, I have no idea what's happening to you. We have Maddy to think about, now."

Matthew holds her tighter, and he can feel that she is shaking even more than before.

"I've had some setbacks at the Standard," he says. "Things I've done that have been pointed out to me. But I have a plan to do some other things that don't involve the company. I'm tired of standing by, waiting for Rockefeller's beck and call...tired of being his errand boy. I'm also worried about what's happening at the company...things the directors are doing."

"Does that mean we'll have more time together?" Melissa asks. "Time to do things like a family should?"

He smiles at her and takes a deep breath, as the light drizzle resumes falling from the sky. "Well, we wanted to come out and see your new statue, and we have," Matthew says. "But I think it's about time to go back inside, warm up by the fire...have you finish that sonata for me."

Melissa turns, embraces her husband and kisses him. "And maybe after that, we'll try and make Maddy a little brother," she whispers. "I told you it's the perfect night for it."

Matthew holds her and stares into the mist at the imposing form of Demeter looming over them. The goddess appears like a ghost in the night, and he notices the falling rain accumulating around her sculpted, passive eyes. He watches the droplets pool on her lower lids. Suddenly, the water overflows, falling like a steady stream of tears upon the brown, barren earth below.

Side Action

James Harris, Matthew's business advisor, stands on the steps of the Standard Oil building and watches Matthew's carriage pull up to the front entrance. The previous night's rain has stopped, and the morning is cool and breezy.

Matthew steps to the pavement and looks around. "God, it's good to be back in Cleveland," he says.

"When did you get in?" Harris answers.

"Late yesterday afternoon, but I went straight home. How are you, James... business been chugging along okay while I've been gone?"

Harris reaches out to shake his boss's hand. "Yes, all's well, sir, no major problems. Welcome back. How was Baku?"

"Have you heard anything?" Matthew asks him. "I bet Archbold's talks with the Rothschilds weren't any better than mine were with those Nobel bastards."

"I've heard Mr. Rockefeller isn't pleased, that I can tell you."

"I heard that, too."

Harris nods. "By the way, there's a fellow named Blaze Clayburn inside waiting for you."

"Did anyone see him come in?"

"No, sir, he arrived early, and I brought him straight to your office."

"Before we go in, James, tell me what you found out about him."

"While you were in Baku, I went to Texas to learn as much as I could about talk of oil strikes there, and also to dig up more about Clayburn."

"Let's start with him."

"Based on what I found out, he's legitimate."

"How legitimate?"

"I can tell you he's the real deal, that's for sure. He comes from a wealthy ranching family who've lived in Texas since the eighteen twenties, and he owns about six oil leases just outside of Nacogdoches."

"Where?"

"Nacogdoches. It's a small town southeast of Dallas. I've been to the clerk's office there, seen the paperwork. He holds rights to about two-thousand acres with a handful of minor partners, you know, small investors … no large speculators."

"Does he have any operating wells?"

"No. In fact, he's drilled two dry holes and is just starting on a third well, although I hear he's already running into problems on that one."

"So, no indications of oil or gas anywhere on his prospects? No signs of success?"

"That's right," Harris answers. As I say, he's only got two dusters to show for, with a third well spudded a week or so ago, so there's no results on that one yet. Maybe he'll have more to say when you speak with him. But I can tell you he's running a seat-of-the-pants operation, as you'd expect at this point. You have to figure he's putting up his own money for the most part, because from what I've heard, his family isn't backing him at all. In fact, they think he's crazy."

"Are there *any* working wells around Nacogdoches?"

"None that I saw."

"Then what's causing all the excitement down there?"

"I'd compare it to everything I've read about the early days in Pennsylvania twenty years ago ... oil seeps, polluted water wells, sulfur smells, gas bubbles coming up in ponds, those kinds of things. All the signs that say there's oil and gas underground."

"Well," Matthew says, "I don't think I've ever told you this, but I've done pretty well speculating on the Oil Exchange the past few years, and I'm thinking of investing in Clayburn's venture."

James Harris appears shocked. "You're putting your own money into this without presenting it to New York?"

Matthew's dark eyes lock on his advisor. "I've thought about this long and hard, James. God knows I had enough time in Russia. First of all, JDR and his directors are far too caught up with what's happening on the world scene to worry about some outback oil play in a place nobody's ever heard of in Texas."

"You're probably right about that, Matthew," Harris replies.

"Second, and even more important, I've no hard facts to show them. Like you just said, there've been no major discoveries, no wells up and running, no refineries being built ... hell, the Standard doesn't even have a majority stake in our marketing outlets there."

"I see your point," Harris says. "I can't imagine Mr. Rockefeller wanting to invest in such a risky place."

"Of course he won't," Matthew replies. "It's too speculative, and there's no way I could guarantee a return on his investment. Why, I'd be thrown out of the room on my ass if I brought up such a proposal. Just like I was that day at the board meeting when I brought up Tarbell and the muckrakers."

"Right."

Matthew smiles at Harris. "But that doesn't mean I can't put some of my own money on the line down there."

"Of course not." Harris smiles and nods, appearing convinced.

They walk up the front steps of their office building, take the elevator to the fourth floor and head their separate ways down the hall.

Matthew opens his office door. Stretched out in Matthew's leather chair with his well-worn black boots resting on top of the large mahogany desk is Blaze Clayburn.

Matthew stands in the doorway for a second in disbelief. He puts his hands on his hips, but then a wide smile crosses his face.

Hell, any guy with the balls to make himself at home in a place like this... I think I like him already.

"Have you made yourself comfortable enough?" Matthew asks. "Is there anything I can get you ... you know, as long as I'm up and all ... coffee, a glass of water, a drink maybe?"

Blaze Clayburn smiles back but doesn't move. "No thanks," he says. "I've had breakfast already, and it's a little early fer that drink ya mentioned. But leave that offer open fer another time, if ya would."

"Sure, consider that a standing offer, no pun intended," Matthew says, still smiling.

Blaze eases his feet back on the floor and rolls Matthew's chair closer to the desk. "I always wanted to know what it's like sittin' in a bona fide oilman's chair." He looks around Matthew's office. "I could get used to this. At least I think I could."

Matthew walks toward him. "From what I hear, you've already become one."

"One what?"

"An oilman. My people tell me you've got some plays going on in East Texas."

Blaze doesn't answer. Rather, he grabs his Stetson from his lap, rises, and walks around Matthew's desk to greet him. They shake hands.

"I like lookin' a man in the eyes when I meet 'em," Blaze says. "What are ya, 'bout six-two?"

"Yeah," Matthew answers.

Blaze shakes his finger at him. "And, I'd guess 'bout thirty?"

"Twenty-eight, actually."

"I jus' turned thirty," Blaze says.

Besides being close in height and age, they are built much the same, with broad shoulders, muscular arms and thin waists.

But the similarities end there. Matthew's hair is the color of black ink, and he has dark skin and dark brown eyes. Blaze, by contrast, has curly blonde hair, deep blue eyes and a ruddy complexion from his days under the hot Texas sun. He has a relaxed manner and an infectious smile that lights up a room, while Matthew projects a cooler, more reserved air.

Blaze grins at his host and gestures toward the empty desk. "I suppose ya should take yer seat back. That is if I'm gonna try an' convince Standard Oil to invest in my operation."

"No, let's sit over here," Matthew says, motioning to a round table next to a window overlooking the Public Square.

"Mr. Clayburn," Matthew says.

"Call me Blaze, please. If we're gonna be workin' together, I think first names will do, don't you?"

"Fair enough," Matthew says. "If you remember, when you first came to us a few months ago and raised the possibility of Standard taking an equity stake in your Texas wells, I told you we'd take a close look at it."

Blaze nods. "I had a feelin' yer company would be interested in comin' in, once 'ya all realized how much oil's down there."

"What makes you think you're going to find oil?"

"I can smell it, I can see it, and if ya want to know the truth, I can do more than that."

"What are you talking about?"

"I can find oil with a divinin' rod better than any man alive."

"Did that divining rod of yours work on those two dry wells you've already drilled in Nacogdoches?" Matthew replies, studying Blaze's reaction.

"How'd ya hear 'bout them wells?"

"Do you think for a minute we didn't check you out?"

Blaze's face takes on a steely resolve, and he looks Matthew straight in the eyes. "Let me tell ya something 'bout those two wells, Matt, and I'm tellin' ya straight. And you probably know we're drillin' a third one. There's oil under all of 'em, I'm sure of it, and I'll bet every nickel I have to prove it. The problem right now is the drillin' equipment. It's not made to go through the gumbo and quicksand we ran into 'bout three hundred feet down each hole. And, we hit pressure pockets that tore up the drill pipe."

Blaze gazes out the window. "But if we can only git deeper, I know we'll hit pay dirt."

"Have you taken any core samples, had any indications in the well cuttings there's oil there?" Matthew asks.

"Yeah, we've seen small bits of carbonous rock comin' up from the hole, and sulfur crystals."

"How much do you think it would take to get drilling back on track?"

"I'm figurin' 'bout ten thousand bucks. That will take care of two new rigs, bits, larger drill stems and casings, lumber to shore up the derricks, payment for the crews, staples and other supplies, and maybe a bit left over to hold as reserve, or to get more land around my leases."

"You hold about two-thousand acres now?"

"That's right."

"And you think it's smart to buy more land, even though you haven't struck oil?"

"No doubt about it. When these wells come in, we want to have the prime drillin' areas locked up ... keep the vultures at bay." Blaze flashes a wide grin.

"What are we talking to buy out your partners?" Matthew asks.

Blaze thinks for a second. "I'd say 'bout another seven or eight thousand."

"What do they have invested so far?"

"'Bout six grand, all told."

"How eager are they to sell?"

"Offer 'em the right price ... they're history."

"What are you looking to do, long term," Matthew asks.

Blaze leans back in his chair and puts his feet on the table. "I don't think I need to own or control everythin' under the sun, like Standard Oil, if that's what yer gettin' at. Why not just *find* the oil and, after you do, hold on to production rights? Leave the headaches of transport, refinin', sellin' ... leave all those problems to somebody else."

"The producers have always been the weakest link in the chain when it comes to setting prices." Matthew points out.

Blaze winks at him. "Not if those producers *own* all the oil in a big area, say, half the state of Texas. Or in a place that's convenient to transport it, like down a river or next to the Gulf of Mexico. Then the power shifts away from the buyer. From what I hear, the problem with Oil City and other places in Pennsylvania was that you had too many producers, all of 'em flush producin' at the same time, all of 'em holdin' too little of the stuff. There was 'jus too much competition among 'em, and they couldn't control prices. They all ended up sellin' their oil for nothin'. It was like takin' candy from a baby, for a guy like Rockefeller."

"You've got a point," Matthew says. "I'll give you that."

Blaze continues. "Hell, Matt, the real fun is findin' the oil! Explorin' the land, chasin' yer dreams, trustin' yer instincts, going fer broke, bringin' in a wildcat and rechargin' the coffers. That's where the action is!"

"So you're saying you want to form an exploration and production company."

Blaze leans toward him. "I'm proposin' we become the greatest wildcatters the West has ever seen. Hell, I'm tellin' ya, there's oil in Texas; there's oil in Louisiana; there's oil in Oklahoma, New Mexico—we already know about California—and I can lead you to all of it, and then some!"

"Those are cocky words, Blaze."

"Confident words, Matt."

"You might be limiting your opportunities."

"Let me get ya down to Texas. You sit with me at night under the big sky, next to a mesquite fire, sippin' whiskey, eatin' a good steak, hearin' the drills workin' away, knowin' that with every stroke yer gettin' that much closer to yer prize. I'll have ya hooked in a week!"

Matthew gets up from the table and begins pacing around his office. "I have to tell you, Blaze, you've got my interest up, and I think you have some good ideas, not to mention the know how to make them happen."

Blaze remains seated, but follows Matthew's motion around the room. "Then I can count on the Standard comin' in?"

Matthew stops and turns toward him. "I'm sorry to say, you can't."

Blaze doesn't say anything.

Matthew walks over to him and extends his hand. "But, you can count on me personally to back you with whatever it takes!"

Blaze gets up and shakes his new partner's hand. "Yer not goin' to regret this, Matt," he says. "They'll be a time you'll look back on today, yer decision, as settin' ya on the path to becomin' a real rich man."

"Let's sit back down and work out the details," Matthew suggests.

"First, we need to come up with a name fer our company," Blaze says.

"Right," Matthew says, "but my name can't appear on any of the incorporation papers, or in the company name itself. I need to keep things secret. I have to be a silent investor, understand?"

"Then I guess my first choice, Clayburn, Strong and Company, is out, huh?"

Matthew smiles.

"What about this one," Blaze says, "Texas Exploration and Production Company?"

Matthew thinks about it for a moment. Then he grabs a pencil and paper. He writes the name, Tex E & P Co., and shows it to Blaze. "What do you think? We can use this for stationery and letterhead, and keep the longer name for official papers."

Blaze slaps Matthew on the back. "Tex E 'an P Co. We got a name, pardner!"

The men work for the next couple of hours putting their deal on paper. When they'd finished, Matthew rings for James Harris to join them, and he enters the room.

"James, you've met Blaze Clayburn before. He's been talking to me about opportunities in Texas."

Harris nods. "Yes, Mr. Clayburn and I met earlier."

Blaze corrects him. "Call me Blaze."

"Blaze," Matthew says. "How did you come by that name?"

"Believe it or not, my daddy named me after a favorite horse he used to own. He and I don't git along too well."

"You and the horse?"

"No, he's long gone. I'm talkin' 'bout me and my daddy. He doesn't much 'preciate the bid'ness I been pursuin'. Thinks I should be a rancher, like him."

"Fathers don't always get want they want," Matthew says.

"Funny thing we should be talkin' 'bout that."

"How so?"

"Because I was just talkin' to daddy a few weeks ago, and he says to me, 'Do you know the difference between you and that horse I used to own?'"

"You and Blaze?"

"Blaze and me. So the old bastard says, 'You know what the difference is? My horse never disappointed me; I can't say the same fer you.'"

They shake hands a final time. "Keep your chin up, Blaze," Matthew says as they walk toward the door. "Maybe what we just put together will make your father real proud someday."

Blaze puts on his Stetson and shrugs. "Who the hell knows? Stranger things have happened!"

STORM CLOUDS

It's a little before 8 a.m., and Matthew is relaxing in a comfortable wing chair in his second-floor study having his first cup of coffee and reading *The Plain Dealer*. He glances at the mantle clock for a second, and then at the newspaper's date on the top of the page: Monday, November 29, 1886.

He takes a sip from his mug, and resumes reading a lengthy story about France's recent gift to the United States, the Statue of Liberty, which had been dedicated in New York Harbor one month earlier. The study door flies open and in bolts Maddy, followed by her nanny, Thelma Jean.

Matthew lays the paper on the table beside him, leans forward and opens his arms. "Well, look who's here!" he says, as Maddy runs across the plush carpet and jumps into his lap.

Thelma Jean smiles at the two of them. "As usual, sir, the little one insisted on seeing you off to work."

"What are you doing, Daddy?" Maddy asks.

"What I do every morning, honey. I'm having a cup of coffee and reading the newspaper."

"Can I taste?"

Matthew smiles. "No, Madeline, Daddy's told you before ... coffee's for grownups. You have to get a little bigger before we let you have some of this. Besides, it's hot."

"Why's it hot?"

"Because that's the way people drink it. It wakes them up and it also warms them up, especially on a cold day like today. Do you want to see what Daddy was just reading?"

"No," Maddy says, looking out the window.

"The *Farmer's Almanac* says there's an early winter storm coming our way this week," Thelma Jean says. "It's supposed to last awhile."

"It looks like it could snow," Matthew replies, picking his newspaper back up. He opens it to the two-page center section featuring the story about the statue. The article contains six large photographs showing Lady Liberty in various stages of assembly, the dedication ceremonies, and a panoramic shot of the New York skyline taken from the observation area inside Liberty's torch.

He points at the photograph of the city. "Do you see these buildings?" he asks Maddy. "The place I visit when I go to New York is right behind them."

"Why?"

"Because that's where it was built. That's where Mr. Rockefeller put our headquarters when he made it."

"Maddy," Thelma Jean instructs, "listen to your father, now. He's trying to show you something." The four-and-a-half-year-old shifts her weight in Matthew's lap.

"Maddy," Matthew asks, "how would you like to come to New York with me on my next trip and visit the Statue of Liberty? They take you to this island on a boat, and we could walk to the top and see the sights ... just you and me."

Maddy looks over at Thelma Jean. "Can Nanny come with us?"

"Of course she can," Matthew replies, "and your mother, too, if she's up to it. But I have one more thing to ask you, Maddy, before I say goodbye."

"What, Daddy?"

"Do you remember the special meal we had last Thursday?"

Maddy appears to be thinking, so Matthew prompts her. We had Thanksgiving together, remember? Remember what we ate?"

Maddy smiles at the memory. "Turkey!"

"You're right. We had a turkey with gravy and stuffing, and mashed potatoes, and green beans, and cranberry sauce, and biscuits with honey and pumpkin pie for dessert."

"It was good!" Maddy says. "Are we going to eat another turkey tonight?"

"Not tonight, honey."

"Why?"

"Because Thanksgiving is a special day when we give thanks for all our blessings. That's why we say that special prayer together."

Maddy hugs her father. "I remember."

"Well, I just want you to know that I say a prayer of thanks every day for you, because you make every day special for me."

"Me, too." Maddy answers.

He kisses her on her head, and Thelma Jean walks over to them and tries to lift the little girl from Matthew's lap, but she hugs her father tighter.

"Don't you and Thelma Jean have something to do today?" he asks her.

"We're going to feed the squirrels."

Matthew smiles. "And what are you going to feed them?"

"Nuts."

"Well," Matthew replies, "when the squirrels come up to you for those nuts, you be sure to drop them on the ground when they get close. I don't want you being bitten. Thelma

Jean's going to make sure you feed them that way, just like I asked you to, okay? Don't let the squirrels take the nuts out of your hand because they could bite your fingers."

"They won't bite, Daddy. They're my friends."

"You be a good girl, my darling, and I'll see you in a few days."

"Another trip, sir?" Thelma Jean asks, taking Maddy off his lap.

Matthew rises from his chair. "No, just three straight days of meetings that will go well into the night. It's more convenient if I just stay downtown."

Thelma Jean nods. "Have a good day at the office, sir. We'll see you later this week."

He kisses Maddy one more time, and walks out the door and down the hallway to Melissa's suite. His wife is sitting up in bed staring at the wall.

"Good morning," he says. "How are you feeling today?"

She doesn't answer him, and Matthew walks over to her bed and sits down beside her.

"Listen," he says, stroking her uncombed hair, "I have refiners coming in from six states for their year-end reviews. The meetings could last at least three days, so I'm going to stay in town until probably Thursday. Will you be okay?"

"I heard you say her name again last night, you know."

Matthew stiffens. "Who's name?"

"Lavinia's," she says, looking at him for the first time. "I was standing by your door, watching you while you slept, and you said her name. I've heard you say it before. Who is she, Matthew?

"No one," he replies, getting up and walking over to the window. He stares at a crew of workmen constructing a huge marble fountain in the center of the circular drive at the front of the mansion. "Whatever I said, it wasn't that. You must be mistaken. I don't know any Lavinia."

"You have to be going somewhere for sex," she says.

"God knows I'm not finding it here," he replies. "We haven't been together since you found out you couldn't have any more children. And that was over three years ago."

"I haven't wanted to," Melissa says.

"You haven't wanted to do much of anything, Melissa. You hardly leave your bed, except at night when you wander around this museum we call a house. You don't even play the piano anymore."

"So who are you screwing? Is it Thelma Jean? Or maybe one of the maids!"

"You're talking like a crazy woman, Melissa. Just stop it!"

"Who the hell's Lavinia? She has to be someone. Are you sleeping with her, too? Is that where you're going tonight... to see her?"

"What do you care what I do or don't do," Matthew snaps. "And speaking of not doing things, the head gardener told me yesterday that nobody's been paid around here in weeks. What's going on? Why hasn't the estate manager paid the staff and the other people you bring in and out of here for your projects... like the men outside building that monstrosity of a fountain?"

"Because I fired him three weeks ago! I didn't like his attitude!"

Matthew reaches into his jacket pocket and pulls out a stack of invoices. "These are just some of the unpaid bills I found laying around. Good Lord, Melissa, there must be a thousand dollars in obligations here alone. Why did you let these debts stack up?"

"Well," she snaps, "you weren't here to pay them now, were you? No, you were too busy out screwing anything with a dress on!"

"I told you to stop talking like that! But answer me this, why have the men stayed and worked, even though they haven't been paid?"

"Some left…you'll see their bills are in there. But I replaced those workers with others willing to wait for their wages."

"I don't believe you did this," Matthew says. "And as soon as I'm back at the end of the week, you can be damn sure I *will* get it squared away. I just don't have time to do it now."

"Do you think for one minute I really believe you're going to your office for three days?" Melissa shouts.

"Believe what you want. It's true," Matthew replies, heading for the door.

He shakes his head as he walks down the hall, hearing her screams behind him: "Lavinia! Lavinia! Lavinia! Your whore! That's who you're going to now, aren't you! I know you are! I just know it!

The dart cuts through the smoke and din of O'Rourke's Pub and buries its tip in the number "15" on the cork board.

"That's a triple!" Rebecca shouts. "I've got you on points. All I need is one more bull's-eye, and you're history, my fine Italian stallion."

"The game ain't over yet," Remo replies, swigging a mouthful of cold beer. Don't be countin' your chickens, grandma."

He wipes his mouth with his sleeve and watches Rebecca strut to the board to remove her darts.

She puts one in her right hand, turns, and wiggles it at him. "You know, Remo, I can hit anything I want with this. So, I'd be careful who you're calling 'grandma,' if I were you."

"Well, you are one, aren't you? You told me Matthew's wife had a kid a few years ago."

Rebecca walks back and stands beside Remo. She takes a drink of her beer, and then kisses him hard on the lips. She jabs him playfully in his stomach with the tips of her darts. "Do I look like a grandmother to you?"

"Ouch! Gimme those things," Remo says, grabbing the darts from her hand. "We've got a game to finish."

She gives Remo a sly look and kisses him a second time. "We may have another game to play later, too … a game we can't play here."

"Don't mess me up," he says. "Can't you see I'm concentratin'?"

Rebecca rolls her eyes. "Frankly, Remo, I hadn't noticed." She takes another drink of beer and watches her lover take aim at the board.

"You got everythin' closed out," he says, "and are up by thirty. All I can do is stay alive on points." He throws his first dart at the bull's-eye, but misses. "Son-of-a-bitch!"

Rebecca goads him. "Only two left, the pressure's on. But you can handle it, right, Remo?" Her eyes sparkle, and her pretty face flashes a carefree smile. After all, it's a relief to be away from the monotony and routines imposed by her husband Philip Fenner. This raucous hideaway with its smoke, smells and salt-of-the-earth people is a welcome escape, and Rebecca's enjoying every moment of it.

"I can handle *you*, bet your sweet ass on that," Remo replies, tossing his second dart. It lands just outside its target, and he steps off the line, walks over to their table and takes a swig of beer. "Like I said, don't be countin' any chickens. You still have to finish off with a bull's-eye."

Like scores of other neighborhood joints in Hell's Kitchen, O'Rourke's is a magnet for a menagerie of working-class characters looking to quaff a few penny beers, play some pool, tell a joke or two and unwind after their shifts. The little hole-in-the-wall on the corner of 10th Avenue and 53rd Street is packed with burly laborers from the docks, slaughterhouses, construction sites, railroads, shipyards, factories—all the places that hire immigrant workers and pay them a pittance for their daily toil.

Owner 'Johnny Boy' O'Rourke runs numbers out of the place, so his regulars also include two-bit street hustlers like Remo looking to place a bet or pick up an inside tip on a racehorse.

And with the men come the women—waitresses, maids, housekeepers and the like, women of all shapes and sizes, from lusty big-boned cooks and washerwomen to mousy freckled-faced colleens who work as governesses for the rich families living in midtown. Like the men, the women are out for some laughs and a good time, sharing stories, beers and bowls of brown stew, sometimes getting lucky by night's end and leaving with what they hope is a halfway decent man for a squeeze and sweaty tumble in the sheets.

Rebecca, with her striking black hair, tailored clothes and sexy confidence, is by far the most beautiful and enticing female who'd ever set foot in O'Rourke's. Every time she walks in, she turns heads, garners glances, fuels thoughts among men of things that will never be.

One such man stands in the shadows in the corner of the pub, eyeing her every move.

"Are you going to throw that last dart, Remo, so I can put you out of your misery? Or are you still 'concentrating', because to tell you the truth, it's a mystery to me what the hell you're doing."

Remo nods. "Just watch … and weep," he says, making his final throw, missing his mark by a mile. "Fuck!" he shouts so the entire bar can hear him, but not a head turns his way as he walks to the board and pulls out his darts.

Rebecca takes them. "It pains me to do this to you, Remo, it really does," she says, looking up at him with a half-serious expression. "Because I know how you hate to lose." She sips a bit of her beer and eyes the dartboard.

She walks to the line, aims, and throws her dart into the very center of the bull's-eye. "Want these?" she says, turning and offering her two remaining darts to Remo. "I'm thinking you need the practice."

"Fuck this."

"Want to dance, then?"

Remo and Rebecca enter a back room with a small stage and four musicians: a fiddler, an accordion player, a man strumming a mandolin, and a hefty red-haired woman with bouncing breasts pouring halfway out her low-cut gingham blouse. She's hard at work alternating between belting out songs and blowing on the harmonica. The floor is mostly filled with couples, but also with a fair number of women dancing in groups.

Remo grabs Rebecca, and they begin to twirl to the beat of the jig. The singer, into her cups as well as her music, sways her big body as she belts out the tune.

"Bought a pair of brogues rattling o'er the bogs
And fright'ning all the dogs on the rocky road to Dublin.
One, two, three four, five, Hunt the Hare and turn
her down the rocky road and all the way to Dublin,
Whack follol de rah!"

At Rebecca's insistence, they stay on the dance floor for several more songs.

"Have you ever noticed that the Irish are the only people in the world who sing happy songs about going to war, and sad songs about being in love?" she asks Remo.

"Yeah, now that you mention it," he replies. "I guess you Micks get things confused sometimes, huh?"

"Not when it comes to you," Rebecca says. She dips her body to the music, grabs the front of his belt and pulls him toward her.

The man who'd been watching them walks up and taps Remo on the shoulder. "Me wants a dance with the lady."

Remo turns and faces the tall wiry character, who has wild eyes and a couple of missing teeth. He's about thirty-five, dressed in old but clean clothes. "What…you just walk off the boat?" Remo says to him. "Get the fuck outta here!"

"Any lass on the floor is fair game for a dance, and maybe more," the man says, eyeing Rebecca.

"What, you a fuckin' poet?"

The man ignores Remo and holds his hand out to Rebecca. "Come on, me girl, what say you and me have a twirl?"

"Didn't you hear me the first time, you Irish asshole!" Remo shouts, stepping closer to the man. "Get lost!" Remo pushes him backwards, away from Rebecca.

"Remo, let's not start anything," she says. "We're having too good a time."

"I *didn't* start anythin'. This blockheaded Mick did!"

The man grabs an empty beer bottle off a table by the dance floor. He holds it by its neck, breaks it in half, and lunges at Remo.

The Italian's hand moves with blinding speed, and he reaches into his jacket and pulls out a knife with an eight-inch blade. He sweeps its edge across the upper wrist of the man's hand, and the bottle falls to the floor. Remo raises the knife and waves it in front of his attacker. "Come on! You want to see what it's like to get cut again! I mean *really* cut?"

"Remo, don't do it," Rebecca pleads, looking at the man, who is trying to stop the bleeding by covering his wrist with his opposite hand.

O'Rourke runs into the back room gripping a bat, and the crowd on the dance floor scatters. "You two stop these shenanigans, or I'll bash yer heads in!"

The bleeding man throws a punch at O'Rourke, and the bar owner smashes the bat against the side of his head. He crumbles to the floor and two of O'Rourke's cronies pick him up and drag him toward the back-alley door.

"Rough him up some," O'Rourke orders. "And tell him never set foot in here again!"

Remo slides his knife back into his jacket and grabs Rebecca's hand. "Let's go up front," he says. "There's somethin' I need to ask you."

They walk back into the front part of the tavern and sit across from each other in a booth along the wall opposite the jammed bar.

"You want another drink?" Remo asks.

"Yes, but I think I've about had it with beer. Get me a gin on the rocks."

"Me too," Remo says. I think I'll switch to grappa." He rises and heads to the bar.

He returns a few minutes later with their drinks. He places Rebecca's in front of her and sits back down on the opposite side of the narrow wooden table separating them. "Listen, we need to talk about somethin'."

"If you're thinking of asking for my hand in marriage after all these years," Rebecca teases, "you know I'm already taken, if you can call it that." She glances at the crowd. "I often wonder, though, what it would be like to live with a real man again."

"No, I'm serious," says Remo. "I need a favor."

"You look troubled, my dear. What's bothering you?"

"I owe some people some money. Money I don't have."

"What people?"

"People you don't string out, and I've reached the end of the line of excuses."

"You're gambling again, aren't you? I thought we talked about that, and you said you were going to try and lay off."

"I did try."

Rebecca gives him a sly smile. "I mean, after all, you've got other vices to keep you occupied. Like me."

Remo looks at his grappa, ignoring the overture. "I guess it's in my blood, in my nature." He picks his drink up off the table, brings it to his lips and belts it down. He winces at the liquor's harshness. Then his face takes on a fearful look.

Rebecca's smile disappears. "How much money do you owe these people?"

He looks away.

"Tell me."

"Twelve hundred dollars."

"How in the world did you get in such a hole?"

"Horses, cards, craps … take your pick."

"Most likely all three, knowing you. That's a lot of money, Remo."

"Are you goin' to help me?"

"You don't have any of your own money to put toward this?"

"Not a fuckin' dime. You should know that better than anyone. Don't forget, you've been the one shorin' me up all these years."

"Supporting your bad habits is more like it."

"You goin' to do it, or not? Don't make me go elsewhere for money."

Rebecca pushes her drink aside and rises from their booth. "Let's talk about it back at your place."

"So, what's it gonna be?"

"Come on, Remo," Rebecca says, extending her hand. "If I'm going to give you twelve hundred dollars, by God, you're going to earn every penny of it ... and then some."

They leave O'Rourke's and strike out for Remo's tenement building. They pass the slaughterhouse down the street from his room. The smell of pigs hangs like a dripping cloth over the cold, damp afternoon. They walk without a word between them, wrapped within their private thoughts. Even the pigs are silent, collectively quiet ... quiet in their contemplation of the impending flash of the butcher's knife.

SORROW'S SNOWFALL

It is a little after 1 p.m. on Wednesday, and Matthew and James Harris are taking a lunch break from their third day of meetings with the refiners. Harris looks out the office window and says, "Do you believe this weather? I don't think this storm's ever going to end."

Matthew rises from the table and walks to the window, not saying a word. The snow descends in what appears to be impenetrable sheets from the slate-gray sky, and as it falls the wind whips white particles of ice against the windows and into the lifeless alleyways, forming frozen drifts on the cold, granite ledges and deserted city streets.

"Are you okay?" Harris asks.

"I'm concerned about Melissa," Matthew replies, staring at the snowstorm.

"She's not getting any better?"

He shakes his head. "No, if anything she's getting worse. I don't know what to do. I think she's losing her mind..."

"What's the doctor say? Does he have any ideas?"

"I mean she makes up things that are untrue, accuses me of things I didn't do. I don't know."

"I'm sorry, Matthew," Harris says. "I wish I could do something to help you with this."

"What time do we pick it up again with the refiners?" Matthew asks. He looks tired, distracted.

"We're due to meet Wesley Tilford and his people at one thirty," Harris says. "But before we do, I wanted you to know that you got another telegram from Blaze Clayburn."

"How much does he want now?"

"He's back in East Texas, and he wants you to advance an additional fifty-five hundred for drill bits and machinery parts. He says he expects to have some good news to report soon. Says his crew is getting close to bringing in those Tyler wells."

"Getting close to sending me to the poor house is more like it," Matthew says. "Every one of those Nacogdoches wells he drilled turned out to be a bust."

"I know. Should I wire him the money?"

"What the hell choice do I have? Between my wife draining me dry and Blaze sucking every last dollar out of me, I'll be lucky to be able to put food on the table. But I made a commitment to him, and I'm not going to leave him high and dry at this point."

Matthew takes a deep breath, shakes his head and looks back outside. The snow's falling so heavily he can't see across the street to the Public Square. He feels a pang of fear shoot through him, and he shudders and stares at the clock. It reads 1:17 p.m. He tries to shake off the gripping anxiety growing inside him, but he's unable to do so. He realizes he's sweating, struggling to breathe.

What's going on? he thinks. *What's wrong? Am I having some sort of attack?*

His office door flies open and in runs Thelma Jean. "She's gone, sir! Maddy's disappeared!"

"What do you mean, 'disappeared?'"

"We can't find her anywhere. We've looked all through the house... outside, too!"

"Is my wife at home?"

"Yes, sir. She's in her bedroom, beside herself."

"Maybe Maddy's with her. Maybe she's up there hiding in one of the closets. She's done that before."

"That can't be, sir. I checked all over Mrs. Strong's room before I came here."

Matthew realizes that Thelma Jean is soaking wet and shivering. He runs over to the coat rack, grabs a wool sweater, and drapes it over the young girl's shoulders. "How did you get here?"

"I took one of the groundskeeper's wagons from the shed, she replies, starting to cry. "I came as fast as I could, but the roads are horrible."

"I want you to stay here where it's warm," Matthew says. "We'll get you some fresh clothes. I'm going back to the house."

Thelma Jean sobs even harder now. "No, I'm going with you! I can't just stay put! I have to explain what happened!"

Matthew guides her over to one of his office chairs, and she sits down, and he stands beside her. "What *did* happen, Thelma Jean? Tell me everything you know."

"It's my fault, sir... it's all my fault!" Tears stream down her face, and she buries her head in her hands.

Matthew places his fingers under the young girl's chin and raises her head. "Look at me," he says. "Tell me exactly what happened."

She wipes her nose with her hand. "Maddy wanted some lunch, and I sent word to the cooks to prepare a plate for her... you know, little portions from last night's leftovers... and Maddy wanted to go down to the basement kitchen to eat it."

Matthew stiffens. "I didn't know she was allowed down there."

"Oh, we don't go often, sir, every now and then, always just for the lunch hour, you know, just to have a different place to eat, instead of taking all our meals in the nursery. Sometimes the cooks will give us treats, some candy."

She lowers her head again and begins bawling.

"Try and stop crying," Matthew says, putting his hand on her shoulder. "It's important you tell me everything you can."

"On the way down to the cellar, Maddy wanted to play hide and seek. She likes doing that … her going ahead, and me trying to find her. You know all the hallways and hidden rooms down there."

"Actually, I don't," Matthew replies, stiffening. "Did you two do that often?"

"Oh, Mr. Strong, you have to believe me. We play hide and seek all the time, but we don't go into the basement often at all."

"Have you and the workers searched every square inch of that cellar?" Matthew asks.

"Yes, sir, we looked everywhere, all over the house for more than an hour. There must have been a dozen of us."

"Are there any open pits or wells in the cellar that she could have fallen into?" Matthew asks her.

"None that I've seen, Mr. Strong."

The office door bursts open once again and in runs James Harris with another man. "Matthew, this is Mrs. Strong's appointments secretary. He's come from the estate."

"I know who he is," Matthew says.

"He has something you need to read," Harris replies, thrusting a handwritten note into his hand. Matthew unfolds it and reads the message:

Matthew Strong: Your daughter won't get hurt if you bring $3,000 in cash to the Old Bridge one mile down Lake Road. Leave the money under the bridge on the left riverbank. You'll get another note there. Come alone. Don't bring nobody with you. I'm watching.

Matthew reads the note a second time, then turns to Harris. "Get a leather pouch. Go to the safe and fill it with three thousand dollars. Do it now!"

His advisor rushes from the room without a word. Matthew opens his desk drawer, grabs a revolver and shoves it into the waistband of his pants. He walks over to the coat rack and removes a long black wool overcoat.

"I want to go with you, Mr. Strong!" Thelma Jean pleads. "I have to go with you!"

"I told you, you're staying here, Thelma Jean!" Matthew orders, turning to Melissa's secretary. "I want you to go back to the house and make sure my wife is okay. Tell her I'll be there as soon as I can, and we're going to get Maddy back. Stay close to her until I get there … do you understand?"

Thelma Jean starts to cry uncontrollably, and Matthew races out of the room to get the money from James Harris.

He reins back his horses with a sharp tug, and the carriage slides to a stop by the Old Bridge. He draws his pistol and jumps to the ground. The snow is deep, falling so hard now he can't see more than ten feet in front of him. He also doesn't see any tracks leading beneath the bridge.

The snow hasn't accumulated under the stone and steel structure, and the ground running along the left riverbank

GUSHER!

is bare. Matthew's eyes dart over every square inch of dirt and fallen leaves, but he can't find the note. He stuffs the pistol back in his trousers and looks up at the bridge's black support beams. He runs his hands across the top of the beams, along sections he can't see standing on the ground, searching for a scrap of paper, an envelope, anything. He finally feels what he hopes is the note. It's folded in half, and he opens it and reads the instructions:

Leave the money on top of this beam out of sight. Go back to your house. Don't go to the police, or you won't see her again.

Oh, God, please protect my precious little girl, he prays aloud. *Don't let anything happen to her. Please, God, bring Maddy back to me safe and sound.*

Matthew leaves the money pouch where he was told and runs up the slippery bank. He jumps into his carriage and tears down Lake Road, heading to his estate.

The incessant snow slows his progress, but thirty minutes after leaving Old Bridge he arrives home. An attendant stands in the center of the drive by the estate's front door, huddled against the cold, waiting to take Matthew's carriage and horses.

He jumps to the ground and runs up to the worker. "Have you found her yet?"

"No, sir, and we've scoured the house. Do you want me to take the horses to the stables?"

"Yes, get them inside but leave them hitched, in case I have to go out again."

Matthew runs to the front door and enters the house. He glances at the large grandfather clock in the foyer. It's 2:38 p.m.

He bolts through the estate's entrance hall and across its ballroom. He runs into the study and sees Melissa sitting in a wingchair, surrounded by several maids.

She looks up as he approaches. "That little bitch!" she screams. "What has she done with my daughter?"

"This has nothing to do with Thelma Jean, if that's who you're talking about," Matthew snaps.

"It has *everything* to do with Thelma Jean!" Melissa shouts back at him. "She was in charge of Madeline's safekeeping. She was responsible for her custody, or so I thought. She was never supposed to let her out of her sight, but it looks like she did, doesn't it?"

Matthew glares at her. "You stupid selfish woman... Maddy's been kidnapped! Here are the ransom notes," he says, throwing them at her. "Read them!"

The notes land in her lap, but she makes no effort to pick them up.

"I bet one of those workers you have traipsing in and out of here all hours of the day and night has taken her!" Matthew hollers. "One you were too damn lazy to pay!"

"Go to hell, Matthew! This wouldn't have happened if that Mick had been doing her job like she was supposed to. That's why this has happened... it's because of her, not because I was upstairs or a workman hasn't gotten paid on time! What's it going to take for that to sink into your thick head?"

Just then one of the gardeners bursts into the room. "Mr. Strong, you'd better come with me. We've found tracks in the snow by the greenhouse leading into the woods."

"Are they a little girl's footsteps?" Matthew asks, not wanting to know the answer.

"I'm sorry to say they are, sir. There are larger ones as well... a man's footsteps next to the small ones." The gardener swallows before continuing. "There are places where it looks like the little one's been dragged through the snow."

Matthew pats the revolver's handle under his coat. "Let's go," he says.

Melissa follows him across the room. "You really *do* think this is my fault don't you, you selfish bastard!"

Matthew stops and turns, hatred filling his eyes. "Melissa, the only thing you ever gave me is my lovely little daughter! And now even she may be taken away! If that happens, we have nothing between us anymore, if we ever did to begin with!"

He storms from the study with the gardener following close behind. They run down the stairs to the basement kitchen and to the door leading outside. Two more workers are waiting there.

"Show me where you found the footsteps," he orders.

"We'd better hurry, sir," replies one of the men. "The snow's coming down harder, and we don't want the tracks getting covered up."

As the snow tumbles from the sky, Matthew and the three men run down the sloping back yard of the estate, and one of the workers falls and rolls a dozen or so feet down the slippery hill. Matthew looks around as he runs and everything he sees—the trees, ground, main house, stables, outbuildings, the statue of Demeter—everything is coated in white.

Dear Lord, why are you doing this to me? he asks, lifting his face to the heavens. *Haven't I suffered enough? Surely you wouldn't hurt a little girl?*

They come to the greenhouse, also blanketed in snow, and a worker bends down to inspect the ground. "They're mostly covered, but you can see footprints right here!"

"Follow them," Matthew orders. "They should become clearer the closer we get. Hurry!"

The men enter the thick woods, and the footsteps do become more distinct. They follow them over a knoll, through a pine forest, and across a small brook, where the footsteps show the man and Maddy must have balanced on several exposed rocks to get across the frigid water. They pursue the footsteps through more forest and into a clearing surrounded by a stone wall, as the sky spews its white wrath.

And then Matthew sees it. In the middle of the field is a small mound of snow. The mound is saturated in a blackish-crimson color.

"No," he screams. "For the love of God, no!

He runs to it, falls to his knees, and begins brushing back the cold blanket of death. His hands are covered in blood and ice as he pushes the snow aside. Curled into a ball on the frozen ground is the lifeless form of Maddy. Her throat has been slit.

Matthew screams louder, and the tears gush from him and fall on the icy earth. He sweeps his daughter into his arms and brings her to his chest. He rocks back and forth, closing his eyes, wishing beyond hope this is another nightmare about to end, a nest of snakes dissipated by daybreak, a dream of despair soon to be gone, cast aside as the sun paints the sky with the purple hue of first light.

He opens his eyes and looks down at Maddy and realizes this is no dream—it *is* happening all over again, and Matthew lowers his head and holds his little girl tight.

The three workers stand in silence over him as the snow coats their bodies—white statues, silent sentinels from another world, devoid of life, of love, descendants of the evil and miseries provoked by man himself.

GUSHER!

❧ ❧ ❧

By Friday the storm has moved east, blanketing New York City with four-foot drifts in six hours of steady snowfall. Rebecca sits stone still in the wooden chair in the corner of Remo's room. The window is wide open and the room is freezing, but Rebecca appears oblivious, her unblinking eyes fixed on the door. Outside the wind howls, and the cries of the slaughterhouse pigs can be heard, their hopeless screams carried in waves in the swirling black night air.

She detects a key being inserted in the slot, and the door opens, and in walks Remo.

"What the..?"

"Where've you been?" Rebecca asks.

Remo looks at her for a second, and then at the window. "What, are you nuts? Why in the hell are you sitting in here in the freezing cold?"

She notices his shoes are soaking wet. "I asked you a question, Remo."

"I've been gone."

"Where?"

"None of your fuckin' business," he snaps, walking over and slamming the window shut.

She glares at him. "What were you doing?"

"Business. I had some business to take care of. What's it to you?"

"That 'business', as you call it, wouldn't have taken you to Cleveland now, would it? Your 'business' wouldn't have involved Matthew and his family now, did it?"

"I haven't seen that hothead of a son of yours since I got into it with him at that boardinghouse. Why you bringin' him up?"

267

"Funny you should say that. I got a telegram from him yesterday. Do you know what has happened?"

"I don't have a clue."

"Do you know what the telegram says? It says my grand-daughter has been murdered…kidnapped and killed, with a ransom note left behind demanding three thousand dollars."

Remo begins pacing around the room. "What's that supposed to mean to me?"

"She was found with her throat cut, slaughtered like those pigs down the street. That's why the window was open. I was listening to the pigs."

Remo turns his back to Rebecca. "You're fuckin' nuts. You're talkin' like some crazy woman. I told you before, what's this got to do with me?"

"You know damn well what it has to do with you. You did it. You killed Maddy."

Remo reels around to face Rebecca and sees the pistol pointed at him. He raises his hands chest high and waves them in front of him. "What do you think you're goin' to do with that?"

"You're going to find out exactly what I'm going to do with this. Now, open the window back up."

"What?"

Rebecca aims the gun at Remo's head. "I said open the window! Now! I want you to hear the screams of the pigs."

"Okay…okay. Go easy with that gun." Remo walks over and raises the window a couple of inches.

"All the way!" she commands.

He opens it as far as it will go. The room fills with the sounds of slaughter, and a blast of arctic air rushes in, dropping the temperature in Remo's tiny hovel even further.

He turns and faces Rebecca, who puts a bullet through his balls.

The Italian screams and doubles over. He falls to the floor, and his hands cover his crotch as if he's protecting it from further assault.

Rebecca rises from her chair, takes a few steps toward him, and stands a short distance away. "I want you to tell me why you killed my granddaughter. Was it money? Was it money you needed? If so, why didn't you come to me like you always have?"

Remo's body writhes and twists in pain, and he begins to sob. His trousers are soaked in blood and urine, and a reddish-yellow pool forms beside him and spreads across the bare wooden floor.

"Or was it that you just had to hurt Matthew after all these years? Had to make him pay for that night when both of you were just boys?"

Remo grimaces and spits out his words. "I told you, you crazy bitch, I had nothin' to do with that."

Rebecca shoots a bullet into his right knee. The jolt makes him roll flat on his back, and he screams again, louder now.

"Oh, God, I'll tell you what you want to know. I did kill her. I wasn't going to. I didn't want to. All I wanted was the money, the three thousand dollars. But she wouldn't stop cryin' and she kept layin' down in the snow, slowin' me up. I had to drag her. I knew they'd be comin' after us. I had to get rid of her, don't you see?" Remo is crying uncontrollably. "Please don't hurt me again. I beg you, Rebecca."

She moves closer to him.

His high-pitched shrieks join the shivering whine of the winter wind outside, and the rising wails mingle with the screams and squeals of the pigs bound for slaughter.

"Do you hear them, Remo?" Rebecca whispers. "Do you hear the pigs?"

"Yes, I hear them!" Remo screams. "I hear them!"

"Do you hear yourself?"

He twists and turns, and his face and hair are now coated in his own blood and filth. He screams again, and cries even harder, pressing his mouth into the worn tenement floor.

"Good," Rebecca says, standing over him. "I want you to hear the pigs. I want you to hear yourself. Do you know why, Remo?"

"Rebecca … help me! I'm beggin' you!"

"Because there's no difference between you … you and the pigs. Do you know something else?"

His answer is unintelligible.

"You're both destined for the same fate!"

She presses the pistol's barrel against his head and squeezes the trigger a final time.

Rebecca turns, drops the gun, and leaves Remo's room for the deserted street below. The snow falls, the wind wails, but the pigs utter not a sound.

THE DEPARTURE

Matthew's hands shake as he reaches across the plain wooden table, grabs the bottle of Early Times, and pours himself another half-tumbler of bourbon. It's going on 9 p.m.

His eyes are glazed and his binge is in full swing, his mind dancing from one tortured thought to another.

He looks old. His black hair is flecked with gray, and his usually dark complexion appears washed out. His face is strained, his eyes haunted.

Matthew pitches his head back and gulps down the bourbon as if he's drinking a cold glass of water. He hears a knock at his door.

"Go away!" he shouts, his words slurred.

"Matthew...open up! It's Daniel O'Day and John Archbold. We need to talk."

Matthew takes a second to answer. "Can't it wait until tomorrow, Daniel? It's late."

"No, it can't! Archbold shouts. "Open the damn door!"

He rises, steadying himself by gripping the back of his chair. "Okay...I'm coming," he hollers, shuffling across the tiny room, flipping the deadbolt and swinging the door open.

Archbold struts in, takes a deep breath and looks around the apartment. "Good God, man, when's the last time you had a cleaning woman in here?"

"You want a drink?" Matthew asks them.

Archbold shakes his head. "I've given up liquor."

"I'll pass as well," O'Day adds, glancing at a pile of unwashed clothes in the corner.

"Suit yourselves," Matthew replies. "Guess you won't mind if I have one." He walks back into the kitchen and fills another tumbler.

"Matthew," O'Day says, "the board has elected John president of Standard Oil. He's succeeding Mr. Rockefeller at the end of this month."

Matthew slugs down his drink, sits back in his chair, and looks at Archbold from the kitchen. "John...you lucky bastard," he shouts. "You know, there was a time I thought I was going to get that job."

O'Day grits his teeth and glances at Archbold. "That's why we're here, Matthew. Mr. Rockefeller wants to see you first thing in the morning."

Matthew clasps the bottle. "What's he want?"

"Do you really need more of that?" O'Day asks him.

"You must know what the old prick wants," Matthew says, pouring himself another.

Archbold walks into the kitchen and stares down at him. "We most certainly do. He wants to talk about your job."

Matthew brings the tumbler to his lips as O'Day pulls one of the chairs out from the table, sits down beside him and looks into his eyes. "You know, Matthew, we tried to keep you busy, tried to keep your mind off things. We thought the jobs we gave you these past months here in New York would help get you back on track. Get you out of Cleveland, away from all the memories. Maybe help you make a new start."

Archbold frowns. "But it's had the opposite effect, that's for sure."

Matthew looks up at him. "What does Mr. Rockefeller want to talk about?"

"Good God, man, have you heard anything we've said?" Archbold shouts.

"Yeah, I heard you the first time, John. He wants to talk about my work. What else?"

O'Day leans forward. "Matthew, Mr. Rockefeller hasn't been well. That's one reason he's retiring from active business...with his stomach problems and the hair thing, both of which are being brought on by stress, he's made the decision to slow down, pursue other interests, like his philanthropic endeavors."

"His what?" Matthew asks.

"Charity work, you fucking moron!" Archbold bellows. "What's with you?"

"What's with me?" Matthew shouts back. "You want to know what's with me? How much time you got, John?"

O'Day sighs. "We know it hasn't been easy for you, Matthew."

Matthew refreshes his glass. "Do you now, Daniel? Do you know what it's like to lose all the people you love?"

"I know what it's like to lose loved ones," O'Day replies. "Yes, of course I do."

"Do you know what it's like to have a wife lose her mind...spend money faster than you could make it, drive you to the poorhouse?" Matthew points around his kitchen and into the living room. "I mean, look at this shit hole."

Archbold smirks. "You've got that right."

O'Day shakes his head. "Matthew, you divorced Melissa four months ago. You've been earning good money for all that time."

"My investments have gone sour...drained me dry."

"Yeah, that's another subject the old man wants to talk about," Archbold adds, "your little secret deals in Texas."

Matthew downs another gulp of bourbon and wipes his mouth. "Everybody's entitled to a few side bucks. What the hell's wrong with that?"

"Yeah, well, you can talk to Mr. Rockefeller about it in the morning," Archbold replies. "Make no mistake…he'll give you a few thoughts on the subject."

Archbold turns to O'Day. "Let's go, Daniel. I think we've given our friend here enough to mull over tonight."

The men head for the door, but Matthew doesn't get up. "You know, we *are* going to miss him!" he shouts.

"You're right about that," O'Day replies from the hallway. "Mr. Rockefeller has been the steady hand that's guided this company from the start."

"You bet your ass we'll miss him!" Archbold shouts back. "Just don't forget to show up tomorrow!" he adds, slamming the door behind him.

Matthew's hands shake even more now. He clasps the neck of the Early Times, turns it upside down, and drains what remains. He brings the tumbler to his lips, trying to decide whether this would be it for the night, or if the evening's sufficiently young to crack open another bottle.

The assistant opens the door to John D. Rockefeller's corner office, turns to Matthew, and says, "You may go in, Mr. Strong. Mr. Rockefeller is waiting for you."

Matthew enters the large room, but he doesn't see JDR. The drapes are drawn, and it's dark inside, which Matthew thinks strange. Then he sees the oil king standing in the corner.

My God, what's happened to him? he thinks.

Rockefeller's appearance has changed radically from the last time Matthew saw him a few months ago. He's lost every follicle of hair on his body—the hair on his head, his moustache, eyebrows, other facial hair, the hair on the back of his hands—all gone. He's also lost his color. He's sheet-white, and his skin has the texture of dried parchment. He's bloated, and in Matthew's mind, JDR looks very much like the octopus the newspapers are fond of calling his sprawling empire.

Ironic, he thinks.

JDR walks across the room and shakes hands with the man who was once his protégé. "You are finding it hard to recognize me, aren't you, Matthew? Don't feel bad, you're not alone. I was at a dinner hosted by J.P. Morgan two weeks ago, and I was seated beside Charles Schwab, president of U.S. Steel. I knew he had no idea who he was sitting next to, so I turned to him and said, 'I see you don't know me, Charley. I'm Mr. Rockefeller.'"

"What has happened, sir?" Matthew asks, feeling JDR's penetrating eyes looking him over. He wishes he'd worn a fresh suit, but he hasn't had one cleaned or pressed in weeks.

"This condition, if one can call it that, is called alopecia. The doctors don't know much about it. They say it may be genetic, or brought on by constant stress. Either way, the result's the same. You lose every bit of hair on your body."

"Is there a cure?"

"None the doctors know of."

JDR walks over to his desk, picks up the newspaper and points across the room to a black skullcap hanging on the coat rack. "Before you arrived, I was reading an article about me. You probably haven't seen me in that skullcap, but I wear it when I go outdoors so my scalp doesn't get sunburned. So listen to this."

JDR puts on his glasses and begins reading aloud. "'Under his silk skullcap he seems like an old monk of the Inquisition such as one sees in the Spanish picture galleries.'" He throws the newspaper onto his desk. "Imagine having to endure such drivel, on top of everything else!"

There's a knock on the door, and an attendant enters carrying a tray containing a glass of milk, a napkin and a plate of soda crackers.

"It's come to this," JDR says, watching the attendant remove the items and place them on the conference table. "I'm reduced to eating milk and crackers, almost for every meal…my digestive problems have acted up so. Let's sit down."

JDR sits in the middle of the rectangular table, and Matthew takes his usual place across from him.

"It's taken its toll," JDR begins, "but the Standard has grown into a giant. We control nearly a third of all the oil produced in the United States. We have twenty thousand oil wells, four thousand miles of pipelines, five thousand tank cars. We employ more than one hundred thousand workers, and ship seventy thousand barrels of crude oil a day to Europe. Our refineries make eighty percent of the kerosene for this country."

"It's a magnificent creation, Mr. Rockefeller," Matthew says. "But the pressure *has* affected you, hasn't it?"

"That's one reason why Archbold is taking over, to get me out from the grind of the day-to-day responsibilities. Henry Flagler has left as well, to operate hotels in Saint Augustine and in Ormond Beach, Florida, plus run his railroads. He has a plan to build a line all the way to Key West. Can you imagine?"

"It must be costing him a fortune."

"Speaking of money, Matthew, did I ever tell you my philosophy of money? It's this: I believe it is a religious duty to get all the money you can, fairly and honestly; to keep all you can, and to give away all you can."

Rockefeller stares at him. "Can you say the same, Matthew?"

"Same what, sir?"

"That you accumulated your money fairly and honestly?"

"I believe that's the case, Mr. Rockefeller."

"You don't think you blurred the line between opportunities that should have been brought to the Standard's attention, and those that you pursued for personal gain?"

Matthew shifts in his chair. "I can't think of an instance."

"Not with your Oil Exchange activities based on inside knowledge of those Pennsylvania wells?"

How in the world does he know about that? Matthew thinks.

"Or your investments in Texas when you set up that exploration and production company. You didn't see a conflict of interest?"

Matthew takes a deep breath. "Sir, do you remember the first night we met?"

"Of course I do," Rockefeller replies. "It was outside the Euclid Avenue Baptist Church in Cleveland."

"It feels like yesterday," Matthew says. "Yet it's going on seventeen years ago. I remember running home; I remember how happy I was you'd given me my chance. I was walking on air."

"Those were heady days," JDR says, nodding.

"But it's like whenever I find happiness, tragedy follows. It's like disaster lurks around every corner. I've lost my brother, my father, my precious daughter ...."

"I know, and I can't tell you how sorry I am, Matthew," JDR says. "I never told you this, but Mrs. Rockefeller and I lost our second child, our daughter Alice, a year after she was born in 1870."

"I didn't know, sir. Tell me, does the pain ever go away?"

"Sometimes," Rockefeller replies. "But these tragedies have changed you, Matthew. Understandably, but nonetheless, they've made you a different person, someone we don't even know anymore."

Matthew stares into the darkened room. "I don't know if I can go on, sir. I can't think of anything but Maddy's murder."

"You do realize, Matthew, it's probably best for you to leave Standard Oil," Rockefeller says. "I don't think this comes as any surprise. Given your performance for the last year or so, I think you know it's time for you to move on."

"That's true, sir," Matthew says. "I know I need to do something different, regain my footing, start again, if I can. Everything I've built has been destroyed."

Rockefeller leans forward in his chair. "Don't take offense at this, Matthew, but I believe you're contributing to your current problems. That's the reason a change could do you good, let you go after something new, something that doesn't involve the responsibilities we face here every day in this business. I'm moving on as well."

Matthew shakes his head. "I can't argue with you, sir."

"Then, we agree your leaving is a mutual decision, something that would benefit all of us?"

"We do," Matthew replies, rising, and JDR gets up as well.

"You were right about one thing," Rockefeller says as they head toward the door.

"What's that, sir?"

"Do you remember that management committee meeting we had here after your Toledo breakfast with Fleshner...the session where you predicted the criticism from the media and others?"

"I remember it well, sir."

"You were right."

"From everything I've read, I'm sad to say, I was," Matthew says.

"Tarbell and that hypocrite, Henry Demarest Lloyd, trashing our good works, everything we've accomplished," Rockefeller adds.

Matthew can see that JDR is getting agitated, and he reaches in his pocket and pulls out his special pen.

"Do you remember this, sir?" He holds it in front of him.

"I certainly do. You still have it, I see. I almost didn't hire you because of that pen. I have always felt it's too ostentatious, too gaudy for a respectable businessman to carry."

"I'm not going to own it for much longer," Matthew tells him. But I do believe this pen had a role in my meeting you that Wednesday night, and in creating many of the opportunities Standard Oil gave me over the years. And for that, Mr. Rockefeller, I can't thank you enough."

JDR extends his hand. "You take care of yourself, Matthew Strong. You did give us many years of fine service, and I honestly thank you for your hard work. I'm so very sorry for your loss. And, the indiscretions we spoke of earlier…well, I suppose they can be seen in the context of an otherwise admirable career. Who knows, maybe our paths will cross again."

Matthew nods, but doesn't say anything more. He ends their handshake, turns and walks out the door.

The trolley stops at 48th Street, and Matthew jumps off and walks into a small storefront with large yellow block letters across its facade: Gold's Pawn Shop. He clasps his pen and approaches the clerk behind the counter.

"What will you give me for this?"

The man puts on an eyepiece that magnifies the diamond, and he studies it closer, rotating the pen to capture the rock's every angle. He runs the jewel over a piece of glass, and Matthew winces at the scraping sound.

"This is a fine, custom-made pen," the man finally says. He reaches into his cash drawer, removes fifty dollars and lays it on the counter.

"I was thinking a hundred," Matthew says.

"How about sixty?"

"Make it seventy-five and you've got a deal."

The clerk pulls out another twenty-five dollars and adds it to the other bills. "Do you want to set up a payment plan so I won't sell it?"

"No," Matthew replies, "I've no idea what my money situation's going to be, so I can't make any commitments."

The clerk shrugs. "Suit yourself."

Matthew leaves the shop and walks to Rebecca's mansion on Park Avenue. He knocks on the door and a maid opens it. "Oh, Mr. Strong, please come in," she says.

Rebecca is having breakfast in the conservatory, and she looks up as her son enters. "Matthew! What brings you here so early?"

He can see her looking him over, and he suspects that she's unnerved by his disheveled appearance, but she doesn't embarrass him by saying so.

"Mother, I've come to say goodbye. I'm going to Texas."

"Texas? For how long?"

"I'm going there to live. I've resigned from Standard Oil."

"Resigned? Matthew, why?"

"I need a fresh start, Mother. I can't face anything anymore."

Rebecca rises, putting her teacup aside. She walks over to her son and hugs him, tighter than ever before. "Oh, my dear boy, I'm so sorry." She rests her head on his shoulder and begins to cry. He throws his arms around her, drawing her closer.

"You sure you want to do this?" she whispers.

"I have to, Mother. I have no choice. I'll write when I get settled, get to feeling better."

Rebecca regains her composure, and she steps back a few feet from her son. "Are you taking your father's gift with you?"

"I'm not...I had to hock it for train fare and pocket money for the trip west and for a stop in Oil City I'm making along the way."

"You did what?" Rebecca says.

"I brought the pen to a pawn shop and hocked it."

"Why would you do that? Why didn't you come to me for the money? I would have given you what you needed. In fact, let me get you some now. You're going to need money in Texas."

Rebecca begins to leave, but Matthew grabs her and throws his arms around her again. "No, Mother, I can't accept your money. I have to do this on my own. It's the only way back."

She starts crying again, and Matthew does, too. They stand in the center of the room, embracing, with Rebecca clinging to her son even harder. Matthew wonders if their tears and their pain will ever go away.

MEMORIES IN THE WIND

Muleface McCoy looks like one of those old dusty-gray donkeys that kids hop on for a two-cent ride around the ring at the county carnival, and Matthew spots him on the other side of the smoke-filled Down Hole Saloon the moment he walks through the door. McCoy is sitting in the same chair, at the same table drinking the same brand of whiskey as on that March afternoon so many years earlier. Matthew had been a teenager in search of his father that day. Now he isn't sure what he's looking for.

Muleface has aged, of course, and Matthew notices he's lost his left arm. But aside from that, he appears pretty much the same: downing his shots, cracking jokes, eyeing the whores, shooting the pretty ones his patented buck-toothed grin.

The old nitroglycerin hauler looks up, drops his drink, and turns white as a ghost. "Blessed Baby Jesus!" he shouts. "It's Caleb Strong, back from the dead!"

"Not Caleb, but his son, Matthew...remember me?" Matthew's words are slurred, and he grips the side of a chair to steady himself.

"Well, I'll be damned, I must say I do," stammers Muleface, turning to the other men at the table. "This here's Caleb Strong's son. I'm certain you never knew 'em, but I used to deliver nitro to his pa. He was a well shooter, one of the best, but he died a good many years back... blown to smithereens on the job. What brings you to Oil City, son?"

"They tell me there's still some good card action to be had around here," Matthew jokes. "Got room for a fifth?"

"Table's always open for more players," one of the men mumbles.

"Bring us a bottle of whiskey and five shot glasses... on me!" Matthew hollers at the barkeep, pulling out a chair and joining the others. "Where's Jack Thackery?" he asks as he sits down.

"Same place my arm ended up," Muleface replies. "Blown to bits 'bout five years back. We knew it would happen one of these days. It always does."

The bartender comes up to the table with the glasses and booze, and he places them in front of Matthew, who grabs the bottle and pours the shots. "Toast," he says, raising his glass as the others follow suit. "To my father, Caleb Strong and to his friend, Jack Thackery, who lived and worked in this town... and to Muleface's left arm, wherever the fuck it is, may they all rest in peace!" They click glasses, drain them, and Matthew quickly reaches around the table, refilling the shots.

After a couple of hours and a second bottle of booze, Muleface's thin lips part to reveal his buck-toothed wonders. "It's time," he mumbles.

"For what?" Matthew asks.

"Time to cut for the poke. Ante up. Buck apiece."

"You guys still drawing for whores?" Matthew replies, watching the men pitch silver dollars into the center of the table.

"Come on, Matthew" Muleface goads. "Cough up a buck. You tellin' me you couldn't use a woman right now, especially after the number of pops you've had? They got some lookers upstairs."

"Yeah," adds one of the men, pointing at McCoy. "Some even stupid enough to go for an old stump mule like him."

"Come on," Muleface implores. "It'll be just like the old days, 'cept you'll be playin' for your pa. It'd make him proud. You know, for old time's sake, you takin' his place and all!"

"Oh, what the hell," Matthew says, reaching in his pocket and throwing a dollar in the pot.

The men draw cards, and Matthew pulls a king; the three others draw a two, an eight and a jack.

Muleface launches into his routine, scrunching up his face up like he's about to eat a sack of sour oats. He bends forward, fans the deck, and pulls out a card. He lays it face-down on the table, pauses for a moment, and flips it over. It's an ace of diamonds.

He smiles and looks at Matthew. "I knew you wasn't gonna win. Your pa never did neither, no offense intended."

"None taken," Matthew says, scanning the room. He sees that the bewhiskered piano player is still plinking the ivories, except now he's so hunched over his nose and white beard appear to be brushing the keys along with his fingers. Matthew looks at the packed bar and the filled tables, and then back at Muleface, who's in the process of scraping his chair across the floor to stand up.

"Pleasure to see ya again, my boy," Muleface says, giving Matthew a slap on the back. "Hope you'll pardon my manners, me runnin' off the way I am, but duty calls." He winks and grabs the money from the middle of the table.

"Looks like things haven't changed that much here after all these years, have they?" Matthew says to him.

His father's old friend makes his way toward the stairs, but before he goes up he turns and replies, "For the most part, I'd say that's true, 'cept we're payin' more for whiskey...and the price of whores' gone up, too!" His gangly frame ambles up the steps, and a moment later, Muleface disappears down the second floor landing.

Matthew bids the others goodbye, and walks outside, heading down Seneca Street toward Doc Willetts' office.

A couple of blocks from the saloon, he comes on an emaciated man in tattered clothes sitting on the stoop of a vacant store. Matthew can tell the man is blind because his eyes look like cloudy dead marbles, and his head bobs from side-to-side in an erratic motion as if it's a broken pendulum. Every twenty to thirty seconds the man erupts into profane outbursts, jerking his body, and screaming in diseased rasps at anyone who happens to be passing by. He wears a rusty tin can on a string around his neck, and on the can is a card with the scribbled words: Dying, please help!

The man is Augustus Clapp, and Matthew can't believe how small he's become. His once massive arms are now mere sticks, and his rat teeth are all missing, rotted from his head. The fearful enforcer is wasting away, disappearing with each passing day.

Matthew approaches him, keeping his distance because Clapp's smell is repulsive, overwhelming.

"Where's your club, Augustus?" he says to him.

Clapp's dead eyes dart aimlessly, and he opens his mouth, but no words come out.

"I thought you went everywhere with your club?"

Clapp cocks his head back and screams, "Rats and razors, bucket o' water at the circus teat!"

Matthew realizes Clapp's club isn't anywhere to be seen. In its place, lying on the sidewalk next to the stoop, are two decrepit wooden crutches.

"I give him another month, maybe less," a voice behind him says. "He's really quite gone." Matthew turns and is amazed to see Doc Willetts standing before him. "How are you, Matthew?" says the doctor. "It's been a long time."

Matthew and his old friend embrace, and the doc seems to catch a whiff of his breath, and a frown crosses his face.

"It's good to see you again, sir. It's been too long," Matthew says.

Willetts walks over to Clapp and puts a bottle of laudanum in his quivering hands. "It's about all I can do for him at this point… try and ease his pain as best I can," he says. "I'm on my way to look in on a sick patient on the other side of town, but I have a few minutes to catch up on things. How's your mother?"

"She's fine," Matthew replies, reaching in his pocket and pulling out a couple of dollar bills. He places them in Clapp's can. "Here's something for you, Augustus," he says. "Don't lose it. Go buy some food or medicine with it."

"He'll just spend that on booze," the doc says, shaking his head and looking down at the syphilis-riddled man. "But one never knows."

"How've you been?" Matthew asks, walking unsteadily down the sidewalk next to the doc.

"All-in-all, getting along fairly well," the doc replies. "No complaints."

"And Lavinia?"

"She's married, has a baby boy. She's happy, still living in Chicago."

"Wish I could say the same," Matthew answers. "Trouble has followed me everywhere since the days I used to work for you."

"Word is you've achieved great things at Standard Oil."

"I've left the Standard, sir. My problems are just too much to handle. Unless I get them under control, they're going to overtake me."

The doc shakes his head again and frowns. "I said a moment ago, Clapp would just take that money you gave him and use it to buy liquor. That's the last thing he needs in his condition, and I could say the same thing about you now!"

"What are you talking about?" Matthew asks.

"It's obvious you've been into the bottle already today. I'd say more than a little, and I'll tell you as we stand here, Matthew, that's not the answer to your problems."

"If it isn't, I haven't found what is."

"Then look harder!" Willetts hollers, grabbing Matthew by the shoulders. "And stand up and walk, and walk tall, walk like a man, don't simply stumble around looking for a handout like Clapp or some other two-bit drunk! The bar and that bottle you're wrapping your life around are nothing more than cheap excuses that cloud your judgment, drain your wallet, and pull you into stinking latrines to piss away your future!"

Doc Willetts lets go of his grip and resumes walking down the sidewalk. He stops and turns to Matthew. "I heard about your daughter, son, and I'm so very sorry. But let me ask you something, Matthew. Why'd you come back to Oil City after all this time?"

"I want to talk to my Pa," Matthew says, staggering a bit, trying to steady himself.

"You're going to his gravesite?" Willetts asks.

"Yes. But first I'm headed to the Farris fields."

"There's not much out there anymore," the doc replies. "Oil production stopped years ago. It's just open land now."

"I bet I can find the spot I'm looking for," Matthew says, stepping closer to the doctor. "You know I love your daughter. I always have. I've never stopped loving her. It's just that I always thought I was never good enough for her."

Matthew's words seem to disarm the old doctor, and Willetts smiles at him. "Why don't you borrow my wagon and team for the ride out to the Farris property? They're in the same stable we used to go to. Just bring them back when you're done, leave them with the livery hand."

Matthew remembers the boy who tended the stable years ago who used to hang around for tips after each fatal nitroglycerin blast, seeming to revel in the constant death and destruction.

The doc appears to read his mind.

"Oh, don't worry," Willetts says, smiling. "That greedy little bastard who worked there when you were a kid is long gone. I hear he went into politics."

It's a bright and clear afternoon, so different from that miserable morning in 1870 when Matthew had last walked this land.

Where there was once only mud, pools of surface oil, fouled water and smoking debris, thick green grass and trees now grow and thrive. There isn't a hint of the derricks that had dotted the Farris tract, or the wagon ruts that had radiated from the wells, or the maze of pipelines that had replaced the wagons as transport for the field's long-lost output. All are gone, restored to a tranquil landscape that belied the hellhole of yesteryear.

Matthew walks to the center of what is now a lush pasture, and he feels a slight depression under his feet.

This is the spot, he thinks. *This is where the blast happened that took Pa.* I'm sure of it.

He tries to remember the boundaries of the destruction, but the place has changed so, and it's difficult to get any bearings. Then he recalls the direction in which he'd first noticed the glimmer of his special pen, the calling of his gift, and he heads up a rise fifty yards toward the forest's edge. The trees are larger now, more majestic in their hypnotic sway, and he stops where he'd once found his rainbow.

He falls to his knees, closes his eyes, and clasps his hands together. "I've let your gift go, Pa, and I don't know why. On this very spot, you gave me the light that cut through darkness and led my way. But that darkness always followed me everywhere I went, and I could never shake it, no matter how high I climbed, no matter what I achieved, or how much money I made. Now, I've let your legacy slip through my fingers for a few measly dollars. And why? I could have gotten the money somewhere else, but I didn't... didn't even try. Was it that I wanted to get rid of my past, rid myself of the demons I thought went along with your gift? The demons you wrestled with all your life? Or was it because I wanted to hurt you... hurt you like you hurt me when you disappeared right here into hell's fire?"

The winds become more pronounced, and the swaying trees surrounding the pasture begin to rock and lean more violently with each powerful gust. The grasses in the pasture undulate like waves in a vast greenish bay. Every time they bend, they reveal their pale undersides.

Matthew opens his eyes and watches the grasses twist.

"Am I like this grass, Pa," he asks, "tough and coated on the outside, but white and weak within? Do I buckle to weakness at the first sign of a storm? I walked away from a loveless marriage, leaving her everything I owned, everything

I'd worked so hard for, but I ask you … should I have been stronger? Should I have tried harder and made my marriage work? But how could it have worked after we lost our little Maddy?"

The trees shake as the leading edge of a spring gale sweeps through the valleys and hollows of Venango County.

"Forgive me, Pa, for pawning your gift, for turning away from it. Forgive me for being unworthy of what you wanted that pen to bring me. That's why I had to let it go. I have to seek my own way now, go to Texas and get back some of what I've lost. Make a life there and not look back on the past. You understand, don't you, Pa?"

Matthew gets up, and the gusts pound him, ruffling his clothes, sweeping his graying hair off his forehead and backwards away from his face. The trees rock under the tempest to come, and a huge limb high in one of the towering pines snaps and plunges to the ground.

Matthew watches it crash at the edge of the pasture, and the broken branch makes him recall the horror of the lost life this place will always hold. He fights his way through the tunnel of wind and memories, and climbs into Doc Willetts' wagon for the trip back to town.

Part III
Corsicana, Texas
Three Months Later

LONE STAR

Blaze Clayburn yanks a faded red handkerchief out of his jeans pocket and runs it across his sweat-drenched brow. He shakes his head and squints at the blistering July sun high in the sky over the parched Corsicana field where he and his men are drilling a new exploration well. The tiny Texas hamlet southeast of Dallas hasn't seen a drop of rain in three months, and this is the eighth-straight day the thermometer has topped a hundred degrees by noontime.

He looks down the dirt utility road through the undulating bands of rising heat and sees a man dressed in a dark wrinkled suit walking toward him. Blaze narrows his eyes even further to catch a better view of the approaching stranger.

"Is it always this hot in Texas?" a famished and overheated Matthew asks, as he comes up to Blaze and his men a few minutes later.

Blaze appears shocked. "Why Matt Strong...I thought ya done fell off the face of the earth!" He takes a closer look at the sunburned man standing before him. "What, ya *walk* all the way here from Cleveland?"

"No, just from the train station."

"That's enough of a hike this time of day." Blaze replies. "Better than three miles, I'd reckon."

"Tell me about it," Matthew says.

"Come on, let's git out of the sun, and git ya some water. You gotta be as parched as a horned toad."

They walk a hundred yards from the drill site to a large stand of pecan trees and into a tent Blaze uses as his prospecting office. Matthew sits down at a table covered with property maps and drawings of well sites, and he sees Blaze's divining rod in a corner, propped up against the canvas wall.

Blaze places a jug of water in front of him and then reaches into a crinkled brown bag and removes two ripe peaches. "The water ain't cold," he says, "but it's wet. And here, eat these ... they'll perk 'ya up."

Matthew takes a long, slow swig from the jug, and bites into a peach, and its juice trickles off his lips and falls on his pant leg. Blaze watches him, smiling.

"So, where the hell ya been hidin', Matt?"

"I really can't say. These past few months have been a blur."

"It's been a hell of a lot longer than a few months, pardner," Blaze replies. "But I'm glad to tell ya Tex E an' P Co. finally hit a couple of wells over in our field in Nacogdoches. They ain't huge, but they been flowin' steady, give or take, fifty-to-seventy-five barrels a day since they come in. I been mailin' royalty checks to ya at yer office."

"I know you sent something, because I'd receive envelopes forwarded to where I was staying in Pennsylvania the past few months."

"Ya never cashed the checks."

Matthew gulps down another slug of water. "Never opened the envelopes."

"Too busy?"

"Didn't give a damn."

"Well anyway," Blaze says, "I been depositin' that money in a special Tex E an' P Co. bank account for ya all this time, once I realized ya weren't cashin' what I was sendin'. 'Course, I been deductin' yer share of expenses from what's been goin' in … costs of runnin' the business and all."

Matthew can't believe it. "How much money do I have?" he asks.

"'Bout seven thousand bucks."

"You've been doing that, putting money in a bank, after not hearing from me all this time?"

Blaze grabs a peach from the bag and takes a bite. "Don't fergit, early on ya backed Tex E an' P Co. every time I asked ya for money, even sometimes sendin' more than I needed. Then ya dropped out of sight, but by the time ya did, the company was makin' a small profit, and we were able to hold our own. Certainly able to hold our head above water. Fact is, I didn't need to come to ya any more."

"Well I'll be damned," Matthew says, shaking his head. "How'd you know I'd show up someday?"

"I didn't," Blaze says. "But puttin' aside what was owed ya, keepin' things square between us, between you and Tex E an' P Co., was the right thing to do."

Matthew looks around the cramped office. "So, Blaze," he says, "what do you have going on here?"

Blaze smiles at him. "You mean, what do *we* have goin' on here."

Matthew nods, still not believing what he's hearing. He glances over at the property maps in front of him on the table.

"Those won't tell ya much," Blaze says with a wave of his hand. "What we got goin' here is an exploration play. We've drilled two dry holes, and we're workin' on a third prospect now. That's the well you passed comin' in. I got a feelin' 'bout that one, though we're hittin' some gumbo and pressures downhole that could foul things up for us real bad."

"What's your drill depth?" Matthew asks.

"Target's two hundred seventy-five feet, and we're almost at two-ten now. If we can push out of the trouble, I think we'll see somethin' good, maybe in the next day or so."

"I want to work on the wells with you, Blaze," Matthew says. "I want to learn the other side of this business, learn it from the ground up."

Blaze flashes wide smile. "Now yer talkin', Matt, and, Lord knows, we could use the help. But if yer goin' to work on the wells, you'll have to ditch that fancy New York suit of yours."

Matthew looks down at himself and laughs. "It's seen better days, that's for sure."

Blaze gets up and walks over to a lock box on the tent floor. He opens it, withdraws a piece of paper, and hands it to Matthew.

"That's the number to your bank account. I'll have one of the boys drive you into town, and after you visit the bank...Wells Fargo, by the way...check into the Texas House Hotel. They got good rooms there, and you'll be able to clean up, eat a decent meal, and git a good night's sleep. But before you do that, go to Carter's Dry Goods and git yourself two or three pairs of jeans, some cotton shirts, underwear, wool socks...make sure they're thick enough to ward off blisters...gloves and a pair of heavy-duty work boots. Oh, yeah, and don't forgit to buy a decent Stetson. You'll need it under that sun ya got a taste of today."

"What time should I be here in the morning?"

"I'll have one of the boys pick ya up at five thirty."

"Where do you stay?"

"I sleep out here in the bunk tent with the other men. We usually have a couple workers on the drill all night, and I like to stick close."

"I'll join you here starting tomorrow," Matthew replies. He takes a deep breath, feeling more alive in the last hour than he has in years.

He emerges from the morning haze like a cardboard cutout that's fallen into a vat of fast-drying glue. His jeans are pressed and stiff, his boots unyielding. His brand-new shirt doesn't have a wrinkle anywhere on it, and his Stetson looks like it's carved from stone. His movements are mechanical and measured, and he walks up to the men at the derrick stiff and slow, as if dressed in a suit of armor.

Blaze takes one look at him and doubles over laughing. "Pardner," he finally blurts out, "either ya bought those clothes two sizes too small, or we got to git ya out for a good day's work 'an loosen 'em up on ya!"

"No offense," jokes one of the men, "but you're walkin' like you got a load in your pants!"

"Yeah, with no outhouse in sight!" Blaze adds, laughing even more.

Matthew knows he looks like an Eastern dandy dressed up like a cowboy on his first day at a dude ranch.

"Come here," Blaze says, waving his arm. Matthew walks up to him, and his partner grabs his Stetson off his head, whacks it against his thigh about five or six times, then tosses it to the ground. He stomps on it as hard as he can, picks it up, and punches it back into some semblance of its original shape.

"Take it," Blaze says, dusting it off. "It ought to feel better after that poundin'. Now, why don't ya git yer gloves on and come with me up on the derrick floor. I'm gonna teach ya how to drill an oil well."

They climb on the derrick and join a worker who's watching the cable rod guide the drill pipe up and down, forcing it deeper into the ground.

"Good job, Chris," Blaze shouts over the pounding of the steel. "We'll take over now. You go catch yourself some shut eye." Blaze walks the man over to the side of derrick and speaks with him briefly.

Then he rejoins Matthew. "Chris tells me he's gotten through that pressure pocket that was worryin' us. I 'spect we should be in good shape now."

Forty-five minutes later, Blaze and Matthew slide the cable tool to the side of the derrick wall and climb down to retrieve another piece of eight-foot piping. Each man takes an end, and they carry it back up to the drilling floor, and together they screw it to the pipe already in the ground. They tighten the connection with a couple of wrenches, pull the plunger back into place, and give the signal to the boiler man to engage the steam engine. In less than a minute, the rod begins pushing the pipe downhole again.

They work side by side, repeating that process five more times over the next eight hours.

The sun beats down, and the temperature climbs, but Matthew can't believe how good he feels. His clothes are soaked in sweat, and he's using muscles he didn't even know he has. It's great to be outdoors, working harder than he's ever worked in his life, and he thinks that this is so much better than sitting in some office pushing paper.

He's excited, too… excited at the chance of finding a prize deep underground, like digging for buried treasure or prospecting for gold. He feels a pure kind of adventure and excitement, like the thrill kids have on Christmas Eve wondering if they're going to get that special gift they want.

He can feel the sensation in the pit of his stomach, and he loves every minute of it.

He sees Blaze look up at the late afternoon sun, pull his red handkerchief out of his back pocket, and swipe it across his face. "Okay," he says to Matthew, "time fer the next crew to take over."

"You think we're close?" Matthew asks.

"I got a feelin' tomorrow's gonna be it," Blaze replies. "With what we accomplished today, plus what Chris did last night, I'd say we only got another forty feet or so to go before we hit pay dirt."

"I can't believe it," Matthew says. "In all the years I've worked in this business, I've never brought in an oil well. I've been around them enough, but I've never brought one home."

"Ya remember when we met that last time in yer office up in Cleveland?" Blaze asks. "Remember I told ya how great it is to work under the open sky, be yer own boss, search fer somethin' that ain't easy to find, but then when ya do find it, the feelin' ya git... the reward, the satisfaction?"

"I remember everything you said," Matthew replies. "But I didn't understand what you were really talking about."

"That's because you'd never experienced it."

"But I do now." Matthew says. "And, do you know what else?"

"Yeah, I do," Blaze answers. "It don't git much better than this, now, does it?"

Matthew just smiles. He looks up at the clean Texas sky and he feels strong. He feels like a man again.

Later that night, Blaze and Matthew sit side by side on a couple of logs eating chili and drinking cold beer. It's dark now, with clouds moving fast across the sky, making the night air cool and refreshing.

Blaze takes a swig and says, "Matt, let me ask ya something. When we were talkin' yesterday, ya mentioned the money problems ya had all those years, yer wife draining you dry and all."

"Yeah," Matthew says. "Even after I divorced her, I was still hit with bills for things she bought that I didn't know anything about. She hadn't been right in the head for years."

"So, why'd ya keep sending money to Tex E an' P Co.," Blaze asks. "Money I'm sure ya could have used fer other things. Money ya may not even *had* when ya sent it my way?"

"Don't give me credit for any of that, Blaze," Matthew says. "Remember, I didn't open a scrap of mail from you or anybody else for going on a year. For all I knew at the time, those letters were requests for more money."

"But, the point is, Matt, they weren't. Like I said, we'd passed that stage, and if I'd needed more cash, I would have found other money people to back me. I would have tracked ya down wherever ya were, and negotiated a buyout, just like you and I did with my investors when ya first came in."

"I still feel I turned my back on you," Matthew says, taking a drink of beer.

Blaze shakes his head. "I don't see it that way. But if *you* do, I'm sure ya have yer reasons."

Matthew looks over at the well and the two workmen tending to the drilling by lantern light. "I'd hit bottom and didn't care much about anything…my life, my job, my future. I fell into the bottle. This last year is a blur."

"Which gits me back to my original question," Blaze says. "Ya had to know you were goin' down before ya slipped off the deep end. Why'd you stick by Tex E an' P Co., when money, and I 'spect jus' 'bout everything else in yer life was goin' to hell in a handbasket?"

Matthew drinks a little more of his beer, and he feels proud of himself tonight, for although he knows Blaze keeps a couple of bottles of the hard stuff in the work tent, he hasn't wanted a drop of it. No shots to bolster his spirits and loosen his tongue. No boilermakers rushing to his brain to erase memories and bring thoughts of better times. None of it, and it's been that way for weeks now ... and he likes the feeling.

He looks at his partner. "I don't know the answer to your question, Blaze. "But if I ventured a guess, I think it's because Tex E and P Co. was my dream ... a dream I never knew I'd attain, but a dream nonetheless. When everything was falling apart, it was the only thing I had to hold on to ... that dream we talked about that morning in Cleveland after I got back from Europe. I couldn't let it go, and there's a side of me that thinks I was meant to come out here all along ... that everything that's happened before was getting me ready for what's about to happen."

"How long were ya married?" Blaze asks him.

"A little over five years. How about yourself." Matthew asks. "You ever been hitched?"

"Nah," Blaze says, shaking his head. "I've been close a couple of times, but bid'ness, or some other damn thing, has always gotten in the way. I've had my share of women, though. When ya get divorced?"

"A few months ago."

"Children?"

"A little girl, murdered at age four. We never found the killer."

Blaze shakes his head. "I'm mighty sorry, Matt. I can't even imagine goin' through somethin' like that. It's had to been tough for ya. Any other family left back East?"

"My mother, in New York. How are your folks?"

"Doin' well. Daddy's still runnin' the ranch and pissed off as ever I ain't a part of it. He hates the oil bid'ness, always will. But he's got a good crew workin' with him, so all the responsibility doesn't fall on his shoulders. Makes me feel a bit better I'm not there to help him, I guess. My momma's healthy and still keeps up the house. My sister Mariah is livin' with 'em, breedin' her quarter horses. How's yer mom gettin' along in New York City?"

"I visited her to say goodbye when I knew I was leaving. She seemed so sad…kind of like in her own world…acting like she did after my brother Luke died. At least that's the way she looked to me. I don't know what's bringing her down, but I know she's not happy with her second husband."

"Yer daddy's gone, too?"

"Yeah…years ago…few weeks after Luke. Lost him doing a well workover. Gone without a trace. He was a well shooter. I got there soon after it happened. I visited the place where it happened on the way here."

"Matt, yer comin' down on yourself way too hard," Blaze says. "You've gotta stop kickin' yourself. Because after what you've gone through, you have every reason in the world to have lost yer way, and no one can fault that. What's amazin' is ya look like yer determined to come back. And that's a good thing, and I hope I can help ya with that."

Blaze stands up. "I have to take a piss," he says. "This beer's goin' right through me. Gimme a minute."

Matthew watches him disappear behind a tree, and he looks up to see black clouds coating the sky, but suddenly the clouds part, and there's an isolated break in the cover. He stares at a solitary star shining above him.

Are you my star of hope? he thinks. *My star of promise? My lone star…come to guide me in this new place? Because, you know, I've been in the dark, looking for light. I've lost most everybody I ever loved, everything I cared about, everything I worked all my life for.*

Blaze returns and sits back down next to him, and the two men continue talking well into the night.

At dawn Matthew stands on the derrick floor next to Chris, his lead driller. The steam engine is cranked up and working hard, as the boilerman stokes the fire and watches the gauge. Behind him, a sliver of purple sunrise creases the horizon.

Blaze walks out of the darkness, smiling. "What y'all tryin' to do!" he shouts. "Make me look like I slept in this mornin'?"

"No!" Matthew shouts back. "But if today's the day...I want to get an early jump on things."

Blaze climbs up to the derrick and joins them. He bends down and takes a long whiff of the odor coming from the well. "Can ya smell it?" he asks.

"Yeah," Matthew replies. "We have to be getting close."

"We're gonna strike oil, fer sure," Blaze says. "Question is, how much she gonna flow?"

After about an hour more of drilling, they can hear natural gas coming out of the hole.

"Shut down the engine!" Blaze shouts, as he and Matthew grab the cable rod tool and slide it to the side. "Go careful, now!" he orders. "Don't hit any metal! We don't want a spark settin' off this gas!"

They can hear a rumbling underneath them, and in a few seconds, a steady stream of greenish-black crude oil starts bubbling up from below.

"You did it!" Matthew shouts, slapping Blaze on the back. "You said we'd hit pay dirt today, and you were right! Congratulations, old buddy! You brought her home!"

"Well, she ain't gonna make us millionaires," Blaze says, looking at the flow coming out of the well. "But if she holds up, I'd say we're lookin' at a hundred or so barrels a day. Tex E an' P Co. can use the cash, that's fer sure."

Matthew bends down and puts his hands in the crude oil coming up from within the earth, and he feels the liquid trickle through his fingers. The well's flowing steadier now, and he looks up at his partner. "There's going to be more, Blaze, a lot more, isn't there? I just know it!"

Blaze nods back at him and smiles. "Yeah, there's gonna be more, Matt, a hell of a lot more. Count on it. It's jus' a question of when and where!"

BELLY OF THE BEAST

B laze Clayburn was right: the discoveries came in rapid succession over the next year, and the once small Tex E & P Co. is now a substantial producer of oil and gas, with operations in Texas, Oklahoma, New Mexico and Louisiana. The company's offices take up the first floor of a brick building on Main Street in Houston.

Like they do most mornings when they aren't in the field working on one of their wells, Matthew and Blaze huddle in their conference room to plan their next exploration play.

"I been hearin' talk 'bout some prospectin' goin' on over in Beaumont," Blaze says. "Couple of fellas named Captain Lucas and Pattillo Higgins are drillin' a well at a place called Big Hill."

"What's so unusual about that?" Matthew asks.

"It got my interest up," Blaze replies. "So, I took a trip over there last week to take a look at things. I walked the entire knob, which is nothin' more than a low-prairie mound. But it's also a salt dome with pools of colored waters all over the place. Everywhere ya walk, yer hit with the smell of rotten eggs, sulfur and lemon phosphate."

"Nothing strange about that," Matthew says. "There's plenty of places around here where you get that."

"Right," Blaze says. "But, this place is different. I been readin' 'bout these salt domes they're findin' here in Texas, and over in Louisiana, and how some people think they're giant plugs in the ground that trap crude oil underneath 'em. But the problem everybody's runnin' into is borin' deep enough through the plug to reach the oil."

"How deep do you figure you'd have to go?" Matthew asks.

"'Bout a thousand feet or more."

Matthew just stares at his partner and doesn't say a word. They're now producing nearly fifty thousand barrels a day from some one hundred and eighty wells on their leases, but none of those wells is deeper than three hundred fifty feet. Blaze is talking about a well three times that depth.

Blaze seems to read his mind. "You know what the problem is?"

"I take it Lucas and Higgins haven't been successful," Matthew says.

"Right," Blaze answers. "And the problem is the equipment they're usin'. The cable-tool drills don't have the power. They jus' won't drill deep enough to git at the kind of oil we're talkin' 'bout. And we could be talkin' 'bout oceans of it. Gusher wells, like over in Russia."

"You're saying we need to buy one of those new rotary-type drills they've come out with," Matthew says. "You're saying that's the only way to penetrate a reservoir that deep. That a cable tool won't do the job?"

"That's the first thing we need to do," Blaze replies. "And those things ain't cheap, but we want the biggest they make. I was talkin' to a couple of drillers out there on the Lucas well and they tell me there are all sorts of problems they're runnin' into tryin' to punch that hill. There's pressure pockets and quicksand, and gumbo clays and calcium rock deposits and other things under Big Hill that people haven't run into before."

"Okay," Matthew says. "What else?"

"We need to lock up all the land around there, more than three-thousand acres, plus we need to buy the option on 'nother six hundred that Higgins and the Captain own, but haven't drilled on yet," Blaze replies. "I figure were talkin' an investment of at least a hundred thousand dollars for the property, drillin' equipment, crews, supplies... everything it's goin' to take to bring in a proper well."

Matthew again stares at his partner, not believing the scope of Blaze's proposal. "You're serious about this?"

"Dead serious," Blaze replies. "And, if yer agreeable, I'd like you to go out to Beaumont beginnin' this week to start lockin' up the land."

There's a knock on the conference room door, and it flys open and Chris Miller, their chief driller, interrupts them.

"Sorry to barge in on you like this, "Miller says, "but we got big problems on that well we're drillin' in the swamp at Sabine Pass. Got here as fast as I could."

Blaze gets up from the table. "What kind of problems?"

"The well's sidewall collapsed and is expandin' somethin' awful. I think it's makin' a sink hole. One of our men got sucked in and disappeared. The rig's gone, too."

"Who'd we lose?" Matthew asks.

"Charley Ingals."

Blaze shakes his head. "How many men you got out there?"

"Six."

"Anythin' comin' out of the hole?"

"She's spewin' gas."

"Shit," Blaze says, "that's all we need. One spark and the whole damn thing'll go up."

"Ain't gonna hurt nothin' 'cept the gators and moccasins," the driller replies.

"I suppose that's true." Blaze says. "That well's in the middle of no man's land."

Matthew stands up. "You head back to the site," he says to Miller. "We'll get a wagon and be right behind you."

It's early evening as Matthew and Blaze near the spot southeast of Sabine Pass where a crew of Tex E and P Co. workers have cut a rough trail through the moss-draped cypress trees, thick palmettos and high grasses of the vast swamp. Where there is more water than ground, which is most everywhere, the men have built wood-planked bridges supported by pilings or suspension cables so wagons and equipment can make the two-mile journey into the endless marsh to the work camp.

Less than an hour later, the partners cross the last bridge over the muck and floating islands leading to the drill site. They can hear the frantic shouts of the workers, for the well has, in fact, ignited. Matthew looks at the black ceiling of soot coating the sky, and he feels the rumble and roar of the inferno. Just above the quivering green leaves of a stand of bald cypress trees he can see yellowish-blue spikes of fire darting into the air. *Devil's fingers*, he thinks, *uncontained, escaped from their subterranean depths to wreak destruction and death. Just like it used to be in Oil City.*

Blaze reins back the horses, and they jump to the ground and run towards the fire.

An old steam pump runs full speed, drawing water from a murky bayou fifty feet away. Two men grip a heavy fabric hose that's spraying a powerful stream of water through its tapered nozzle toward the flames. A third worker mans the steam pump, watching its gauge, making sure the pressure's right.

"Aim the flow lower!" Blaze shouts to the men, who are dripping in sweat, their faces reddened by the heat. "More to the ground, not so high!"

The water from the hose has no effect on the column of fire vaulting from the blown-out well that's now expanded into a sinkhole forty feet across. Golden and reddish flames shoot from its center, and the flames are as thick around as sequoia trees, and nearly as tall. The ignited gases propel the deadly column skyward, dwarfing the men trying to bring it under control. The fire roars with the deafening, consuming intensity of a blast furnace.

"I told you to keep back from that hole, for Christ sakes!" Blaze bellows at the crew.

Suddenly, the ground gives way, and one of the workers holding the hose cascades into the cavern like a toy toppled from a table. Matthew rushes to the edge, but Chris Miller catches up with him, grabbing his boss from behind with both hands and spinning him around.

"Wait!" Miller shouts. "If you get too close to that hole, you're goin' in, too!"

The man below is hanging from the fire hose and crying for help. "Let's find some rope first," Miller says. "We'll tether ourselves to somethin' that's not goin' to get sucked in...just in case this thing gets bigger."

Blaze cups his hands around his mouth and shouts at the man tending the steam pump. "Drop what you're doin' and turn that pump off! Water's useless! Might as well be pissin' in a tornado."

Matthew singles out a worker. "You...go fetch us two ropes. Make sure both are plenty long enough. Go on now, and make damn sure they're not rotten or frayed!"

Once the worker returns with the ropes, Matthew and Miller each tie their lines to a tree a good distance from the sinkhole. They secure them around their waists, double-checking the knots. The men edge forward to the drop off and peer into the morass, recoiling from the intense heat.

The fire rages straight up from the center of the cavern, causing the watery mud around it to boil. Every few seconds they see the charred remains of Charley Ingals rise and disappear again in the percolating caldron. The heat continues to assault them, but they can't escape it if they are to save the stranded man. They see him suspended twenty feet down the sink hole, hanging above the flames. Suddenly, he slips to the end of the hose, and all that's keeping him from plummeting into oblivion is his grip on the brass nozzle, getting hotter by the second.

The stranded worker looks up and shouts: "Help me, I beg you! I can't hold on much longer!"

Matthew turns to Miller. "Chris, we can't risk pulling the hose up now or we're going to lose that man. I'm going down to get him."

"One of us has to, and fast," Miller replies.

Matthew motions for two other workers to come to the edge. "Get your gloves on and grab hold of my line!" he shouts. "Hold on tight!"

The men do as instructed and Matthew prepares to rappel down the side of the sinkhole. "Keep a good grip on the rope," he orders. "Make sure it's taut, and feed it out to me as I need it." Blaze joins them, grabbing a hold as well.

Matthew feels the fire's heat on his back, and he can feel the slushiness of the sinkhole wall as he kicks it and propels his body backwards into the pit. The stench of burning sulfur and methane begins to overtake him, and he shakes his head to clear his thoughts. He pushes off again, dropping another eight feet closer to the man.

"Help me! Oh God, help me!" screams the worker clinging to the nozzle. "I'm not going to make it!"

"Yes, you are!" Matthew shouts down at him, knowing time is working against him. He pushes off once more, dropping deeper, and he rappels a final time and comes even with the worker, who appears frozen in fear with a death grip on the hose, his clothes and hair singed from the heat.

"Take my hand!" Matthew shouts. Without wasting a second, the worker grabs Matthew's wrist, and he swings his other arm over Matthew's shoulder. He interlocks his hands around Matthew's chest, so he is now riding on his rescuer's back.

When Blaze sees both men on the rope he orders Miller and the other workers to begin hoisting them up. "Bring 'em up!" Blaze barks. "But go easy! I don't want 'em fallin' loose! Be careful!"

At that moment a column of fire shoots from the hole, and a section of the rim crumbles, and Blaze and his workers jump back to escape the cave in. As the edge of the sinkhole continues to give way, Matthew and the man drop several feet, but the rope draws tight again, and the crew at the rim is back in control, pulling them up higher, out of harm's way.

Matthew crawls from the sinkhole with the man on his back. He helps him to the ground, and the worker collapses on his back in exhaustion. "I didn't think I was goin' to make it," he murmurs. His body is shaking, and he looks like he's about to pass out.

"Let me see your hands," Matthew says.

The worker opens his palms, and Matthew sees the large, whitish-yellow blisters covering his skin.

"How the hell did you manage to hang on?" he asks.

"I've no idea," the man replies. "It was like claspin' a red-hot stove. I couldn't have lasted much longer."

Matthew motions for a crewman to come over. "Take this man to the work shed and give him water. He's got to be dehydrated. When you're in the shed, look for a large jar of salve. It should be in the medicine kit. Tend to his hands, after you get him comfortable. Make sure you put some blankets over him. I want you to stay with him until you're sure he's okay."

Later that night a thick mist envelopes the swamp, making the men barely distinguishable, even from a short distance away. Behind them, the fire still rages, and surrounding the massive flames, a moist cloud glows with a ghoulish greenish-blue hue, illuminated by the fire spewing from the belly of the beast.

Matthew and Blaze sit on a work bench down by the water, not saying a word, looking up at the inferno. Miller ambles up and stands in front of them. "What are you goin' to do," he asks. Leave 'er burnin'?"

Blaze wipes some sweat off his face. "As much as I'm tempted, we'll be comin' back, probably in a couple weeks, to tap this field again at a different location. If we let the gas burn off, we'll ruin the reservoir for extractin' oil."

"What ya got in mind?" Miller asks.

"Nothin' tonight," Blaze replies. "But I brought down a case of dynamite in the back of my wagon. In the mornin', in the daylight, we'll load a canister and put 'er into the pit. See if we can snuff this fucker out."

"Want me to git the explosives?" Miller asks. "Git 'em ready fer tomorrow?"

As the men talk, a pair of cold yellow eyes in the bayou watches them with unblinking resolve.

A worker walks out of the fog with a bucket in his hand. "The cook's makin' a meal for us," he says. "I'm gettin' him some water to boil for coffee."

Miller jumps up and grabs the pail. "I'll git it. You take a break. You already done enough today."

The eyes, invisible in the mist, follow Miller as he walks to the water's edge. The swamp has fallen silent, and all that can be heard or seen is the column of fire vaulting into the dripping heat of the summer night.

Miller bends down and puts the bucket into the bayou. He swishes it around a couple of times to try and remove the surface scum. Suddenly the monster shoots out of the water and grabs Miller's head in its jaws. The huge alligator disappears in a flash, swimming away from shore with its prey. A second later it goes into a death roll, keeping its flailing victim from taking a breath, clamping its crushing, tearing teeth down harder on Miller's neck.

Matthew and Blaze spring to their feet and rush to the spot where the creature has snatched up their friend. They can hear the roiling waves as the reptile continues thrashing, and Blaze pulls out his pistol and aims it in the direction of the sounds. But he hesitates and doesn't shoot.

"Shit! I can't see a thing!" he hollers to Matthew as a few other men run down and join them on the shore.

"What happened?" shouts one of workers, staring at the bucket laying on its side in the mud. "Where's Chris?"

"Mark my words," Blaze replies, turning to him. We're gonna find him," "I want two of you men to go up to my wagon. Bring back the dynamite ... and my shotgun!"

A few minutes later, Matthew maneuvers a rowboat into the mist. Blaze stands at its bow with a burning torch in his left hand and a stick of dynamite in his right. Behind them, obscured by the cover of fog, the dull glow of the well fire can barely be seen.

"Sometimes gators will take their prey to the bottom and jus' sit there," Blaze says, lighting the dynamite. "If that's so, this will bring 'em up."

He throws the explosive about fifteen yards to the right of the boat, and he watches the waterproof fuse sparkle as the bomb sinks into the murky depths. The blast is muffled, but a broad dome of water bursts up from the swamp. A few seconds later several dead carp, a water moccasin and a small alligator float to the surface.

Blaze draws another stick out of his belt. "Row us over that way, Matt," Blaze orders, pointing to another spot nearby. We'll see if we have any luck there."

After several more blasts, Blaze sits down in the bow of the boat and grabs his shotgun. "Okay," he says, "the damn thing must have taken him back to its den. Let's drift up 'an down the shore on the opposite side of the camp. We'll find the son o' bitch."

"We need to make sure Chris gets a proper burial," Matthew says.

"We will," Blaze replies, scanning the water. "Mark my words, we'll find 'em."

"We can't leave him out here." Matthew reiterates.

Blaze turns around and flashes an annoyed glance at his partner. "I jus' told ya, Matt. We ain't gonna leave him out here. How many times do I have to say it!"

They drift past the lairs of countless alligators, their dens cut deep into the muddy banks, half submerged by the swampy waters. Blaze crouches low in the bow of the boat, extending his torch into each entrance. Through the darkness of the subterranean tunnels he can see reflected in the flames bloodthirsty yellow eyes following his every move. A few of the creatures have their jaws open, baring inch-long teeth. As Blaze's eyes adjust, he sees the mouths and masses of muscles surrounding gullets throbbing with primal anticipation.

"We're lookin' fer a big 'un, a man-eater," he whispers to Matthew. "He's nearby. I can feel it."

Suddenly, out of the fog, the men see the headless body of Miller floating in the swamp. Several alligators swim around him, tearing chunks of flesh off his bones.

Blaze doesn't say a word. He draws his pistol from his holster and begins unloading bullets into the heads to the reptiles, singling out one after another. Matthew paddles to Miller's body, and they lean over the side and pull his remains into their boat.

Blaze notices something nearby on the water. "Hold up," he orders.

"You see something?" Matthew asks.

"I think we've found 'em."

Blaze lowers his torch closer to the swamp. "You see it?" he says.

Emanating from one of the largest dens is a bluish-green trail of crude oil, a nearly imperceptible slick sitting ghost-like on top of the mirrored water.

"Miller always had oil on his clothes from all the drillin' he did," Blaze whispers. "The gator's in there. And so's the rest of Chris."

Blaze stretches out in the front of the boat, leaning over the bow with his torch to get a better view. "Get me in closer," he tells Matthew.

Then he sees it, in the far corner of the den. The monster's eyes are wider apart than the others, and larger, and as the boat drifts nearer, it makes a harsh hissing sound like a rush of steam escaping from a broken steel pipe.

"Check with yer oar," Blaze orders. "Tell me how deep is it here."

Matthew stands up, removes the oar from its lock and juts it into the water. "About three feet," he says.

Blaze reloads his pistol and hands Matthew the torch and firearm. "I'm goin' in and shoot the damn thing. If any of his buddies come to his rescue...you know what to do with that gun."

Blaze double checks that his shotgun's loaded and the safety's off. He jumps out of the boat into the swamp, and the algae-riddled water rushes up to his waist.

"As I git closer, you follow me with the torch, so I can see," he tells Matt. "And keep yer finger on the trigger of that pistol. Don't be afraid to use it! On anything but me, that is."

Blaze inches his way toward the den, and can feel his boots sink into the mud. He points his shotgun straight in front of him and holds it high so it won't get wet.

The creature explodes out of its cave with the speed and force of a runaway train, and Blaze is momentarily blinded by the wall of rushing water and death propelling toward him. A second later, he regains his bearings and pulls the trigger to the right barrel of his gun, sending a load of number six steel shot into the reptile's mouth. A cloud of blood and broken teeth fly into the air, and the alligator crashes into the water, clamping its jaws around Blaze's thigh. He can make out the broad outline of the gator's head beside him, and it tightens its grip, and he can feel the monster begin to pull him under. He lowers the barrel of the shotgun into the water between the creature's eyes and pulls the other trigger. The second blast hit its mark, penetrating the beast's brain. The huge reptile releases Blaze from its clutches, and the creature begins to twitch and writhe on top of the water.

"Throw me my Colt, Matt," Blaze orders, clutching his shotgun with his left hand and snatching the pistol out of the air with his right one. He sinks deeper into the muck, and the water now comes up to his chest, but he makes his way over to the alligator that's now spinning aimlessly in its own death roll. Blaze unloads six consecutive shots from the pistol into the top of the animal's head.

"If it weren't dead before, it sure the hell is now," Blaze says. "Let's git a rope around this thing and bring it back to camp."

They row across the swamp and drag the alligator up on dry ground, well away from the water. The crew surrounds them, seemingly in shock at the size of the creature before them.

"Anyone with a weak stomach better take a walk," Blaze says, drawing an eight-inch knife from its sheath. "What I'm about to do ain't goin' to be pretty."

No one leaves.

"Turn this thing over," Blaze orders, and two workmen come forward and flip the beast onto its back. Blaze leans down and begins slicing the underbelly of the reptile, cutting it open in a long straight line. A few moments later the maimed head of Chris Miller can be seen between the fleshy folds of the animal's skin and scales. The gator's gastric juices have already begun their work, and Miller's face is shriveled and deformed, and the men lift it from the sickening stench of the creature's stomach.

Blaze turns to Matthew. "Let's bring him back to Houston tonight. We'll make sure he gets a proper burial. Let's leave now. I don't know about you, but I feel like gettin' the hell outta this place."

What about Charley Ingals?" Matthew asks.

"I hate to say it," Blaze replies, "but when the men dynamite that well later tonight to git that fire under control, there's gonna be nothin' left of Charley to take home."

Matthew stands silently as he watches the men place Miller's head beside his body, and wrap the remains in a gray tarp for the ride back to the city.

A MOTHER'S FAREWELL

Matthew stands on the south side of Big Hill and closes his eyes. He can feel the Gulf breeze blowing off the water, caressing the tall marsh grasses and infusing the air with a salty, coastal smell.

Behind him, Blaze walks the hummock with his divining rod, looking for the perfect spot. After about ten minutes of what appears to be aimless meandering, Blaze stops and shouts, "I've got it, ol' buddy! This is it!"

Matthew turns to see his partner standing over three fat hogs lying on their sides in a pool of yellow sulfur water. Around the pool is a crude fence made out of discarded wooden boxes.

"I'd wager farmers bring their pigs up here to git rid of fleas and kill the mange," Blaze says, eyeing the largest hog, a huge beast with red-brown skin and patches of bristles running from its neck to its ass.

"Lemme have the stake!" Blaze says, and Matthew hands his partner a marker. Blaze takes it and forces it into the soft ground next to one of the boxes.

"You think this is the spot, huh?" Matthew says.

"I'm sure of it," Blaze replies. "This is the place fer our first well on Big Hill. 'Bout a thousand feet straight down from this marker is the biggest pool of oil this side of Baku."

"With the money we got into this, I hope to hell you're right," Matthew says. "When are our men getting here?"

"I'd say any day now," Blaze says. "I'm bringin' in Al and Curt Hamill, and Henry McLeod to help us with the drillin'. And Peck Byrd will be our fireman for this job."

The crew arrives two days later, and it takes about a week for the men to construct the derrick above the former hog wallow. They're assembling Tex E and P Co.'s new rotary rig, which consists of a rotary, draw works, heavy-link chains, pump, swivel and steam engine. Stacked next to the sixty-five-foot-high derrick is drill pipe, casing and six steel-forged drilling bits.

The day they are to begin drilling, Blaze and Matthew stand on the derrick floor next to the Hamill brothers and McLeod. Blaze removes his Stetson and waves it at Peck Byrd. "Crank 'er up, Peck." he shouts, "We're ready to spud."

Byrd opens the engine's firebox and throws in a couple more pieces of wood, checking the gauge and putting the engine into gear. The chains begin to rotate, and as they do, an assembly on the derrick floor makes the drill stem turn.

After two hours they are down sixty feet, but the pipe isn't rotating properly, and Blaze stands by the well trying to figure out what's gone wrong.

Matthew walks up to him. "I bet we've hit that quicksand you were talking about," he says.

Blaze seems lost in thought and doesn't answer, but after a minute or so he turns to his partner and says, "I've got a notion that if we were able to counteract that sand gummin' up the works downhole with somethin' heavier—say some thick mud we'd pump into the well to hold the sidewalls—I bet ya we could penetrate whatever shit's bindin' the bit." He points at a herd of cattle grazing in the distance. "Who owns them cows?"

"Beats me," shouts Curt Hamill.

"Well, we're gonna borrow 'em fer a spell, Blaze says. "Come on, boys, let's drive that herd over to the slush pit. Let 'em walk around in it. Git things good and sloppy."

"Why in the hell you want to do that?" McLeod asks.

Blaze smiles and says, "Because, we're gonna use them cattle to make us some drillin' mud. Now, let's go git 'em over here!"

In a little more than an hour after the cows have trampled around in the pit, the crew is back at work pumping mud down the borehole, and eliminating the quicksand problem.

But big trouble comes when the well reaches one hundred-sixty feet. There, even the mud isn't heavy enough to stop the sidewalls from collapsing, and the formation is coarse and pitted with rocks.

Blaze bends down and picks up a handful of drill cuttings. "Will ya look at this crap," he says to Matthew, holding out his hand. "This stuff's big as eggs." He glances back at the pipe, which isn't rotating, even though the steam engine is cranked up to full power. "Shut 'er down, Peck," he shouts. "We're gonna have to think long and hard on this one!"

The next day, the five of them are back on the job before dawn, joined by Captain Lucas, a powerfully built man in his mid-forties.

"I think I've come up with a solution," Blaze says. "We're gonna have to find a way to flush that hole to bring the cuttin's to the surface and, at the same time, drive the bit through this formation. This ain't gonna be easy. In fact, it's gonna be back-breakin' work, because we gotta pull everything we got down the well back out, and replace the bit we're usin' with a special drivehead that will cut through the rock. I also figure if we put four-inch pipe inside the eight-inch, we can pump the drillin' mud down the smaller pipe to get circulation goin' to flush the cuttin's from the hole."

Blaze looks at his men. "Here's the bad news, boys. We're gonna have to find the heaviest block of steel we can git our hands on, rig it to the cathead line, and set up a makeshift pile driver."

"What's so bad about that?" McLeod asks.

Blaze shakes his head. "Ask me that question in a day or two, Henry."

"Why?"

"Because we're gonna be doin' the pile drivin' by hand."

"You're all nuts," McLeod shoots back, looking at the men. "This well just ain't meant to be … and I'll guarantee you, it's goin' to be just as dry as the other three they drilled on this hellhole of a hill before we got here … all dusters, every one of 'em!" He spits a wad of brown tobacco a couple of inches from his feet.

"There's a bonus fer every man who sees this through." Blaze says to him.

"Screw that," McLeod says. "What good does a bonus do if it kills you to get it? I've had it. I'm retirin' from this business, that's what I'm doing … and don't try and stop me."

"Suit yourself, Henry," Matthew says. "But you're making a big mistake. When this well comes in, Blaze and I are going to make sure every worker is taken care of. You can bank on that."

McLeod bites off another chuck of tobacco. "Don't take no offense, fellers, but I've been at this type of work a long time, and I ain't able to do it like I used to." He points at the derrick. "I don't believe you're goin' to strike oil here. And that contraption yer talkin' 'bout … that pile driver? That'd be downright man-killin' work … and I can't take it no more."

Matthew shrugs. "I'll send word to Houston to square away what we owe you, Henry. You take care of yourself."

He watches McLeod walk down the dirt path off the knoll to the road below.

In less than three days, they've made the necessary alterations to the rig, and the crew begins the back-breaking job of driving the pipe through the troublesome zone by hand. Matthew and Blaze take the first two-hour stint, raising the three-hundred-pound block of steel above the pipe by pulley. When they've hoisted it twenty feet in the air, Blaze shouts, "Let 'er go, now!" and the partners release their grip and watch the steel fall on top of the pipe like a giant hammer. But the drill stem barely moves.

"Get that circulatin' going," Blaze shouts to Al Hamill. "Let's see what we can flush out."

They repeat the process for the next two hours under the late summer sun suspended high in the sky. They're dripping with sweat, and as they work, fat mosquitoes buzz and torment them like legions of black, bloodthirsty vampires.

"Curt!" Blaze hollers. "Go over to that sulfur pool yonder and bring us back a bucket o' water!"

Matthew and Blaze raise the weight again, letting it smash back down on the pipe. The sweat falls from their faces, and the perspiration from their bodies saturates every inch of their clothes.

Curt Hamill comes back with the bucket, and Blaze takes it from him. "Close yer eyes and hold yer nose, ol' buddy," he says to Matthew. "Because this stuff ain't gonna feel too good, and Lord knows it smells like shit. But it should keep these sons o' bitchin' mosquitoes away. I'm gonna pour half of this on you, then I want you to pour the other half on me."

The two men take turns covering each other with the malodorous repellent, and Blaze puts his sweat-soaked Stetson back on his head and hollers to the rest of the crew. "You boys ought to try this. You won't be attractin' any pretty young ladies with this stink-um, but ya won't be courtin' no blood suckers, neither."

"Speakin' of blood suckers," Peck Byrd shouts, "you should have met my first wife!"

"Lift 'er back up!" Blaze shouts to Matthew, and the pair raise the weight again and let it fall.

"Al, anything comin' up from the hole?" Blaze hollers to Hamill.

"Nothin'," Hamill shouts back.

"Keep tryin' … we're bound to break somethin' loose!"

The partners lift the weight once more. They release the cathead line, and the steel hammer crashes onto the pipe, which moves a fraction of an inch.

Two more hours pass, and the pipe's down about four inches. Matthew feels like he's going to drop.

"Al, Curt … you fellows take the next shift," Blaze orders.

He and Matthew let the weight fall one more time, and then they tie back the pulley line, suspending the hammer above the drill pipe. Al and Curt Hamill climb up the side of the derrick and join them.

"Have fun," Blaze jokes, handing the line to the two men. "If this don't put ya in shape, nothin' will. Curt, maybe you'll even work off some of that beer belly of yers."

He turns to Matthew. "I'm gonna relieve Peck on the circulatin' pump, so why don't ya git us some more buckets of sulfur water, and we'll do another drenchin' all 'round.

We ought to be smellin' real good by the end of the day, but I ain't intendin' on going nowhere!"

By 6 p.m., the pipe has only been lowered an additional three inches into the earth. Matthew has just covered himself with another half bucket of sulfur water and is sitting on a large round log by the steam engine, when he sees a young man in a uniform charging up the hill toward him.

The man is from the Western Union office, and he stops in front of the derrick and shouts, "Anyone here named Matthew Strong?"

"You got something for me?" Matthew shouts back.

"Telegram, sir. It's urgent."

Matthew rips it open. It's from Philip Fenner:

Rebecca critical, failing fast.
Come immediately to NYC.

He reads the words a second time, not believing them. The sulfur water on his face mingles with the beads of sweat, and the mixture runs into his eyes and onto his lips, making them sting, and he tries to blink away the pain as his eyes well with tears.

He can't tell if the tears are caused by the mosquito repellent, or the note he clasps in his shaking hands, and he wonders if it matters.

Matthew knocks on the door of the Fenner mansion, and after what seems like an eternity Philip Fenner opens it and stands before him. He's tight-lipped as he shakes Matthew's hand.

"How long has she been sick?" Matthew asks.

"Not long," Fenner answers. "The doctors believe it's cancer, but it's come on so fast. She was fine two weeks ago."

How the hell would you know? Matthew wants to say, but doesn't.

Fenner leads him to an elevator, and they ride silently to the second floor. The elevator door opens, they emerge into a hallway, and Fenner points to the last door on the left. "You'll find your mother in there. We've had a nurse staying with her for the last few days. She may be asleep. She's being given morphine for her pain, so you probably won't be able to talk with her for too long. She's delirious most of the time."

Fenner turns, walks away from Matthew and disappears into one of the rooms down the hall.

Matthew walks to the bedroom with the hollow steps of a man condemned.

His mother lays in bed with her eyes open and fixed on the door, as if she's waiting for him to arrive. He enters her room, directs the attendant to leave, and takes a seat beside her bed.

Rebecca smiles and opens her hand, so small, yet so purposeful.

"You've come," she says.

"Of course."

"It's good to see you, Son."

Matthew clasps her hand.

"I've been so selfish," Rebecca whispers.

"I have, too," Matthew replies.

"I want you to know I loved your father. And I have always loved you, even if I haven't shown it."

"I know, Mother. You don't have to say that."

Rebecca closes her eyes, appearing to search for strength.

The smell of death pervades the room, and Matthew lowers his head. "It all changed when we lost Luke," he says.

"Your father was never the same," Rebecca whispers.

"I know."

"Yet, he always believed you'd make good. And you did, didn't you?"

Matthew stares at his mother. Her hair is white, her eyes distant.

"That's why he got you your pen," Rebecca says. "Do you remember how Caleb and I argued about that?"

A pang of guilt courses through Matthew.

"I want you to promise me something," Rebecca says.

"Yes, Mother. Anything."

Rebecca draws her left hand from under the covers. She clasps his special pen, and she motions for her son to come closer.

Matthew can't believe what he's seeing, for the pen is more beautiful than he remembers, its glow more radiant than ever.

"This was Caleb's gift to you and to your promise ... your future," Rebecca says. "I'm giving it back to you now, and I don't want you to ever let it go again."

"How did you find it?" Matthew asks.

"I want you to consider this as your gift from your father *and* your mother. If you ever have another child, I want you to pass this pen on. Will you do that for me?"

"I will, Mother."

He looks down at her, holding back his tears. "I'm the one who's been selfish, and I'm so sorry for the things I said to you that night in the rooming house."

Rebecca closes her eyes and shakes her head. "I said some terrible things, too. We were angry at each other. But I hurt *you* more, in ways you don't even know."

"You were my rock, Mother," Matthew says. "Always there when I needed you."

Rebecca grimaces as a bolt of pain shoots through her disease-wracked body. "I destroyed our family," she whispers. "Your family."

"Mother, don't... now's not the time to say things like that."

"I was the one who caused it."

"Caused what, Mother?"

"If it wasn't for me ..." she whispers, gazing into another world."

Rebecca shuts her eyes again, and her head falls onto the pillow.

"... Maddy ... our little girl ... your little baby ... would be with us today."

Matthew holds Rebecca's hand as tight as he can, and he counts her breaths, now so shallow, so soft. Mothers' breaths, sustainers of life. Of comfort. Breaths children believe continue forever.

REVELATION

Matthew stands before the small gathering at Grove Hill Cemetery in Oil City dressed in a black business suit. Seated at the gravesite are Blaze, Philip Fenner, Doc Willetts, Charles Wharton, Matthew's ex-father-in law, and Reverend Hill, the preacher who used to give Matthew the stubby pencils. Lavinia and her husband, John Spencer, sit on either side of her father. In a chair next to Lavinia is a young boy with hair the color of coal.

Matthew takes a deep breath and glances at Rebecca's casket. She is to be buried beside Caleb's marker, adjacent to Luke's grave, and a short distance from Maddy's.

"Thank you, Reverend, for those kind words you said earlier...I appreciate them," Matthew begins. "She was born in eighteen-thirty-four in County Donegal, and her maiden name was Rebecca McCann. Her father, Brendan, was a professor at the college, and Morna, her mother, was a homemaker. Her family came to America in eighteen-forty-eight, settling in Philadelphia. That's where she met my father, Caleb Strong, who worked in the dry goods business before entering the oil trade."

Matthew looks down at Caleb's marker. "For many years, as most of you know, my father was a well shooter. He worked in these parts in the late sixties for the Roberts Petroleum Torpedo Company. He died in eighteen-seventy trying to open a well on the Farris tract, not too far from here, in fact."

He glances at Luke's grave. "My brother, Luke, was eighteen when he was taken from us in a well fire. My parents never recovered from that loss, and I believe it was Luke's passing that preoccupied my father's mind and contributed to his death."

Doc Willetts raises his head and stares at Matthew.

Matthew continues. "My mother and I moved to Cleveland soon after pa died." She then went to New York and remarried."

He looks at Philip Fenner. "Philip, I thank you for taking care of her for all those years, and for being a good provider. I especially thank you for the care you made sure she had at the end."

Fenner stares at his shoes, and Matthew looks over at Maddy's tombstone:

Madeline Abigail Wharton Strong
April 1882 – December 1886

I've lost them all, he thinks. *Everyone I ever loved. They are all here.*

Matthew looks back at the group. "My mother not only gave me the strength and desire to achieve, but also the freedom and courage to fail. And when I did fail, as we all do in one way or another along the way, she understood, and didn't judge me or hold against me the consequences of my actions."

He clutches his pen and glances at Lavinia, who is staring straight at him.

"I picked out the inscription on my mother's tombstone. I thought it was appropriate for what she and I have been through. I'm going to read it to you.

"There is a spot mid barren hills,
Where winter howls, and driving rain;
But if the dreary tempest chills,
There is light that warms again."

Matthew bows his head. "God bless you, Mother. May
you find peace and comfort in the arms of our Father, and
warmth in his eternal light."

He walks over to Reverend Hill and shakes his hand. As
he turns, he sees the boy sitting next to Lavinia is also just
staring at him, not moving or saying a word.

Matthew is transfixed, and his jaw drops because it is
like he's seeing a mirror image of himself. The boy has the
same eyes, hair and cheekbones, and his physique, while
undeveloped, hints at the strength and broad muscles that
will someday come. Matthew senses mannerisms he'd seen
in Caleb and Luke, and that he knows he has as well.

Lavinia and her husband stand up, and Lavinia takes
the boy by his hand, and the three of them walk over to
Matthew.

Lavinia is more beautiful than ever, and Matthew
notices a confidence and a vitality that he hasn't seen in
her before. Her husband isn't anything like he'd imagined,
either. John Spencer is trim and tall, with clear blue eyes
and distinguished white hair. He has immaculately clean
and strong hands—the hands of a surgeon, Matthew notes.

Lavinia walks up to him and embraces him briefly, kissing him lightly on his cheek. "Oh, Matthew, I'm so sorry
about your mother," she says. "We stayed in touch all these
years, writing to each other almost up to the end. She's in a
better place, you know."

"Thank you, Lavinia," Matthew says. "I appreciate you
and your family coming back to Oil City."

"You've never met my husband, John," Lavinia says to him.

"No," Matthew replies, extending his hand, feeling like he's in the middle of a dream. "Pleased to meet you, sir."

Lavinia puts her arm around her son. "And this is Nate. Say hello to Mr. Strong, Nate."

Mathew can hear Lavinia speaking, but her words seem like they're coming from miles away.

"Mr. Strong and I used to live in this town years ago, Nate," she says. "We were friends growing up, and we went to school together here, just like you and your friends back in Chicago. But then we both had to move to other cities."

Lavinia takes her husband's hand and says, "Before we go, Matthew, I want you to know how devastated we were to hear about your daughter Maddy."

"Yes, we're very, very sorry," John Spencer says. "What a terrible thing to lose someone that young."

"She was murdered," Matthew replies. "They've never caught the killer."

"Your mother wrote me about it," Lavinia says. "It was awful, and I can't even imagine what you and your wife must have had to go through. No one should have to endure something like that."

"Melissa and I are divorced," Matthew says. "She couldn't bear it, and she became very sick."

"Our condolences, sir," Spencer reiterates. "We're so sorry."

Lavinia begins walking to the carriage with Nate and her husband. Then she turns and says. "Goodbye, Matthew. Please try and take care of yourself. Please believe better times are coming."

Matthew stands and watches them leave, and after they're gone, he bids the few remaining guests goodbye and thanks them for attending. Charles Wharton stands a short distance away from him, and after everyone leaves, he approaches his former son-in-law.

"Join me for a drink?" he asks.

"I think I could use one," Matthew replies.

Less than twenty minutes later, the two men sit across from each other in the bar of the Drexler Hotel in Oil City.

Wharton takes a drink of scotch. "I never told you this, Matthew, but I want you to know how appreciative I've always been at the effort you made with Melissa. I know how difficult she can be."

"How's she doing?" Matthew asks.

"Not good. We've had to hospitalize her. She's been going steadily downhill, and the doctors say her mind's not right. Unfortunately, things seem to be getting worse."

"I tried, you know," Matthew says. "But after Maddy was killed…"

"Melissa was never an easy woman to be with," Wharton says. "She's always been high strung and emotional. Both Mrs. Wharton and I know that, probably better than anyone. We know that when she found out she couldn't have any more children, she began to change."

"I did try," Matthew says. "I hope you believe me."

Wharton nods. "I also want to tell you how destroyed we were when Maddy was lost," he says.

Matthew closes his eyes, fighting back tears. "I finally had someone I could love."

"You're a good man, Matthew, and I respect you," Wharton says. "Rest assured, you'll love again. It's just a matter of time."

"And now my mother's gone..."

Charles Wharton catches the waiter's eye. He rotates his finger in a circle above their drinks, signaling another round.

GUSHER

Matthew and Blaze step off a passenger train at the station in Humble, Texas, about seventy miles west of Beaumont. The weather's turned cold, and the men are dressed in long leather overcoats and gloves, their Stetsons low on their heads. It's a little before 10 p.m.

They walk from the platform to the darkened street where almost every building is closed, shut for the night.

"Can ya see 'em?" Blaze asks.

On the outskirts of the small town, Matthew can see a yellowish glow above the trees. Stars fill the blackened sky, and in every direction he turns, he sees shimmering lights, just visible above the tree lines.

"Let's get a closer look," Matthew says.

They walk a short distance into the countryside where they come on the source of the illumination.

"I'll be damned," Blaze says. "You ever seen anythin' like this?"

Stretching before them are acres of cabbage fields, row after row of plump, dark-green vegetables. Beside each plant is a small steel tube stuck in the ground. The fields contain hundreds of these tubes, and at the top of each one a yellow-blue flame burns about two to three inches high. Matthew and Blaze enter the patch, and it's like walking

335

into a heated room, for the difference in temperature is astounding.

"I've heard 'bout these Humble field fires," Blaze says, taking off his gloves and sticking them in his coat pocket. "I've always wanted to see 'em fer myself. The farmers up here been doin' this fer the past few winters, from what I hear...keepin' their crops from freezin' with these gas lights, ever since they discovered shallow gas deposits 'round here."

He stoops to the ground and picks up a spare rod. "Lemme show ya something."

Blaze reaches underneath his coat and pulls his pistol out of its holster. He grips the gun by its barrel, and with the butt of its handle he coaxes the rod a couple of feet into the loamy soil. He sheathes his weapon and takes out a small box of wooden matches from his shirt pocket.

"This is the shallowest deposit of natural gas I ever seen," Blaze says. "And, where there's gas, there's usually oil." He lights a match, places it over the top of the tube and a small burst of flame erupts.

Blaze smiles and surveys the surrounding fields of light. He looks all around, taking in the glow coming from fields he can't even see beyond the tree line.

He turns to Matthew. "We ought to hedge our bet, since we've made the decision to lay our nuts on the line at Big Hill. You and me ought to scrape up every dime we can git our hands on, have Tex E an' P Co. buy up every acre of dirt around this town and then some. I know it's gonna stretch us mighty thin, probably back us to the wall financially, but there's a fortune to be made here."

"We're already through the wall financially," Matthew replies. " I have no idea where the money will come from, but I'll get our landman looking at this place first thing in the morning."

"I didn't mention this to you before, ol' buddy," Blaze says. "But right before yer mother's service, Charles Wharton pulled me aside. He said he'd been hearin' good things 'bout Tex E an' P Co. and the work we been doin' down here. He said if there was a chance to come in, he'd be interested, and to let him know."

Matthew shakes his head. "I don't think that's a good idea, Blaze. I felt beholden to that man from the moment I married Melissa. I'll be damned if I'm going to open that door again. It's shut for good."

"Jus' think 'bout it," Blaze says. "It'd be a way a lockin' up this land. I can't see us turnin' our backs on somebody that believes in us, especially when we're so tight fer cash. Besides, we wouldn't have to give away much … maybe five percent, tops."

"I don't know," Matthew says. "We already have Captain Lucas and Patillio Higgins as minority partners. Now we're talking about bringing somebody else in?"

"All I'm sayin' is think 'bout it," Blaze reiterates.

"I will," Matthew replies. "I'll give it some thought."

The men leave the cabbage patch and head back toward town.

"Let's hitch the last train out and git back to Beaumont," Blaze says, looking up the tracks. "There's no reason to stay. Nothin' goin' on here."

Matthew is deep in thought, and he turns and stares at the bands of glowing fires beyond the loblolly pines and yaupons, and he feels excited.

"Did you happen to take a close look at Lavinia's son at my mother's funeral?" Matthew asks Blaze.

"How could I miss 'em," Blaze says. "I 'spect it was like lookin' back in time at you."

"I need to see him again," Matthew says. "I need to talk to Lavinia. I can't believe she didn't tell me about him."

Blaze stops in the middle of the street, turns and places his hand on Matthew's shoulder. "Careful ol' buddy. A boy isn't meant to have two fathers. And I guarantee ya … as far as that young un's concerned, he's already got one."

The next evening, the partners sit across from each other in the dining room of the Crosby House Hotel. It's Christmas Eve, and they have two piping-hot turkey dinners in front of them.

"Well, we've drilled through everythin' this hill's thrown at us," Blaze says, "but did ya see how slow the pipe was rotatin' today?"

"Yeah," Matthew says. "You worried about that?"

Blaze sighs and reaches for the gravy. "It could mean we're on top of the dome formation, but it could also mean sand is gummin' things up."

Matthew glances out the window of the dining room. "Good God … will you look at that!"

They get up from the table and hurry outside to the street, and they gaze up at Big Hill.

Covering the entire knoll is a great shimmering light. It grows larger and seems to hover and move across the ground, glowing ever brighter with dancing hues of blue, yellow and green. They can hear a hissing sound coming from the hill, and they are joined by dozens of onlookers.

"You know what that is?" a man standing next to them says. "It's Saint Elmo's fire. People say it's been seen here off and on for centuries."

Matthew turns to Blaze. "You know what I think it is?"

"Yeah, ol' buddy, I think I do. I think it's our beacon that's goin' to lead us to our treasure... our sign lightin' the path to our fortune!"

They stand with the crowd in the cold night, mesmerized by the beckoning beams.

By early January, the crew has solved the collapsing sand problem, and has penetrated the rock to a depth of one thousand twenty feet.

Suddenly, the pipe stops rotating, and the rotary chains jerk and break into pieces.

"Shit!" Blaze shouts. Peck Byrd disengages the steam engine, and hollers, "What the devil now?"

Blaze climbs up on the derrick floor. "I 'spect the bit's chewed up, so let's start pullin' this pipe back outta the hole. We'll need to change 'er out."

Matthew runs up to him. "What do you think happened?"

Blaze shakes his head. "I've never seen anything like it. 'Course I ain't never drilled a well this deep, neither."

"It has to be the downhole pressures," Matthew says. "They must be immense."

Blaze shakes his head. "Could be pressure, could be gumbo, could be harder rock, nasty sands or some other confoundin' formation. Who the hell knows?"

For the first time since they spudded the well, Matthew's concerned. *What if we fail*, he thinks. *How will we ever pay back all we owe?*

The men pull the drill pipe out of the well during the next twenty-four hours. The crew replaces the chewed-up bit with a new one, and they begin lowering the stem back into the hole.

They'd reach about seven hundred feet, when Matthew hears it…a deep rumbling sound coming from the well. He stops what he's doing and he looks up at Blaze, who's perched forty feet over the derrick floor helping guide the pipe.

Thick globs of brown mud begin flowing up over the rig's rotary table. Peck Byrd and the Hamill brothers back away as the force becomes greater, and the mud spurts almost to where Blaze is standing. Blaze scrambles down the derrick's side, moving as fast as he can.

"Run…get the hell outta here!" he shouts to the men. "This well's about to blow!"

Matthew, Blaze and the others start running, and in a few seconds, a great roar comes from the earth, and six tons of piping shoots skyward, knocking off the top of the derrick.

"Heads up for that steel!" Matthew hollers. A six-foot section slices into the dirt beside him as other pieces of pipe pierce the ground like spears falling from the clouds.

Then everything goes silent.

The men stop and begin walking back toward the well. The derrick's destroyed, and there isn't much left of the drilling floor, either. The crew wades through mud two feet deep around the hole, looking at the mess.

Peck Byrd turns off the boiler and turns to Al Hamill. "What the hell are we going to do with this damn thing now?"

"Well, Peck," Hamill answers, "I guess we'll just have to shovel this mud away and see if…"

He never finishes his sentence. The ground begins shaking, and there's a tremendous roar like cannon fire.

"Here we go again!" Blaze shouts, as a great geyser of mud erupts from the hole and the roar grows louder. In less than a minute, the mud disappears, and in its place a huge column of natural gas bursts high into the sky.

Blaze, Matthew and their crew start running from the well again.

"If that gas gets anywhere near the boiler, everything will blow!" Matthew shouts, turning back around. "I've got to go back and douse the box."

Blaze grabs him. "Wait on that. It's too dangerous. Let's see what happens."

Peck Byrd is running so fast away from the gas stream that his feet slip out from under him, and he falls headfirst into the slush pit. He gets right up, shakes himself off, and joins the others a safe distance away.

The eruption of gas stops as abruptly as it started. In its place a massive stream of green-black oil shoots a hundred sixty feet into the air. The well on Big Hill now sounds like ten speeding freight trains tearing down the tracks.

"Peck!" Blaze yells. "Go fetch Captain Lucas. He should be at home. Tell 'em we've struck oil. Tell 'em to come. Hurry, now!" He looks at Matthew who, like his partner, is drenched in crude.

Matthew wipes the oil away from his eyes. "What do you think she's flowing at?" he asks.

Blaze sizes up at the column. "Hard to tell. But I wouldn't be surprised if she's spurtin' a hundred thousand barrels a day."

"You're kidding?"

"No, I ain't."

Matthew reaches into his pocket and pulls out his prized pen. He holds it tight in his right hand, and with his left he wipes away oil and tears of joy.

He closes his eyes for a moment and lets his mind drift. He sees the smile on his father's face as Caleb gives him his special pen. He sees Luke standing on the green grass outside under the summer sun, skimming flat rocks across the mirrored surface of their backyard pond. He sees little Maddy a short distance away feeding peanuts to the plump gray squirrels. He sees Rebecca come out the front door of their home with a blanket and a picnic basket in her arms. He sees her smile and beckon him, and he joins his family as they climb into their wagon, all of them, undivided, inseparable—a family forever bound by love and devotion—his family, never to be taken away again.

He remembers the excitement he felt the night JDR gave him his chance outside the Baptist church. He recalls the heady power of rising up the Standard Oil ranks, and the satisfaction of negotiating those Toledo contracts with Fat Freddie Fleshner. He remembers everything he'd accomplished with the oil barons, and realizes that this is so much better, so much more meaningful.

Matthew opens his eyes and shouts, "We're rich, partner…rich beyond our wildest dreams!"

Blaze puts his arm around his shoulders. "Yep, ol' buddy, we are rich, richer than anything we could have imagined!"

"Rich to have traveled this road together," Matthew says, gripping his pen harder.

"I can't wait to see what's around the corner," Blaze says.

"I can," Matthew answers, "I'm just going to enjoy what we've got right now. Do you know why?"

"I believe I do," Blaze replies.

"Because it's better the second time around!" Matthew says.

"Ain't that the truth," Blaze says. "But ya know, first things first. You and me got a well to git under control."

The friends walk side by side toward the mighty gusher, and disappear into the black torrent of falling gold.

AUTHOR'S NOTE

I'd like to express my sincere appreciation to Keith Urbahn and Matt Carlini at Javelin for believing in this story, and for guiding it to publication. While the agency specializes in the representation of nonfiction authors only, an exception was made in this instance, for which I am extremely grateful. Also, thanks to Marion Forcht, Ashley Timm, Jason Wilder, Jim Pitts, Kent Barry and Mike Long for reading the *Gusher* manuscript, and for providing suggestions and encouragement. I wish to extend special gratitude to Jim Pitts for hiring me into ExxonMobil, and for all his kind help in making me a better writer.

The initial idea for *Gusher* came a number of years ago, while attending a lunch at the Houston Club to hear a presentation by Ron Chernow on his book, *Titan*, the Pulitzer-nominated biography of John D. Rockefeller, Sr.

Mr. Chernow began his lecture by revealing the shadowy, contradictory nature of the elusive industrialist, who spent many of his days sequestered within the confines of his vast estates or cocooned inside his impregnable offices.

A financial and organizational genius, Rockefeller embodied the free-spirited, anti-competitive practices prevalent in the post-Civil War Gilded Age. This period witnessed the rise of other fabulously wealthy moguls such as

Cornelius Vanderbilt, Andrew Carnegie, J. P. Morgan, Jay Gould, Henry Flagler and Andrew Mellon.

Arguably, Rockefeller was the smartest and richest of them all. He certainly was the most austere and idiosyncratic.

During the lunch, Chernow spoke of JDR's fetish for secrecy, his unwavering Baptist faith, his all-consuming predatory business practices, his legendary philanthropy, and his many quirks, which included routines that never deviated, such as chewing each bite of food precisely the same number of times, or employing an identical number of steps every time he'd walk across a familiar room.

In the book's introduction describing Chernow's initial reservations regarding Random House's proposal that he write a Rockefeller biography, he wrote, "In the existing literature, he came across as a gifted automaton at best, a malevolent machine at worst. I couldn't tell whether he was a hollow man, deadened by the pursuit of money, or someone of great depth and force but with eerie self control."

The Standard Oil Company, formed by John D. Rockefeller more than 135 years ago, evolved into more than 50 entities, including Exxon Mobil Corporation, one of the most complex and profitable enterprises in the world. There, vice presidents run divisions larger than most *Fortune* 100 companies.

I joined ExxonMobil in 1989, first as a consultant and then as an employee until my retirement in 2017. I held positions as senior media advisor, editor of the corporation's quarterly shareholder magazine, *The Lamp*, and as executive speechwriter to the Chairman and CEO.

My job took me to Japan, Singapore, Thailand, Indonesia, Venezuela, Guyana, Newfoundland, Western Canada, Africa and Europe, as well as to numerous oil-producing regions within the United States such as Alaska, California, West Texas, Louisiana and offshore Gulf of Mexico.

My job also gave me routine access to the corporation's understated yet elegant Irving, Texas, headquarters and, on occasion, to its executive wing, facetiously known among employees as the God Pod.

In one section of the first floor, set apart from the others, there are two executive dining rooms: the John D. Rockefeller room, commemorating the founder, and the John D. Archbold room, named for the fascinating, paradoxical man who succeeded JDR as president of Standard Oil. Every business day at noon, when they are not otherwise traveling, the chairman and his top officials gather in the Rockefeller room for lunch, a practice begun by JDR himself more than a century ago.

There are other qualities evident in the contemporary headquarters that seem to be carryovers from past Standard Oil days. For example, the 350 or so people who work there interact with quiet, respectful decorum. You won't find any back-slapping camaraderie or water-cooler joke-telling in the immaculate halls or corridors. Rather, the daily business of the corporation is conducted with precision and predictability. That's not to say the place is devoid of emotion, for expectations run high, performance is closely scrutinized, and only the most dedicated, smartest and most capable rise to the highest positions of operational power.

As one employee with an appreciation for Standard Oil history recently put it, "One can sense John D. Rockefeller's DNA throughout the place." Indeed, I'd contend one would find his imprint to varying degrees at every ExxonMobil office, production unit, refinery, chemical plant and marketing facility in the 200 countries and territories where the company operates.

Gusher is a product of my twenty-eight years' of employment at ExxonMobil. It's the story of the origins of the American oil business as seen through the eyes of Matthew Strong, an ambitious but poor young man who breaks free of his troubled past and attains great wealth and power in the Rockefeller empire. While Matthew is taken under the titan's wing, his rise comes at a great price that tears his family apart and nearly destroys him.

The story begins in 1870 in the oil regions of Pennsylvania and ends with the discovery of Big Hill, America's first gusher, a number of years later. It traces Matthew and his family's lives through these tumultuous times.

This is also the first work that brings the enigmatic John D. Rockefeller, Sr. to life in a novel. There are other true characters in the book as well, including the aforementioned Archbold, who used to whistle *Onward Christian Soldiers* wherever he went, and who fought a life-long battle with alcoholism (it's ironic that he was named JDR's successor, since Rockefeller deplored liquor); Henry Flagler, who was later to develop the east coast of Florida, from Saint Augustine to Miami and the lower Keys; Daniel O'Day, Standard Oil's tough field commander in charge of the conglomerate's sprawling oil and gas pipeline networks; and the Nobel brothers, Robert and Ludvig, as well as the champions of Big Hill, Patillo Higgins and Captain Anthony F. Lucas, among others.

Fictional characters include the Strong family, Matthew and his mother and father, Rebecca and Caleb; Jack Thackery, Muleface McCoy, Doc Willetts, Remo Carbone, Augustus Clapp, Helmut Weiss, Lavinia Spencer, Melissa Wharton, Blaze Clayburn and a host of minor characters.

While *Gusher* is based on actual events, it is first and foremost a work of fiction. Any inaccuracies or errors are solely the responsibility of the author. There are sections in the book where I have had to adjust time several years forward for the sake of story continuity. A case in point is the chapter about the discovery of the huge oil well at Big Hill, which is actually Spindletop, one of the largest oil finds in the United States. The discovery was made in 1901, not earlier, as inferred. These instances are relatively infrequent.

Gusher was written chiefly to entertain. But I also believe it gives the reader a memorable excursion into the world's biggest business, and an intimate, behind-the-scenes look at the powerful, iron-fisted men who created it.

Bob Davis
The Woodlands, Texas

ABOUT THE AUTHOR

During his 28-year career with Exxon Mobil Corporation, Bob Davis was a senior advisor and press spokesman as well as executive speechwriter to the Chairman and CEO. A long-time resident of Ridgefield, Connecticut, he now lives in The Woodlands, Texas, with his wife, Linda.

35918194R00199

Made in the USA
Lexington, KY
08 April 2019